"Sheer fun… filled with down-home humor, realistic characters and pure romance. The characters… are all so well-written, they leap from the pages."

—Romance Reader at Heart

"Carolyn Brown takes her audience by storm… I was mesmerized!"

—The Romance Studio

"Compelling from page one… The delightful humor, the uniquely regional sayings, and the appealing setting along with sassy dialogue… make this love story enchanting."

—The Long and Short of It Reviews

"The writing is first-rate—it's smooth and enticing and makes you want to read every word… Carolyn Brown wowed me with her expertise in crafting a perfect romance."

—Cheeky Reads

"A very entertaining romp."

—Drey's Library

"The passion is red-hot. Smart dialogue and unmistakable characters will leave readers wanting more."

—Affaire de Coeur

"The down-home Texas feel comes through in spades in Brown's writing."

—Leslie's Psyche

"Wonderful characters, seamless writing, and a firecracker romance have Carolyn Brown at the top of her game. Loved it!"
—Wendy's Minding Spot

"Carolyn Brown has done it again... Word of warning—you will not be able to put this one down."
—Fresh Fiction

"The chemistry is electrifying."
—Literary Escapism

"The Luckadeau men are H-O-T!"
—Cheryl's Book Nook

Published by Sourcebooks Casablanca, an imprint of Sourcebooks, Inc.
P.O. Box 4410, Naperville, Illinois 60567-4410
(630) 961-3900
FAX: (630) 961-2168
www.sourcebooks.com

Printed and bound in Canada
WC 10 9 8 7 6 5 4 3 2 1

Also by Carolyn Brown

HONKY TONK
CHRISTMAS

Carolyn Brown

Thank you to all the women who have served or who are serving in any branch of the United States Armed Forces.

Chapter 1

THE WHIRRING OF THE HELICOPTER BLADES CUT through the hot Iraqi desert wind. It was late summer and the Shamal wind was throwing enough sand around to limit visibility. But she could make out the target in her crosshairs and the sand kept the choppers from getting a direct bead on her and Jonah. They'd already made four passes. She had sand in her mouth, sand in her boots and in her ears. She'd been trained to ignore everything and take out the target, but that damned buzzing noise reminded her of a bunch of swarming bees—and she hated bees.

"Keep focused on the target," she whispered so low that Jonah couldn't hear the words.

She set the crosshairs on the terrorist behind the machine gun mounted on the hood of a military jeep. She'd never missed yet and didn't want to spoil her record.

"Convoy is less than a mile from the ambush," her commander's voice said on the radio. "Fire when ready."

"Yes sir," she said. "Adjustments, Jonah?"

Her spotter ran his finger down a column of numbers and called out the wind velocity. She made adjustments in the blistering heat. She took a deep breath and blinked twice for good luck. If she took out the ambush, the convoy took her friends back to base. If she didn't, there'd be widows and orphans crying that night in the States.

Sweat trickled down between her breasts to puddle at the bottom of her bra where a sand trap waited.

Evidently God knew what he was doing when he gave breasts to women and not men. Boy soldiers wouldn't last ten minutes out in the heat with bras biting their ribs and shoulders. They'd scratch and fidget until the enemy blew their weak little asses all over the sand. She wiped moisture from her brow, inhaled, and blinked twice again for good luck. Then she pulled the trigger and the target dropped graveyard dead.

"Mission complete. Convoy can proceed. Send in rescue," she said.

Gunfire started and the sand kicked up all around her. She looked over at Jonah to tell him to keep his head down and get ready to run when their rescue team lit. His chin rested on his chest and blood was everywhere.

"Jonah's down!" she screamed into the radio. "Send me some help now. Jonah is shot."

"Hello, anybody home?" a deep Texas drawl yelled and light from the open door filled the Honky Tonk.

She jerked her head up and scanned the area. It was dark and cool. Where had the desert gone? Where was her rifle and why was she wearing cowboy boots? She looked to her right and Jonah Black was gone. She drew her eyebrows down. He'd been there the last time she blinked. Then the past faded into the dark corners of the beer joint and the present brought a cowboy across the hardwood dance floor.

"Back here." Her voice was hoarse and her mouth dry. She'd fallen asleep on the table when she sat down for a rest. Her arms tingled as the feeling returned and her heart pounded. It was the same thing every time she went to sleep. Recurring dreams of Iraq, of the job that women did not do and were not trained to do in the

Army. But Sharlene had done the job and when she was discharged she'd brought it home with her in the form of nightmares.

The sound of cowboy boot heels on hardwood floors coming toward her sounded like gunfire. She covered her ears and shook her head. She needed another second or two to bury the visions and pull herself away from the sight of Jonah and his dark brown dead eyes.

"I'm looking for Sharlene Waverly. I was supposed to meet her here at one o'clock," the Texas voice grew closer.

She stood up and extended her hand. "I'm Sharlene. You must be Holt Jackson. Have a seat. Can I get you a beer?"

Holt's big hand swallowed hers. He noticed that her hand trembled when he shook it.

"No, I'm fine. *You* are Sharlene Waverly?" He frowned as he let go of her hand.

She had kinky red hair and green eyes. She didn't look old enough to work behind the bar much less own one. She barely came to his shoulder and would have to produce an ID to get out of a convenience store with a six-pack.

"Yes, I am. Sit and we'll talk." She motioned toward the table with four chairs around it and an empty beer bottle on the top. "I was just about to start cleaning up the place from last night's business. I fell asleep with my arms under my head and they're still tingling." She shook her arms to restore feeling.

He pulled out a chair and sat across the table from her. He was tall with thick dark hair that tickled his shirt collar. His mossy green eyes scanned the beer joint, finally coming to rest on her.

"So where do you want to build an addition to this place?"

She pointed toward the north end of the Honky Tonk. "I want to knock out half of that wall and make a room as big as the original Honky Tonk. I'll put the pool tables and jukeboxes back there and that will leave more room in here for a bigger dance floor. Hardwood floors, paneling on the walls. The good stuff, not that stuff that looks as cheap as it is."

"Why not go to the south?" he asked.

"Because I'm barely over the county line as it is. Erath County is dry. Palo Pinto is wet. If I get over into Erath County I couldn't have a beer joint," she explained.

He stood up and reached for a steel tape fastened to his belt. A vision of someone grabbing a gun made her flinch but she covered it well by throwing her hand over her mouth to cover a fake cough.

He pulled a small spiral-topped notebook from the pocket of his chambray work shirt and began measuring and making calculations. "Twice as big? That's a hell of a big addition."

"I need a big addition. Folks are waiting in the parking lot now because my max says three hundred or less. I want to be able to bring in more customers."

Holt made notations and measured some more. "Windows?"

"No. Solid walls. No windows and no frilly curtains. I run a beer joint here, not a boarding house for proper little girls."

"Why?" Holt asked.

"Because I like running a beer joint and I would not like a bunch of whiny little girls fussing all day long about having to learn the proper way to set a table," she said.

"Why no windows? It's your business what you do for a living, lady, not mine. I'm just here to build an addition." Holt grinned.

"Sorry that I bit at you. I'm grouchy today. It's not your fault. Drunks aren't real good with windows. If they get into a fight before Luther can break it up, the walls don't break. I'm going to clean while you figure, then we'll talk when you get the estimate worked up," Sharlene answered.

Holt worked for half an hour then slipped the tape back on his belt and hiked a hip onto a bar stool. "I'll take that beer now, Miz Waverly. If you like my estimate and can find me a rental house with a yard in Mingus, I can do this job for you."

"Call me Sharlene. Miz Waverly makes me look behind me to see if my momma is in the place. Let's see, it's mid-August. I'd like to have it finished and ready by Christmas…" She hesitated because it was on the tip of her tongue to tell him that she'd give him her apartment if he could have it done by Thanksgiving.

"You don't know much about building, do you?" he asked.

She shrugged. "Not really. Is that not doable?"

"I can get this done by Halloween if we have good weather. Probably within eight weeks, which would finish it by mid-to-late October," he said.

"Really?"

"I'm figuring we can have it done in eight weeks, maximum," he said.

"How big is your crew?"

"I've got three men who work for me. If it's a long distance from home we live in our travel trailers. If it's close by we commute. I see you've got some spaces over there. Interested in renting two of them?"

"Two? Why only two if you've got three men who work for you?"

"Two are from up close to Wichita Falls. That'd be a pretty long commute and they are both single so they don't mind staying on the site. The other is from Palo Pinto. I reckon he'd rather commute since he's married and has kids."

She nodded. "I've got plenty of spaces back there. Plumbing, water, and electricity go with the rent."

He glanced at the bar. "Pretty nice location for Kent and Chad. They're brothers, by the way, and they'll love the idea of being close to a beer joint so they can get a brew after working all day."

She set a beer in front of him. "Estimate?"

He handed her the paper and tipped up the bottle.

It was twenty percent higher than she'd figured but less than Merle had thought it could be. She could afford it. "I can live with these numbers. When can you start?"

"Monday morning. I'll call Chad, Kent, and Bennie and tell them. They'll be here sometime over the weekend to get the trailers hooked up. We'll get our equipment set up, the materials ordered, and hopefully get it stringed up and leveled on Monday. Then Bennie will begin the concrete work Monday morning. I figured you'd wrangle with me on the price. I allowed ten percent for some haggling room."

"Then take ten percent off. But I don't want concrete floors."

He held up his palm. "I know what you want. The concrete is for the foundation. I know what I'm doing Miz... Sharlene."

"Then yes, we have a deal and you can start the job."

He set the bottle down. "Not so fast. I'll need a place to live. I was renting a trailer up in Palo Pinto and I could commute, but the hot water tank blew a gasket and flooded the whole thing. Owner doesn't want to fix it so we've got to find a place to live. Find me a rental house by tomorrow and then we'll have a deal."

Sharlene cocked her head to one side. "How about a side bet? You get the trailer spaces and a house free of rent if you promise you can get the job done by Thanksgiving. If you fail, then I get to take your rent out of the final payment. I'll pay you half now and half when it's finished. That all right with you?"

He extended his hand. "Sounds pretty good to me."

She shook with him. "Good. I'll get the keys from my purse."

"You own a rental house?"

"I do."

"And where is this house?"

"Which way did you come into town?" she asked.

"From Palo Pinto."

"Did you see that house by the post office? The turquoise one with hot pink trim and yellow porch posts? It's got two orange rockers on the porch."

He shuddered. He'd seen the house all right and wondered what drunk had painted it. "So you own that white frame house just west of it?" he asked.

Sharlene handed him the keys. "No, I own the turquoise one. It's yours until the job is done."

Holt groaned. "How big is it and does it have kitchen appliances?"

She nodded. "Kitchen, living room, two bedrooms. Larissa left living room furniture in there. You can move it out into the garage out back of the Tonk or use it. Stove, refrigerator, and the washer and dryer are in the kitchen. You still interested?"

"You think I'll turn it down, don't you," he said.

"Lord, I hope not."

"Are there any other houses in town?" he asked. He'd gladly pay rent to live in something that didn't look like a human-sized Barbie doll house.

She shook her head and grinned.

"Okay, then, it'll do until after Thanksgiving. Now there's one more little matter we have to discuss before I actually take a check from you. I've got two kids. They'll start first grade in a couple of weeks but I bring them to work with me every day. They won't get in your way, I promise. If that's a problem then the deal is off."

She frowned. "Ever think of a baby-sitter?"

He shrugged. "Tried it. Didn't work. Won't try again."

"If that's the only problem, then welcome to Mingus, Holt Jackson," Sharlene said.

—◆—

Holt picked up his sweet iced tea, sipped it, and then set it back down. He reached across the table and touched Nikki's hand. Perfectly white-tipped fingernails, a nice diamond dinner ring, and skin as smooth as silk. She wore one of those little black dresses with thin straps and a ruffle at the knees showing off her legs, browned to the right shade from daily visits to the tanning bed during her lunch break.

"So where are we, Holt Jackson?" She laid the menu to the side and looked him in the eye.

Tonight her eyes were crystal blue and matched the color on her eyelids. Holt should have thought it was sexy but it reminded him of the skin on a dead chicken's eyelids. Three years ago in the fall he'd helped Kent and Chad's parents kill and freeze a hundred fryers and Nikki's eye shadow was that exact same shade.

"I like your eyes better their natural color," he said.

"My eyes, like my hair, change with my mood. Tonight I was blue thinking about how long we've been going out and how you run from commitment. And this week I wanted to be a blonde," she said. "Would you please give me a straight answer?"

"I've got the kids and they take a lot of my time. You knew that from our first date," he said.

The waitress appeared at their table. "You ready to order now?"

"I'll have the chicken parmigiana and bring a bottle of Principato Rosato wine," Nikki said.

"And you, sir?" the waitress asked Holt.

"The lasagna, please." He handed the waitress the menu.

"May I suggest a bottle of Rocca Delle Macie Chianti Classico Riserva with that?"

"Sweet tea is fine. I'm driving so I'd better not be drinking," he said.

"Kids!" Nikki muttered.

"It's against the law to shoot the little critters and I've taken a real likin' to them so I don't reckon I'd shoot 'em anyway," he drawled.

She jerked her hand out from under his and held both of them in her lap. "This isn't going to work for me, Holt. It's bad enough that you run all over creation with that job of yours, but now the kids…"

He leaned back in the booth, lowered his chin, and looked at her from under thick dark brows. "You knew what I did when we started dating."

"I guess I thought you'd change for me. I love Dallas and Fort Worth. You could do your little construction jobs in Dallas until you could find a decent office job," she told him.

He frowned. "I don't want a decent office job. I love my job and my business and I don't like big cities."

The waitress brought their salad in a big chilled bowl and set it on the table between them, along with a basket of warm garlic bread sticks. She placed chilled bowls and plates in front of Nikki and Holt.

"Would you please bring my meal in a to-go box?" Nikki said. "I won't be eating here."

Holt put both hands on the table. "Nikki, I'm all they've got. I can't forsake them," he said.

"There are dozens of good boarding schools. Couple right here in this area where they'd be taken care of and given a wonderful education. I attended them when I was their age. You don't have to have them underfoot twenty-four-seven."

He sighed. "But I like them underfoot all the time. That's why I take them to work with me. I wouldn't put them in a boarding school even if I had the money."

"I've got the money and I'll pay for it. You commit. I'll pay. Last chance. Going, going…" she hesitated.

He shook his head.

"Gone!"

She picked up her purse and slid out of the booth. "I'll pick up my dinner at the front counter. Have a nice life, Holt. You're a good man, just not good for me."

"Good-bye, Nikki," he whispered.

———m———

"One more tequila shot and I'm calling it a night," Sharlene said.

Her four friends all hooted.

The tall blonde patted her on the arm. "You've been saying that for the last six. I haven't seen you this wasted since the night we had the party in New York when you came home. Remember when you sober up that we are holding you to your promise to come see each of us and sign books in our town this winter. That's only three months away and we aren't going to let you back out."

"I deserved to get plastered out of my mind when I got back stateside. You fair-weather friends left me over there the last two months all by myself. And I'll be there. I'll feel like a big celebrity signing books. Three months? What month is this anyway?" Sharlene slurred.

The short brunette giggled. "It's August 15, darlin'. Four years to the day since we left you in Iraq and came home without you. It wasn't very nice of us to leave you like that, was it? But if they'd have given me a choice of staying and sleeping with Brad Pitt every night or coming home, old Brad would have been sleepin' alone."

Sharlene laughed with her. "We got to do this more often."

"What? Get drunk?" Kayla asked.

"No, get together and talk about it. No one but a vet understands what went on over there. Was it hard for you to leave behind?" Sharlene rubbed her eyes and smeared mascara.

"Hell, yeah," Kayla said.

Sharlene nodded. "I still hear the helicopters in my sleep."

"We all do," Kayla whispered. "Bringing the dead and maimed to the hospital."

"That sound of them buzzing around haunts my dreams and…" Sharlene clamped a hand over her mouth. Not even her four best friends were privy to the classified ops she and Jonah shared. She'd been in hospital administration and only she and a handful of top officials knew what else she did.

"It'll get better with time." Kayla patted her arm.

"When I'm so old I have demen… dement… whatever the hell that word is that means I can't remember, I'll still hear them," she said.

"Well, it's midnight and I've got to drive this bunch to the airport in five hours so I'm going to call it a night for all of us," Maria, the short dark-haired one of the group, said.

"Not me. I'm going to sit right here and watch you all go. Just like I did back then. I'm going to drink one more beer and then go to my hotel. It's just a couple of blocks from here. I'll be fine," Sharlene told them.

"You sure?" Maria asked.

"Sure as sand will sneak into your under-britches." Sharlene laughed at her own joke. "Call me when you get home, all of you."

Group hugs. One more toast with one more round of

tequila shots. One more suck on a lime wedge. And they were all four gone.

Sharlene looked at all the empty bottles and shot glasses on the table. "Shhhtory of my life," she muttered. She pushed the chair back, staggered to the bar, and slapped it with her fist. "One more Coors."

Holt could hardly believe his eyes. It couldn't be Sharlene Waverly of Mingus, Texas, slapping the bar right beside him. He'd just visited with her yesterday and moved into her rental house that very morning. The kids had been elated to have a house again. Judd had done a jig all the way to the front porch when she saw the hideous multicolored house.

"I'll give you one more beer for your car keys. I can call you a taxi but I can't let you drive as drunk as you are," the bartender said.

"Over my dead body. I can drive an Army jeep back to the barracks through a Shaqi windstorm after an all-night mission. I can drive anything with four wheels and can shoot the eyes out of a rattlesnake at fifty yards, so give me a beer and I'll drive myself to the hotel. Besides, it's only two blocks from here," she argued loudly.

"She's with me," Holt said. "Give her a beer and I'll see to it she makes it home."

"And who the hell are you?" Sharlene turned bloodshot eyes at him. Was there one or two fine looking cowboys sitting on the stool? Dear God, was that Holt Jackson, the man she'd hired to add the addition to the Honky Tonk?

"Don't you remember me? I'm Holt, the man who's going to put an addition on your beer joint in Mingus," he said.

"Well, slap some camouflage on my sorry butt and call me a soldier, I believe it is." She picked up the bottle of beer and turned it up. "And you're going to take me home?"

"Wherever you need to go. Boss gets killed, I don't have a job."

She set the bottle down with a thump. "Well, pay the man and let's get out of here, Mr. Jolt Hackson."

The bartender waved away the bill Holt held out. "Her friends took care of their bill and paid for her last drink. They made me promise to call a taxi for her. She's pretty wasted."

"Shit-faced is more like it," Holt said.

Sharlene laughed and stumbled when she slid off the bar.

Holt hooked an arm around her waist and slipped his fingers through her belt loops. He led her outside where the hot night air rushed to meet them as if someone had opened a giant bake oven in the parking lot.

"Hot, ain't it? That's my pink VW Bug over there. Just put me in it and follow me to my hotel, cowboy." She tried to drag him in that direction.

"You are not driving anywhere, not even out of this lot, Sharlene."

"I been to Iraq. I could take you in a fight. I'm that good. Don't let my size fool you," she said.

Holt grinned. "Where's your hotel key? I'll take you there and you can get a taxi to come get your car in the morning."

She fumbled in the back pocket of her jeans and brought out a paper envelope to the Super 8 with the room number written on the outside. "If you look that way…" she squinted to the south and tilted her head to one side "… nope, guess it's that way…" she turned too quickly and fell into his arms "… there's that sorry sucker. Do you reckon they moved the sign while me and my friends were in the bar?"

Holt laughed. "Surprising how those things happen when you've had too much to drink."

"I'm not that drunk. I was worse than this when I came home from Iraq. They all came to New York to welcome me home. Did I tell you that I was in Iraq two years? They killed Jonah. Sand was everywhere. Blowing in my eyes and sneaking down my bra. It was everywhere. It was hot like this, only hotter. Take me to my hotel. It's cool there," she said.

He put her in the cab of his pickup truck and drove to the Super 8. She was snoring when he parked.

"Hey, wake up, Sharlene; you are home," he said.

She didn't move.

"Damn!" he swore as he opened the door and rounded the back end of the truck. He opened the door and she fell out into his arms but didn't open her eyes. He carried her like a bride through the front door, across the lobby, and down the hall to the right to her room. It took some maneuvering to get the key out of his shirt pocket without dropping her, but he managed.

He laid her on the bed, removed her boots and denim miniskirt, pulled the comforter up from the side of the bed, and started to cover her when her eyes popped open. "Shhhh, if you make a noise they'll see us. You have to be very quiet. They're up there but you might not hear them yet. I hate this place. I want to go home where it's green and there ain't burned up trucks and bombed out buildings."

"What do you hear, Sharlene?"

"The helicopter blades. They buzz like flies lighting on cow patties. Shhh, they'll be here soon and we haven't finished the job. If we don't do it, the men will be in trouble."

He sat down on the other side of the bed. She grabbed his arm, looked him right in the eyes, and pulled at his arm. "Get down or they'll see you. Don't make a noise. I can't get you out of here if you talk. Just lie here beside me until they are gone."

"I'll be quiet." He stretched out beside her.

Her eyes snapped shut and she snuggled up to his side. He decided to wait until she was snoring again before he left. As drunk as she was, she might see aliens the next time her eyes opened and if the hotel owner had her committed he wouldn't have a job come Monday morning.

So she'd been in Iraq, had she? Was that the demons that made her get drunk? He thought of his sister and the night she died because of a drunk driver. He fell asleep with his sister on his mind and a strange woman in his arms.

A sliver of sunshine poured into the room in a long uneven line through a split in the draperies. Sharlene grabbed a pillow and crammed it over her head. She hadn't had such a hellish hangover since she got home from Iraq. They'd had a party to celebrate her homecoming and they'd really tied one on that night. The next morning her head had been only slightly smaller than a galvanized milk bucket. Her head throbbed with every beat of her heart and she'd sworn she'd never get drunk again. But there she was in a hotel room with the same damn symptoms.

She needed a glass of tomato juice spiked with an egg and lemon and three or four aspirin. Somehow she didn't think raw eggs and tomato juice would be on the free continental breakfast bar in the hotel dining room. She peeked out from under the pillow at the clock. The numbers were blurry but it was nine o'clock. Two hours until checkout. That gave her plenty of time for a shower. Maybe warm water would stop her head from pounding like a son-of-a-bitch.

She and her friends had hit four... or was it five bars? She didn't remember dancing on any tabletops or getting into fights. She checked her knuckles and they were free of bloody scabs. No bruises on her arms or legs. She wiggled but didn't feel like she'd been kicked or beaten. Either she didn't start a fight or she won. She frowned and in the fog of the hangover from hell she remembered arguing with a man. Then the helicopters were overhead and she told him that Jonah was dead.

Then they all left and the man brought her to the hotel. She sat up so quickly that her head spun around like she was riding a Tilt-A-Whirl at Six Flags. She was hot and sweaty, barefoot and her skirt was missing. She was still wearing panties, a T-shirt, and a bra, so evidently the man had put her to bed and left.

The newspaper reporter in her instantly asked for what, when, who, and how. She drew her brow down and remembered the what. She'd been drunk and passed out in his truck. The when involved after all the bars closed. The rest was a blur.

She moaned as she sat up on the edge of the bed and the night came back in foggy detail. Four of her girlfriends who'd served with her in Iraq had come to Weatherford for a reunion weekend. One from Panama City, Florida; one from Chambersburg, Pennsylvania; another from Orange Cove, California; and the fourth from Savannah, Georgia. Sharlene could only get away for Sunday so they'd flown into Dallas and saved the best until she arrived. One beer led to another and that led to a pitcher of margaritas and then the tequila shots. She vaguely remembered a tequila sunrise or two in the mix. Her stomach lurched when she stood up and the room did a couple of lopsided twirls.

She leaned on the dresser until everything was standing upright and her stomach settled down. If she waited for her head to stop pounding she'd be there until hell froze over or three days past eternity—whichever came first.

She held her head with both hands as she stumbled toward the bathroom. Hangovers had been invented in hell for fools who drank too much. Or maybe the angels developed them. A good hangover would keep more people out of hell than a silver-tongued preacher man ever could.

"Holt Jackson! Dear God! That's who brought me home. Lord, he'll think I'm a drunk and a slut."

She'd slept in his arms and had *not* dreamed. Even with a hangover, she knew she hadn't dreamed. She hadn't seen Jonah's eyes the night before and she'd slept for the first time in years without the nightmares. She looked back at the tangled sheets on the king-sized bed and the rush of what might have happened made her even dizzier than the hangover. She grabbed the wall and scanned each corner of the room.

"Did we? I can't remember. Oh, shit! I can't remember anything but getting into his truck," she whispered. She reached for the knob to open the bathroom door: It swung to the inside and there stood Holt Jackson, drying his hands on a white hotel towel. She had to hang onto the knob for support or she would have fallen into his arms.

"Good morning," he said.

She rushed inside, shoved him out, and hung her head over the toilet. When she finished, she washed her face and brushed her teeth. She heard deep laughter and bristled. Sure, she was in misery, but he had no right to laugh at her unless he was a saint or an angel and had never had a hangover. When she opened the door, he was sitting on the end of the bed putting on his boots and watching cartoons. He ran his fingers through his dark brown hair and green eyes looked at her from beneath thick deep dark eyelashes. His face was square with a slight dimple in his chin and his lips were full.

The anger left and was replaced with remorse. "Sorry about that. I haven't been drunk in many years."

"Not since Iraq, huh?" he said.

She glanced at the bed. "We didn't... did we?"

"You snored and I fell asleep. Didn't mean to but it had been a long day with the moving and then driving to Fort Worth for supper. I apologize. Other than that, nothing happened."

"How did you know about Iraq?" she asked cautiously.

"You tried to convince me that if you could drive an Army jeep to the barracks from something or somewhere named Shalma that you could drive your pink Bug to the hotel," he said.

"That all I said?"

"There was something about sand and helicopters, then you passed out. What did you do over there?" Holt asked.

"My job," she said. "Thanks for taking care of me. I appreciate it. I'm going to take a shower and go home."

"Sure?" he asked.

"My head is throbbing and my stomach isn't too sure about whether it's going to punish me some more, but I'm sober. Still being drunk wouldn't hurt this bad." She tried to smile.

"Okay, then. I'll see you tomorrow at the building site. Be careful." He waved at the door.

She nodded and threw herself back on the bed.

Holt had seen her in her white underpants and heard her throw up. Nothing the day could bring could top that. She waited five minutes and went back to the bathroom. She stood under the warm shower for twenty minutes, shampooed her hair twice, and could still smell smoke so she washed it a third time.

A bass drum still pounded out a thump-thump-thump when she threw back the shower curtain, wrapped a towel around her body, and a separate one around her head. Using the back of her hand, she wiped a broad streak across the steamed up mirror and checked her reflection. Dark circles rimmed her green eyes. Every freckle popped out across her nose. Kinky red hair peeked out from under the towel.

She shut her eyes to the wreck in the mirror and got dressed. The last bar where she and her friends had landed was located close to her hotel. She could easily carry her tote bag and walk that far. She didn't need to waste money on a taxi.

The free continental breakfast offered doughnuts, cereal, milk, juice, and bagels. The thought of any kind of food set off her gag reflex so she bypassed all of it and checked out. The girls had said they needed to get together once a year from now on. Sharlene thought once every five years would be enough if she was going to feel like this the next morning. Hells bells, if she was going suffer like this she didn't care if she never saw any of them again.

The noise of the heavy equipment doing road construction between the hotel and the bar ground into her ears like artillery fire in the desert. Her cowboy boots on the sidewalk sounded like popping machine gun chatter and the bag on her shoulder weighed twice as much as her pack in Iraq. The July sun was doing its best to fry her brain and sweat beaded up between her nose and upper lip. It wasn't anything compared to the Iraqi desert, but heat and hangovers did not make good partners no matter what country they met up in.

"If I ever get back to Mingus I'm never drinking again. I may not even have my nightly after-hours beer," she said.

Her hot pink Volkswagen Bug looked lonely in the bar parking lot. The night before she'd had to circle the lot a dozen times before she finally found a place to squeeze the little car into, but that morning it was the only car in the place. She opened the door, slung her bag into the passenger's seat, started the engine, and turned on the air conditioning.

She bought a cup of coffee from a McDonald's drive-by window before she got out on Interstate 20 and headed west toward Mingus. It was only forty miles from Weatherford to Mingus, but the way her head ached it could have easily been five hundred miles. She hadn't gotten relief when she parked her car in the garage behind the Honky Tonk. She carried her bags out across the grass to the door of her apartment located right behind the beer joint. She'd thought she'd move into the house in town that she'd inherited right along with the Tonk, but it was too convenient to walk through a door back behind the actual bar and be home at two o'clock in the morning.

Ruby Lee had built the Honky Tonk back in the sixties and nothing had changed since then. The outside was rough barn wood with a three-level façade and a wide front porch. Inside a long room served as poolroom, dance floor, and bar with a few tables scattered here and there.

Ruby had lived in the apartment in those first years before she bought a house in town. She died and left the Honky Tonk to Daisy, her bartender and surrogate daughter. Less than a year later, Daisy fell in love and married Jarod. She gave the joint to her cousin, Cathy. Then Cathy and Travis got married and she gave the bar to Larissa. Now Larissa was married to Hank and she'd passed the bar and her house down to Sharlene.

By the time Sharlene inherited the Tonk, it had a reputation for having a magical charm that created happy ever after marriages. Women flocked to it with a gleam in their eyes that reflected three-tiered cakes and big white wedding gowns. Sharlene could have made a fortune if she'd put a little statue on the bar and charged five bucks to rub the place where its ceramic heart was located.

In the beginning Sharlene had come to the Tonk looking for a story that would get her a better office and a promotion at the *Dallas Morning News*. She'd offered to shadow Larissa looking for that human interest story and they'd become friends. Before long she was living in the apartment back behind the Honky Tonk and helping Larissa out at the bar on weekends. When she got the pink slip from the newspaper, Larissa hired her full time. Going to Mingus for a story was the best thing she'd done since she came home from Iraq. She'd found a home, written and sold a book instead, and wound up owning the beer joint.

She forgot about the Honky Tonk charm when she slung open the door and yelled for Waylon. Usually he came running from the bedroom the minute he heard her but that day he must have been in a pout because she'd left him alone. She checked the bed to find the pillows mashed down where he'd taken a nap. He wasn't under the table or behind the sofa.

"Waylon, where are you?" she sing-songed as she held her head. "Damn cat, anyway. I've got a hangover and he's in a snit. I'd trade places with him. He can have a headache and I'll hide and pout."

She found him curled up behind the potty. When she called him he ignored her. When she picked him up he wasn't breathing.

"Waylon!" She sat down in the bathroom floor and wept, her tears dripping off her jaw and onto the dead cat's fur.

—///—

She held him until she got the hiccups, then laid him gently on the bed and went to find something appropriate to bury him in. She found a boot box and lined it with his favorite fluffy blanket, laid him inside, and taped the lid down with duct tape. She carried the box out to her car and gently laid it on the passenger's seat right beside her.

"It's a hell of a hearse but it's all I've got, old boy. At least you'll have a proper burial," she said. She wiped away tears several times during the two-mile drive from the place of death to the house where she intended to lay Waylon to rest at the edge of the garden plot.

She pulled up in the driveway and removed the boot box casket from the car and carried it to the garden. Two miniature bicycles were propped against the front of the shed and toys were lined up on the back porch.

"Crap! I forgot they were moving in over the weekend," she said.

She knocked on the back door to let Holt know she was there and exhaled loudly when no one answered. She dang sure wasn't ready to face him again that day so she would get her cat buried, leave, and no one would be the wiser.

The house had been the talk of Mingus when Larissa had painted it turquoise with hot pink trim and yellow porch posts. Then when she painted two rocking chairs bright orange and set them on the porch everyone in town had a hearty laugh at the sight. It looked like a massive hurricane had picked it up in the Bahamas and set it smack down on the edge of Mingus, Texas, without damaging a single board.

She found the shovel in the tool shed, dug a good deep hole in the softened dirt, and laid Waylon in it. After she filled the dirt back in, she found a couple of boards and some wire in the shed. She made a small cross to set on his grave and painted his name on the crossbar in bright yellow paint.

She tapped it into the ground with the end of the shovel and began her eulogy, "Waylon, you were a good friend. I will miss you. You've listened to so many stories and helped me talk my way out of many problems."

She wiped sweat from her brow and fanned her face with the black straw hat that she only wore when she mowed the yard. She was gearing up to preach a sermon when she felt a presence behind her. Not another soul in Mingus even knew Waylon. Not even Merle, Luther, or Tessa. He'd been a very private cat and hid under the bed when anyone came inside the apartment. So who in the world would be coming around to his graveside services?

She heard the doors of the truck slamming before she realized it had driven up in the driveway. When she turned around, Holt stood there with a kid hanging on each of his long legs.

"Waylon died," she said flatly.

A little boy poked his head out from behind the man's leg. "I'm not dead. I'm right here. Tell her I'm not dead. Don't let her cover me up with dirt like they did Momma. I'm scared, Uncle Holt."

She dropped down on one knee to be at the little boy's eye level. "I'm sorry. Is your name Waylon too? My cat was Waylon and he died."

A girl about the same age with the same brown hair and big brown eyes walked past both man and boy right up to Sharlene. "Ain't no need to be scared, Waylon. I ain't lettin' her put you in the ground like they did Momma." She looked at Sharlene. "Waylon ain't dead, so why are you havin' a fun'ral? And what's your name and why are you havin' a fun'ral in a yard? You're 'posed to have them things in one of them places what has gots lots of other dead people in it."

Sharlene touched her black cowboy hat and realized what a crazy picture she'd presented in her hot pink boots, a denim mini-skirt, and a bright yellow tank top. "I'm Sharlene Waverly. Your dad is going to work for me."

Holt held up a finger and both kids hushed. "We just got back from Palo Pinto where the kids stayed last night. We're on our way to Stephenville to buy groceries. We'll let you get on with burying your cat."

Sharlene slowly removed her hat and nodded.

Holt stopped on his way to the truck. "I wanted to measure one more thing. All right if I stop by the bar?"

"It's locked. I'm finished here. I'll follow you," she said.

"What about the kids?" he asked.

"They're not twenty-one but then the bar doesn't open until eight so I don't think the cops will come and take them away," she said.

"I don't want to go away with the cops," Waylon whined.

The little girl rolled her dark brown eyes and sighed. "They don't take you away unless you are twenty-one. Damn, Waylon, we ain't but six."

"You better not say that word, Judd, or you'll get in big trouble. We won't get to watch television if you say bad words."

Judd popped a fist on her hip. "He likes cartoons in

the afternoon because he don't like to be outside when it's hot. He's the smart one. I'm the mean one. Uncle Holt says we're playing at your house. Can we watch television there?"

Sharlene laughed again. "There's one in the bar and you can watch it all day if you want."

"Then let's go see this place where my Uncle Holt is going to work. I don't have to drink beer, do I, Uncle Holt? I can still have juice packs and peanut butter sandwiches, can't I?" Judd snarled her nose.

Waylon tilted his head up and looked down his nose at his sister. "I like beer."

"When did you drink beer?" Holt asked him.

"Momma left some in a bottle and I tasted it. I liked it. Judd made an awful face and tried to puke when she tasted it so she ain't so mean."

She shook her fist at him. "Am too!"

"Mean girls could drink beer," Waylon said.

"Okay, okay, that's enough," Holt said.

Sharlene touched Waylon's tombstone one more time and walked away listening to Waylon, the boy, and Judd, the girl, argue.

She smiled for the first time that day.

Chapter 2

"So who's the new family moving into your hideous house?" Merle Avery set her custom made cue stick case on the bar and motioned for a pint of Coors.

Merle had seen customers come and go in the Tonk for more than forty years. She and her best friend, Ruby Lee, had blown into Palo Pinto County at the same time. Ruby built a beer joint and Merle got rich designing western shirts for women. She was past seventy, still shot a mean game of pool, could hold her liquor, and spoke her mind. She wore her dyed black hair ratted and piled high; her jeans snug, and her boots were always polished. She was part of the fixtures at the Honky Tonk and anyone who could whip her at the pool table had something to go home and brag about.

"That would be Holt Jackson and two kids," Sharlene said.

"The carpenter, Holt Jackson? The one you've been trying to hire for weeks?"

Sharlene blushed. "Yes, that's the one. He needed a house and no one was living in mine. Rent is his bonus if he finishes my job by his deadline. He says it'll be a piece of cake with his crew. Tell the truth, I don't care if he nails up every board single-handedly or if he gets a hundred people to work for him. I just want it finished in time for the holidays. Did you see all those pink strings and little yellow plastic flags? The flags mark the electric and telephone buried wires. The string is where the foundation will be."

"I didn't know he was married, much less had two kids," Merle said.

Sharlene looked down the bar to make sure no one needed anything. "It's his niece and nephew. I thought they were his kids when he mentioned them but they call him Uncle Holt. I don't know the story behind why he's got them. Don't really matter to me, long as he gets the job done."

"So who's keeping them while he works?"

Sharlene wiped the already clean bar. "He is going to bring them with him. Today they stayed with some friends up in Palo Pinto because he and his crew had to get the equipment down here. Tomorrow they start coming here."

Merle frowned. "He's the best carpenter in the area and from what I hear he's damn fine looking, but he's not that good or that pretty."

"What does that mean?" Sharlene asked.

"You will figure it out the first time two little kids wake you up before noon. There's Tessa. Ask her what she thinks of that situation. And hot damn! There's Amos. He'll give me some competition tonight." She picked up her beer and cue case and nodded at Amos. He headed in the same direction and they reached the pool table at the same time.

"Ask me what?" Tessa asked.

Larissa hired Tessa back when she owned the joint and Sharlene kept her on when she inherited the place. Tessa and Luther, the bouncer, lived together out on a ranch between Gordon and Mingus. Someday they'd get married and the Honky Tonk could add another notch on one of the porch posts out front.

Sharlene pulled clean Mason jars from the dishwasher as she explained. "Holt Jackson is willing to put the addition onto the Honky Tonk. He needed a house so I threw in my Bahamas Mama house for free rent if he will get the work done by mid-December. Only thing is he's raising a niece and nephew and they will come to work with him."

"So?" Tessa asked.

"Merle thinks that's going to be a big problem."

"I disagree with Merle. I used to go to work with my dad. He ran a bulldozer and dug farm ponds for folks. We played and he worked. Don't remember it causing a problem," Tessa said.

A customer called from the end of the bar, "Hey lady, could we get six pints of Bud and a pitcher of tequila sunrise down here?"

Sharlene looked at the tray where Tessa already had six pint jars and a pitcher of tequila sunrise waiting. Her eyebrows rose and she cocked her head to one side.

"How'd you know what they'd order?"

"I'm not blessed with ESP, believe me. I heard them talking when I was on that end of the bar a while ago. They couldn't decide whether they wanted tequila sunrise or margaritas with their six beers. They'd made up their mind about the mixed drinks and were deciding whether they needed five or six beers. We'll just get these filled and it'll be ready." Tessa laughed.

Tessa was taller than Sharlene's five feet three inches standing five feet eight in her stocking feet. Add boots to that and it pushed her up another two inches. Her nose was a little too big for her face and she wore black-rimmed glasses that made her green eyes look enormous. She was slightly bottom heavy with wide hips and narrow shoulders. That evening she wore a sleeveless red western shirt with pearl snaps tucked into denim shorts.

"Love that shirt. Is it new?" Tessa drew up the beer and made change for a fifty dollar bill.

"Thank you. I bought it yesterday in Weatherford." Sharlene's shirt was white with pink rhinestone buttons and the traditional Texas Longhorn symbol in pink stones across the back yoke.

"So how did the big reunion day and night go?" Tessa asked.

"Fun. Hangover. Never again," Sharlene said.

"Girl, something happened. You told me the first time I met you your biggest failing was that you talked too much. Now you tell me in four words about the reunion you've talked about for a month. I figured you'd be gushing and all I get is four measly words. What happened? So you got drunk. Did you dance on the bar or take a cowboy home to the hotel with you?"

Sharlene blushed.

"That proves it. 'Fess up. What's his name? Please don't tell me you did a one-nighter and don't even know his name."

"Got customers. Nothing to 'fess up about. Didn't do a one-nighter and why does everyone think all roads lead to a member of the male species?" Sharlene hurried to the other end of the bar.

"Apple martini," the middle-aged woman said. "Where's all the good lookin' cowboys? I was told they were six to every woman over here."

Her light brown hair sported blond highlights straight from a bottle. She wore a slinky little gold sequined top that didn't have enough material in it to sag a clothesline and tight fitting jeans. Her boots had sharp toes and walking heels and they didn't come cheap. Eel seldom ever got put on a sales rack. The best makeup in the world couldn't fill in the crow's-feet or the lines around her mouth, but the dim lights in the Honky Tonk were kind. She might pass for forty after four beers. After six she could probably convince a cowboy that she was thirty-five. It would take a bottle of Jack Daniels Black Label to make her twenty-nine.

"Got to give 'em time to wash the dirt from behind their ears and brush the hay off their boots. This is hay season. They work until it's all in. They'll be along in a little while and you can take your pick. Got bikers until they get here." Sharlene motioned toward a table of Amos's friends. "And those Harleys they rode in on cost more than a custom ordered pickup truck, darlin'."

The woman rolled her eyes dramatically. "Those old geezers couldn't keep up with me."

Sharlene frowned. Amos could out two-step and out drink any of the young cowboys. "Be careful. Those *old* fellows know more about how to treat a woman than the young bucks can learn in a decade."

"Maybe I got a mind to teach the cowboy, rather than them teach me. Grab 'em young and raise them up to suit me." The woman smiled.

Sharlene set the martini on the bar. "If you are interested in quantity rather than quality, then take a look at the door. Those three all look teachable."

The woman wet her lips and stood up straight. "Yum, yum!"

Sharlene leaned on the bar and watched her paint an imaginary red laser dot on the prettiest blond cowboy's belt buckle and head that way with an extra wiggle under her tight jeans and a smile on her face.

Toby Keith had a song on the new jukebox called "I Love This Bar" and it described the Honky Tonk along with every other beer joint in Texas and Oklahoma. He said that it had lookers, hookers, all nighters, preppies, and bikers among other things. Well, the lookers just walked through the doors and the pseudo-hooker was marking her territory. Bikers would be Amos and his crew of retired businessmen who rode up from Dallas a couple of times a week to drink and dance. Preppies came from all four directions to listen to what they called vintage country music and learn to two-step in their loafers with tassels and pleated dress slacks.

Since it was Monday night the new jukebox had been turned off and the old one took center stage. Three songs for a quarter just like in Ruby's first days had become the Tonk's trademark. When the last bar owner, Larissa Morley, came to Mingus, she'd been instrumental in putting the news out on the Internet that there was a quaint little beer joint just over the border separating Erath and Palo Pinto Counties. It didn't take long for the word to spread and for Luther to have to count customers to make sure they stayed under the maximum quota for their space.

"Trip to Heaven" by Freddie Hart was playing when the woman stuck her fingers through the young cowboy's belt loops and led him to the dance floor. Freddie sang about not needing wings to fly and said that he just took a trip to heaven and he didn't even have to die. If that greenhorn got drunk enough to let her pick him up that night, he'd think he took a trip to heaven, got rejected at the door by St. Peter, and been sent straight to hell come morning time. He'd have a hellacious hangover and a nasty taste in his mouth when he figured out the sweet young thing he'd gotten lucky with was as old as his mother.

A blushing sting crawled up Sharlene's neck. What did Holt Jackson think when she passed out cold as a mother-in-law's kiss in his pickup truck? And if he hadn't been a gentleman, where would their business relationship be? Lord what a tangled mess!

The music changed to a slow Alan Jackson song and the middle-aged woman kept her cowboy on the dance floor for another round.

"What are you smiling about?" Tessa asked.

"Chigger," Sharlene said.

"Yep," Tessa agreed.

"What's a chigger?" a blonde woman asked from a bar stool right in front of them. She'd been nursing a beer for the past half hour and brushing off every man who approached her.

Tessa leaned on the bar and explained above the noise of the jukebox and the boot heels on the floor as the dancers did different versions of a fancy two-step. "A few years ago a woman used to come into the Tonk every weekend. Her nickname was Chigger."

"Was she a hooker?" the girl whispered behind her hand.

Sharlene laughed. "No. Hookers charge and Chigger said sex was too much fun to make a dollar on. She said she could put an itch on a man just like a real chigger and only a weekend in bed with her could make the itch disappear."

"What happened to her?" the woman asked.

"She got married, had a baby girl, and is expecting another baby by Christmas. She's happy as a kitten with its nose in a bowl of warm milk. You'd never guess that she used to try to put the make on every good lookin' cowboy who walked through the doors. The Honky Tonk charm worked for her," Sharlene said.

"I heard about that charm. That's why I'm here. I heard that more people have met and gotten married out of this beer joint in the last three years than on those Internet dating services," she said. "I'm Loralou, by the way."

Tessa motioned toward the packed dance floor with a bar rag. "Don't see anything you like yet, Loralou?"

Loralou shook her head. "Chigger woman got the one I might have liked."

Tessa patted her hand. "Don't give up, darlin'. See that big old bouncer back there?"

Loralou glanced at Luther standing in front of the door with his arms across his chest. He was as big as the broad side of a barn. His hair was cropped short and his round face serious. She shivered. "Don't tell me that he's interested in me, please. Just looking at him makes me want to run home and hide under the bed."

Tessa laughed. "He's harmless unless some idiot starts something in here. What I was about to tell you is that he belongs to me. You get a Chigger itch for a big man, you just remember that you got to go through me to get at him. The rest of the peacocks in here are free territory. You don't like the way that Chigger woman is trying to superglue her boobs to that cowboy, you go out there and tap her on the shoulder. She creates a problem, Luther sends her out the door and lets the next one in."

Loralou shook her head. "I'm shy."

"Shy don't cut shit in the Tonk. We got charm, darlin', but you got to make your own miracles. You like the cowboy then you make a move," Tessa said.

"Hey, could I get a bucket of Coors, Tessa? Merle just whipped me and now I got to buy a round for all the boys," Amos said.

A black leather do rag covered up his bald head with a gray rim showing around the edges. His black vest covered a T-shirt and black leather chaps covered the front and sides of his jeans. When he went to work the next morning in one of the biggest oil companies in Dallas, he'd be dressed in a three-piece custom made Italian suit and few people would believe that he rode Harleys a couple of days a week. He'd been Ruby Lee's best friend and possibly her lover for many years.

Tessa crammed six longneck bottles of Coors into a galvanized milk bucket, shoveled two scoops of ice on top, and handed the bucket to Amos. Sharlene filled an order for three quarts of Miller. When they looked down the bar Loralou tossed back the rest of her drink, took a deep breath, and plowed right out into the middle of the dance floor. She tapped the Chigger woman on the shoulder and stood back.

The cowboy smiled at Loralou and wrapped his arms around her.

The Chigger woman headed for the bar. "Give me

one of them longneck bottles of Coors. I need some beer on my breath."

"Yes, ma'am," Sharlene said.

"Damn young cowboys ain't got a lick of sense. Don't even appreciate the taste of a good apple martini. I was going to throw him back to the pack anyway before that Sunday school teacher tapped me on the shoulder. I wonder if her preacher knows where she is tonight. If he does, he's on his knees at the altar praying for her wanton soul. I bet she don't even know how to two-step," she said.

"That so?" Sharlene asked. From where she was standing it looked like Loralou had a real good handle on two-stepping and the way the cowboy was looking at her, Sharlene wouldn't be surprised if the Honky Tonk charm had just pierced her heart.

The woman fluffed back her hair and pulled a tube of bright red lipstick from her hip pocket. She used the long mirror behind the bar to apply a fresh coat and did a lip-pop to even it out. A quick smile at her reflection said she thought everything looked wonderful. "There's got to be a happy medium. Woman with class like me don't want a man with a foot in the grave and the other on a piece of boiled okra. But them young ones, fun as it would be to break them in, just don't see a good thing even when it's lookin' them in the eye."

Sharlene set a cold beer in front of her and made change for the bill she laid on the bar. "Guess you are right."

She downed half the beer, made a face, and pushed it back. "Well, here goes. I'm going hunting again."

"Good luck," Sharlene said.

"So when is a cowboy going to claim a bar stool and the charm going to work for you?" Tessa asked.

"Never. Three times, remember. A genie only gives three wishes when he floats up out of the lamp. Larissa, Cathy, and Daisy got the wishes. I got the Honky Tonk. Wishes are over for the bartenders. Only the customers get the luck of the draw these days."

———

The joint closed down at two o'clock just like usual. All the customers were out of the place and Luther and Tessa left by ten after the hour, just like normal. But Sharlene's routine was all messed up. She paced the dance floor, plugged three quarters into the jukebox, and listened to three songs by Ricky Van Shelton.

Usually she had a beer while she sat in a chair with her boots propped up on a table, listened to a quarter's worth of music, then turned out the lights. That wound her down enough to go back to her apartment and tell Waylon all the news. He would have gotten a big kick out of that night's stories. Loralou stole the cowboy from Miss Redder-than-red lipstick. The Chigger finally went home with a middle-aged rancher with a little gray in his temples. Merle had whipped everyone who'd challenged her at the pool tables like always. Amos bought one round of beers for the pool sharks. One of his biker friends, Wayne, bought a round and Derrick, a Monday night truck driver who sometimes rented trailer space out behind the Tonk, bought another. She'd sold enough beer and pitchers of mixed drinks to keep the *Titanic* from sinking and the cash register was bulging. Tessa took home a pocket full of tips and Luther had only had to break up two fights.

Sharlene went straight into the apartment and settled down on the sofa. Waylon didn't come out from the bedroom to snuggle up against her. She'd been interrupted at his funeral and never did really tell him good-bye. He'd been her friend for a long time. It wasn't right not to tell him a final adieu.

"It's the middle of the night. They're all asleep. They'll never know I was even there," she said.

She picked up her purse from behind the bar and headed toward the garage out behind the Tonk. She got out into the yard and went back into the apartment. She couldn't go to Waylon's grave at two thirty in the morning. The guys in the white coats with straightjackets in their white vans would jump on her and carry her to the nearest mental facility.

She tossed her purse on the sofa and sat down beside it. "This is crazy. It's my house and my garden spot and my cat's grave. If I want to go talk to him then I can do it and to hell with anyone who doesn't like the idea."

She grabbed up her purse and marched out the door without stopping to lock it and went straight toward the garage. She hit the remote door opener and left it up when she pulled the VW Bug out of its slot.

The moon hung in the sky like a king with all the twinkling stars acting as subjects in the lunar kingdom. She didn't pass another vehicle, but then normal people were in bed sound asleep. Hopefully, Holt and the children would be snoring too. If there were lights on in the house she promised she would drive back to the Honky Tonk and forget about telling Waylon good-bye.

The house was dark so she parked at the end of the driveway. Holt's truck and trailer with Jackson's

Carpentry written on the side separated the back porch from the garden plot.

She laid a hand on the cross and whispered, "Waylon, I missed your furry old hide tonight. I never did tell you good-bye so that's what I came to do tonight. You can't be expecting me every night but it's been a hell of a twenty-four hours. I could have bent your furry old ear for an hour tonight."

"Who's out here?" Holt whispered loudly from the back door.

"It's me, Sharlene," she said. "I'm here to visit Waylon one last time and you were supposed to be asleep. Besides, I wouldn't even be here if you hadn't interrupted my funeral today. I never got to tell him good-bye so I needed closure."

He rounded the front end of the truck and leaned against the fender. "This going to be a habit?"

He was shirtless and wore some kind of baggy pajama bottoms. His chest was broad and his dark hair stuck up every which way, testifying that he'd been asleep. Sharlene felt guilty that she'd awakened him when he had to get up early the next morning and work.

"I'm sorry I woke you up. I was trying to be quiet. And no, it won't be a nightly thing. I usually tell Waylon everything that goes on in the Tonk every night before I go to bed and I missed him. I'm not crazy."

"What kind of work did you do in Iraq?" He changed the subject abruptly.

"I'll be leaving now. Good night," she said.

"You were the one who kept talking about being there when you were drunk. I've never known a woman who was over there," he said.

"I could talk all day and you still wouldn't know how things really were in that place."

"Kind of like raising two kids. Folks can talk about it all day but until they've actually done it, they can't understand the job."

"What happened to your sister?" Sharlene asked.

"Stupidity."

"There might not be a cure for that disease but it's not fatal. I see living proof every night. I *am* living proof after Saturday night. Took me all of Sunday and until Monday at noon to get rid of the headache." Sharlene sat down in front of Waylon's cross, pulled her knees up to her chin, and wrapped her arms around her legs.

Holt's voice sounded weary when he started talking. "She got pregnant right out of high school and married the loser. He got drunk one too many times and tried to straighten out a curve before the kids were born. He wasn't even old enough to buy the beer that killed him. She went from job to job until last May. She was partying with some of her friends and shouldn't have driven home. Kind of like you were at the bar on Sunday night. She made it all the way home, got out of her car, and opened the front door to her house when her little dog ran out into the street. She ran after him. A drunk driver swerved to miss the dog and hit her. Impact killed her instantly. The dog ran off and no one ever saw it again. Her in-laws shifted the kids around among them for three weeks and then they called me and said they didn't want to raise two kids forever so I inherited them."

"I'm sorry. So the kids have been shoved from baby-sitter to grandma's most of their lives?"

He nodded. "They need stability. You heard what

Waylon said about drinking beer. She was too young
for kids and too pretty for the men to leave alone."

A hot summer wind picked up strands of Sharlene's
red hair and stuck them to her sweaty forehead. She
brushed them back and blinked away the tears.

"Hot night, ain't it?" he remarked.

"It's not as bad as the Shamal wind," she whispered.

"The what?" Holt asked.

"The Shamal winds. They're not as strong as the
Sharqi wind but they are just as wicked. We'd go hours
and hours with restricted visibility. It was like a blizzard
only with sand instead of snow. It gets into everything.
Your hair, your ears, your boots, even between your
teeth. The Shamals aren't as strong as the Sharqi but the
temperature is higher. More than a hundred degrees and
thirty mile winds make you feel like you're up against a
sand blaster. I'm sorry. That's just an information dump
that wouldn't make a bit of sense to you. The hot wind
reminded me of the first time I encountered the winds
of Iraq."

"Well, thanks for the info dump. Go on and tell your
cat the beer joint news. And Sharlene, it's all right if
you want to come around and talk to him in the middle
of the night. Most of the time, I'll be sound asleep." He
raised his arms over his head and stretched. His chest
and abdomen were muscular and ripped like he'd been
spending hours at a gym.

"Thanks, Holt. I'm sorry about your sister," she said.

"Me too," he said softly.

He disappeared around the front of the truck and she
heard the door close softly. The yellow glow of the light
coming out the kitchen window went out. She patted

the cross a couple of times and went back home to the Honky Tonk.

She parked the small car in the garage and pushed the button to lower the doors. The steady hum of truckers' engines out in the trailer spaces provided background music for the crickets and tree frogs. She opened the back door of her apartment, peeled off her clothes, and left them on the bathroom floor. A quick shower and shampoo and a favorite old nightshirt with a picture of Betty Boop on the front and she was ready for bed.

She laced her hands behind her head and stared at the dark ceiling. It became a screen for mental pictures from Iraq. The bombed out buildings. The little children in a war-torn country. The fear that was always right behind her. The joy when someone finally got to go home. The sorrow at leaving comrades behind maybe to never make it back to the States.

Chapter 3

EVERYTHING WAS EERILY QUIET UNDER THE HEAVY layer of camouflage. Sharlene missed Jonah. Even when they didn't talk he was there beside her, but now he was gone. She'd flown with him back to the hospital praying all the time that he wasn't really dead; had stood beside his body while Joyce and Kayla tried to resuscitate him; had saluted the coffin when they loaded it on the plane; and had refused to answer questions from her four best friends about why she was so sad.

Sweat ran down the bridge of her nose and dripped off the end. It reminded her of the icicles hanging on the house in Corn, Oklahoma, in the winter. When they started melting they dripped just like the sweat dripping off her nose.

The sun came up different in Iraq. She couldn't explain the odd way it looked as it jumped up from the end of the earth and into the sky. She'd been hunkered down on the top of the building across the street from the store for the last hour. She'd had a late supper the night before at the hospital with her friends before she got *the call*. After she finished the job, she'd go back to the hospital and do her job without nearly enough sleep. But that was Sharlene's life. At least once a week she got a call that meant she had extra duty. If she didn't keep up with her regular routine at the hospital, questions would be asked that had no answers because the army didn't train women to do what Sharlene did best. Hells bells, they didn't train her either. They came one day and talked to her, sent her to a psychiatrist who said she could do it without falling apart, and then they put her on a plane to Iraq.

Kayla always asked the most questions and teased her about having a secret boyfriend who kept her out all night. Letting her think that was easier than telling her the truth. Sharlene stopped thinking about Kayla's teasing the minute the store opened and the target stepped out into the light. He raised his hands. He looked like dozens of harmless old fellows who sold fruit and bread. No one would have ever mistaken him for a terrorist, yet intel said that he was the center of a cell that had been killing American soldiers. She blinked twice for good luck. Then laughter rang in the streets and children ran in front of the store. She wiped her brow and waited. How could the children laugh and play?

Same way that they did in godforsaken Corn, Oklahoma. That town and its way of life put you in this army, but it's still home. This is home to these children. They might jump at a chance to leave it but it'll always be home.

She couldn't shoot into them. She waited until they had run into the store next door and the man started back inside. She blinked twice and squeezed the trigger. The terrorist dropped to one knee and fell forward onto the sidewalk as if he was praying, but he was kneeling in the wrong direction.

She awoke sitting up in bed holding her pillow like a rifle. The noise of kids giggling outside her bedroom window was very real. Why on earth would Iraqi children be in the Honky Tonk yard? And that absolutely could not be sunshine peeking through the mini-blinds. She hadn't had time to get back to the makeshift barracks she shared with the four nurses.

Reality replaced the past in a jolt. She threw the pillow on the floor and moaned. "I've become just like Larissa and Cathy." Both of those women hated, no, they abhorred (that sounded so much worse than merely hated) mornings. And now that she'd owned the Tonk a few months she was growing up to be just like them.

She sat up and peeked out the mini-blinds to see Waylon and Judd playing tag. Their hair was plastered to their heads with sweat. They both wore shorts and knit shirts. Other than Judd's dark ponytail flying in the hot Texas wind, they were two identical blurs as they sprinted in a foot race from the end of the Tonk out to the first trees beyond the trailer park.

She remembered playing like that with her brothers until they each got too old to run and romp with her. Nostalgia and homesickness hit and she was glad she'd planned to go home to Corn, Oklahoma, for a couple of days. She'd watch her nieces and nephews play in the big backyard and listen to her mother scold her about her biological clock being broken. She'd tell her mother the same thing she had ever since she'd come home from Iraq. Women didn't marry at sixteen anymore. They waited on marriage and children. It wasn't unusual for a woman to be forty or even more before starting a family. At which time her mother would cluck her tongue and say the whole world had gone plumb crazy.

She stretched and was about to throw back the sheets when she heard Judd screaming at Holt. "I got to go right now. Where's the bathroom, anyway?"

Sharlene ran to the apartment door and swung it open. "In here, Judd. You can use my bathroom."

"Sorry," Holt said.

Sharlene ignored him. When a boy child had to go really bad and couldn't find a bathroom, he could always find a tree or a bush to hide behind. It wasn't so easy for the girl children.

Sharlene put a hand on her shoulder and ushered her through the living room, down the short hall, and right into the bathroom. "Right in here."

Judd yanked at her shorts on the way and she settled her fanny on the potty. Her feet didn't touch the floor and she swung them as she looked around at the room. It wasn't as big as the bathroom in their new house. That one had a bathtub that Uncle Holt said was as old as God. Judd wondered how Uncle Holt knew God's birthday and how old He was as she rolled off a fist full of toilet paper.

"I'm getting dressed. If you need anything, holler at me," Sharlene said.

"You got a pretty bathroom. How old is God?" Judd yelled.

Sharlene smiled. "Thank you. I don't know how old God is. Why are you asking me?"

"Because Uncle Holt says our bathtub is as old as God. I wondered how old it really is. What do you do in here all day?"

"I don't spend my whole day in the bathroom," Sharlene hollered back and looked up to see Judd standing in her doorway.

"I'm right here now. I got finished in there and I didn't mean in the bathroom. I mean in this house. If you don't have to build stuff like Uncle Holt does, then what do you do?"

"I write books."

"Like Bambi books?" Judd asked.

"Something like that."

"Oh. I like Bambi and Cinderella. Uncle Holt reads to us before we go to sleep at night. Waylon likes Bambi better than Cinderella. Someday I'm going to grow up and be just like her. I'm going to wear pretty dresses and the fairy godmother is going to make my hair all pretty. Hey, you want to come outside and play with me and Waylon? You can be it and chase us," Judd said.

"I think I'd better stay inside and get some work done but thank you. You and Waylon can come in and use my bathroom anytime you want," Sharlene said.

"How about Uncle Holt? Can he use your bathroom? I'll tell him to put the seat down," she whispered.

Sharlene bit her lip to keep from grinning. "If he can remember to do that, I suppose it's all right."

Judd took off like a jackrabbit with a coyote snapping at its fluffy tail, yelling at the top of her lungs. "Uncle Holt, Sharlene said you can use her bathroom if you put the seat down. That goes for you too, Waylon Mendoza. If you don't put the seat down I'm going to slap a knot on your head."

"No you won't," Waylon yelled. "I can outrun you."

"But when I catch you I can whoop your ass. Whoops!" She looked at Holt.

"You better learn to watch those bad words or you'll get in big trouble when you start school," Holt said. "And Sharlene, Judd can use the bathroom out in Donnie's trailer. They won't bother you again."

"Sorry," Judd sing-songed and ran off to play with her brother.

Sharlene poked her head out the door. "That's a long way to run. You might want to let them come on in here when they've got to go. It's closer and could save you a lot of laundry."

"If it becomes a bother, just tell me." He waved.

She stepped out onto the tiny back porch and leaned on a porch post. Three men were busy hammering boards into a framework for the foundation support. She hadn't realized the addition would take up so much space. There would be no side yard to mow anymore and she wouldn't be able to step outside her back door and see all the way to the road. But change was good... wasn't it?

Kayla said it had been good. Even Baghdad was better than Oklahoma according to her. She'd finished her tour and went home to get a master's degree in nursing and nowadays she was pulling in a good salary in Savannah, Georgia. Yes, change had been good for Kayla, but Kayla had been trained as an army nurse so she had something to fall back on when she got home. Sharlene had been trained as a glorified secretary and a sniper. One she could use on the outside; the other she'd sworn not to talk about once she was discharged.

At least I got away from wheat and cows in Corn, Oklahoma. And now I own a beer joint, a house, and I've written a book—which is all a miracle. Not many authors can say they got an agent and a publisher for their first rattle out of the bucket. If I had to enlist again, would I? Even with the nightmares? Who knows?

She shook off the memories and looked at the men working on her addition. It was hard to think that in a few weeks there would be walls and a roof, hardwood floors. And it all started with strings and a foundation.

Holt wore bibbed overalls that were stained and faded with a gauze muscle shirt underneath. She'd never thought the day would dawn when a man in bibbed overalls was sexy, but he was. Sweat poured off his forehead and he kept wiping at it. She vaguely remembered seeing him wipe at his forehead when they got into the pickup truck at the bar where she'd gotten so drunk.

And spilled my guts. What is it about him that gets me to talking about things like Shamal winds? I never told anyone, not even Larissa, about Iraq, other than to say that I'd been there and here I am talking to Holt Jackson about it. I can always blame tequila shots for the first time and grief for Waylon for the second, but it will not happen again. Drunk is over. Grief is past.

Folks on this side of the big sand pile didn't need to know what she did over there. If they thought owning a beer joint tainted her reputation, they'd fall off the edge of the earth if they ever found out her classified job description. She went back in the house and made a pot of coffee.

She drank two cups while she made corrections on what she'd written the week before but couldn't keep her mind on the screen. Her editor wanted the second book done by the first of December with a publication date of November of the next year. A book a year was her goal and so far she was ahead of schedule. The first one would hit the racks in November. She started another chapter, but the hero kept looking more and more like Holt rather than the blond-haired Texan she'd described earlier.

The computer screen was blank and she couldn't find words to fill it. For the first time in her life she had a dose of writer's block and it scared the bejesus out of her. Writers had to make things happen on paper. If they couldn't, they were finished.

Finally she shut her laptop and slipped her bare feet into a pair of old boots sitting beside the door. The noise had stopped and all she heard when she stepped out on the small porch was one lonesome truck engine going up the road toward Mingus and a couple of dogs barking in the distance. The kids were sitting on a blanket eating sandwiches and the men were lazing in the shade of an old pecan tree with their lunch buckets open beside them.

"Y'all need ice or anything?" she asked.

"We're all right," Holt said.

"Sharlene!" Judd ran to her side. "It's hot. Can we come inside and watch cartoons?"

"Judd!" Holt scolded.

"Well, it is hot. I'm even sweating in my under-britches."

"Then I suppose you'd better come on inside where it's cool. A girl can't have sweaty under-britches," Sharlene said.

"Come on over and meet the crew." Holt motioned her that way with a wave of his hand.

Judd hugged up to her side and kept in step with her the whole way. "Waylon still takes a nap but I don't."

Holt winked at Sharlene. Her heart tossed in a couple of extra beats but she told it she'd be stone cold dead if she didn't think he was good looking. And he had seen her without her boots on—a feat not many men could lay claim to. Not to mention he'd heard her hugging the toilet the morning after she'd tied one on and listened to her ramble on about Iraq. One more drink and she would have told him classified information. Thank God and good tequila she passed out when she did.

"This is Kent and Chad Stigler. They're brothers from up around Wichita Falls. Little community called Jolly. And this is Bennie Adams. He's from Palo Pinto. Guys, this is our boss, Sharlene Waverly."

"She's the one who painted our house all the pretty colors," Judd said proudly.

"Actually I only helped with the painting. Larissa, the lady who owned the Tonk before me, picked out the colors. I wanted to paint the Tonk just like it but she wouldn't let me. I'm pleased to meet all of you. Y'all got set up all right in the trailer spaces? You need anything else?"

"We're fine. We laid claim to the two at the very end of the lot," Kent said.

"You didn't really consider painting the beer joint those gawd awful colors, did you?" Holt asked.

"I did but Larissa convinced me it would look more like a hippy flower shop than a beer joint so I left it alone."

Kent nodded. "Well she was a wise woman. It would sour the beer and turn the whiskey to water. Why'd you put trailer spaces behind a beer joint?"

"I didn't. That happened when Cathy owned the place. Amos Lambert owns the land and he put in the trailer spaces to accommodate his oil well crew. When they finished up in this area he leased the land to the owner of the Tonk for ten years. I inherited the lease with the business," she explained.

"Well, it's an ideal situation for us. We can walk to work and we got a place to get a cold beer after we finish," Chad said. "What nights are you open? You got a live band?"

Waylon edged his way to Sharlene's other side but he was careful to keep space between them. She reached down and pulled him close.

"Open six nights a week from eight to two. No live band. We've gotten a reputation for being a vintage bar. Got an old jukebox in there that still plays three songs for a quarter. The old stuff, like Hank Williams, Waylon Jennings, and Willie. Friday and Saturday nights I plug in the new box. Blake Shelton, Miranda Lambert, the Zac Brown Band, and Josh Turner."

She clamped her mouth shut. Her biggest failing was that she talked too much, especially when she was nervous, and Holt Jackson sure enough made her nervous. She'd left Corn because she didn't intend to ever get entangled with a man who wore bibbed overalls, and there she was, panting at the sight of Holt in striped overalls.

Kent looked over at Chad. "Sounds like my kind of place. We go home most Friday nights but we like the old stuff, don't we?"

They were definitely brothers with their sandy blond hair and brown eyes, but Kent was taller and lankier than Chad. Both good looking men but neither was sexy as Holt. On a scale of one to ten, they were a good solid six and Holt was an eleven or maybe a fifteen.

"I'll have to bring Coralynn down some weekend. She's been after me to go dancing for a month. She heard about this place from a friend who comes down here pretty often when you got the old music going," Bennie said.

He was the shortest one of the three, had a receding hairline, a white rim where his cowboy hat kept the sun from his wide forehead, and a round baby face. His eyes were crystal blue and his arms bulged beneath the knit of a faded T-shirt.

"Bring her around and the first beer will be on the house," Sharlene said.

Chad chuckled. "Coralynn don't drink beer. Will the first margarita be on the house?"

"You got it," Sharlene said. "All right with you if I take these kids inside for a while?" she asked Holt.

"If they won't bother your work," he said. "Judd, don't you shut your eyes. Waylon, you wiggle every now and then so you don't fall asleep. Get your pillows out of the truck."

"I got pillows they can use. Come on, kids. I've got that satellite stuff that gets the Disney channel. I don't know if they've got cartoons in the afternoon but we'll see," she said.

Waylon shyly reached up and put his small hand in hers. Judd ran on ahead to the door and waited.

When she was in the house, Chad whistled under his breath. "Now that's one sexy lady."

Bennie grinned. "She'd be your dream girl, Chad. Owns a bar and plenty of beer."

Kent pushed his brother's shoulder. "This ugly old boy ain't got a chance when I'm here. Besides, Gloria would beat him to death with a broom handle if he looked at another woman. I'm the good lookin' brother and I'll be the one who takes her home. Bet you ten dollars I've got that pretty redhead in my trailer by the time we finish the job."

A shot of pure jealousy heated up Holt's veins. If Kent got her drunk he might win the bet. Holt had seen what happened when Sharlene had too many shots. He wasn't about to let himself get involved with another woman so soon after Nikki, especially one who owned a beer joint, but he dang sure didn't want any of his crew to go after her either.

Bennie finished off a bottle of water. "Okay, let's get the rules laid out before we bet. She can't just go in your trailer. You got to get her into bed."

Chad shook his head. "No, that ain't going to work. He could get her to sit on his bed and we'd lose. He's got to have real sex with her. Like Bill Engvall says, he's got to have some hot pig sex with Sharlene or all bets are off."

"Hell, that's worth a fifty dollar bet," Kent said. "How many of you are willing to give me fifty bucks if I sweet-talk Sharlene into a bout of sex?"

Holt stood up. "She's our boss. All bets are off and the first one I catch flirting with her is fired. You're all being disrespectful when you talk like that."

"Whew! Who pissed on your scrambled eggs this morning?" Kent asked.

"Let's get back to work. We've got a trench to dig, forms to build, and concrete to pour before we quit tonight," Holt growled.

Sharlene turned on the television and tossed each child a pillow. Waylon laid on his back and laced his hands behind his head. Judd flopped down on her stomach and propped her face in her hands.

"*Little Mermaid* is coming on Disney in about one minute," Sharlene said.

"Yes," the kids said in unison.

"You want to watch it with us?" Judd asked.

Sharlene sat down on the sofa. "Maybe for a few minutes. Anyone need to go to the bathroom before it starts?"

"Where is it?" Waylon asked.

Sharlene pointed.

"You put that lid down," Judd said.

Waylon frowned at her. "Don't boss me. I know what to do."

Judd rolled her eyes. "Men!"

Sharlene grinned. "Where did you hear that?"

Judd sighed. "From my momma. Sometimes I miss her but I don't tell Uncle Holt acause he misses her too and it makes him sad if I cry."

Waylon came out of the bathroom when the music started at the beginning of the movie and threw himself down on his pillow. "I put the seat down."

"That's good. We don't want Sharlene to fall in the potty like Momma did that time," Judd giggled.

Waylon's eyes twinkled. "She said some bad words, didn't she?"

Judd poked him on the arm. "She said it was your fault that she cussed. And besides, she got her whole as... hind end wet and that ain't funny. I fell in one time in the middle of the night when you didn't put the seat down."

"Well, it was your fault that she cussed more times than it was my fault," Waylon argued.

"Which one of you is the oldest?" Sharlene asked.

"I am but only by four minutes," Judd said.

Sharlene looked from one to the other. "You are twins?"

Waylon nodded. "Yep, we're twins but I'm smarter than she is."

"Well, I'm tougher than you are," Judd said.

"Is your name short for something?" Sharlene asked.

Judd grinned. "Nope. It's for the Judds. Them singing girls. Momma didn't know which one to name me for, Wynonna or Naomi. I'm glad she didn't name me either one of them names. I don't like them. So she named me for the one that's on television sometimes. Her name is Ashley and that's my name too. Ashley Judd Mendoza. And Waylon is Waylon Jennings Mendoza. Uncle Holt is going to 'dopt us and then we'll be Ashley Judd Jackson and Waylon Jennings Jackson. He said we could keep our names but we decided if he was going to be our 'dopted daddy then we want to have a name like his."

"Momma said that the reason we call her Judd is acause I couldn't say Ashley when I was a little kid but I could say Judd," Waylon said.

"Shhhh, the movie is startin'. If we talk, we'll miss the good parts," Judd said.

Waylon settled into his pillow more comfortably. "I thought we were going to watch TV in the bar where we went yesterday."

"It only gets the sports and news channel. I thought you'd be more comfortable in here," Sharlene said.

"I like it in here. It smells good," Waylon said. He was asleep in ten minutes.

Judd forced her eyes to stay open, blinking only when her eyes stung so badly she couldn't bear it. She finally picked up her pillow, put it next to Sharlene on the sofa, cuddled up next to her thigh, and went to sleep.

Sharlene leaned into the corner of the sofa. She and the mermaid had a lot in common. They were both misfits in the world. Sharlene had grown up in Mennonite country where the puritanical influence was still prevalent. Her parents weren't of that faith but they were very strict, very religious, and still adhered to the old ways. Girls grew up to be women who stayed home, raised babies, cooked three meals a day, and kept a spotless house. If they did work outside the home, they didn't neglect their first duties to the family. They even ironed pillowcases and tea towels and God forbid that they ever had frozen dinners for supper. Sharlene wasn't sure that a wife and mother could even look at the Pearly Gates if she didn't make supper from scratch and that involved going to the garden to gather it in the spring and summer.

Boys grew up to be men who had jobs outside the farm only if necessary and who milked cows, ran cattle, plowed, planted, harvested, and brought home the bacon. Men did not do dishes, cook, or wash clothes even if they had the time and the wife had a job in town. One sink full of dishes would rob them of their masculinity for all eternity. Sharlene figured if her mother died before her father that he'd starve to death. She might need to suggest to her mother that she start putting frozen dinners in the extra freezer out in the garage so he'd survive long enough to rope in another wife.

She went to sleep with a smile on her face. If Claud Waverly looked at another woman before or after Molly died, he wouldn't have to die to get a taste of hell. Molly would deliver it to him on a shiny silver platter.

The minute she drifted off to sleep the dreams started. Jonah was beside her in this one, asking her if she was ever going to ruin her perfect record. According to the U. S. Army, the average soldier would hit a man-sized target ten percent of the time at 300 meters using an M16A2 rifle. Snipers were required to hit the same target ninety percent of the time from 600 meters out. Sharlene was one of the elite who could hit it ninety-five percent of the time from 1000 meters. So far she hadn't missed. Jonah kept joking about her falling apart the day that she did.

They were belly down in the sand under deep camouflage waiting for the white limousine. Her first bullet was to take out the front passenger tire, then fire the RPG, rocket propelled grenade, and to leave no one alive. She blinked twice and fired and awoke with a start before it hit the target.

She wondered what Iraqi children were doing in her bunker. The noise of hammers sounded like machine gun fire. She looked up expecting to see Jonah's dark eyes but instead the credits rolled at the end of the movie on the television. Waylon's eyes popped open and he gasped when his sister wasn't lying right beside him. He slowly scanned the strange room and finally sighed when he found her on the sofa beside Sharlene.

Sharlene inhaled deeply and banished the dream from her mind.

Judd wiggled and then opened her eyes. "Did you have a good nap?" she asked Sharlene.

"Yes, I did. How about you?" Sharlene hugged her closer.

"I didn't go to sleep. I just gotted up here on the sofa and got you to sleep. I used to do that for Momma. She'd let me get her to sleep and then she'd feel all better after a good nap," Judd said.

"Well, thank you for a wonderful nap," Sharlene said. "Are you two hungry? I always wake up hungry when I take a nap."

Both heads bobbed up and down.

"How about some cookies and milk? I've got those soft chocolate chip ones and some Oreos."

"Oreos." Waylon put his pillow on the rocking chair and pulled out a kitchen chair.

Judd followed his example. "The other kind and do you have chocolate milk? I don't like white so good."

"I like white," Waylon said.

"You are so different to be twins," Sharlene commented.

"That's acause he's a boy and I'm a girl," Judd giggled.

They ate their snacks, made a hurried rest room stop, and ran out the door yelling at Uncle Holt. She stood on the tiny back porch and watched him stop work, gather them up in his arms, and listen to their chatter for a few minutes. Then they raced toward the oak tree with Judd yelling that the last one there was a dummy.

She walked out to the work site where a noisy concrete mixer turned slowly, getting the cement ready to pour into the foundation forms.

"Is all this machinery yours?" she asked.

Holt stopped and leaned on a hoe. "It belongs to the company and the four of us own the company equally. Do you want the outside to be rough wood like that part or are you going to paint it?"

She looked at the weathered wood. "Just like that if you can get it. Got any ideas about the front to make it look connected?"

"I'd just put two levels of the façade up, leaving three above the old part to hold the sign. That way it would look like it's been here forever. That old stuff is weathered cedar. New cedar would be a different color. I've got some barn wood stored up in one of Bennie's barns. There's probably plenty to cover the outside and it'd look identical to what you've already got."

"How much?" Sharlene asked.

"I reckon we could make a deal. You got time for two kids to take a nap and give them cookies and milk in the afternoons, it would make us even on the wood."

She smiled up at him. "Sounds like a good deal to me."

She turned around too quickly and ran into Kent. She started to tumble and he reached out and caught her pulling her close to his chest.

"I'm so sorry." She pushed away and blushed scarlet. "Grace is not any part of my name."

"Not me. That was the highlight of my day," Kent said.

"Well, thank you for not letting me fall on my face." She hurried toward the apartment.

"Might as well give it up, brother," Chad said.

"Why's that? She's a fine looking lady."

"Take my word for it. You ain't got a chance. She's already set her sights and they ain't on you," Chad told him.

"Who's she got her sights on, then?"

"Boss man over there."

Holt threw up both palms defensively. "Don't go gettin' me involved. I've got kids to think about, jobs to line up, and I sure ain't got time for romance."

Kent grinned. "Never know when romance might make time for you. I got to get me a couple of kids. They are regular chick magnets. Want to rent yours out for a night or two?"

"I'd sell them to you some days." Holt grinned.

Chad turned off the cement mixer. "Don't sell them to him until after Friday. Me and Gloria are taking them to see that new Disney thing. She says that you got to have kids to go to it and I was supposed to ask Holt already but I just now remembered."

"Why do you have to have kids to go to the movies?" Bennie asked.

"Because Gloria says it'd look weird for us to go without them. It's a cartoon movie and besides, she loves Judd and Waylon. Almost as much as she loves animated movies and musicals," Chad said.

Bennie wiped a hand across his forehead, leaving a streak of dirt in its wake. "That mean you don't get to watch R-rated blood, guts, gore, and war movies anymore?"

"Sure I do," Chad said. "Just not with Gloria. So can I have your kids that night? I'll take them with me after work and we'll bring them home to you after the movie. We're staying in the trailer that night and then going over to Weatherford to do some shopping on Saturday."

"You sure she wants to spend her time with kids?" Holt asked. He'd never hear the word *Weatherford* again without thinking about taking Sharlene to her hotel and accidentally falling asleep with her in his arms. She hadn't mentioned it and he sure wasn't going to. This job was working out too well for all of them to jeopardize it by saying something about how drunk she'd been or how unladylike she had been the morning after.

"Says she does. We have a blast every time you share with us," Chad answered.

"You better run, boy. Next thing she'll be wanting a couple of her own," Bennie chuckled.

Chad grinned. "Never know."

———

Sharlene fell back on the sofa and willed her heart to stop racing. It wasn't fair to be so attracted to a man who'd seen her piss drunk.

"But I am," she said breathlessly. "But that don't mean I can't get over it. I had the chicken pox when I was sixteen and I got over that so I can damn well get over this. So settle down, heart—and brain, you stop throwing up those naughty visions. Think about Larissa and her new baby and the new addition to the Honky Tonk. Don't think about Holt Jackson."

She smiled when she remembered her first impression of Larissa in the Honky Tonk. She had wondered what a classy woman like that was doing running a two-bit bar and she'd been right. So was her first impression of Holt right? Was he even remotely interested in Sharlene?

Her cell phone rang and she finally located it in her purse on the third ring. "Hello," she said without looking at the caller ID.

"I heard Holt Jackson is down there building an addition onto the Tonk," Larissa said.

"Speak of the devil and he shall appear. I was just thinking of the first time I came into the Honky Tonk and my first impression of you and how wrong I'd been. I hear a baby in the background. Let's talk about babies. That's a lot more fun than talking about men or two-by-fours." Sharlene sidestepped the Holt issue.

"Ruby is beautiful. She's sleeping four hours at a stretch now and has Hank wrapped around her finger so tight that he's become a contortionist. Now, about the Tonk. You think that addition will put an end to the cowboys and owners magic charm? That you'll be free of it if you make the Tonk look different?" Larissa said.

"Hell, I don't know," Sharlene said.

"Aha! I hear frustration in your voice so I know something is going on. I'm driving down there if you don't talk to me," Larissa said.

"Okay, but you're going to get stars in your eyes and get all romantic and it wasn't like that. It was a big mistake that's circling around to bite me on the ass and it's got big teeth and I'm scared I might have said some things I shouldn't, but he's not actin' all strange so I'm hoping I didn't..." She stopped to inhale.

"Good God, there's a cowboy involved, isn't there?" Larissa said.

"Yes, but not like Hank or Travis or Jarod. This time it's not even a thinkable situation. I got drunk and we'd met the day before when he came to give me an estimate so he took me to the hotel room. I passed out and he was a gentleman," Sharlene explained. "Wait a minute, Waylon is at the door. He must need to go to the bathroom."

"Waylon stays in the house. He has a litter pan in the bathroom. Are you still drunk?" Larissa asked.

"Come on in, honey," Sharlene said.

"Judd chased the pee out of me," Waylon giggled.

"Who are you talking to?" Larissa asked.

"I told you, Waylon had to use the bathroom. He's kind of shy but Judd is a brassy little thing and she bosses him just like I used to try to do to my brothers," Sharlene said. "He's finished and leaving now."

"I put the lid down," he said.

"That's good, kiddo." Sharlene shut the door. "I guess I'd best start at the beginning, huh?"

"That sounds like a perfect place to me and don't leave out anything. Do one of your 'in the beginning God made dirt' because I want to hear it all," Larissa said.

Sharlene took a deep breath and began.

When she finished Larissa was laughing so hard she couldn't talk.

"It's not that damn funny," Sharlene said.

"Oh, yes it is."

"How can it be funny? I was piss drunk."

Larissa got the hiccups. "I'm imagining your face when you swung that bathroom door open and there he stood. Bet that knocked you on your hungover ass, didn't it?"

"My ass wasn't what was hungover and it didn't waste a bit of time shoving him out the door and slamming it so I could throw up. Real romantic, huh?" Sharlene snapped. "And if you tell Hank one word of the story, I'm going to ban you from the Tonk forever."

"I won't tell Hank but I can't wait to call Cathy and she'll tell Daisy. Now that idea of having a Honky Tonk Christmas is even better. When all the girls come home, you'll have a cowboy too."

"I will not! I swear you've got romance on the brain."

"And you don't?"

"Hell, no. Lust occasionally but not with Holt Jackson. Can't you just imagine it? We'd get all into the kissing and foreplay and then he'd remember me smelling like a brewery and upchucking. Like I said, real romantic. Our Honky Tonk Christmas is going to be the grand opening of the new addition and the celebration of my first book being published. I'll have copies for all four of you that day and my Honky Tonk Christmas doesn't have a damn thing to do with a cowboy."

Larissa hiccupped again. "I've seen the front cover of your book and honey, it has everything to do with cowboys."

Sharlene laughed with Larissa. "I'm hanging up now before you get me all tangled up in words. One last thing, Judd—who is named Ashley Judd Mendoza, soon to be Jackson when Holt gets her and her brother adopted—loves the colors of our house. I'm letting them live in it as part of the payment for the job."

Larissa cracked up again. "I will tell Hank that part of the story. He thought my colors were butt ugly and now a man has to live there."

"Waylon says they're butt ugly too."

"You buried the cat and he never did see the house so what's he got to do with anything?" Larissa asked.

"Remember what I told you? Waylon is Judd's twin brother. My cat Waylon died and yes, I buried him there and that's why I was at the house when Holt came home with the kids Sunday." Sharlene went on to tell the part about burying Waylon and the boy, Waylon, thinking she was going to bury him.

"It just gets better and better," Larissa said.

"I think that's all and I'm really hanging up. I'll call later in the week," Sharlene said.

"Bring the kids up to the ranch for a day and we'll really catch up," Larissa said.

"Good-bye and no thanks. I'm not getting roped into anything. Kids, cowboys, or lust."

Sharlene was deep into a scene where her heroine and hero were arguing about whether or not the hero had been flirting with the local hussy at a barn dance when a loud rat-a-tat-tat on the door made her grab both ears and duck her head.

"It's just one of the kids. It's not gunfire," she said as she made her way across the living room floor.

She slung open the door to find Holt leaning against the door jamb, dirt smeared across his face and the knees of his overalls green with grass stains.

"Just wanted to thank you for letting the kids run in and out of your place all day. You didn't have to do that," he said.

"They are great kids. I loved having them around. Want a glass of iced tea? It's made," she asked.

"Love one but I'm way too dirty to sit on your furniture. Can you bring it outside?"

She nodded. "Wait for me under the shade tree."

She popped ice from two trays and filled two quart jars, poured tea over it, and carried it out to the yard where Holt was sprawled out in a fold-out lawn chair. He took the jar from her and nodded toward the construction site.

"Don't look like much but it'll go fast from this point," he said. "How'd your writing go today? Did the kids interrupt too much?"

"They were fine, really. I'm ahead of schedule and believe it or not, Judd and Waylon are wonderful role models for a couple of the kids in my story. It's hard to visualize the whole thing all finished." She waved toward the lines of concrete that would hold the foundation blocks. "It doesn't look so big right now."

"Never does. When we put up a house, that's the first thing the owners mention. That it looks so much smaller than their plans," Holt said.

"Guess it's like a book. First few pages look pretty small compared to the finished product."

"That's right. All things start small, even humans, and grow into something bigger," he said. "This tea sure hits the spot. Hey, kids, get your messes cleaned up. We've still got unpacking to do at home."

"Maybe we'll find my Barbie dolls," Judd said. She and Waylon started picking up their toys and putting them inside a big blue tote bag.

Holt handed the empty jar to Sharlene and stood up with a groan.

"You're not that old." She smiled.

"No, but I'm that sore," he said. "Thanks for the tea. We'll be back tomorrow and you'll see more progress."

"I'm looking forward to it," she said.

Merle was the first customer in the joint that night when Luther opened the doors. She grabbed a stool at the end of the bar and set her cue stick case beside her leg. "The parking lot is full and they're chomping at the bit out there. Lord, you'd think it was Saturday night instead of Tuesday the way they're all lined up."

"Coors?" Sharlene asked.

"No, I'm not drinking until I win a game then someone else can buy. I heard you got a couple of permanent trailers out there with the guys who are helping Holt put on the addition. Are they any good at pool?"

"Didn't ask them," Sharlene said. "How'd you find out about Chad and Kent so fast?"

"Honey, like I told Larissa last year, you can't fart in Mingus without everyone in town knowin' what you had for dinner. Talk don't cost a thin dime and it travels fast. I heard that the Stigler brothers were part of Holt's crew. Them and Bennie Adams. You flat out got the best carpenters in the state workin' for you. Just be damn careful. Three of 'em ain't married and you know what they say about this place. Seems like we change owners more often than a hooker changes her underpants and I'm getting tired of it. I hated change when I was a young person. Now I'm old and cantankerous and hate it even worse. So promise me you won't let any of them three sweet-talk you into leaving," Merle said.

"I promise," Sharlene said.

"That was too fast and you didn't even think about it for a minute. Something ain't right," Merle said.

Sharlene bristled. "I just met those men and everyone is trying to hook me up with one of them. I'm not interested in a cowboy, a preppie, a damn biker, or even a millionaire. I'm not ever getting married. You've lived without a man all these years so why are you pushing me at Holt Jackson?"

Merle cracked up. "I ain't pushin' you at anyone, kid. I just wanted my sassy Sharlene back and I've got her now. Talking too damn much. Making promises she probably won't keep but she's home and I'm fine for tonight. I'm going to go shoot some eight ball. I was worried you'd gone down there to that reunion shit and decided to re-enlist and be a GI Jane woman again. Then I got to thinkin' maybe you'd fall for Holt and I'd lose you that way."

"Been to the army, did my job, finished with it, and came home. Don't plan on falling for Holt Jackson or any other cowboy," Sharlene said.

Merle had no idea just how finished she was with the army, and how much she loved the solitude of the Honky Tonk.

The jukebox cranked up to a slow Hank Williams tune and the people coming inside hit the dance floor in a country waltz.

Loralou took Merle's stool.

"Hi," she said.

Tessa pushed the swinging doors at the end of the bar and grabbed a tray. She placed six Mason jars on it and got ready for the first rush when the dancers worked up a sweat and were ready for beers and mixed drinks. "You're back again. Must've liked that cowboy a lot."

"Actually, not. I found out the sorry sucker is engaged. That's my luck," Loralou said. "I'm out licking my wounds tonight and hoping there's still a charm hiding somewhere just for me."

Chad and Kent claimed a stool on each side of her before Sharlene could answer.

"Give us two of them big jars full of Miller," Chad said.

"Kent, meet my friend Loralou," Sharlene said.

"Right pleased to meet you, ma'am. You want to dance?" Kent said.

Sharlene smiled. That could knock all but Holt out of the running. Bennie was already married. Chad was seeing a woman. If she could fix Kent up with Loralou that only left Holt. If she kept telling Merle and Larissa that she wasn't interested in Holt, then pretty soon everyone would believe it and maybe she'd even convince herself. Life was getting better with every hour.

"You any good with a pool stick?" Sharlene asked Chad.

"I can hold my own but I didn't bring my cue stick."

Sharlene's smile broadened. A damn fine night all around. If he had custom made sticks then he was probably pro-quality and that would make Merle real happy. "Take those two beers and give one to that lady back there with black hair who's claiming that first table. She'll give you some competition."

"Is that a joke?" Chad asked.

"Hell, no. Don't bet with her or you'll go home without anything but your underpants. She's damn good."

Chad picked up the beers. "Tell Kent he'll have to buy his own tonight."

"I'll do it."

Kent and Loralou claimed a table in the corner and talked through several songs then Kent plugged a couple of quarters into the jukebox and they swayed together on the dance floor for thirty minutes. He led her back to the table, kissed her fingertips, and crossed the floor in a few long strides.

"Two pints of Millers. Holt don't know what he's missin' out on," Kent said.

"So you and Loralou gettin' on pretty good?" Tessa asked.

"Better than pretty good, I'd say. Is there something wrong with her that I should know about?"

Sharlene shook her head. "Is there something wrong with you that she should know? If you have a woman up in Wichita Falls, tell me now. I don't want her heart broke."

"No woman. Cross my heart and hope to die. Chad has Gloria, but I'm free as a bird," Kent said.

"You heard of the curse of the Honky Tonk?"

Kent's smile vanished. "What?"

"We don't usually tell the cowboys. You think we ought to clue him in on the curse?" Tessa asked Sharlene.

"Well, he does work for me and we probably should."

"What?" Kent asked.

"Women come in here to find husbands. There's this charm on the Honky Tonk put on it by the first owner. To the cowboys it's a curse; to the women it's a charm. I'll tell you up front, the cowboys don't have a chance. When a woman sets her sights on him, he's as good as bitin' the dust," Tessa said.

"Ah, y'all are joshing me," he said.

"Yeah, we are. It's an urban myth," Sharlene giggled.

"Whew! I was about to tell you to pour the beers down the drain and that I was goin' to light a shuck for home."

"Naw, we was just teasing," Tessa said.

He carried the beers back to the table where Loralou waited.

"How long before he realizes we were telling him the truth?" Tessa asked.

Sharlene shook her head. "Hell if I know. I just hope that fat naked little cupid keeps his arrows away from me."

Chapter 4

It was a busy Friday night with customers standing in line outside and the dance floor crowded. The jukebox hadn't been silent a single minute. Sharlene put six beers into a bucket, shoveled ice in on top of them, made change for the customer, and went on to the next one. It was routine work and she'd loved every minute of it from the time she first set foot in the bar and Larissa had put her to work drawing beers behind the bar. The story she'd intended to write never did materialize but everything had worked for the best because when she lost her job at the newspaper she already had the bartender job to fall back on. She'd had time to write a book, which had started out to be a loose biography of the first owner of the Tonk and evolved into a paranormal romance about an enchanted bar with a beautiful bartender named Rose who was a secret matchmaker. The only trouble was she forgot to take a dose of the antidote and wound up falling in love with a charmed man who was determined to prove his power was stronger than hers.

"What are you thinking about?" Tessa asked when their paths crossed from one end of the bar to the other.

"Why?"

"You looked so serious."

Sharlene drew up beers as she talked. "Probably my mother. She's the only one that can make me look serious."

"Still haven't told her, have you? It ain't goin' to get any easier. Especially when she finds out how long you've been doin' it. Besides, it's on the back of the book. You showed me the jacket cover and it's right there under your picture that you own the Honky Tonk and it gave you the inspiration for the book. Does she at least know about the beer joint?"

"No. I haven't been home since I inherited the place. The book comes out in time for Christmas. I figure I'll tell her before then," she said.

A customer pushed a shoulder between two barstool warmers. "I need two martinis and a bucket of Miller."

Thirsty, hot customers lined up four deep at the bar after a line dance that lasted through four songs. While Tessa filled the orders for daiquiris and two buckets of Miller beer, Sharlene made single pints and pitchers of mixed drinks.

Sharlene had done the job so long that she could think and work at the same time so her mind went back past six years. Her relationship with her parents had hung by a thin frayed thread after she joined the Army rather than staying in Corn, Oklahoma, and marrying the boy she'd dated all through high school. He'd proposed on graduation night but she couldn't accept the little diamond ring he had in his pocket. There had to be more to life than wheat fields, cotton plants, tractors, and cows. And she intended to experience part of it before she settled down.

"It's not as bad as the other stuff, Momma," she muttered.

"What's not that bad?" Holt asked from a stool.

She blinked three times and he was still there. He had

kids at home in the evenings and… what in the hell was he doing there and where was Judd and Waylon?

"Telling Momma that I own a beer joint," she spit out and immediately wished she could reach up into the air and cram the words back into her mouth. "I've got 'til November to tell her and I'm putting it off until the last minute."

"Be glad you got a momma to tell. I'd like a Coors, longneck, please," he said.

She pulled a beer out of the cooler, dried the cold water from the outside of the bottle, removed the top, and set it in front of him. He handed her a bill and their fingers brushed. Something tingled down her spine but she attributed it to going-home nerves.

"Where are the kids? They've talked about going to the movies all week. What happened?" she asked.

"Chad and Gloria took them for the night. Gloria likes kid movies. They'll be home about midnight. I thought I'd come take a look at this place when it had noise in it. You were right. Those are *old* songs." He nodded toward the jukebox where Buck Owens was singing about there being blue skies again when she opened up her heart and let his love come in.

"It's just for an hour. We usually don't plug up the old box on Friday night but the customers begged. Luther is putting the other one into play at ten o'clock."

George Jones's "Who Shot Sam?" put the line dancers back on the floor in a frenzy of back kicks, shuffles, and hip slapping.

"Back when that was recorded they didn't do that kind of dancing," Holt said.

"The beat of pure country music doesn't change all

that much. A few instruments get added but the solid beat is the same so the dance steps are pretty easy to adapt," she said.

She heaved a sigh of relief when Tessa hollered at her that she needed two pitchers of strawberry daiquiris. She mixed ingredients in the blenders and hoped that Holt being in the Tonk was a one-night thing just like her visiting Waylon's gravesite.

"Is that the one?" Tessa asked out the side of her mouth.

"What one?"

"Holt Jackson?"

"Well, it's Holt Jackson all right and he's the one who is making the Honky Tonk bigger," Sharlene said.

"But he's not your cowboy?" Tessa teased.

"I've only known the man a week," Sharlene snapped as she poured a blender of daiquiris into a pitcher and set it on the tray with half a dozen empty pint jars. Tessa had finished with half a dozen quarts of Coors so she left her to figure up the bill and went on to the next customer.

"Where's my carpenter?" Merle asked from the end of the bar.

"Chad is off to the movies with Holt's kids and his girlfriend. Was he any good at pool?" Sharlene asked.

"He made me sweat worse than a cowboy in tight jeans and a duck tail haircut back when I was a young filly. That boy could go pro if he ever got tired of hammerin' nails in two-by-fours," Merle said.

"Well, Holt is sitting down there at the other end. Don't know if he's any good but…"

Merle started in that direction before Sharlene could finish talking.

"It's worth a try," she threw over her shoulder.

Sharlene stole glances toward the tables as Holt and Merle battled it out with cue sticks and wooden balls. He looked almighty fine stretched out over the table to make a difficult shot in those tight jeans and turquoise plaid western shirt. His face lit up when he put the ball in the pocket and he frowned when Merle got the best of him. He made one trip to the bar for two beers before Luther plugged in the new jukebox. Half an hour later she looked up to find him standing there with a boot propped up on the foot rail as Blake Shelton sang "Hillbilly Bone."

"That's me," he said.

"You aren't a hillbilly," she argued.

"Oh, yeah, I am. Every bone in my body just like Blake is singing. I need two more beers and then I'm going to call it a night and Merle can keep her crown."

She wiped off a couple of longneck bottles of Coors and set them on the bar.

"Hey, I didn't expect to see you here tonight," Kent said.

"I work here." Sharlene wiped her sweaty palms with a bar rag.

"Yep, but Holt… oh, yeah, Chad and Gloria have the kids. Why are you buying two beers? You already got a woman picked out?" Kent asked.

"See that woman over there at the pool table?" Holt nodded in that direction.

Kent's lower jaw dropped. "You got to be kiddin' me."

"That's Merle Avery."

Kent swiped a hand across his forehead. "She as good as Chad said?"

"Better," Holt said.

"Playin' for beers or money?"

Holt held up the two beers. "Want to give it a try? I can't beat her."

"But I'm better than you. Hey, Sharlene, is Loralou here yet?"

"Haven't seen her," Sharlene answered.

Kent clapped a hand on Holt's shoulder. "Then introduce me and give me one of them beers. I been savin' your sorry ass all our lives. Guess I can do it again."

Holt's green eyes glittered as he led the way to the pool tables. "We won't discuss what happened in Jolly two years ago in front of Sharlene, will we?"

"Hey, now, don't air dirty laundry on a Friday night when we've got a pro waiting." Kent almost blushed.

Tessa wiped her hands on a bar rag and asked, "What's the difference?"

"In what?" Sharlene asked.

"In those two cowboys. Kent tried to put the make on you before he got interested in Loralou. He fills out them jeans real good. He's handsome and he can dance, plus he ain't afraid of good old hard work. Holt fills out his jeans just as good. He's not a bit more handsome. I don't know about the dancin' part but he ain't afraid of good old hard work either. So why does Kent make you smile and Holt makes you sweat?" Tessa asked.

"I'll admit he's attractive and I admire him but it will go away if I ignore it. Lust, like stupidity, isn't fatal and can be cured," Sharlene said.

Tessa threw back her head and laughed. "When you find a pill for either one, call me. We'll patent it and make so much money we'll build Honky Tonks all over the state of Texas."

Just before midnight Sharlene told Tessa she was

stepping out on the front porch for a breath of fresh air. "Be back in five. I'll see how many we got standing in line and dancing in the parking lot."

"Take ten. I can handle it that long," Tessa said.

A tailgate party was going on not far from the front porch. A group of young girls wearing jean shorts, halter tops, and boots were dancing with a bunch of guys about the same age. Sharlene could see a red and white cooler filled with beer and ice and the smell of fried chicken wafted across the lot on the hot night breezes. It brought back memories of that night when she'd come home from her final tour and danced with her friends out by the river. They'd had cold beer and watermelons one of the boys had brought straight from the patch. And they'd danced to country music from a radio in a pickup truck. Her best friend and new bride, Dorie, had been there with her husband. Jason, the boyfriend she'd turned down when he proposed, danced with her and whispered it wasn't too late for them to start over. But it was. She couldn't tell Jason what she'd done and she couldn't marry him without telling him. And she still didn't want to live in Corn, and… the ands outweighed the buts.

She noticed a couple of trucks with fogged up windows on her way across the lot and giggled. It had been a very long time since she'd found a handsome hunk and gotten in all kinds of positions in the front seat of a pickup truck. Suddenly she felt old at twenty-six.

She sat down on the foundation blocks and pulled a knee up to rest her chin on. Was the addition a mistake? Would it put a hex on the charm of the Honky Tonk? Would it make it more modern and less vintage? Would her customers stop coming and would the few that still hung on look like a dozen marbles rattling around in a big old watering tub?

"Penny for your thoughts," Holt said from the dark shadows next to the Honky Tonk.

She jumped and shivered at the same time. "You scared the devil out of me. My thoughts aren't up for sale, and if they were they'd cost a hell of a lot more than a penny. I'm not sure there's enough money to buy them. When did you leave the Tonk? I didn't see you go."

He'd been sitting with his back to the Tonk, facing the road. He moved down to where she was and sat down beside her. "Few minutes ago. Needed some fresh air and besides, I didn't know if I could even hear my phone in there in all that noise. You didn't see me leave because you were so busy filling orders at the bar. You could use at least one more bartender. Two would be even better. Then you could get away and check out Weatherford bars once in a while."

"For the record, I don't drink like that very often. My friends came for a reunion. We hadn't seen each other since… well, in several years. We let the moment get ahead of us. And Tess and I do pretty good most of the time keeping up. This is just a bumper crop tonight."

"Is that what you were thinking about?" Holt asked.

"Okay! Put your shiny new penny away and I'll tell you my thoughts for free. I was thinking about whether or not I'm making a mistake building this addition. Would Ruby like it? Will it destroy the ambiance of the place? It's gotten a reputation for an old western type honky tonk with vintage music most of the week. We're packed almost every night. When more can get in is it going to wreck the aura?"

Holt pointed to the parking lot. "Look, Sharlene. They're bringing their own beer and dancing under the stars. How can you let doubts rise up when you think about how many more drinks and beer you'll sell? You should be charging a cover charge too."

Sharlene shook her head emphatically. "The old saloons in the western movies didn't charge the cowboys to push open the swinging door. If I had my way I'd pay you to install that kind of door but it's not a smart thing in today's world. It would invite vandalism." The night was scalding hot even at that late hour, but it was nothing compared to the heat that sucked the oxygen from her lungs when Holt was that close. It had to be his shaving lotion and the black hat he had tilted down over his eyes. She'd always been a sucker for Stetsons, both in shaving lotion and hats.

Tessa was right. He did make her sweat.

"Install a folding wall. If it becomes more space than you need then you can move the jukeboxes and the pool tables back to their original places and use the big room for storage," he suggested. She was a cute little thing in those jean shorts, that bright pink stretchy top, and cowboy boots. The kids talked about her every night over supper and Judd thought she was the grandest thing since Barbie dolls. It would be easy to let her get under his skin but she was a bartender for heaven's sake.

She clapped her hands. "That's a wonderful idea. I've been wondering how in the devil I'm going to keep it closed off until the grand opening at Christmas anyway. That solves the problem and I like your idea of being able to shut it off if it becomes more room than I need."

"Why Christmas?" he asked.

"It's a long story," she said.

He swatted a mosquito. "Heat don't seem to affect the bugs. I swear that one was as big as a buzzard. It would have sucked all my blood out in five minutes. Now about that long story, I've got at least half an hour until Chad and Gloria get here with the kids."

She giggled nervously. "Promise you won't laugh."

He crossed his heart like a little boy and held up two fingers.

She inhaled deeply and began, "I came here a year ago to write a story about the Honky Tonk. I was working for the *Dallas Morning News* in the obit section and had my eye on advancement. So I got a bright idea for a story when I heard some of my friends talking about the Tonk. It was getting a reputation for vintage country but it's not really that old. That would go all the way back to Hank Snow and Porter Wagoner, but I suppose to today's bar hoppers the sixties and seventies music is vintage. And the other reputation that it's famous for is the charm. Have you heard of that?" She didn't wait for him to answer but went on. "Ruby built the place in the sixties. She ran it for almost more than forty years before she died. She was a salty old girl who rode a Harley with Amos and his crew and died in a motorcycle wreck up in Oklahoma. She left the place to Daisy who'd worked for her about seven years. Daisy was determined to run the place until she died too."

"Sounds like she had a little salt too," Holt chuckled.

"She did right up until the time that Jarod McElroy swept her off her feet and they wound up married. By then her cousin, Cathy, had come to stay with her and she gave the Tonk to her. Amos put in the trailers and brought an oil crew to town. Travis was the engineer and lived in the first trailer spot out there. Didn't take Travis and Cathy long to figure out they were made for each other when Amos talked Cathy into running the office for him. She was a high-powered accountant and knew the oil business upside down and backwards. Only trouble was Travis had wings and didn't want to settle down and Cathy had put down some roots like I have in the Honky Tonk and she didn't intend to leave. So they had to jump a lot of hurdles before they figured out their hearts weren't going to be happy without each other. Meanwhile Larissa Morley blew into town and that's a very long story that would take half the night to tell. Cathy left her the Honky Tonk when she and Travis got married. At first it looked like Larissa was going to run Ruby some competition for not letting the charm beat her. But then there was the deer and that's another story. Anyway, after a lot of ups and downs, she and Hank Wells got married and now she lives in Palo Pinto on a ranch. Do you know him?"

"I know his dad, Henry, really well. Met Hank last spring when Henry hired us to build a hay shed. I'd have never pictured his wife as owning a beer joint. She seemed like someone who'd come from money. Kind of genteel. Lovely lady with dark hair. Hank seemed to be real possessive of her." Holt was amazed.

"Yes, she did and yes, he is. She inherited the Tonk from Cathy. Did you know that Hank was also Hayes Radner? Heard of him?"

"You're shittin' me. Hayes Radner is a big-name Dallas businessman," Holt said.

"No, I'm not and yes, he was. He about blew his chances with Larissa because he didn't tell her that in Dallas he was a Radner and in Palo Pinto he was Hank Wells."

"Tell me that story another night. You were telling me about you tonight," Holt said.

Sharlene smiled. "I get sidetracked and I always talk too much and when I explain something I start from, 'In the beginning God made dirt.' So in the beginning I smelled a story about Honky Tonk owners and cowboys falling in love so I asked Larissa if I could shadow her a few weeks to see if the charm was going to hit her like it did the previous two owners. That led to me living in the apartment and then working full-time."

Holt was still frowning. "And?"

"And I gave up on the newspaper article and wrote a romance novel. It kind of veered off into another line of thought rather than being solely about Ruby, but she was the inspiration for the book. Never thought I'd sell it so fast but Larissa knew an agent who took a look at it and the next thing I knew I was signing a contract and now it'll be on the stands in November. Anyway, the reason I want to have a grand opening on Christmas Eve is because I've invited all the girls who owned the place before me down here to christen the new addition. And to see my new book, *Honky Tonk Charm*, which I plan to have on hand to sign for anyone who wants to buy a copy."

Holt laughed. "You do talk too much but now I understand everything from the beginning of time. You forgot to throw in the part about Moses and Jonah, though."

A cold shiver ran down her spine at the mention of Jonah. Of course, he didn't know about her spotter or his death. He'd been talking about the Jonah that got swallowed by the whale, but still hearing the name brought back memories she didn't want to think about.

She slapped his arm and felt the heat from the sparks dancing all around them. "If you want a sermon, you can go home to Corn with me and I'm sure my father will be glad to preach one to you."

"Corn? Where's that? Your father is a preacher? And you own a beer joint? No wonder you don't want to tell your momma," he laughed.

"Corn, Oklahoma, is where I grew up. Daddy is not a preacher but he is a deacon. And my momma almost had a heart attack when I didn't get married right out of high school. She doesn't even think I should be working when I could have a good husband and a farm. When she sees the front cover of *Honky Tonk Charm* she's going to faint and tell me that I'm kissing Lucifer's forked tail for writing such porn. When she reads on the back of the book that my beer joint was the inspiration for the book, she'll probably go into hiding."

Holt shook his head. "Why? She should be proud of your accomplishments."

"Momma won't be able to hold her head up at the Ladies Circle meetings once a week or at the grocery store or the post office when everyone in town knows her daughter is writing trashy romance, but throw that in with owning a beer joint and the sun will stand still. Oh, they'll all buy a copy the next time they get into a town where no one knows them and they'll drool on the cover but they'll never admit that they read it to Momma."

Holt chuckled. "Small towns, huh?"

Sharlene threw up her hands. "Corn, Oklahoma, huh!"

"Never going back there to live, I take it?"

"Hell would have to put in an ice skating rink and a snow cone stand for me before I'd consider such a thing," she said.

His cell phone rang. He pulled it from his shirt pocket and answered it. "Hello. Will do."

"That was short," she said.

"Got to go. Chad and Gloria are about five minutes from my house. Both kids are asleep in the backseat and we're going to try to get them inside without waking them. Thanks for the conversation, Sharlene. And don't worry about the addition. When I get finished, it's going to look like it was always there, I promise." He held out a hand to help her stand.

The electricity between them sparkled even brighter than the twinkling stars overhead. She looked up at him and he looked down, their eyes locked in the distance between their lips. She shifted her gaze to his mouth and before she could look back into his mesmerizing eyes, his sexy mouth covered hers. The kiss was intense and passionate, holding the promise of a wild night in bed. She wished it would go further and she'd wake up tomorrow morning in his strong arms.

He broke the kiss and stepped back. "I'll be seeing you," he said hoarsely, wondering the whole time why in the devil he'd kissed her. It had stirred him to painful desire, but it had also awakened things he didn't want to think about. Not with a bartender.

"I expect you will on Monday morning. Tell the kids not to forget anything that happened at the movies. I'll want to hear all about their night." She clamped her mouth shut. God, what was she thinking? He'd just kissed her and caused her knees to go all rubbery and she was talking about kids?

"Will do. Good-bye." He jogged across the parking lot.

She leaned against the outside wall until her breath came naturally instead of in short gasps as if she were in labor. Then she walked across the parking lot, opened the door to go inside, and the young folks who'd been dancing and drinking at the tailgate party set up a howl.

The spokesperson for the group shouted as she marched up on the porch and bowed up to Sharlene. She was at least thirty pounds heavier, had long black hair that Sharlene could use to cause a little pain if the woman didn't back down, and enough beer in her to make her cocky. "Hey, lady, how come you get to go inside when we have to wait for someone to leave? That's not fair!"

"I get to go inside because I own the joint and I'm the bartender," Sharlene said.

"Whoops!" The woman clamped a hand over her mouth and backed away. "Don't tell that big old bouncer to ban us. We drove two hours from Wichita Falls and we've been waiting forever to get inside. It's all our friends talk about. They got off work earlier than we did and they're already in there."

"Come back in the fall and the place will be twice this size. We shouldn't have to turn folks away very often when the addition is built," Sharlene said.

"We'll be here every week until we get inside. We heard it was the most fun bar in this part of Texas. Is there really a woman in there who is pro at pool?"

"There is and a jukebox that plays three songs for a

quarter on weeknights. It's not nearly as crowded then as it is on the weekends."

"Well, damn. Hey, y'all, guess what?" The girl went running back to her group.

Sharlene went on inside and found Tessa hustling to get the orders out.

"That was a hell of a long ten minutes. We need to think on hiring another bartender. This is getting crazier every night," she fussed. "You out there kissin' on that cowboy?"

"I was not!"

"You ain't never lied to me but I still don't believe you. Was he kissin' on you?"

Sharlene smiled sweetly. "Just which cowboy are we talkin' about, Tess? There was a lot out there who might have been kissin' on me. There was a bunch with fried chicken in a bucket and beers in a cooler and at least two Chigger women were doing business in the front seats of pickups. Thank goodness the windows were fogged over or it would have been pure old Honky Tonk porn out there."

"Oh, hush and make two pitchers of Coke and Jack while I fix a couple of buckets. You might talk too much but you sure know how to beat around the bush and I ain't got time to kick every bush between here and Houston to get the truth out of you," Tessa said.

"I see Loralou made it." Sharlene changed the subject.

"Yes, and Merle is in a pout. She says that Kent is almost as good as Chad. She's down at the far end with her third beer for the night. You'd think she'd be fat as much of that as she puts away every night," Tessa said.

"I'll work my way toward her. She might want to prop her feet up with me after two and bemoan the fact that lust will win out over eight ball most of the time," Sharlene said.

Merle left an hour before closing at two a.m. Tessa and Luther were out of the joint by ten minutes after. The parking lot was empty when Sharlene carried her bottle of beer to the porch.

Strange as it was, those same stars up there in the sky sparkled down on Baghdad the same as they did Mingus, Texas. There were still women over there saving lives, filling out papers, carrying guns, and doing what they'd been trained to do. She didn't figure there was another woman doing what she did because that job was closed to women. Some kind of special decree from two notches under God had to be signed in blood before she was allowed to get her name on the sacred classified list.

She sat down and leaned against a porch post with her feet on the steps. She could see the very place where she and Holt sat on the block foundation, where he'd kissed her, and where she'd come close to swooning. Lord, but that cowboy could have caused a holy woman to fall backwards and pull him down on top of her.

"It would be so easy, but it ain't happenin'," she said. She left her half empty bottle on the porch and went back inside. She turned out the lights and went straight to the shower.

It didn't do a bit of good. Relaxing wasn't possible. She paced the floor and finally picked up her purse and headed back to the rent house north of the Tonk. She parked on the road to keep from waking anyone and sat down in one of the orange rockers on the porch where she often went in the middle of the night to think. She pulled her knees up and propped her chin on them.

Holt also had trouble sleeping that night. Every time he shut his eyes he saw her lips, felt the warmth of them as their tongues did a mating dance. He sat straight up in bed when he heard a strange noise. It sounded like footsteps across the front porch so he looked out the window and saw someone curled up in one of the rocking chairs. Figuring it was a drunk from the Boar's Nest beer joint not even a block away, he didn't even bother with shoes. Sending a staggering fool on his way wouldn't take long enough to get his feet dirty.

He went out the front door and touched the person on the shoulder, only to have Sharlene come up from the chair ready to fight.

"What? Don't say a word. They'll… oh, my, I woke you up. Was I screaming?" she stammered.

"No, you were rocking and I heard a strange noise. I still haven't gotten used to the house so I hear every strange noise. What are you doing out here in the middle of the night?"

"Thinking. I have nightmares and can't sleep… sometimes."

"Well, hell, Sharlene. Come on in the house. I'll make you some hot chocolate. Mother always said that would put a person to sleep."

"I can't bother you like that," she said. "I'll just go on home."

"I insist. I'm awake now. I'll make us both a cup and put in an old movie. I don't have to get up tomorrow morning and the kids will sleep late from being out so long tonight." He offered her his hand.

"Are you sure?" she whispered.

"Very." He led her around the corner and into the

back door. He turned on a table lamp and pointed to the sofa.

She sunk down into it and pulled a lightweight throw over her legs. She listened for the ding of the microwave bell but it never sounded. In a few minutes he returned with two cups of steaming hot chocolate complete with marshmallows and whipped cream.

She reached for one. "I didn't hear the microwave."

"That fake stuff wouldn't put anyone to sleep. This is the real stuff, made with cocoa, sugar, and vanilla." He poked a button and the DVD tray slid out. "How about *Lucky Seven*?"

"You're willing to watch a chick flick?" she asked.

"Sure." He settled in on the sofa beside her.

She took a sip. "God, this is wonderful."

Almost as good as the kiss, she thought and blushed.

She'd seen the movie so many times that she knew the dialogue. Who would be her lucky number seven? Had there been six already and was Holt the seventh? She didn't think so. She damn sure couldn't remember six and there had been none that had turned her insides upside down with a single kiss.

She finished the chocolate and set the cup on the end table beside the lamp. Her eyes grew heavier and heavier until it was an absolute chore to keep them open. Finally, she figured she'd only close them for a minute.

Holt smiled when she slumped against him. He slung an arm around her and let her sleep. She awoke with a start when the noise of the movie ended.

"Have a good nap?" he asked.

"You will never know how good it was but I've got to go now. It's almost daylight," she said.

"Want some breakfast?"

"No, I want you to get some rest before the kids wake up," she told him.

I'd rather take you to bed, he thought.

"Thank you, Holt," she said as she stood up and headed for the door.

"For what?" He followed her.

"For the chocolate and the sleep."

"Thank you, Sharlene," he said.

She frowned. "For what?"

"This." He leaned forward and kissed her, long, hard, and lingering through several kisses that would probably send him straight to a cold shower when she left.

"Wow!" she said when he broke away.

"Yeah," he said hoarsely.

"See you Monday," she mumbled as she stumbled out the door. If his kisses could make her need to change her underpants, she couldn't imagine what a night in bed would do. She shivered as she got into the car and slapped the steering wheel. Determination to not be attracted to him just ended in pure frustration.

Chapter 5

ONLY AN IDIOT WOULD BE SITTING IN THE HOT afternoon sun when they could be inside with air-conditioned comfort. The temperature was kissing the hundred degree mark even though it was mid-September. It might be hot but it hadn't rained but once since Holt and the guys started working and that was on a weekend. So it looked like the deadline would be met in plenty of time.

The kids were running around for another half hour before quitting time. Holt and the guys were putting up studs and the addition was beginning to look like something other than a row of concrete bricks with floor joists running from one side to the other. Now it had a floor and the walls were going up.

She kept her head down and her sunglasses pushed up on her nose, but she stole long glances at Holt while he worked. No wonder she'd felt so safe in his arms that night in Weatherford. It had been the first night she'd slept without dreams of bombs and guns and Jonah's death, but they'd returned every night since other than the night she'd fallen asleep on his sofa after a cup of hot chocolate. She'd tried drinking the same thing for a whole week after that but it hadn't worked. She'd still had the nightmares. It must have been the security that she felt snuggled up in his big arms that had brought on peaceful sleep.

"Yeah, right! It was the booze the first time and the kiss the second time. Knocked me on my butt and my brain cells were so fried they couldn't dream. The second time it was the kiss. It created so much havoc in my heart that the nightmares couldn't get inside my head," she mumbled.

She forced her eyes away from Holt's arms and back to the notebook in her hand. If she didn't work while she was using the excuse to get some fresh air, then she'd have to go back inside because she had to get the book finished. She began to note out another chapter as she watched the children crawl all over the new jungle gym out behind the Honky Tonk. Holt and the guys had put it together in an hour out of scrap lumber from the project. Then at her suggestion they'd hung a couple of round discs from long ropes attached to limbs of the pecan tree. Judd and Waylon ran from one to the other, playing everything from robots to Tarzan.

Wouldn't Ruby think that was a hoot? Play equipment on the beer joint lawn. Can't get anymore redneck than that, can I? At least the new addition hides the whole backyard and no one can see it. I'm not going to tell Larissa. I can just hear her giggling about Holt working his way into my life through the children. If it did work it wouldn't last. First time I told him the whole story he'd grab those kids and run for the woods. No man would ever live with a woman like me.

"Watch me, I'm a monkey," Waylon shouted.

Sharlene looked up to see him hanging upside down from a crossbeam. "Don't fall," she called out.

"Watch me, Sharlene!" Judd ran past her and plopped her fanny down on one of the swings. "I'm Jane from the Tarzan cartoon." She gave out a bloodcurdling yell that sounded more like a half-dead starving coyote out in the woods behind the Tonk than Tarzan. If he'd sounded like that back in the day when he was the star at the movie theaters, there would have been more people rushing out than paying their quarters to get inside.

"I think Tarzan did that, not Jane," Sharlene told her and went back to brainstorming in her spiral notebook.

The new book wasn't a sequel to the first one even though her editor would have liked that. She'd started with a whole new cast of characters and timeline. This one was a time travel about a woman who went to sleep in the late eighteen hundreds and woke up the next morning in a small town in north Texas a hundred years later with a redneck husband, a double-wide trailer, and pregnant. All she could think about was getting back to her own world but then her husband won her heart and they lived happily ever after.

"Then I'm a girl Tarzan." Judd let out another whoop that had all four men looking in that direction. When they didn't see broken bones or blood, they went back to work.

Waylon left the jungle gym and claimed the other swing. "You can't be a girl Tarzan. He's a boy so I get to be him. You can be his monkey or Jane but you can't be Tarzan."

"I will *not* be a monkey. They're ugly. I'll be Jane and you be Tarzan. If you can't holler like he does then I'll do it for you. Me Jane. You Tarzan. Monkey is Chee-Chee."

"My monkey ain't Chee-Chee. That's a dumb old girl's monkey. My monkey is Hoss."

"That ain't a monkey's name. You can't name a monkey something like that. It'll think he's a horse and horses can't climb trees," she argued.

For the next hour they lived in a jungle. Their bickering and giggles blended in with the sounds of nail guns putting up two-by-four studs and men discussing what was next on the list that day and when they'd have the whole building in the dry. If they kept on at the rate they were going, it would be finished before the end of September. That meant she'd have to make a decision whether to go ahead and open the room up for customers before the grand opening or to wait.

She'd filled three pages with notes before she laid the book on the grass beside her folding lawn chair and watched them play. Her phone rang and she ignored it the first time but then it started again.

"Hello," she said.

"Sharlene, where are you? What's all that noise I hear in the background?" her mother, Molly, asked.

"I'm outside. I brought my work with me so I could get some fresh air," she said honestly.

"I'm making final dinner plans for Sunday and I'm not taking no for an answer. Your brothers and their families are all going to be here right after church and then the next day we're having a picnic in the backyard with the whole family plus friends and neighbors. You will be here. We haven't seen you since Christmas."

"I haven't changed all that much since Christmas that you wouldn't recognize me, and the road runs both ways, Momma," Sharlene said, hoping the whole time that her mother wouldn't get a wild hair and come south to see her.

"Yes, it does and if you don't come see me this weekend like you've been promising, I'm coming to Dallas the next one. I mean it, Sharlene. Your dad said he'd let the boys take care of the chores and we'd drive down there. Eight months is too long."

"I was gone a year two different times to Iraq, Momma."

"That was more than five hours away and it was impossible for you to come home. It's not now." Molly's tone didn't leave an ounce of wiggle room.

"I'm coming to Corn, I promise. So don't pack your bags and make Daddy put on dress clothes just yet," Sharlene said.

"Just you?"

"Did you want me to bring someone, Momma?" The idea was born in an instant and she rejected it just as quickly. She would not ask Holt to go with her to Corn. As much fun as it would be to take the children, she couldn't ask.

Or could she? All he could do was say no.

"You're not getting any younger. I had five kids when I was your age," Molly was saying when Sharlene snapped back to the present and stopped entertaining crazy notions.

"Can you hold just a minute?" Sharlene asked. If he went, he'd understand why she could never live in a place like Corn, Oklahoma.

"Yes, I can. Why?" Molly asked.

"I need to ask a co-worker a question," she answered. She pushed the mute button and crossed the small yard to where Holt was measuring studs and cutting the ends off with a chop saw. She tapped him on the shoulder. "Hey, I've got a favor. Do you have plans for this weekend?"

He rolled the kinks from his neck and looked at her. "Other than laundry? You want to come over and help me do laundry?"

"I do not!"

"Then why are you asking?"

She wished he'd bring those arms down and wrap them around her. "I want you to go home with me. We'll leave at the break of dawn Sunday and not get home until Monday night. You up for a five-hour drive to Corn, Oklahoma, and another one back here on Monday afternoon?"

Holt frowned. "Are you asking me to meet your parents? We haven't even gone to dinner or had a date. I mean, we did sleep together, but I don't think…"

She slapped him on the arm. "Not in that sense. I just thought the kids might like to go to the farm for a couple of days. I've got tons of nieces and nephews and there'll be family and food everywhere. If you don't want to go, can I at least have the kids?"

He grinned. "Are we going to have a custody battle if I say no?"

"My momma is waiting. She asked if I was bringing someone. I'm asking you. It's not a marriage proposal."

"Good. I don't get engaged without a ring and I don't see one in your hands. Yes, Sharlene, the kids and I would love to get away for a couple of days. The only condition is that we take my truck. I refuse to show up anywhere in a pink Volkswagen."

She bristled. "What is wrong with my car?"

"It's pink. It cramps my long legs. It doesn't have enough room for the kids to cuss a cat without getting hairs in their mouths and I don't like it. So it's up to you—are we still invited? I'll drive up and back. You provide us with a place to sleep and lots of food. Sounds fair to me."

"Can I tell the kids?" she asked.

"I don't care. You might wait until they wake up from their naps or else they'll be so hyped they won't sleep and then they'll be cranky as hell the rest of the day. I'll have to deal with them all day tomorrow wanting to know how many hours it is until we leave and how many kids will be there as it is." He went back to measuring studs and wondered why in the devil he'd just agreed to her invitation. Sure, it would be nice to get away for a couple of days and the children would love the country. But five hours up there and back with Sharlene? Just the touch of her palm on his sweaty bicep had glued him to the ground. No woman had ever affected him like that.

"I have twelve nieces and nephews, all totaled. I'd have to count how many of each but it's a good mixture so you can tell them that much. And they'll have to be ready to leave Mingus by seven and we'll get there by noon. That's five hours any way you look at it." She pushed the mute button on the phone and walked away from him.

"Hey, Sharlene," he hollered.

She turned around with the phone at her ear. "What?"

"Do I have to pretend to be something other than your employee?"

She shot him a mean look and shook her head.

"Who was that?" her mother asked.

"Someone working on a building beside my park bench," she said.

"You've got to get out of that big city, Sharlene. It's not safe for a woman to be wandering around in a place as big as Dallas with men yelling at you that you don't even know. You need to come on back home and find a good husband," Molly said.

"Maybe someday I'll get out of Dallas, Momma. But I'm not ever coming back to Corn to find a husband. Are you making ham?" She changed the subject.

"Yes and the kids are out of school up here on Monday for a teacher's meeting so we're having two days. Sunday it's ham and the family. Monday your dad is grilling burgers and hot dogs and we're inviting friends, but you didn't answer me a while ago. Are you coming up here alone? Is there finally someone in your life? Please tell me there is. Folks up here are beginning to say that you are an old maid or worse."

"Is there anything worse in Corn than being an old maid?"

"Yes, there is. Being one of them women who sell themselves or being one that don't like men," Molly said sternly.

"Well, I'm neither of those so I guess I'll just be a disgraceful old maid. Maybe I'll get a dozen cats and be a crazy old maid cat woman," Sharlene teased.

"Don't you go on like that with me when I'm worried about you ever finding a decent man at your age."

"Sorry, Momma. It was going to be a surprise but I'll tell you so you can quit fretting. I'm bringing a co-worker with me. His name is Holt Jackson and he's raising his niece and nephew. Their momma died in May. Kids are twins. Six years old. Is that all right?"

Molly squealed. "Oh, honey, I can't wait to go to Ladies Circle tomorrow morning and tell everyone. Is it serious?"

"No, Momma, it's not serious. We're just… friends."

"Once he eats my cooking, it could get serious. A mother can always hope and pray," Molly said.

"Yes, you can. Good-bye, Momma," Sharlene said.

Her conscience nagged at her. She and Holt weren't even friends. They were business associates. Of course her momma would read all kinds of scenarios into the visit and once she met Holt with his deep voice and big smile, she'd be on the sidelines with a John Deere tractor pushing Sharlene at the man. Thank God it was only for two days and then she could come back to her Honky Tonk. She'd just have to remember to go home more often.

At five thirty the hammering stopped and the work came to an end for another week. What had happened to the last four weeks? It seemed like only yesterday that Sharlene had hired Holt and now the job was nearly half done.

Sharlene and Judd helped gather up small pieces of scrap lumber and throw it in an ever growing pile in the backyard. The kids scattered it most days building forts or playhouses, but at five o'clock it was their job to get it all gathered up. As they picked up the pieces, Sharlene ran across several small end stud pieces that Judd had used for art. She'd colored them in bright colors and then stacked them up like a totem pole. The pictures made Sharlene smile and she couldn't bear to throw them into the trash heap to be carried away.

"You want to keep your colored ones over by the back door so you can play with them next week?" Sharlene asked.

Judd nodded and carried them in that direction.

"Did you tell them?" Holt whispered when Judd was out of hearing distance.

"No, I thought I'd let you have some peace tomorrow. You can tell them whenever you want," she answered.

He wiped the sweat from his brow with a bandana he kept in his pocket and slumped down into one of two old lawn chairs under the shade tree. "Sit down here with me and tell me what to expect. Am I walking into a hornet's nest? I probably shouldn't mention that I'm building an addition on your beer joint, huh?"

Sharlene sat in the chair beside him. Her sweaty thighs immediately stuck to the plastic webbing. "That would be a very good idea. I might tell them the news while I'm there. The stuff is going to hit the fan and stink to high heaven when I do."

"You're not a little girl anymore, Sharlene. You've been to Iraq and you can drive a jeep to the barracks in a hellacious sand storm," he said.

"That's a lie." She blushed.

"Oh?"

"I was just making that up but I have no doubt I could've done it," she said.

"What else did you make up? Did you really go to Iraq?"

She nodded slowly. "I really did go. Two tours. One for a year, came home and got sent right back a couple of weeks later. So it was more like one tour with a two-week break."

"What'd you do over there?"

"I'd rather talk about my family," she quickly changed the subject. "Momma is Molly and she will try to win you into the family with her cooking. I can't help that. She'd feed a homeless serial killer to find me a husband. Don't encourage her or she'll have you talking to a preacher before we leave on Monday afternoon. Oh, no! I wasn't thinking about Judd and Waylon missing school on Monday."

"Statewide teacher's meeting on Monday. I'd been meanin' to tell you but I only got the note in their backpacks yesterday," he said.

"Good. Oklahoma has a teacher's meeting that day too, so my nieces and nephews will be out," she said.

"Go on. Tell me about your dad," Holt said.

"Daddy is Claud and basically he's pretty quiet. He has to be because Momma is like me. She talks all the time. His ears probably scarred over years ago and he could be deaf by now. They've built on to the house so there's enough room. They've got two spare bedrooms and a big family room. Momma says Monday is going to be with friends invited and Sunday is family only but both days will be out in the yard. The house isn't big enough for that many to sit down to dinner. I have four brothers; Jeff, Matthew, Bart, and Miles, and four sisters-in-law and a dozen nieces and nephews."

"What kind of clothes do I need to pack?" he asked.

"Play clothes for the children. Casual for you but tuck in a set of work clothes in case the men folks decide to do something."

Holt cut his eyes around at her. "Like what?"

"Don't get that deer in the headlights look, Holt. Corn is out in the middle of nowhere but it's not *Deliverance*. They don't wear their starched and ironed jeans out to feed the cows or to harvest watermelons for the party," she said.

"Okay," he said slowly. "I'm not going to have to ride a horse or wrestle a bull to the ground, am I?"

She laughed. "No, maybe toss some feed out to the livestock or… you haven't ever ridden a horse?"

Judd came running up to them. "What horse? Is there a horse back in those woods? Can I ride it? I want to ride a horse so bad."

Sharlene patted her shoulder. "I thought you wanted to ride in a carriage like Cinderella in a fancy dress with your hair all fancy."

"And glass slippers too. But after the party at the castle, I want to ride one of them big old white horses," she said.

Sharlene hugged her tightly, not even minding the sweaty smell of a child who'd been running and playing in the hot Texas afternoon. "Someday a prince will ride up on a big white horse and he'll reach down his hand and…"

"And help me up on his horse and we'll ride off to live happy never after," she said wistfully and then ran off to tell Waylon about her prince.

"On that note, I'm taking them home. You've still got a busy night ahead of you and I've got laundry to do. See you at seven o'clock on Sunday morning. I'll pick you up so you don't have to get your car out."

"Don't want my pink car sitting in front of your Bahamas island house? And you didn't answer me. Are you a city boy who's never been on a horse?" she asked.

"I have been on a horse a few times. And your pink car wouldn't even show up in the driveway of that house. It'd be like wearing camouflage into battle. Don't oversleep, and get ready for the ride of your life. Five hours in the pickup with those two will have you pulling out all that pretty red hair," he teased.

She sat there for a long time after he and the children left with three words playing on a loop through her mind—*pretty red hair*.

———

It was one of "those" nights. Luther shooed everyone out of the Tonk at closing time. Tessa wiped down the bar one more time. They sat down at a table and talked about the new addition for ten minutes while they had their after-hours beer and then she was alone.

She tried a hot shower but it didn't work. Neither did hot chocolate. Finally she put a pair of rubber flip-flops on her feet and headed for the orange rocking chair on Holt's porch. She'd be extra quiet so that she didn't wake him. He'd had a long week of hard work in the hot sun. He needed his sleep.

She drove to the house, parked, and shut the car door as quietly as possible. She was halfway across the yard when her right foot sunk into a gopher hole in the yard and she went down on one knee.

"Well, shit!" she whispered.

"If you keep sayin' those words you'll have to stand in the corner at school," Holt said.

Thinking she'd imagined his Texas drawl, she jerked her head around in the direction from where she thought she'd heard it. Sure enough there was Holt stretched out on his back on an old quilt in the middle of the front yard.

"What are you doing?" she asked.

"I might ask you the same thing. Did you stump your toe?"

"No, I think it's a gopher hole but I'm all right. I was stealing time on your porch. I couldn't sleep." She retrieved her flip-flop from the shallow hole and stood up. When she took a step, her knee didn't hurt so evidently she was fine.

"Need some hot chocolate?"

"Already had some. It didn't work."

"I'll share my blanket. Forget the rocker and join me. I couldn't sleep either. I let the kids stay up late and watch movies since it's Friday night. They'll have to go to bed early tomorrow night so we can go to Corn on Sunday."

She sat down on the edge of the patchwork quilt. "Why are you out here again?"

"When I can't sleep this old quilt and the yard is my orange rocking chair. I watch the stars or the moon or even the clouds and think through my problems," he said.

"What are your problems tonight?"

"Sometimes I worry that I'm not enough for the kids; that they need more. Maybe we should settle down in one spot since they've started to school. Up around their dad's people so they'd at least have family around them. Lay down here beside me." He moved to one side and patted the quilt.

She stretched out and folded her arms over her chest. "You are doing fine, Holt. There's lots of single parents in today's world."

"I know that but I want them to grow up happy and well adjusted. I want Judd to go to school with her hair all fancy and I can't fix it like she likes. Everything is overwhelming when I think about them growing up and I'm all they have. What if something were to happen to me, Sharlene?"

She patted his arm. "Stop worrying. Momma says worrying about tomorrow robs us of any joy we might have today."

"Thank you," he said around the lump in his throat.

"Hey, look at that cloud. Does it remind you of anything?"

He smiled. "Which one?"

"The one just shifting over the moon. That one." She picked up her hand and pointed toward the sky with both their hands.

"A marshmallow," he said.

"No, it's a big fat elephant with his trunk hunting for peanuts. The stars are the peanuts," she laughed.

"I can see the trunk now." He laced his fingers through hers.

His touch set a tingling up her arm, down her chest, and all the way to her toes. She definitely felt like a seventh grader who finally held hands with her pimple-faced boyfriend the first time.

Hell, no! I didn't feel like this when Jason first grabbed my hand after church that Sunday night, she thought.

"Sharlene, is it Iraq?"

"In the clouds?"

"No, is it what happened over there that keeps you awake at night?"

She nodded.

"Want to talk about it?"

"I don't think it would help. It's something I have to work out for myself."

"Okay, but I'm here anytime you need to talk. You listened to my worries. I'll be glad to listen to yours."

"Thank you, Holt."

He rolled over and propped up on an elbow. "Did you see a lot of soldiers in the hospital who'd been wounded?"

She nodded again. "The helicopters brought them in."

Her drunk rambling made more sense to him. He scooted over closer to her and wrapped her up in his arms. "Nine-eleven sure blew the bottom out of our peace, didn't it?"

"Yes, it did," she said.

But not as much as you do when you touch me. How can that be possible? The very thing that sets me on fire is the thing that made me rest without dreams. It's a physical oxymoron. Right along with the idea that of all the men in the world, Holt Jackson is the very one I shouldn't want. He needs a role model for those kids who isn't a bartender.

She stayed awake longer than he did, watching the clouds take their place on center stage over the moon and then leave by stage left for the next set of animals to have their time in the spotlight. Then her eyes grew heavy and she decided it was time to go home, only she didn't want to wake him. She promised herself that she'd only shut her eyes for a minute.

The sun was the tip of a big orange ball when they awoke at the same time.

She set up with a start. "I've got to go home. Good lord, what if the kids saw us sleeping on the front lawn?"

His smile was lazy and slow as he brushed a sweet kiss across her eyelids. "Good morning, Miz Sharlene. Don't worry about the kids. I expect they'd want to join us. They'd think it was a party."

"Well, I'm going home. Thanks," she said.

"For what?"

"Sharing your quilt." She smiled.

"You are very welcome."

She rushed to the car and was back to the Honky

Tonk before she remembered that she had not dreamed. Not about Iraq or about kids. She'd slept peacefully and completely snuggled up against Holt's chest.

She touched her eyelids where his lips had been and moaned.

———

Kent grabbed the first available barstool the next night and asked Tessa, "Seen Loralou?"

"Not yet," Tessa said on the run.

"I heard you and Holt are taking a weekend trip together." He pointed to a pint of beer Sharlene was holding. "One of them."

She finished the order she was working on and filled a jar for him. By the time she set it in front of him, Merle was sitting beside him. "Where's your brother?"

"He goes home every weekend to see his girlfriend," Kent said.

"And Holt?"

"He's at home with the kids, I suppose. Got to get a good night's sleep so he can drive to Corn tomorrow." Kent talked to Merle but looked at Sharlene.

"Why would he go to Corn?" Merle asked.

"Ask Sharlene," Kent said.

She threw up both hands, one with a bar rag and the other with an empty beer bottle. "Because I asked him and the kids to go home with me for the weekend. Don't worry, the Tonk will open on Monday night as usual. If I'm not back right on the minute then Tessa is opening for me and she can go home early and I'll close up."

"Why?" Merle asked.

"Because Momma is bugging me to bring someone

home or else she's going to start combing the wheat fields again for me to find a husband. She even threatened to come to Dallas."

"Dallas?"

"Momma has no idea that I'm in Mingus or that I own the Tonk or the house. She doesn't know about my book either. And she threatened to have Daddy drive her down here to see me," Sharlene said.

Merle shivered. "Go home, kiddo. That could be disastrous."

Sharlene nodded rapidly. "I know. It's easier this way. I told her that Holt was my friend but she's already thinking about three-tiered cakes. It's not such a big deal. The men congregate in one place. The kids go wild. The women sit around the kitchen table and catch up on gossip. We won't even see each other except at meal times and then there's so many of us, it's served buffet and sit-where-you-find-a-place."

Merle fluffed at her freshly done hair. "You trying to convince me or you? Come on, boy, you'll have to do tonight since your brother has to go chase his woman."

"When Loralou gets in here holler at me," Kent said.

"Y'all been seein' a lot of each other," Tessa commented.

"It's not a big deal." He grinned.

Sharlene cocked her head to one side. "Don't look at me. I told you about the curse of the Honky Tonk. You want to take your bachelorhood in your hands, that's your decision."

"I'm not superstitious," he declared.

Tessa pushed her black-rimmed glasses up on her sweaty nose. "Well, good for you."

"What are you doing for the holiday?" Sharlene

turned around with her back to the bar and asked Tessa.

"Luther and I are going up to Ardmore to see his parents. I'm nervous as a long-tailed cat in a room full of rocking chairs. I know how Holt must feel."

Sharlene rolled her green eyes toward the ceiling. "You and Luther have been seeing each other a year. He's in love with you. It's a whole different situation. I asked them to go with me because Momma was pressuring me and besides, I wanted to take the kids up to the farm and let them play with all my nieces and nephews. I'm *not* taking Holt home to meet the family."

"Did you sleep with him yet?" Tessa asked bluntly.

Sharlene went scarlet in a flash and stammered, "Why in the hell would you ask me that dumb question?"

"Because I wanted to know. Here comes a whole new bunch in the door. Get ready for a rush," Tessa answered.

Thank the lord for thirsty, lusty women and dusty old cowboys who are tired after a week's work, Sharlene thought as she started getting clean Mason jars out of the dishwasher and setting them up six to a tray.

Loralou timed her entrance perfectly. Kent had lost his first game to Merle and there was a line of preppies itching to try to beat the pro they'd heard so much about. Kent bought her a martini and led her to the nearest table where they sat close together and talked until a slow song started. Then he led her out to the dance floor and they two-stepped to Alan Jackson, to a Blake Shelton song, and finally to a faster tune by the Zac Brown Band.

Sharlene liked the last song. It talked about having his toes in the water, his ass in the sand, and a cold beer in his hand. She'd like to take a long vacation where the waters were clear and there was nothing between her and sky but ocean. After a couple of days in Corn, she'd be ready for a trip to the sand and a cold beer. Iraq sounded good compared to Corn.

Then things got so busy that she and Tessa didn't have time to talk about anything other than mixed drinks and beers. It was like that record-breaking Saturday night that she decided to open the new room as soon as possible and christen it at the Christmas party in December. She would definitely need to hire a third bartender. Luther said the parking lot was jam packed all night and the line waiting to get a foot in the door was all the way out to the new addition. At closing more than a hundred people still hadn't gotten past the porch.

She glanced at Loralou. Maybe she'd be interested in making a few extra dollars.

"No, wouldn't ever work," Sharlene muttered. The woman was smitten and Kent was about to feel old Cupid's arrow piercing his little heart.

At five minutes until two Luther unplugged the juke-box and pointed at the clock. Amidst moans and groans, the customers left and Tessa wiped down the bar one more time before she swung the doors open at the end of the bar and joined Luther.

"Have fun in Ardmore," Sharlene said as Tessa and Luther started out the door.

Tessa held up the keys to the Honky Tonk. "Don't rush back. I'll open and you can close."

"Thanks, Tess."

"Keep your running shoes right handy. You might need them if your whole family gangs up on you."

"Got 'em packed. It's not me that'll need to outrun

'em though. It's Holt. Bless his heart, he doesn't have a clue."

"Don't tell him. He'd back out. Good night," she called as she and Luther disappeared out into the night.

Sharlene popped the top off a beer and carried it to the nearest table. She usually waited until morning to clean up but that night she started in as soon as she locked the door. The mess wasn't too bad considering the amount of people who'd come and gone in the six-hour shift, but it still took until almost four to get it in shape for Tessa to open on Monday evening.

Chapter 6

THE SUN WAS MAKING A GLORIOUS ENTRANCE ON THE eastern horizon when Holt pulled up in the Honky Tonk parking lot. By the time afternoon arrived it would be another hot day. The addition was a skeleton with a roof but it was coming along very well. Even if they did get rain for a whole week, he'd still meet his deadline. He stepped out of the pickup truck, shook the legs of his jeans down over his boot tops, and ran his fingers through his dark hair. When he stepped up on the porch, Sharlene opened the Honky Tonk door and set her bags out.

She wore an emerald green sleeveless western cut shirt with lace accents, a belt with a double heart rhinestone buckle, and snug fitting jeans. Her boots were shined to a high gloss and the same color green as her shirt. A chunky rhinestone heart pendant on a silver chain dropped down between her breasts. Just looking at her made his mouth go as dry as if he'd just eaten a sawdust and dirt sandwich and washed it down with a healthy dose of alum laced iced tea.

He tried to whistle but it came out too weak to be a whistle and sounded more like a dying groan. "You look very nice today."

"Thank you. You look mighty fine yourself," she said. His boots had been polished jet black, his jeans creased and starched and bunched up just right over his boot tops, and his dark brown hair feathered back. He wore the same turquoise plaid western shirt that he'd had on the night he came to the Honky Tonk and the colors brought out the green in his eyes. He tipped his black hat when she complimented him and she caught a whiff of his aftershave and almost melted at his feet in a puddle of whining hormones. Stetson aftershave and a Stetson cowboy hat both on a morning when she hadn't had enough sleep. What sin had she committed to be punished like that?

Damn! Damn! Damn! She had no time for any kind of relationship in her busy life. She'd finally gotten where she wanted to be and her roots ran deeper than any of the previous bartenders at the Tonk. Besides, there was that business in Iraq and if she told him the whole story, he wouldn't be available anyway. Her conscience argued that she should spit out the fact that she was a shooter in the army right then and there and see what happened. But she didn't want to arrive in Corn without him and the kids. Her mother would hang her from the nearest pecan tree.

"Perfect timing. You packed light." He was amazed that words flowed from his addled brain to his mouth and he could speak intelligently.

"It's just for one day and I didn't know how much room you had." He might not hear the heat from her unnaturally high-pitched voice but she dang sure felt it.

He pointed to the back of the truck. "I put the cover on in case it rains so nothing would get wet. I threatened to put the kids back there if they weren't good."

The corners of her mouth turned up in a brilliant smile. "Shame on you!"

He opened the tailgate, slid her duffle bag under the cover, and snapped the tailgate back shut. When he rounded the end of the truck to open the door for her she was already in the passenger's seat and talking to the children.

He kept walking and crawled in his side, sending another wave of the aroma of his cologne her way. She inhaled deeply and let it out slowly, savoring the sight of him all cleaned up and smelling like heaven.

He fastened his seat belt and started the truck. "Okay, I know we're going north but which way is best? I'm not sure where Corn is. Somewhere up in the panhandle?"

"Not that far. It's just west of the middle of the state. First you go to Wichita Falls, then to Vernon, and then I'll tell you which turns to make. Can't ever remember the highway names but I can get there blindfolded in the middle of a…"

"Shalaka storm?" His eyes glittered.

"What?" she asked.

"One of those things in Iraq."

"Shalma or Sharqi. But I was about to say a blizzard. I'd rather face off with snow as sand," she said.

"How far is it?" Judd asked.

"Five hours. Member, that's what Uncle Holt said. Five hours. That's two movies or ten times watching cartoons," Waylon said.

"But that's forever," Judd moaned.

"Just think how long you get to play with the kids when you get there then it won't seem so long," Sharlene said.

"Okay," Judd sighed. "Let's color. I betcha I can stay in the lines better than you can."

"Can not!"

"Can too and I don't color hair purple and green, either," Judd said.

"Well, I don't color it pink!" Waylon shot back at her.

"The joys of parenting," Holt said.

"There were five of us acting like that most of the time in a car. I usually sat between Momma and Daddy in the front seat and all four boys were in the back. Now I understand why we never went anywhere five hours away," Sharlene said.

"What was the longest distance you'd been before you moved to Dallas?"

"I left home right out of high school and I'd never been out of the state of Oklahoma. My grandparents were raised in Corn, so were my parents. Both sets of my grandparents are still alive and farming still yet. So I went from Corn to army to Dallas."

Holt twisted his neck around and looked at her. "You've got grandparents still alive?"

She nodded.

"And you haven't been home to see them in how long?"

"I was there for Christmas."

He slowly shook his head. "Shame on *you*!"

"Don't you talk to me like that! How long has it been since you've seen your folks?"

"My grandparents died when I was a little kid. My parents both died the year that Callie, the twin's mother, graduated from high school. They never saw their grandchildren. Car crash got Dad. Momma died with a brain aneurism. She was washing dishes and gone before she hit the floor. Don't take family for granted, Sharlene. Things can change pretty damn quick."

She felt horrible that she'd been so rude. "I'm sorry. How old were they?"

"Dad was seventy and Momma was sixty-eight. They

were both older than most parents with kids our age but they didn't marry until they were past thirty," he explained.

"My mother was sixteen when she and Daddy married. He was twenty. By the time she was my age, she had five kids," Sharlene said.

Holt's eyes twinkled when he grinned. "You really are behind, aren't you?"

They made it all the way to Wichita Falls before Judd began to squirm and fuss about needing to go to the bathroom.

"How far is it, Uncle Holt? I really, really got to go," Judd said.

"And I'm hungry. Can we get some pancakes at McDonald's?" Waylon asked.

"I don't want pancakes. I want eggs," Judd said.

"How about you? Are you hungry? Do you need to find a little girls' room?" Holt asked Sharlene as he took the next exit advertising a McDonald's.

"Both," she answered.

Holt pulled into a parking space and Judd fumbled with the seat belt. She jumped out of the truck, grabbed Sharlene's hand, and tugged on it. Sharlene jogged along beside her all the way inside where Judd came to a screeching halt and looked up at Sharlene.

"Where is it?" she whispered.

One glance toward the back and she saw the signs pointing toward restrooms. "This way."

When they were in the ladies' room Judd jerked her shorts down and sat down on the nearest potty without shutting the door. "You look pretty today," she said as she swung her feet.

"Well, thank you, so do you. I'm going in this stall

right here. When you get finished wash your hands and do not leave the bathroom without me," Sharlene said.

"Okay. Why?"

"Because Waylon and Holt might not be out in the restaurant yet and you wouldn't know where to go," Sharlene explained.

"I like you," Judd raised her voice. "I wish you would come live with us."

Sharlene gasped. "I like you and Waylon too, but I have a job at the Honky Tonk and I can't live with you."

"You don't like Uncle Holt? He's nice and he knows how to cook and wash clothes. I bet he would even make you macaroni and cheese and he don't use that kind in a box; he makes it with real cheese and butter. I bet if you lived with us he'd make you some and maybe even hot dogs. I'm going to wash my hands now and then I'll wait right by the door for you," Judd announced.

"Thank you." Sharlene was glad that six-year-old little girls didn't wait for answers to their questions. Of course she liked Holt but wild horses or promises of riches could never drag the words from her mouth aloud. Simply seeing Holt all dressed up that morning and then sitting so close to him for a couple of hours had already shaken the devil out of her resolve to keep Holt completely across a barbed wire fence from anything more than friendship.

"It won't do a bit of good anyway because I'd have to be honest and that would send the best man in the world off in a dead run," she muttered as she flushed and went to the sink to wash her hands. Judd pushed the button on the dryer and she held her hands under it until they were dry. Then she pulled a hairbrush from her purse and did what she could with her curly hair. She reapplied a coat of lipstick and leaned in closer to the bathroom mirror to check her eye makeup, running a finger under the lower lashes to smooth out the liner.

"I do not need complications and Holt Jackson is an enormous complication," she whispered.

"Uncle Holt isn't one of them things, whatever they are. Now you are beautiful. I used to tell my momma that when she fixed her eyes in the bathroom," Judd said.

Sharlene blushed and hoped that Judd didn't spit out the news that Sharlene was talking to herself in the mirror. "And I'm sure she appreciated it. Are we ready to go eat now?"

Judd reached up for Sharlene's hand.

"I'm hungry to death," she said dramatically.

Waylon and Holt were sitting at the nearest booth from the bathroom doors and Waylon sighed deeply when he saw them. "I thought you'd stay in there forever. I'm so hungry I could eat cold mashed potatoes."

"That's pretty hungry since you don't like mashed potatoes when they get the least bit cold," Holt said.

He'd stolen long glances at Sharlene all morning, but seeing her standing there made him want to take her on a real date, not just a hot chocolate or watching the clouds type of date. Every afternoon when she and the kids went inside her apartment for a nap and snacks, he wanted to go with them. When she sat in the ratty old lawn chair with her notebook and pens, he wanted to sit beside her and ask about her writing career. In the evenings when he left he wished she was going home with him. But common sense told him that the children did not need a bartender for their role model. Still, no woman had ever set his heart to racing and his hands to itching like Sharlene did when he held her.

"Are we going to eat or just sit here?" Waylon asked.

"I was trying to decide what I want to eat," Holt said.

"Well, I want pancakes and Judd wants eggs. Can we tell the lady while you think about it?" Waylon asked.

"I want pancakes too," Sharlene said. "Momma's making ham for dinner."

"Ham?" Holt stood up and followed the kids to the counter.

"You don't eat ham?" Sharlene asked.

"Yes, I do," he said.

Granted he'd been thinking about Sharlene rather than listening to her when she told him what they'd be doing at her family gathering, but he could have sworn that the next day was when the whole clan arrived for a get-together.

"Both. Sunday dinner is always a family thing at Momma's. My brother's wives all bring a couple of side dishes or desserts. Nothing is ever laid in stone since new recipes are always cropping up," Sharlene said.

"I want pancakes," Waylon told the cashier.

Holt hurried to the counter to order for him and both children then turned back to Sharlene. "What do you want?"

"Pancakes. The meal deal. Orange juice instead of coffee." She fished in her purse and handed Holt a twenty dollar bill.

He shook his head. "Put that away. I'll buy breakfast if we're having ham for dinner."

"The deal was that you'd provide transportation and I'd provide food," she argued.

"That was before I realized there would be that much food. I'm just leveling the playing field here," he said.

She put the money in her purse. He didn't have any idea that it would take a hell of a lot more than pancakes to level out the hills and rough spots. Larissa once said that the heart would have what it wanted or else the person it lived in would be miserable. When she got back to Mingus, Sharlene intended to have a long sit-down conversation with her heart. It got its way when it didn't want to stay in Corn and marry her high school sweetheart. It got its way when it wanted adventure instead of a home and children. It got its way big-time when it got the Honky Tonk. So it could damn well be satisfied with past victories and stop aggravating her about Holt Jackson.

All that went into the trash can was empty containers and plates when they'd finished eating. Judd and Waylon hadn't wasted a single bite of food and they'd sucked their milk cartons completely dry just to make noise. They'd barely gotten settled back in the truck and headed west toward Vernon when Waylon grabbed his pillow and shoved it up against the back door.

"Shhhh," Judd said. "Waylon is sleeping."

"I don't suppose you need to rest your eyes for a little bit, do you?" Holt asked.

"I'm not sleepy, but if I put my pillow on Waylon's side and lay on it, it'll keep him from waking up," she said.

Holt looked up in the rearview mirror and talked to Judd. "Well, we wouldn't want him to wake up, would we? He gets pretty grouchy if he wakes up too soon."

"If he's grouchy, he'll color outside the lines and get mad at me when I don't. I'll just keep him asleep for a little while and then he'll be nice." She snuggled in next to his side and shut her eyes.

Sharlene poked a finger in Holt's arm. "You're a sneaky son of a gun."

"Parenting takes being sneaky," he said. "I'm just repeating tricks my mother used on me and Callie when we were kids."

"How much older are you than Callie?"

"Four years. She would have been twenty-four in June but she died a few weeks before her birthday. She was eighteen when the twins were born. I'm twenty-eight. And you?"

"It's not polite to ask a woman how old she is, but I'm twenty-six. My brothers are thirty, thirty-two, thirty-three, and thirty-four. Momma had three in three years, waited a couple of years, had Miles, and then I came along four years after that."

"What are their names?"

"Jeff is the oldest. He's married to Lisa. Then there's Matthew and Clara, and Bart and Fiona, and Miles and Jenny," she said.

"They all redheaded?"

"No, I'm the only one with red hair. They say that Great-Grandma Waverly had red hair and it waited a few generations to pop back up. Momma says that I'm just like her. Independent. Willful and headstrong. What about Callie? Did she have green eyes and dark hair like you?"

Holt chuckled. "Callie had light brown eyes like Waylon and her hair was blond. No, that's too general. It was corn silk yellow like Mother's. She was almost as tall as I am and very slim built. Her husband was

full-blood Hispanic. They'd gone to school together
from kindergarten up. Ray might have grown up to be a
good man but he was just a kid with too many respon-
sibilities. They were barely eighteen when they married
and they both still had a lot of running around and play
left in them. Then he was killed and Callie had to grow
up too fast. She had two kids to raise and she couldn't
even take care of herself. Her in-laws did what they
could, but hell, they weren't even forty yet so they didn't
want to be strapped down to the job of raising two little
babies. I did what I could. I was out in east Texas on a
big job trying to make enough money to help support her
and the kids when the accident happened."

"Why didn't you take them all with you on jobs like
you do now?" Sharlene asked.

"Hey, don't take that tone with me. I did what I could.
Callie refused to leave Mineral Wells. Her in-laws
moved there when she and Ray were in high school so it
was only natural for them to rent a place over there when
they married. Her excuse was that she had Ray's rela-
tives to keep the kids while she worked, but I knew she
liked her wild friends. I don't see a one of your brothers
setting the road on fire from Corn to Mingus to drag
you out of a beer joint. There's not a lot of difference,
is there?"

"Not a one of my brothers knows I have a beer joint
and besides, it's different. I don't have two children,"
she smarted off.

"Yeah, that really does make it different," he answered coldly.

She clamped her mouth shut. There wasn't a single
doubt in her mind that all four of her brothers and her

father would blaze a trail to Mingus if they knew she was a bartender. They'd be worse than Ruby Lee's preacher father had been. He would have stood in the parking lot thumping on his Bible and saving souls from the scorching fires of hell brought on by beer and loose-legged women. Her brothers would storm past Luther and carry her out like a sack of potatoes over their shoulders back to Corn where they'd put her in chains in the storm cellar until she agreed never to go back to the Honky Tonk.

And that would mean I'd grow old and gray surrounded by Momma's canned peaches and jelly because they'd never get that kind of promise from me. And Holt Jackson had better keep his mouth closed tightly or I'll show him just how much temper a red-haired Waverly has.

"Tell me more about Iraq," he said.

"Why?" She wasn't through pouting.

"Because it's still a long way and I don't like this uncomfortable silence."

"What do you want to know?" Sharlene asked.

"Did you know anyone that left kids behind and their folks had to take care of them?" he asked.

"My friend Maria was a nurse in the hospital. She had a little daughter, Abby. She used to kiss her picture a dozen times a day. I caught her crying in the supply room more than one time when they brought in the children who'd been hurt," Sharlene said.

"Did Maria come home?" Holt asked softly.

Sharlene nodded. "She was one of the four friends who I was with that night in Weatherford. Abby is in first grade now and Maria has remarried."

"That would be tough, dealing with the hurt children," Holt said.

"It was. One night Maria called me down to the emergency bay from the office and she was holding a blanket. They'd brought a baby no more than six months old in wrapped up in that blanket. Her mother, father, and older sister were all dead. Her grandmother brought her in but it was too late. The grandmother was wailing and Maria just stood there holding the bloody blanket."

"What did you do?"

"I put my arms around the grandmother and sat with her until she got it under control. She'd lost four that night to a suicide bomber. The family had been in the marketplace buying food for the next day."

"And Maria?"

"She had trouble letting go of the blanket. Abby is a dark-haired, part Hispanic child, like Judd, and she had a security blanket." Sharlene hesitated and looked out the side window for a while before she went on. "It's not something that you can put into words. The feeling when they bring our troops into the hospital all blown to hell. And all I did was the paperwork. I never had to shove my hand inside a wound to stop the bleeding until a surgeon could get there."

She thought about Jonah and the night she sat beside his body in the hospital. The hole in his neck and the blood. His dark eyes staring off into nothing.

She went on, "But the children are the hardest part. They should get to grow up and run and romp. They should color outside the lines and get yelled at when they don't put their toys away. They shouldn't be carrying rifles or letting some zealot tell them they are dying for the greater good when they strap enough C4 on them to blow up fifty people in a marketplace."

"I'm not sure I even agree with this war," Holt said.

"Well, I'm sure I don't. We're over there fighting a civil war that's never going to end. It's another Viet Nam and there will be no winners, only losers. And the children are the biggest losers. They'll never know a country that isn't blown to hell and back. And our troops… it changes everyone who goes there. One way or the other, they don't come home the same person that first set foot on the desert sand."

"How did it change you?" Holt asked.

"It made me appreciate things like quietness and grass. The little things that I got up every morning and took for granted."

"Wouldn't want to go back then?"

"After the first tour I didn't want to go back but that's where they sent me after a two-week leave. I thought since I'd already done my year it was over but it didn't work that way. I was deployed right back to my same old duty station. And no, I don't ever want to see that kind of pain and suffering again," she said.

"But were there good times that you can latch onto and remember?" he asked.

"Of course. There's a camaraderie that can't be explained. It goes almost as deep as blood kin because you have to depend on each other so much. But it's crazy because when you come home, you aren't so sure you want to see those people again."

Holt nodded. "Because even though there were good times, seeing them reminds you of the bad ones?"

"That's right," she said. "It took four years for the five of us who shared a barrack to get together again. We enjoyed a day and night and we had a good time but we couldn't get that feeling of dependence on each other back again. We've each moved on and it's in different directions. I'm not so sure that we'd have even been friends if we'd all known each other in high school."

"Tell me about the other four. You ever plan on seeing them again?"

"I made a drunken promise to go see each of them this fall when my book comes out. They're setting up book signings in each of their towns for me. It's a big thing for them and me too. Now I wish I hadn't made the promise but I'll keep my word," she said.

"Why do you wish that?"

"I don't do so well with public appearances," she said.

"Hey, just remember the people who attend are interested in your writing and want to hear about it," he said.

"Thanks." She smiled.

"Now tell me about the other four."

"Okay. Kayla was from a little podunk town in Oklahoma just like me. She joined the military for the training and for the GI Bill benefits when she got out. She was smart but poor and grew up on the wrong side of the tracks. She'd seen more in her eighteen years than any of the rest of us. Her mother was a drunk and her father had flown the coop when she was too little to even remember him. She used to say that war wasn't anything compared to the fights she'd seen between her mother and her boyfriends."

"And Maria?" Holt asked.

"Half Hispanic. Got married her first year of college and let her sorry husband talk her into joining the Air Guard with him. It would only be one weekend a month and just look at all the money they'd have for that week-end's work. She got pregnant. He finished his time with the Guard and decided not to reenlist but she still had a couple of years. He filed for divorce when Abby was born and her unit got sent to Iraq."

Holt shook his head. "That's sorry luck. Two down, two to go. Tell me about the others."

She almost smiled.

"What?" he asked.

"Lelah. She could make you laugh even in the worst of days."

"What's her story?"

"She joined when she was hungover. Got drunk the night of her bachelorette party and decided she wasn't ready to get married. The next morning she walked into the recruiting station and joined the army. Her fiancé called off the wedding the day before the ceremony be-cause he said he couldn't be married to the military. She told us that's exactly what she wanted him to do. She's the oldest one of us and had a degree in nursing. The army didn't even hiccup when they shoved the papers at her. She's in Florida now. Says she likes that sand better than Iraqi sand."

"And the fourth one?" Holt asked.

"That would be Joyce. The quiet one. Her mother sent her a food package every week and she shared with us. We ate lots of Skittles and beef jerky because that's what she liked."

"What was her story?"

"She believed in the war, that we should take out all the terrorists."

"And?" Holt pressed.

"After a tour, she changed her mind. She heads up a committee against it now," Sharlene said.

"And now the fifth one of the bunch? What about Sharlene?"

"Sharlene is nearly home where she will be a good daughter for a couple of days then go back to being a barroom hussy," she laughed.

He reached across the back of the seat and massaged her neck. "You are too tense, Sharlene. Loosen up or you'll have a headache before we even get there."

"You can't understand until you've been to Corn," she said. His big callused hands felt so good on her tight neck muscles.

"That family can be a nightmare. I believe I do, lady."

She leaned forward and tilted her head to the left. "Right there. God, that feels so good."

"You've got a knot as big as a baseball. Stop worryin'. I promise I won't pick my nose or spit on the carpet," he said.

She smiled. "For a massage like this, I'd…"

He chuckled. "You'd what?"

"Nothing." She blushed.

She'd been about to say that she'd take him to the hay barn and spend the night with him if he'd give her a full body massage. But if he did, her skin would be so hot that she'd set the barn on fire.

"Come on. Tell me what you'd do for a full body massage with good smellin' oil and maybe candles and music?" he teased.

Judd stretched and asked Waylon if he'd had a good nap. Holt looked back in the rearview at them.

"Saved by the bell," he said.

"What bell? Was there a bell? I didn't sleep. I just rested my eyes and thought about all them kids we get to play with," Waylon said.

"Me neither," Judd said. "How much more is it 'til we get there? And who has got a bell?"

"Just a few minutes." Sharlene looked out the window in hopes that the blush would fade and Holt would forget about what she'd do for a massage. Just thinking the word kept her face a bright scarlet. She couldn't imagine the color it would be if they really did wind up in that kind of place.

Good Lord, I've got to rein in my wicked imagination, she thought.

"That's forever." Holt did his best imitation of Judd whining.

Sharlene smiled. "No, it's not. Five hours is forever. A few minutes is just a little while and besides, I don't color outside the lines."

"If y'all fight you'll have to stand in the corner," Waylon said seriously.

"Or you won't get to play all day and that's even worse," Judd chimed in.

"It is not!" Waylon declared.

"Is too," Judd shot right back at him.

They argued about which punishment was worse.

Holt looked over at Sharlene and winked.

"You want to play nice?" he asked.

"I'll decide later. Right now I'm hungry and I get real cranky when I'm hungry," she said.

He chuckled.

"What's so funny?"

"Your grandma Waverly must have been a handful."

She pointed a finger at him but was careful not to let it touch him in any way. "Yes, she was and I didn't dip into her gene pool. I fell into it and almost drowned before they fished me out and named me after her. So don't you forget it, mister. Make a right turn at the next crossroads."

"Bossy as well. Was your grandmother's name Sharlene?"

"No, it was June and that's my middle name. And Mr. Jackson, you're skating on some thin ice saying that I'm bossy."

"Don't be silly, Sharlene. Uncle Holt ain't skatin'. He's driving us to see the kids and play. Are we almost there? How much farther is it?" Waylon asked.

"Not very far now," Holt told him. "I bet if you look at the Bambi book real slow and really study the pictures we'll be there before you get it done."

Waylon turned the pages as fast as he could. When he reached the last page, a very loud voice piped up behind Sharlene, "The end."

"Are we there yet, Sharlene? Is that the house where all them trucks and cars is parked?" Waylon look at the swings in the backyard. "Can we play on them too, Sharlene?" If Judd hadn't been strapped down with seat belts she would have hit the ceiling the way she was jumping around and trying to see everything at once.

"After dinner, you can run and play all you want and since you rested your eyes on the way up here, I bet you don't even have to take a nap today. Don't be shy with the kids," Sharlene said.

"I'm not ever shy with anyone. I walk right up to

them and tell them my name and if they want to be my friend then we are friends and if they don't want to be my friend then I go find someone who does. Waylon is shy, but not me," Judd said.

"Am not," he said.

"Yes you are but I'm not," Judd defended her stand.

He crossed his arms over his chest. "Are too."

Sharlene didn't care who was the introvert or the extrovert. She just wanted the first five minutes to be over and done with. After that she could hold her own. Dread and excitement both filled her as Holt parked the truck beside the others. Her mother came out on the porch and started toward them as Sharlene opened the truck door.

Molly wrapped Sharlene up in a hug. "You are just in time. We're ready to say grace in five minutes. Lord, girl, you are too thin. Have you been sick?"

"This is your mother?" Holt asked. The woman was nearly six feet tall, had blond hair without any sign of gray, and crystal clear blue eyes. There was no way someone as lanky as Molly Waverly had given birth to five kids and yet there she stood, living proof that she had. Her flowing floral skirt stopped at mid-calf. A soft blue knit shirt was belted at her narrow waist with a wide yellow belt that matched her sandals.

"I already like him for just those four words. Y'all come on in the house and meet the rest of the family," Molly said.

"Momma, this is Holt and this is Waylon and his twin sister, Judd," Sharlene said.

"You can call me Molly and you kiddos can call me Granny like the rest of the kids do." She threw an arm around Sharlene's shoulders. "Their momma must have liked country music, so that makes her our kind of people."

Chapter 7

CLAUD MET THEM AT THE DOOR AND WRAPPED Sharlene up in a fatherly hug. "Lord, girl, it seems like ten years since I've seen you. I'm Claud Waverly, Sharlene's daddy, and you must be Holt Jackson. We're glad to have you, son. Make yourself at home." He shook Holt's hand with his right one but kept his left arm around Sharlene's shoulders for a minute longer before he stooped down to talk to the children. He was as tall as Molly, had thick brown hair and green eyes. He wore creased jeans, boots, and a white pearl snapped shirt and a wide smile split his angular face.

"We're glad you kiddos could come see us this weekend. We got lots to do on the farm and there's plenty of other folks your size to play with but first we have to make Granny happy and eat all this food she's cooked up for y'all. You can call me Gramps like the other kids do. That all right with you?"

Waylon nodded seriously.

"I am hungry to death," Judd said.

Claud chuckled. "Then let's get on in here. Everyone is gathered around the table and waiting for y'all to get here so we can say grace. Come on in and then we'll let you eat and get acquainted with the other kids."

He led them inside where everyone waited. "Okay, Jeff, will you give thanks for us so these kids won't starve and then we'll visit?" Claud looked at his eldest son.

Silence filled the big kitchen while Jeff prayed. Holt opened one eye a slit and studied the man. He was the image of his father. Same height. Same build. Same thick brown hair. He held a woman's hand as he prayed. That had to be Lisa, his wife. She barely came to his shoulder and carried twenty or thirty extra pounds. She was blond-haired and Holt caught a glimpse of icy blue eyes before she shut them for the prayer.

"Amen," Jeff said.

"Amen," Claud echoed. "Now these kids need to get their plates first. Once they're settled then us adults can take care of ourselves. There's tables set up in the backyard for everyone and if you go home hungry, it's your own fault. This here is Waylon and that's his sister, Judd. You Waverly kids make these two feel welcome now."

Sharlene joined her sisters-in-law helping the children get their food on their plates. "Okay, Waylon and Judd, come over here and show me what looks good to you."

Claud clapped a hand on Holt's shoulder. "Did y'all have a good little drive up here from Texas?"

"We did," Holt said.

"But they almost had a fight," Judd said.

"And we told them they'd have to stand in the corner if they did," Waylon piped up.

"We didn't really have a fight," Sharlene yelled above the din of fourteen kids ranging from a very independent four-year-old girl up to a thirteen-year-old boy.

Claud shook his head slowly. "It's the red hair. She is the image of my grandma. Thought we'd gotten those genes weeded out but they popped right back up again."

Molly threw up her hands. "That temper of hers comes from his side. Mine is all good-natured German stock without any of that Irish blood. I begged for a daughter and I got one but Claud's grandma marked her."

Holt grinned and looked over the huge family. He'd never seen so many blonde women in his life. The daughters-in-law looked more like Molly Waverly than Sharlene did. Lisa was taller than Sharlene and a few pounds heavier. Fiona was rail thin and tall. Clara was about Sharlene's height but slightly heavier, and Jenny looked like a high school cheerleader. But they were all blonde and blue-eyed.

Sharlene stuck her tongue out at the whole bunch of them and carried two plates outside with Waylon and Judd following her.

"Where do you want to sit?" she asked.

Miles' daughter, Jodie, piped up. "Aunt Sharlene, bring them over here. Me and Tasha and Matty want them to sit by us."

Sharlene set Waylon's plate down beside Matty. "Matty, aren't you six? Waylon and you should be about the same age."

"I'm seven, Aunt Sharlene. I'm in first grade. What grade are you in, Waylon?" Matty asked.

"I'm in the first grade too. Was you scared on the first day?"

"Naw, it wasn't no different than kindiegarden," Matty said. "Want to go see the goats when we get done eatin'?"

"Can I pet them?" Waylon asked.

"Sure, but we can't chase them or the sheep. Gramps says that'll make them hot and they'll die," Matty said seriously.

Sharlene took a couple of steps and set Judd's plate beside Jodie. Her niece had lost two front teeth and looked like a Halloween pumpkin when she smiled. "Jodie and Tasha, this is Judd. Y'all got any kittens out in the barn?"

Judd's eyes sparkled. "For real kittens? Not just stuffed ones?"

"Granny's got two old momma cats with babies. After we eat me and Jodie will take Judd out to see them. Granny says we can play with them if their eyes are open and we can find them. If you play with them before their eyes are open they'll get sick but Granny says they're probably open by now so we'll hunt them when we get through eating," Tasha said.

"You going to be all right for me to go back inside?" Sharlene whispered.

Judd nodded.

"I ain't never heard of a girl named Judd before," Tasha said.

"My momma liked them singing women, Wynona and Naomi Judd. There was another one named Ashley but she don't sing. Momma didn't know whether to name me Wynona or Naomi. Since she couldn't decide she just named me Ashley Judd Mendoza," Judd explained.

"Where is your momma?" Jodie asked.

"She died," Judd answered.

Sharlene stopped on the other side of an enormous pecan tree and listened.

"What color is them kittens?" Judd asked.

"All colors. Some is black and white and some is orange. Do you like cats?" Tasha asked.

"I like cats and dogs. Who made these beans? I like them too," Judd said.

"My momma," Tasha answered. "She makes the best baked beans in the whole world."

Sharlene exhaled loudly. Kids were so flexible. One minute they could be fighting and the next playing together. Thank goodness. An adult would have talked about the idea of Judd's mother for hours.

Men were gathered around the buffet table when she went back inside the big country kitchen. Molly Waverly had never wanted a separate dining room but had always been content with a kitchen the size of a hay barn. U-shaped cabinets covered the west end, part of the south side, and a portion of the north with the kitchen table placed so they could watch the sun come up in the east. An archway opened into the living room creating an enormous great room. Two sofas that made out into beds faced each other with a coffee table between them. Recliners were on either end and a big screen television took up the south wall. A toy box overflowing with trucks and Barbie dolls sat in one corner and pictures of the Waverly children and grandchildren decorated the walls.

Holt looked up from the buffet table and winked at Sharlene. She hoped his wink was proof that he hadn't told them he was building an addition on a beer joint for her. There were so many little secrets lying around like TNT with a short fuse. They'd all hit the fan someday and a class five tornado would look like a sweet little summer breeze. But she didn't intend to fan the winds that day, not unless she had no other choice.

Holt followed the Waverly men out the back door. He carried his overloaded plate in one hand and a glass of iced tea in the other. He didn't look too shabby from behind either, Sharlene was thinking when Fiona nudged her.

"Tell us about Holt," Fiona said. "We had a little meeting last night and Momma told us you were bringing him, but we didn't expect him to look like he walked out of a movie star magazine, though."

"He's a friend and he and the kids don't have family. So I invited him for the weekend. So you think he's a handsome hunk, do you?" Sharlene picked up a plate and forked a slab of ham to start with.

Jenny was right behind her. "What does he do for a living?"

Sharlene got a wicked gleam in her eye. "He models for trashy romance novels."

"Well, I could believe that. He's a fine looking man," Molly said.

"Momma!" Sharlene's voice was shrill.

"Hey, I look at those books when I'm in the Wal-Mart store just like everyone else does and he could do that job, but you are joshing us. What does he really do?" Molly asked.

"Would you believe he's a homeless bum that I picked off the street?" Sharlene teased.

Molly shook a finger at Sharlene. "I would not and I've had enough of your sass, girl."

"Okay, don't get your underpants in a twist, Momma. He has a construction company with three other guys. They build houses, do remodeling, build barns, whatever comes their way, and they stay very busy because they are the best in the whole state of Texas." Sharlene stopped before she said everyone in Palo Pinto County was after them to do carpentry.

"Hard workin'. Good lookin'. How come he's only your friend? Bad divorce?" Lisa asked.

"No, he's never been married. The kids are his niece and nephew. Twins. Their mother was killed in a drunk driver accident."

"Oh, those poor babies," Clara gasped.

"Holt is the only one left in his family and the kids' paternal grandparents didn't want the responsibility," Sharlene explained. Anything to keep the spotlight from her.

"Where is their father?" Fiona asked.

"He got killed before they were born. He was only eighteen and he and their mother had just been married a little while. Let's eat. I'm starving. And what's this about having a meeting before I got here? That's not fair," Sharlene said.

"It wasn't a bare-thy-soul meeting like we will have later on today; just a visit while we planned today so everyone would know you were bringing company home. And we are not eating until you tell me if there's a chance you might be more than friends with Holt," Molly asked.

Jenny giggled. "She's got a new neighbor. Man bought out the Kalanski place next farm over and he's not married. He's not as pretty as Holt but he's a decent man. Goes to church with us and teaches the teenage boys' Sunday school class. He wears glasses and his hair is thin but he's kind and patient. He'd make a wonderful father. You could do a heck of a lot worse."

Sharlene took a deep breath and lied. "Sorry, there's a big chance this could turn into something more than friends. Y'all fix Dorie up with the new farmer. She's been a widow for more than a year now."

"Well, why didn't you tell us to begin with?" Excitement filled Molly's voice.

"I didn't want to jinx it."

"If that's the case then today we're sitting beside our men, girls. Not a word of this leaves the kitchen. If it gets jinxed it won't be because your husbands and my sons got wind of it." Molly issued orders.

They filed out of the kitchen door, each holding a plate in one hand and a glass of tea in the other. Jeff looked puzzled when Lisa sat in the chair next to his. They'd all been married long enough that the men usually congregated around one end of the table to talk about sports, politics, and farming. The women gathered up at the other end to visit about things so secret they were discussed in quiet whispers. He'd learned early on in the marriage not to ask about what went on at that end of the table. Either it bored him nigh unto death or else Lisa would say that she was sworn to secrecy.

When Lisa sat down all the men scooted around leaving empty chairs between them.

"Y'all ain't got no secrets today?" Claud asked Molly.

"Y'all got some you don't want us to hear?" she asked right back.

"We were talking about remodeling that old house we bought in town and maybe selling it, then using the profit to buy a couple more and fixing them up. I think we could make a few dollars after talking to Holt here. He's into that kind of business. What were y'all talking about?" Claud asked.

"We been discussin' tomorrow," Molly answered. "Did you make all these boys known to Holt?"

Holt nodded. The tallest one and the image of his father was Jeff. The next one, Matthew, looked more like Molly. The third son, Bart, was shorter with the lightest hair and bluest eyes. Miles was more like Jeff as if the cycle was starting all over again.

Sharlene settled in between Holt and her youngest brother, Miles.

"So are you going to help Dad do reconstruction work?" she asked Miles.

Her brother shook his head emphatically. "Not me! I wouldn't know a two-by-four from a sledgehammer. I can fix a tractor or a combine or work cattle, but carpentry is not my strong point," Miles said. "But I'd better not be telling you that or you'll go into the construction business just to make me look bad."

"Not me! I got no desire to use a hammer," she said.

"I know how to make you," Jeff said. "Hey, Matthew, let's go into the construction business. I betcha we could put up a barn better and faster than Sharlene could."

"You could not," she said before she thought.

"Sibling rivalry! She's always tried to outdo her brothers. But Miles is telling it right," Jenny said. "I've been trying to get him to build me a deck for five years. Finally I got tired of nagging and went hunting a carpenter. Know what I found? Not a blessed one. No one does individual work up in this area. If they do construction at all they go into Sayre or Weatherford and work on the big crews. If you find someone to remodel a house, you hang on to him, Gramps. I'm next in line for his work."

"And when he gets done at your place I want a chance at him to redo my bathrooms and build us a family room," Clara said.

Claud looked at Fiona and Lisa. "What about you two?"

Fiona laid her fork down. "Bart and I've been talking about building a new house. It's still in the thinking-about stages but I'll wait in line if you find someone to rework the old house because when I get my hands on him, I'll keep him busy for six months to a year. We also need a new hay barn over on our place."

Sharlene's shoulder brushed against Holt's when she reached for her tea and the shock gave her the jitters. That's what she got for lying to her mother and sisters-in-law about this having the potential to be more than friendship.

It don't have a thing to do with what I said to Momma. He just flat affects me that way even though I wish he didn't.

"What do you intend to do with the house you are living in now?" Sharlene asked.

"My grandparents on my momma's side are retiring. They're selling their farm to my brother in another year and we'd like to remodel the old house for them to live in. They'd never be happy in town and Grandpa has to have animals around him or he gets cranky. Grandma likes to garden. They'll have what they like without the responsibility of a big farm and harvest season," Fiona said.

Holt was grinning when Sharlene looked at him.

"And you?" He nodded at Lisa.

"Oh, honey, I could keep a crew busy for a year all by myself. Jeff needs at least two new barns. I want a deck, a family room, and a new garage," she said.

"Sounds like there's plenty of work up here if a person would relocate," Holt said.

"And that's not even counting the women we know whose husbands can bring in a hay or wheat crop but can't figure out how to put in a lightbulb," Molly said.

Sharlene almost choked on a bite of sweet potato casserole. Dear Lord, they were trying to move Holt to Corn. If she was truly interested in him then they'd lure him into their net and she'd follow. She wasn't totally stupid and they weren't as sly as they thought they were. Well, if they could talk Holt into moving to Corn, Oklahoma, they could have him. She wouldn't even fight for him. She'd joined the army to get away from Corn. No way in hell was she coming back to it.

Judd tapped Holt on the shoulder. "Daddy, can we go play now? We ate all our dinner and throwed away the plates in the trash can like Jodie and Tasha. And there's kittens out in the garage and Waylon and Matty are going to go see the sheep and goats and he's all finished too and the ham was so good. Did Granny make it or did God?"

Sharlene rolled her eyes at her beaming mother. "Granny made the ham, Judd. She's got a secret she won't tell anyone about how to make it so good."

"Yes, you can both go play. Have fun," Holt said.

Dinner took the better part of an hour with the conversation going from construction to wheat to hay to cattle. Sharlene didn't pay attention to any of it. She had enough on her hands just keeping still when Holt's thigh accidentally brushed against hers. Add that to every time one of them reached for their iced tea their shoulders touched. She could have sworn something was on fire close by and the embers were falling on her skin. Heat like that should be extinguished in a bedroom or in a hayloft on a nice soft blanket. And where had it come from, anyway? Why did she have to say that there might be something brewing in the wind between them? That one admission, which was a lie to begin with, had sure fanned the embers that were already there to create a full-fledged forest fire.

There was little chance of anything happening with four brothers and fourteen kids all around, not to mention her mother and four sisters-in-law. She felt like one of the women in Iraq who was never allowed out in public without a male escort to be sure she didn't do anything ornery.

Holt studied the house, the yard, and the livestock on the other side of the yard fence while he ate. A carpenter could tell where the additions had been made even though the whole outside had been sided afterwards. It was light gray with white shutters with a white picket fence surrounding it. The huge backyard had two swing sets in addition to a couple of tire swings hanging from tree branches. He'd noticed roses and flower beds in the front yard and thought of the roses climbing up the back porch posts in the abominable multicolored house where he and the kids lived.

He looked out further and saw the barns. Good sturdy buildings that had been well maintained. Her leg brushed against his again and he inhaled deeply and let it out slowly. If she didn't stop touching him, even thinking about houses and barns wasn't going to keep down an embarrassing physical reaction. He might have to "accidentally" spill his ice cold tea right in his lap just to cool things down.

Jenny looked across the table at Sharlene. "What's the matter? Are you sick?"

Sharlene looked up at her sister-in-law and realized she was talking to her. She'd been trying to come up with an excuse to go into the house and wash her face with ice water. Hell's bells, she might need to soak her whole body in cold water the way it was reacting to every brush of his leg or hand or even the scorching look in his eyes when they landed on her.

"No, I'm not sick." She quickly put a fork full of sweet potato casserole in her mouth. All she needed was for them to start some balderdash about her being in love.

"Then why aren't you eating? I swear when she came home from Iraq both times we thought we'd never get her filled up on good common food," Jenny said. "She went there for a year, came home for two weeks, and they sent her right back."

Jenny reached for her tea and Fiona picked up the story, "Just about killed Molly the first time and we won't even discuss the second time around. She didn't think she'd ever see her daughter again but Sharlene came home after a year. There was talk they might station her out at Fort Sill. I remember the day she got a call and said she was going back for another year. It was not a good day around here."

"Why on earth a woman would enlist is beyond me," Clara said. "But Jenny is right. She ate like she'd never get full both times when she came back home. When Sharlene isn't eating, something is the matter. So 'fess up, girl. Don't tell us you went back in the army?"

"I did *not* join the service again," Sharlene said.

"Then what's got you off your food?" Jeff asked.

All eyes were on her and the adult table went silent. The kids' laughter blended with the bawling of cows and neighs of horses but all that was in the distance, like music playing softly in a movie scene.

"The heat," she said honestly. "I'll outdo you all come supper time when it's cooler. And tomorrow when there's homemade ice cream and watermelon, you'd best get in line before me."

Holt bumped her knee when he wiggled in his seat. Heat that had nothing to do with the weather radiated from her thigh all through his body. It might take more than ice water to put out the fire. He wondered how much a plane ticket to the North Pole cost these days. And when did he get so damned attracted to her, anyway?

"So you want banana or chocolate chip?" Molly asked Sharlene.

Sharlene looked bumfuzzled. "What?"

"Ice cream! I swear you're comin' down with something," Molly said.

"Both," Sharlene said hurriedly.

"I'll do the banana. You do the other." Fiona looked at Clara.

She nodded.

Molly stood up. "It's time to put away the food until supper."

All five girls started inside to help her.

She waved a hand at Sharlene. "Not you. You take Holt and show him around the place."

"I'll do that," Claud said. "Your mother's been fussin' for months about not getting to see you, girl. You go on in there and visit with her."

Molly narrowed her eyes and shot Claud a look that left no doubt he would hear about his big, big mistake later.

"What'd I do?" he asked.

"Nothing, darlin'," Molly said syrupy sweet.

When the ladies were in the house Molly stomped her foot on the wooden floor so loud it sounded like a shotgun blast. "Man doesn't say three words all week and today he decides to be a magpie and take all Holt's time. I'm sorry, Sharlene, I tried."

Sharlene threw her arm up around her mother's shoulders. "Hey, I see him almost every day. It's all right if Daddy steals him."

"He works in Dallas? I got the feeling he worked in a small place like Corn." Molly studied her daughter intently. Something wasn't right and she'd ferret it out before Sharlene left the next day or she'd flatten all of Holt's truck tires and keep them until she did.

"He works wherever his job takes him. Now tell me who all is coming for dinner tomorrow?" Sharlene said.

"Don't test her mettle. She knows something is going on. You might as well 'fess up and tell all. You know very well she won't abide secrets," Fiona whispered.

Molly put plastic wrap over the platter of ham and set it in the refrigerator. "You asked who is coming to dinner tomorrow. Well, we have invited Dorie and her two kids and the new neighbor. His name is Wayne Mulligan, by the way. And both sets of your grandparents. And two ladies from the Circle didn't have kids coming home. And Fiona's in-laws and then there's Jenny's aunt and uncle. Did I forget anyone, Lisa?"

Lisa shook her head. "That about gets it."

"Why did you invite the whole county?" Sharlene asked.

Fiona's giggle was high-pitched and always sent them all into laughter just listening to her. "She didn't,"

Fiona said between giggles, "until we found out you were bringing home a bachelor."

"Mother!" Sharlene exclaimed.

"Well, if you aren't interested in Wayne then Dorie might be and if you aren't really serious about that pretty cowboy, then Dorie might be. Then again, even if you are interested in him, he and Dorie are more fitted to each other since they both have a boy and a girl and they're about the same age. And Wayne is a good man. You could do a lot worse. I like what I've seen in Holt. He's seems like a hard-working, honest man with a future but I'm not so sure he's for you," Molly said.

Sharlene popped her hands on her hips. She'd known coming to Corn would be a mistake. What was she thinking anyway? Inviting Holt to the land before time? "What if I don't want a husband at all? I've been doing very well without a man in my life."

"Just don't come whining to us when you get that urge for kids and you're too old to have any," Fiona said.

"Or when all that's left are dregs," Lisa chimed right in. "The good ones in this area are taken by the time they're twenty-five. Lots of them younger than that. By the time a woman gets thirty the pickin's are slim as a bad year's cotton crop."

Sharlene glared at her other two sisters-in-law. "Well?"

"Don't get me into this. I'm the shy one, remember," Clara said.

"Shy, my ass. I've heard you fight with Matthew," Sharlene said.

Clara raised an eyebrow. "Well, if you want my opinion you can have it. Just remember, you asked for it. You've always been a temperamental handful and you might be doing the male population in the world a big favor by not marrying. I wouldn't want to be your husband. You could probably chew up old Holt and spit him out in little pieces. I like the man. Bless his heart, raising two kids alone can't be easy. He needs a good strong woman like Dorie, not an overbearing snit like you."

Sharlene set her jaw in anger. "I'm not a snit, darlin'. I'm a full-fledged red-haired bitch and don't you ever forget it. Okay, Jenny, throw your two cents in before I slam the back door and go for a long walk."

"Love you, honey, but I dang sure feel sorry for any man you set your sights on. He'll have a hell of a life. I wouldn't want Holt to live that way or for Wayne to be miserable the rest of his natural born days either," Jenny said.

Sharlene glared at them all, slammed the back door with enough force to rattle the dishes in the cabinets, and took off across the yard. She ignored the gate and climbed over the yard fence.

Claud shook his head and set his mouth in a firm line. "Looks like Grandma's temper has surfaced in my daughter this afternoon. Them women do that sometimes. They get to talkin' around the table and before you know it, one of them is hotter'n sheet metal in July. You might want to go attempt to pour some water on the fire, Holt."

"Why me?" Holt asked.

"Ain't none of us ever been able to put it out. Ever since she was born she's been feisty. You might as well try," Claud said.

"I guess I can try but don't expect miracles. Judd, you and Waylon be good and mind Claud and Molly. I'm going to take a walk with Sharlene," Holt called out.

"You mean Granny and Gramps?" Waylon yelled.

"Yes." Holt put a hand on the fence, hopped over, and began to jog toward Sharlene.

Cows and horses looked up from grazing to see what was making so much noise. He would have loved to stop and pet that big roan horse but there wasn't time. He'd grown up outside of town. His mother had a garden. His father had one cow, a horse, and a few chickens. He always loved that old mare. Sharlene's strides got longer and longer and pretty soon she was running toward a barn in the distance.

She disappeared inside. When he reached the door he caught a glimpse of her climbing up into the hayloft and followed. She was sitting on a bale of hay, looking out the door at the end of the loft when he reached the top.

"What are you doing here?" she asked icily.

"They sent me to put out the fire of your temper," he said honestly.

"They ain't got much sense if they thought one man could do the trick."

His gaze locked with hers and he took two steps forward, scooped her up in his arms, and landed a hard, passionate kiss on her lips before she could protest. She melted into his embrace and kissed him back, tasting sweet tea and smoked ham and inhaling the aftershave that had set her desire meter on the high level that morning when he showed up at the Honky Tonk looking like sex on a stick.

Where had she heard that expression? And what a hell of a time to wonder about it right in the middle of a kiss. Oh, yeah, it was when Larissa told her about Cathy and Daisy. One of them referred to the cowboy who made them leave the Honky Tonk as sex on a stick.

He broke the kiss and she pulled his lips back down for another. As the kiss deepened she forgot all about the Honky Tonk ladies and let the heat flow through her veins like hot lava.

He broke away again and buried his face in her hair. "Cooled down yet? And what set you off anyway?" he asked in a hoarse whisper.

"Hell no, I'm hotter than ever only in a different way," she said.

He sat down on the bale of hay but kept her in his lap. "Me too."

"Right now I'd like a cold beer or even a shot of Jack," she said.

"We could sneak off to a beer joint," he suggested.

"It's Sunday. Liquor stores are closed. Might buy some beer at the convenience store in town, but if Momma got a whiff of it? Let's just say we wouldn't be eating supper here or having a party tomorrow either. Now, why didn't I think of that? She could kick me off the farm and I could go to Mingus and run my beer joint in peace."

She should make an excuse and stand up but she didn't. She shouldn't sit there all cuddled up in his lap like a lover after a wild passionate romp between the sheets but she didn't move. She leaned back and looked up at him. His mouth was on the way to hers so she shut her eyes and got ready for the sensation. Her veins felt like she was hooked up to a tequila IV, with heat flowing through every part of her body. She pressed closer to him and he ran a hand up her back under her shirt.

When he fumbled with the hooks, she shifted to make the job easier. One hand cupped her jaw line with his thumb making soft lazy circles on the soft sensitive skin on her neck. The other inched its way around to cup a breast. Add that to kisses that made her hotter than the front gates of hell and she wondered if she'd survive the fire.

"You taste and feel wonderful," he said. "I've wanted to kiss you and touch you all day."

"Mmmm," she mumbled as she blindly sought out his mouth for another kiss.

Judd's voice drifted up the ladder. "Sharlene, come and see the kittens."

Tasha's followed. "We thought they were in the other barn but the momma cat moved them. We're going to climb up there, okay?"

"No, it's not okay. There's an open door and you might get hurt. We'll come down and see the kittens," Sharlene yelled.

"Okay, but hurry. The momma cat is gone and we can hold them and she won't hiss at us," Tasha said.

"If it weren't for bad luck." Holt buried his face in her neck and kissed the tender spot right under her ear.

She shivered in spite of the heat.

"I know we'd have no luck at all." She stood up, fastened her bra back, and started down the ladder.

Chapter 8

WHEN SHARLENE OPENED THE DOOR ALL FIVE WOMEN went silent, which was proof positive they'd been plotting against her. Not a one of them could stand to see a woman past twenty-one without a husband. That might be the reason the Ladies Circle met once a week. The idea of studying the women in the Bible was probably a cover-up. Kind of like the mob laundering money through something clean and righteous. The Circle probably did a quick five-minute study of Esther or Hannah and then they put away their study guides and got down to serious business.

Sharlene imagined the conversation when her mother locked the door and the president of the LC, which stood for Love Cupid instead of Ladies Circle, started the real meeting. Someone would list the names of local lasses and hers would be at the top where it had been the past eight years. They thought they had her matched up with a good decent man right out of high school and she'd foiled their wedding plans. She bet they even had Loma buying up extra flour to make a nice five-tiered carrot cake and Dotty lined up for the groom's cheesecakes. If she looked in the attic, she'd find at least one issue of *Bride* magazine hidden away in a cardboard box. Her mother might have even dog-eared the pages of the dresses she thought would be nice on a short red-haired girl.

They'd never give up on a mission but they'd gone on to the name under hers. No sense in wasting time over someone who moved so far away. No wonder her mother was in such a rush to get to the Circle meeting that week. Sharlene was coming home and Molly had a new neighbor, Wayne. And if not with Wayne, well, she was bringing a co-worker home with her and Molly could always work her magic through her cooking. They'd all breathed in relief and said a prayer. If they could just get Sharlene married off they wouldn't be complete failures and there would be a chance they wouldn't miss out on heaven's glory. She wasn't sure that St. Peter would let them through the doors if they didn't get every woman who'd been born or ever lived in Corn happily married.

When they heard that she was writing hot romance books and she owned a bar they'd ban her from ever being on their list again. St. Peter would give them a second chance in those circumstances. The devil had been working against them the whole time would be their defense.

Jenny filled a tea glass with ice and handed it to Sharlene. "Are you over your snit?"

"I was never in a snit. I just had to get some air and get away from all you matchmakers. The harder you push me, the faster I'll run. So stop," Sharlene said.

"We just want you to be happy," Molly said.

"I am happy. I've got… a good job and…" she stammered before she gave away too much.

"What are you hiding?" Jenny asked.

"What are *you* hiding?" Sharlene turned the question back on her.

Jenny blushed.

"Aha, Momma, we've got a secret. Think we need to ferret it out or can it wait until Saturday for the Circle?" Sharlene asked.

Molly pointed at Sharlene. "What's the Circle got to do with our family?"

Sharlene ignored the question. "What is it, Jenny? I'm going to goad until you 'fess up."

Jenny folded her arms under her breasts. "I'll do the same to you. I can tell when you aren't telling the whole truth. You're hiding something big and important. So you've got a good job and what else is there that made you stumble on your words? This is our Waverly round table. What we talk about stays here and goes no further and we haven't had a real one since you left and something has happened. What is it?"

"Truce? Just forget that I had a brain fart and couldn't think." Sharlene grinned.

"It's too late for that," Fiona said. "Now you've got our curiosity all worked up. We won't be able to sleep for trying to figure it out and then when you tell us we'll be angry that it wasn't anything to be losing sleep over."

The smile on Sharlene's face faded quickly.

Oh, honey, you'll be thinking that you didn't lose enough sleep when you find out my secret. But you're not getting it that quickly.

Sharlene propped her elbows on the table and rested her chin in her hands. If they wanted to play with the big dogs she'd show them how it was done. She'd know every one of their secrets before she told them a single thing about the Honky Tonk and then it wouldn't be such a big thing. "What's your secret, Fiona? You jumped in there too quick so you're covering up something too."

"I'm not doing any such thing." She blushed.

Sharlene went on. "And you, Lisa? What's under your hat this week?"

Lisa pointed a long, slim finger at her. "Not one thing and I won't lose a bunch of sleep worrying about you so if you don't want to tell us what's going on between you and Mr. Handsome then that's fine with me. I'd rather talk recipes and get Momma to tell me how to handle a boy going through puberty than talk about your problems anyway."

"So Creed is giving you problems and you've got two more coming right up behind him and you're wondering how you'll keep all that pretty blond hair from going gray before you get them all raised, right?" Sharlene asked.

Lisa grimaced. "You got it."

Sharlene listened with one ear and wondered what the men were discussing as they toured the ranch. Right after she and Holt had crawled down the ladder to see the kittens, her four brothers and father had appeared in the doorway and asked Holt if he wanted to check cattle with them. She didn't know how he fared, but she'd kept her head down and didn't look at her father or brothers. They didn't need to know that she and Holt were up there acting like two love-struck teenagers making out in a hayloft.

"Go on. If you don't there'll be more questions than either of us want to answer," she'd whispered to Holt and he'd left with them without even a peck on the cheek. Was that so she wouldn't be embarrassed or was it because he didn't want anything but a making out session?

She'd played with the new kittens a few minutes then left them with the little girls and went back to the house. That comment he'd made about being sent to put out the fire suddenly surfaced and she knew her father had been behind it. Did her father and her mother have a bet going as to who could get Sharlene married off first? Did she have a snowball's chance in hell's furnace if they were both determined? If she ever got back to Mingus she didn't intend to return to Corn until every bachelor in a fifty mile radius was happily married.

Lisa was still talking about her oldest son, Creed, when Sharlene made herself stop thinking about Holt and listen.

"He wants to argue about everything and fight with his brothers all the time. He's too old to play with them and too young to be interested in girls."

Sharlene laughed. "Old enough to sleep by himself but too old to want to."

Lisa glared at her. "That's enough of that kind of talk. He's not even fourteen yet and that's too young for girls."

"Betcha he's got one in his sights. She might be the most popular little blonde in his class and he's afraid to ask her to whatever it is they call it these days," Sharlene said.

"Talk to her. That's the lingo today. They don't go out or date, they talk to each other. I guess that's because of Facebook, cell phones, and all that stuff where they can text message twenty-four hours a day," Jenny said.

"Christina Alvarez," Lisa whispered.

"That little Mexican girl whose dad came up here to help with the harvest and then brought his whole family? The one that lives out in the trailer on your property?" Molly asked.

"That's the one. That's why he's so irritable. I've seen them riding horses together but I just figured they were the same age and friends. Her father is the hired help and I'll betcha he thinks that me and Jeff will pitch a fit if he likes her. Who knows how in the devil a boy's mind works anyway. Now what do I do? I should've had girls," Lisa asked.

"Sure, and then you'd be fighting with her over wearing thong underpants and wanting to line her eyes with so much black that she looks like a hoot owl," Clara said.

"Amelia is only eleven. She's not into those things yet, is she?" Sharlene asked.

"No, but the thirteen-year-old girls at school are doing those things so it's coming and I dread it," Clara said.

Molly held up a hand and everyone looked at her. "I'll tell you what you do. Invite her to dinner tomorrow. Invite the whole family. It'll show Creed that we aren't that kind of people."

"What kind is that, Momma?" Sharlene asked.

"The kind that looks down on people for what they do or who they are," Molly said.

"Promise?" Sharlene asked.

"Why would I promise such a thing? We never have been ugly to our neighbors or friends," Molly said.

Lisa sighed. "I remember when I was in love with Jeff and I wasn't but a year older than they are. I'll invite them and that should show him we aren't going to be upset that he likes her."

"Okay, Clara, you're next in line. What's on your mind today?" Sharlene asked.

Crimson crept into Clara's cheeks. "Not one thing."

"Then why are you blushing?" Lisa asked. She'd confessed her problems and now she'd join forces with Sharlene and they'd dig the secrets out of the rest of the family. They'd done this many Sundays around the kitchen table while their men talked politics and wheat harvest.

Clara sighed. "I'm going to work Tuesday morning."

Molly spun around in her chair so fast that her neck popped. "Where?"

"The principal at the school called yesterday. The teacher's aide they hired decided not to work at the last minute. He offered me the job. Matty is in first grade and I was dreading staying home all day alone."

"Good for you," Sharlene said.

"You'll be swamped with a job and taking care of the kids and the house after working all day. What does Matthew think of that idea?" Molly asked.

"We talked about it. We're going to bank my salary and not get used to having a second income. If I don't like it or if it's too big of a job I can quit without a problem. But if I do, then once a year we're going to use my salary to take a vacation with the kids. To go somewhere we couldn't afford otherwise," she said.

"I love it," Sharlene said.

Clara pushed a strand of hair behind her ear. "I knew you'd think I was independent and give me a thumbs-up. You've always been independent and sassy. What do you really think, Momma?"

"If you want to give it a whirl, go for it," Molly said.

"Thank you," Clara sighed. "I've been afraid to mention it for fear there'd be a…"

"Shit storm," Sharlene giggled.

"Potty mouth." Clara looked at her.

Sharlene nodded. "You got that right on the nose. Add brassy and sassy to it and you've got a picture of your sister-in-law. It's your turn, Fiona. What is going on in your world that you wouldn't tell another soul outside the family?"

She covered her face with her hands and spoke from behind her fingertips. "Bart has been flirting with another woman."

Molly grabbed her heart. "Who?"

"Some new woman at the bank. He's still good looking and all she has to do is look at the accounts to know that he's not a poor pauper. And she's only about twenty-two or three. Still young and firm and hasn't had four kids," Fiona whispered.

Sharlene reached across the table and touched her shoulder. "What have you done about it and how far has it gone?"

"Nothing and last week he sent her flowers," Fiona said.

Molly gritted her teeth. "I'll talk to him."

"How'd you find out about the flowers?" Jenny asked.

"My second cousin works in the bank." Fiona dropped her hands and knotted them together until her knuckles turned white.

Sharlene covered Fiona's hands with hers. "Bart didn't marry a mealy mouthed woman who walked two steps behind him, girl. He married you because you were the only woman in town who made him toe the line. He'd dated those sweet little prissy girls but it was you who made him fall in love. Remember how you used to get right up in his face and argue with him? I was twelve when y'all got married and I always wanted to be just like you. So go get up in his face and tell him you're going to move the whole bank account into one with your name only and you're going to take the kids with the money. Right after you mop up Main Street with that hussy's tight little ass."

"I feel fat and ugly," Fiona said.

"Don't you tell him that," Sharlene said.

"Then what do I tell him?" Fiona asked.

"You tell him if he sends flowers to that woman or any other woman again that he'll be pushing up daisies when you get done with him. That you are willing to give him one more chance since he hasn't slept with the hussy. But if it happens again, you will own his farm, his kids, and you'll put his ass through a wood chipper," Sharlene said.

"Good advice," Molly said. "All men let their eyes stray but when it goes beyond that, it's time for you to step up and take care of it. Do it tonight because we won't have time for a meeting like this tomorrow with all the people who'll be here."

Sharlene appreciated her mother for not asking Fiona what she'd done wrong in the relationship, or for saying that if Fiona was keeping her man happy that his eyes wouldn't be straying.

Fiona took a deep breath and looked around the table. "Thank you all for being my support group. Sharlene, my sass is ninety percent pure bullshit bluff but don't tell anyone I admitted it."

"I guess I'm going to need the support group too," Jenny said.

They all looked at her.

"I'm pregnant," she blurted out.

Silence filled the room for a good minute.

"It was an accident. Remember when I had the flu? I forgot that the pills sometimes fail when you are on antibiotics," Jenny finally whispered.

Sharlene started to giggle. "Congratulations."

"What's so funny? I only wanted two kids, a boy and a girl, and now they are both in school."

"And now you will have a Sharlene." Molly started to laugh too.

"That's what I'm afraid of. What if it's a red-haired girl with a temper?" Jenny moaned.

Sharlene's laughter was infectious and everyone joined in.

Molly wiped at her eyes. "Or worse yet, a red-haired boy with a temper."

When the giggling stopped, Jenny pointed a finger at Sharlene. "It's your turn."

"Not yet. Momma hasn't told us what her secret is. It's been eight months since we've done this so surely she's got something to say," Sharlene said.

"Only thing I'm guilty of is trying to find you a decent husband. I miss our table discussions and confessions and I want you back home," Molly said.

"And what makes you think if you did find me one that I'd be living in Corn?" Sharlene asked.

"Because you miss us as much as we miss you," Molly said. "And if I remember right, what started this whole thing was Jenny accusing you of having a secret. So out with it."

Sharlene's news wasn't any worse than Jenny being pregnant or Bart sending flowers to another woman. Or was it? Should she wait and tell her mother first or spit it out right then so she'd have the other women to help her if Molly dropped with an acute heart attack?

"I own a beer joint in Mingus, Texas. It's called the Honky Tonk and Holt is putting an addition on it because business is so good that I've got customers waiting in the parking lot to get inside and my maximum load limit is below four hundred. Mingus is even smaller than Corn. And I wrote a romance novel last year and my friend knew an agent who was willing to take me on. She sold it, which is a miracle for a first time author, and now it's coming out in November. The name of the book is *Honky Tonk Charm* and I've got a copy of the cover in my suitcase if you want to see it." She said it in a hurry before she lost her nerve.

It started with a tiny high-pitched giggle from Jenny and within seconds had every woman except Sharlene roaring so loud that Judd and Tasha came in the back door to see what was so funny.

Sharlene hugged Judd up to her side. "Judd, darlin', tell these folks where you go every day."

"To school in the mornin' after we eat breakfast and brush our teeth. And then after school we got to work with Uncle Holt at Sharlene's beer joint."

The laughter stopped as quickly as it started.

"And what do we do when you get home from school?" Sharlene asked.

"Sometimes we play outside after we have a snack in Sharlene's house at the back of the beer joint. Well, it's really part of the beer joint acause there's a door from one to the other but we don't go in the beer joint acause the television in there only gets football games and President stuff. So we have a snack in Sharlene's house and then we go outside and play. Sometimes Sharlene takes her writin' stuff out in the yard and sits under the tree while Uncle Holt builds the big old room for the people to... what is it they do with them sticks and them balls?"

"Shoot pool," Sharlene said.

"Yeah, that's it. The music boxes and the shoot pool tables are going in the new room so the rest of the beer joint can be a dancin' place. We got a jungle gym and two swings in the trees and we live in Sharlene's other house. You got to see it sometimes. It's all different colors and Waylon is buried out in the yard and we have to be careful not to knock his cross down. I like the orange rocking chairs on the front porch and I like the pink windows."

All five women stared at Sharlene like she had two heads and sixteen eyes.

"Waylon is buried?" Molly asked.

It took a ton of willpower to keep Sharlene from rolling her eyes. All that and her mother worried about a cat?

"Waylon was my cat before I met Judd and Waylon Mendoza," she said.

"Where did you get the money to buy a beer joint? And why?" Molly asked.

"It's a long story. A hell of a lot longer than any of your stories," Sharlene said.

"Well, afore you begin it can me and Tasha have a drink? We're thirsty and the other kids said they are too and they said for us to bring them out something to drink too," Judd said.

"Of course you can, sweetheart. Granny bought a whole case of those little juice packs for you kids. I'll load up a sack full and you two girls can pass them out. I've got a platter of cookies I made for afternoon snacks. You can carry them, Tasha," Molly said.

When the children had carried their treats to the yard, Molly sat back down and pointed at Sharlene. "We've got at least two hours before the men come in wanting supper. So talk!"

"In the beginning God made dirt," Sharlene teased.

"Girl, this ain't no jokin' matter. You get serious," Molly told her.

She began when she first had the idea to write a story about the Honky Tonk and ended with that very day, leaving out only the small little detail of the trip to Weatherford and getting so drunk that Holt Jackson had to carry her into her hotel room. Well, that and kissing him in the barn just a couple of hours before.

"The end," she said.

"Well, that explains a lot," Molly said.

"Such as?" Sharlene asked.

"Why you never answer your phone after eight at night or before noon and why you've been so secretive about where it is you live in Dallas. Why didn't you tell me this in the beginning?" Molly asked.

"Good lord, Momma. I was afraid you'd have a heart attack. I waited until the sisters were here so they could hold you off while I got a head start back to Mingus. I figured you'd cut a pecan switch and start beating on me," Sharlene said.

"I can't believe you got published that quickly!" Molly exclaimed.

She nodded. "It's a sheer miracle, I'm telling you. And I got an option for the second one, which I will have finished by Christmas. Which reminds me, we're having a Honky Tonk Christmas at the beer joint on Christmas Eve. Y'all want to come down to the grand opening?"

"Hell no!" Molly said.

"Momma cussed," Fiona said.

"I always knew that if anyone could make her lose her religion it would be Sharlene," Jenny said.

Molly held up her palms. "And Larissa just handed the deed to that beer joint and the house over to you?"

She nodded again.

"What do these places look like?"

Sharlene went to her duffle bag and brought out a small album and a manila folder. She'd put them in and taken them out a dozen times before Holt arrived that morning. First she was going to come clean with only her mother and see what kind of stinky storm that brewed up, but it didn't work that way. Now it was out there for the whole family to see and it hadn't been so very bad. Hopefully they wouldn't faint dead away when she presented living proof of the story she'd just told them.

She laid them both on the table and the four sisters gathered around Molly as she opened the folder first. "Well, I'll be danged. There's your name right there on the front and your picture on the back."

"I'm going to visit my friends that I met in Iraq when the book comes out. They made me promise to come to their towns and sign books for them. Four states in one week. You want to go with me?" Sharlene asked.

"I'd love to but I couldn't. Besides, your dad would die in a week if I wasn't here," Molly said.

Sharlene almost choked to death. Her mother had actually said she'd like to go with her and she hadn't said a word about the hunky man on the front cover in nothing but tight fittin' jeans, a Texas Longhorn belt buckle, and cowboy boots.

"That hunk must be the hero. Where's the sassy witch lady who puts a charm on everyone and then forgets to protect herself from the charm?" Fiona asked.

"Read it and find out," Sharlene said.

"Oh, honey, I will. I intend to own it as soon as it hits the market," Lisa said.

"I'm going to parade up and down Main Street and tell everyone that my sister is a writer," Jenny declared.

Sharlene pinched her leg. It hurt like hell so she wasn't sleeping. They should all be gathering firewood to burn her at the stake instead of drooling over her book cover.

"You don't have to wait for them to be for sale in stores. I'll have author's copies. I'll send you each a copy."

"If you can do all that, by damn, I can straighten out Bart," Fiona said.

Sharlene grinned. "That's the spirit. And if he don't like what you tell him, remind him that his sister has a beer joint and a house. You and the kids can move to Mingus and you can bartend for me. After you sell his farm and take all his money."

Molly quickly shut the folder and opened the album. "Don't you be leading these four astray."

Her nose snarled when she saw the house. "That looks like shit."

"Momma, two dirty words in one day!" Sharlene exclaimed.

"Well, there ain't another word in the English language to describe that thing. And you need to paint this honky tonk. It looks like something out of a John Wayne movie instead of a modern business," she said.

"That's the charm. Vintage music and vintage looking building. Holt is making the new addition look just like the old part. And I love the Bahamas house. I wouldn't dream of painting it white."

"Well, I'm not sleeping in that place when I come to visit." Molly pointed at the picture of the multicolored house. "I'd have to take Pepto to stop the diarrhea. I can feel my stomach grumbling just looking at the picture."

They all giggled.

Sharlene pointed at the picture of the Honky Tonk. "You can stay in my apartment. I'll take the sofa and you can have my bed. Maybe it won't be too noisy for you."

"The day I sleep in a beer joint ain't dawned yet," Molly huffed.

They were still talking about the beer joint when five men filed into the kitchen door but the conversations stopped and the room went silent. Claud went to the refrigerator and took out a gallon jar of sweet tea. Jeff filled glasses with ice and Matthew poured.

"What've you girls been doing? I see you got some pictures," Claud said.

"I need to prepare your dad before he sees this stuff," Molly whispered.

"We've been having some time with Sharlene," Fiona said. "I'm gathering up the kids and we're going home, Bart."

"We haven't had supper yet," he protested.

"We're eating at our house tonight," she said.

"Why?" Bart asked.

"I'll tell you when we get home." She yelled out the door to Tasha to take her younger sister and brothers to the truck.

"But…" Bart started to argue.

The look Fiona gave him would have put a grown grizzly bear in the praying position. Bart knew he was in hot water. His face was a picture of pure guilt.

"Well, I suppose Fiona's got her dander up about something." He tried to make light of the situation. "I'll see y'all tomorrow at noon. Enjoyed your company today, Holt. Tomorrow we'll talk about all the carpentry we could use in this family."

"Thank you," Holt said.

"What was that all about?" Claud asked when they were gone. "I haven't seen Fiona act like that in years. I thought the children tamed that temper down."

"You ever send flowers to another woman?" Molly asked.

Holt looked at Sharlene.

She shrugged.

"No, ma'am, I ain't that stupid," Claud said.

"It's a good thing," Molly said.

"We'd best be leaving too," Jenny told Miles.

"I didn't send flowers to another woman. What are y'all talkin' about? Is Fiona mad because Bart sent a bouquet to that little filly down at the bank? The woman helped him get his business checkbook straightened out. He'd made a couple of mistakes," Miles declared.

Sharlene poked Miles in the arm. "He should have told Fiona. She's always managed the books. If he made a mistake he should've owned up to it with her, not gone flirting with a younger woman. And don't take up for him. He was wrong and he's about to find out what happens when you're wrong," Sharlene said.

"Well even if he was wrong, why do I have to go home? I didn't send flowers to anyone," Miles said.

"Under the circumstances, I hope not," Molly said with a chuckle.

"What are you talking about?" Miles asked.

"It's a big surprise," Jenny said as she made her way to the door to call their son and daughter into the house.

"You didn't tell him yet?" Sharlene whispered in Jenny's ear.

"No, but tonight's the night," Jenny answered.

"We stayin'?" Matthew asked Clara.

"I told them all about my job," Clara said.

"You're going to work?" Claud asked.

Matthew finished off his tea and said, "Yes, she'll be working at the school, Dad. Teacher's aide position came up and they asked her to fill it. What do you think?"

"That'd be between the two of you. Wouldn't be any of my business," Claud said.

Molly looked around at who was left. "It's supper time. Clara, you go on and get the leftovers out and put them on the buffet table. I made a big salad to go with the cold cuts and just in case we needed it I made Sharlene a couple of extra pecan pies. Figured we could use them tomorrow if we didn't eat them all up tonight."

"What can I do to help?" Lisa asked.

"Go make that phone call to the Alvarez family so they'll have plenty of time to whip up something to bring along. If you give them too short of a notice they'll feel like they can't come," Molly told her. "And then you get out the plates, napkins, and cups. Holt, you and Sharlene go wipe down the tables where the kids made mud pies and put on those new plastic tablecloths. Bart, you can fill glasses with ice and Matthew, you call the kids in and make sure they get their hands all washed."

"What about me?" Claud asked.

"You come over here and sit down on this sofa and listen to me," Molly said.

Sharlene wasted no time getting to the backyard with a bottle of spray cleanser and a roll of paper towels. She hadn't been this nervous when she told her father that she'd enlisted in the service. That time he wouldn't speak to her for days. She might have heard the last words from his mouth for the next decade if her mother showed him the pictures of the Honky Tonk.

"What just happened in there?" Holt asked.

"We had our meeting of the Waverly women. Miles is about to find out that Jenny is pregnant and they weren't planning a third child. Bart is fixing to find out that he'd best not ever send another woman flowers again. Lisa and Jeff's son is going through puberty. Clara went to work. And I told them about my book and the Honky Tonk. Momma is cluing Daddy in right now. After the army fit, I'm not sure whether to take off for Mingus or stay and fight."

Holt wiped one side of the table and she got the other. More than once their hands met in the middle and white heat passed between them. "Do I need to put Judd and Waylon in the truck and point it south with the pedal to the floor? Sounds to me like what's about to hit the fan is going to stink really bad."

Sharlene wiped fast and furiously at the mud stains on the table. "Don't know just yet. Momma can work wonders when she wants to. She didn't want to when I joined the army. I'm not sure if she's got a big enough miracle up her sleeve to get me out of trouble this time. We might want to tear out of here if Daddy comes outside with steam coming out his ears."

"Did your momma take it well?" Holt asked.

Sharlene tossed him the paper towels when his got too wet and dirty to use anymore. "Surprisingly, yes. If she hadn't I was going to blame it on you."

Holt caught the roll mid-air. "Why me?"

She sprayed a heavy layer of cleaner on a dirt smear. "Because you made me feel guilty because your family is all gone."

"They're going to crucify me right along with you because they asked several times what I was working on and I evaded the issue," he said. He liked her family and her brothers. It had been a wonderful afternoon and he looked forward to more of the same the next day but it could be coming to an abrupt halt.

Matthew joined them and winked at Sharlene. "Clara filled me in on the skeleton of why you haven't been home in eight months. She said I can have details later tonight."

"Daddy?" Sharlene asked.

Matthew yelled at the children to come wash their hands and get ready for supper. "Momma's still talking. I heard something like 'looks like shit' and 'a beer joint' but that's all I can tell you. Fire isn't shooting out the top of his head yet. It would be mine if one of my girls grew up to be a bartender in Texas, let me tell you."

"Why are you so afraid of your dad? Good grief, Sharlene, you are a grown woman," Holt said.

"Thank you for that reminder. It just makes me feel so much better," she snapped.

"You are *so* welcome. Now I'm going back inside to see what else I can do," he said as they smoothed the last tablecloth. "Are you coming with me?"

"Yes, I am. You are my buffer."

Holt shot a look across the table at her and grinned. "Well, damn! Those hayloft kisses were just mercy kisses because you brought me here to stand between you and your folks if they threw a fit?"

"If you think that, then they might have been."

Claud looked up from the picture album and cocked his head to one side. "That has got to be the ugliest house I've ever seen, Sharlene. I don't like you running a beer joint but you are a grown woman and if that's what you want to do then I can't stop you. Don't expect me to come down there and go inside that place though. And the book? Congratulations on that. You've always had a way with words. Momma says you made a bunch of money already with it and that's good. Now let's eat supper," he said.

It was more words than he usually spoke at any one time and Sharlene was very grateful to hear every one of them.

"Thank you," she said.

Holt slipped an arm around her waist and she trembled at his touch. "Now that wasn't so difficult was it?"

"How do you feel about your woman running such a place?" Claud asked.

Holt let his arm fall away from her. "Sharlene and I are just friends. I guess it's her business what she does for a living."

"I see. Well, you kids all ready for some supper?" Claud nodded seriously.

"Yes!" Yells from all the kids echoed through the house.

Claud reached down and took Molly's hand. "Momma, you say the blessing and we'll let these young'uns get after it."

Holt noticed that Matthew was holding Clara's hand and Jeff had an arm around Lisa's waist. He held his hands behind his back and wished he had the same right to Sharlene.

The pillow was too firm. The bed was too soft. The air conditioner made too much noise. A lonesome old coyote howled in the distance. All of it combined to keep her awake. She looked at the clock. It was ten thirty. No wonder she couldn't sleep. She was just catching a second wind at two in the morning most nights. She was never in bed before three. If she was in the Honky Tonk she'd be hustling around drawing up beers, making buckets and pitchers full of mixed drinks.

It didn't help that Holt was in the next room. Right through that wall. She looked at it as if she could see through the two layers of sheet rock and into the other bedroom. His bed was no more than five feet from hers but a solid wall separated them. Not totally unlike the wall that would always keep them apart. Fathers and bartenders did not mix.

A ten thirty bedtime was one of the reasons she'd left Corn. Granted, it wasn't the major one but it did contribute. Get up with the chickens, go to bed with the cows, and start all over the next morning before dawn. Sharlene was not cut out to be a farm wife. Besides, if she shut her eyes the nightmares would start and she hated them worse than anything.

She eased out of bed, checked the children, and pulled the sheet up over each of them, then carefully went down the hall to the kitchen. Maybe a glass of milk or a piece of pecan pie would make her sleepy. If not, she'd turn on the kitchen light and look at magazines and catalogs until she couldn't keep her eyes open anymore. That beat flipping from one side of the bed to the other.

There was one piece of pie left so she ate it in the dark with her fingers instead of dirtying a fork. She looked out the kitchen window while she washed her hands. It was hard to imagine that just hours before kids had been yelling and screaming as they tried to touch the tree branches in the old swing set. That she'd sat beside Holt and his leg had brushed against hers sending heat flowing through her body like hot lava. She wandered out to the backyard, tucked the tail of her mid-thigh knit nightshirt up under her rear end, and sat down in a swing.

She pushed off with one foot and let the motion take her mind back to when she was a teenager and couldn't sleep. She often worked out her problems in the night air on the same set of swings. It was there that she decided she was not going to marry her high school sweetheart. It was there that she decided to join the army. And when she came home, she was swinging when she made up her mind to go to Dallas, rent an apartment, and look for a job.

When she was a little girl the swings were bright red and shiny. By the time she was in high school they were dark green. When she left for Iraq the first time her father had painted them yellow. Now they were red again. The chains had rusted and been replaced several times and the original metal seats had rusted years before and were now wooden.

Did Holt grow up on a farm or a ranch? There was so much she didn't know about him and she wanted to know everything. If she did would it make it easier to find a chink in his armor? One little rusty hole called a major fault that would be something she couldn't stand? Maybe when he got angry he slapped his women around? No, that wouldn't hold water. Holt was the kindest, most decent man she'd ever met.

----∿∿----

Holt laced his hands behind his head and stared at the bizarre patterns on the wall and ceiling created by moonlight drifting into the room through lace curtains. It had been a strange day with Sharlene finally coming clean with her parents and two of the brothers being hauled home by their wives. He remembered family life when his sister and parents were alive and missed it. Not that they'd ever had the big booming family with kids and food everywhere but it was exactly the atmosphere he'd always wanted when he was a child. If he had the privilege of choosing a family for Judd and Waylon, he would pick one exactly like the Waverly bunch. Grandparents who cared about their children and grandchildren; lots of kids to play and argue with at family gatherings; aunts and uncles who weren't perfect but had love in their hearts.

He shut his eyes tightly to force sleep but it didn't work. He kept seeing Sharlene in those tight jeans and boots stomping out across the pasture toward the barn; in the hayloft with a good dose of mad all over her; sitting in his lap and sharing those hot, passionate kisses.

Finally, he crawled out of bed, checked the kids, and went to the kitchen for a glass of water. He caught a movement out in the yard while he was standing at the sink. One glance told him it was Sharlene on the swings. It was barely eleven o'clock and she wasn't used to finishing up her night until two and then there was wind-down time before she could sleep.

He eased out the back door and pulled up a chair not far from her. The moonlight framed her in silhouette against a sky of sparkling stars. If a painter could catch a woman's profile on a child's swing with a big lover's moon hanging in the sky he would have a true masterpiece. It was a good thing an artist didn't create a picture like that because if they did, Holt would have to own it and it would bankrupt him.

The stars were just beyond her reach when she was on the swing. She was a little girl again with no worries about relationships or problems. She caught a movement off to her left and felt someone watching her. She stuck her bare foot down and skidded to a stop with her heel. The same feeling that she had in Iraq when the enemy was close behind her flooded over her. She turned slowly and saw Holt sitting not ten feet away in one of the folding chairs they'd used around the tables.

"You scared me," she said.

"Sorry," he said.

"What are you doing out here? You don't usually stay up until two in the morning like I do," she asked.

"Strange bed, maybe. Too many things on my mind. Want to take a walk and talk where we don't have to whisper?"

"In our bare feet? There's goat heads out there in the pasture," she said.

"Then let's go back in and get our boots," he said.

She hopped out of the swing. "All right. You want a shirt?"

"No, I'm all right."

But I'm not. That broad chest and knowing there's probably nothing under those knit pajama bottoms is giving me hives.

She tiptoed to her bedroom and slipped her boots on without socks. His were sitting beside his bed when she peeked in the door. She checked on the kids one more time. They were both still covered and sleeping soundly. She could hear Claud snoring as she passed her parent's bedroom door.

Holt startled her when she opened the kitchen door and found him waiting on the porch. "Don't sneak up on me. It scares the devil out of me."

"I wasn't sneaking. I thought maybe you'd had a change of heart," he said.

She handed him the boots and he jammed his feet down into them.

"Which way?" he asked.

"Out toward the barn where the kittens are. That should be far enough that we won't have to whisper," she answered.

His hand brushed against hers and he laced his fingers through hers. She led him to the fence where she opened the gate. The metal was still warm from the sun that afternoon but it wasn't nearly as hot as the hand that Holt held.

"You think it's all right to leave the kids? What if they wake up?" he asked.

"I'll be surprised if they even turn over as tired as they are. They've run all afternoon. Judd almost went to sleep in the bathtub," she said.

Sharlene used her free hand to point. "Look."

The mother cat came out of the barn with a kitten in her mouth. She moved past them to the wood shed and went back again to fetch another baby.

"Guess she got tired of little girls handling her litter," Sharlene said.

"She'd better hide them very good. Judd loves kittens," Holt said.

"Tasha will turn the farm upside down looking for them." Sharlene sat down on a hay bale just inside the door.

Holt let go of her hand and sat down beside her. He looked down at Sharlene at the same time she looked up at him. Their eyes locked and the world disappeared. The barn was the Garden of Eden. Holt and Sharlene were the only two people in it but there was a serpent. Only he wasn't interested in pushing his apple tree; he had something far more exciting than a Red Delicious in mind.

Holt ran the back of his hand down her jaw. No makeup, bedroom hair, a sprinkling of light freckles across her pert nose, and a cute little nightshirt and cowboy boots. Yet, the fire in his gut and the ache in his heart said that she was absolutely stunning. He cupped her face in both his palms and leaned forward.

The soft touch of his rough hands on her face caused emotions deep inside her to quiver. His bare muscular chest, his broad callused hands, his square jaw with dark scruff created even deeper shivers but it was his lips that she focused on. Then suddenly, their lips were so close that she barely had time to shut her eyes before they met in a clash of passion.

The ever loquacious Sharlene Waverly had no words when he broke away and moved his hands from her face to hug her tightly. Face against bare chest made every nerve ending in her body hum with desire. She wrapped her arms around his neck and snuggled in closer, listening to his speeding heart for the second time that day.

"You are lovely in that getup, madam," he whispered.

"Flattery will get you in trouble," she mumbled.

He tipped her chin back up for another hard kiss that was as earth shattering as the first and held her close to his chest when it ended. "We'd better stop there or there's no telling where we'll wind up."

The fast beat of his heart was like a drum beat in her ear. "You are so right. This is too fast, Holt. But I'm not ready to go back inside. Let's go up in the hayloft and watch the moon come up out the loft doors."

He nodded and started up the ladder with her right behind him.

She sat down where she could get a good view and he settled in a few inches from her. "Talk to me," he said.

"About what?"

"Just talk. I love the sound of your voice and the way you put words together."

"I talk too much," she said.

"Not to me."

She threw herself backward and looked at the moon hanging in the sky like a fancy queen with the stars as her subjects. "So what do you think of the Waverly clan?"

"It's been a wonderful day. I've never seen Judd and Waylon so happy."

"And you? Are you happy today, Holt?" she asked.

He stretched out beside her. "Today, I'm happy. You have a gold mine here, Sharlene. Don't forget to visit it often and take a few nuggets home."

She yawned. "I'm sorry. That looks like you are boring me and you aren't. I can't sleep in the house and can't keep my eyes open in a hay barn. Something must be the matter with me."

He slipped an arm under her and pulled her to his side. "It's been a physically exhausting day having to get up that early. And it's been an emotional upheaval what with telling your folks about the secrets. Take a nap. I won't let you sleep but a little while."

She pressed her whole body close to his and looped an arm around his neck, bringing his lips to hers for a kiss that created a delicious oozy warmth in the core of her body. "I couldn't actually sleep right now. If it meant sleep or firing squad, I have to shut my eyes and get ready for a bullet."

He chuckled and kissed her again. So much for stopping. His hand slid up her inner thigh, setting fires all the way to her underpants. His tongue danced with hers in a sensuous mating ritual that lit up the whole hayloft in sparkling fireworks.

She was entertaining thoughts of kicking her panties over in the corner and letting nature take its course when a rat the size of a baby possum ran across her bare legs, up her chest, and looked her in the eye before it disappeared in a flash into a pile of loose hay.

She jumped up and did a dance, wiping at her legs and arms, trying to get the feel of the nasty critter from her body. "Dammit all to hell and back. If it's not kids it's rats. I swear my mother sent that damn rat out here."

Holt laughed. "Guess it's an omen. We are not supposed to make out or make love in the hayloft on the Waverly property. Maybe someone is watching out after us."

"I wish they'd stop," she mumbled.

"Lie down beside me and take a nap. I'll watch for rats," he said.

"They'll crucify you if they find us in here in our pajamas in the morning. So you'd better wake up in time to get us back in the house before daybreak." She yawned and settled back down beside him.

"Trust me," he said.

She wiped a hand across her neck one more time. Trust wasn't something she did very well. And it was something he wouldn't do when and if he read the classified file on Specialist Fourth Class Sharlene Waverly. Maybe there was a higher being watching out for them. It would be so much harder to watch him leave when the job was finished if they'd had sex.

She didn't intend to go to sleep at all because she didn't want to wake up all wild-eyed after one of her famous nightmares. But she did and she did not dream about bombed out shells where buildings used to stand, people who didn't want the U.S. military in their country, and secret assignments.

Instead her dreams were filled with sunshine, fields of wild yellow daisies, and Judd and Waylon chasing butterflies. She could hear Holt's deep Texas drawl behind her and feel his strong arms slipping around her waist as he called out to the children not to go too far. Then he kissed her on the neck and told her she was beautiful.

Chapter 9

SHARLENE ROLLED OVER, STRETCHED, AND REACHED for Holt, but he wasn't there. She was in her bed in the house. Her boots were sitting beside the door and she was wearing her nightshirt and underpants. That was a good thing because if he was beside her, Molly would make Claud load the shotgun and the Waverly brothers force Holt to marry her on the spot. She touched her forehead where he'd kissed her when he carried her into the house and laid her on the bed.

Molly poked her head inside the door. "You going to sleep all day? Holt and the kids have already had breakfast. Bart and Fiona are on their way and Judd and Waylon are waiting for their kids on the front porch."

"What time is it?" Sharlene asked.

"Ten o'clock. Figured I'd let you sleep in since you had a hard day yesterday," Molly said.

Sharlene jumped out of bed, grabbed her duffle bag, and headed toward the bathroom. "Bart and Fiona get things settled? I'll be on the porch by the time they arrive. I'm starving. Did they leave anything on the back burner for me for breakfast?"

"Fiona said things were back to normal. There are some sausage and biscuits still on the back of the stove. All the gravy is gone and there's no more pancakes. I could mix up another batch," Molly offered.

"That's all right. Don't make anymore gravy. I'll stuff sausage and grape jelly in a biscuit and call it breakfast. Be there in five minutes."

Sharlene shut the door to the bathroom and checked her reflection in the mirror. She still looked the same as she had the day before. Unruly red curls, green eyes, a few freckles that she could erase with makeup. She tilted her head to one side and then the other. There was something else; a glow or a glitter in the eyes, something that hadn't been in the mirror the day before. She hoped her mother hadn't picked up on the difference.

Fiona and Bart were getting out of the truck when she stepped out on the porch in her denim miniskirt, boots, and a bright orange tank top. Fiona walked with her head held high and the old determination in her step. If a bouquet of roses or daisies or whatever Bart had been fool enough to send to the hot little teller woke them both up, then they were worth the price and the fight.

Tasha and four-year-old Betsy grabbed Judd's hand and away they went toward the barn where the kittens would not be hiding. Their boys, Dylan and Tyler, asked Waylon if he'd like to toss a football around. Bart kissed Fiona on the forehead and headed to the backyard where Holt and Claud were firing up the grill and setting up more tables.

"So?" Sharlene followed Fiona into the kitchen.

"It's finished and it won't happen again, believe me."

"If it does, you call me and I'll bring an extra shovel. Even if he is my brother, I'll help you bury his body so deep that the coyotes won't even smell him," Sharlene said.

"Who are we burying?" Molly asked from the stove where she was stirring a pot of pinto beans.

"Any fool husband who sends flowers to another woman," Sharlene answered.

"Add a shovel to the list," Molly said without hesitation.

"Thank you, but it really is over. We got it straightened out." Fiona set a lemon layered cake on the table. "I've got a cobbler and potato casserole in the truck. Come help me bring them in, Sharlene. By the way, you look cute today. Something is different about you. Must've done you good to 'fess up to your evil deeds yesterday."

"Does everyone good to come clean," Molly said.

"Amen to that," Fiona agreed.

Sharlene kept her mouth shut. She wanted to slip around to the backyard and see if Holt had a different expression than he'd had yesterday. But common sense told her to steer clear of him for fear that everyone in the family would see the invisible sparks and aura that surrounded them. She followed Fiona to the truck and picked up the long glass pan containing hash brown casserole.

"Y'all need some help?" Bart and Holt jogged from around the house.

Bart took the cobbler from Fiona and said, "I'll carry that. You got anything more in there?"

Sharlene handed the casserole off to Holt. "This."

Their hands brushed in the transfer and she felt a tingle down to her toes. She hadn't set out to be more than friends with Holt Jackson but those kisses the day and night before had nixed that idea. Her mind argued with her heart and everything went in circles as she tried to hang onto a single decision about Holt. It might have helped if the sparks between them didn't keep heating up her body hotter than the hot tin roof of a barn that was in blazes.

"Did you sleep well?" Holt whispered.

"Wonderful well," she smiled.

"I didn't."

"I'm sorry."

"Don't be. It was worth it. Rat and all."

She giggled.

"What's so funny?" Fiona asked.

Jenny and Miles drove up before Sharlene could answer and two kids were out of the truck and running toward the backyard before Sharlene could turn around.

"Hey, you two without something in your hands, come and help me," Jenny called out to Sharlene and Fiona.

Miles had a sack of ice in each hand. "I'm taking these in before they melt," he said.

Jenny pointed to several covered dishes in two cardboard boxes located in the bed of the truck. She and Fiona each grabbed the edge of one box and Sharlene picked up the last dish from the remaining box.

"What's in this?" she asked.

"It's corn salad. We'll put the corn chips on top just before we serve it. Got the recipe at Dolly Benton's funeral last week. No cooking to it. Just mix up cheese and corn and the rest of the ingredients, then you add chili flavored corn chips to it right at the end so they'll stay crispy," she answered.

"Sounds like it would go wonderful with cold beer," Sharlene said.

"It does, but don't tell Momma I said that," Fiona whispered.

"My lips are sealed," Sharlene said. "How'd things go last night with you? Did Matthew about come unglued at the hinges?"

Fiona laughed.

"No, he grinned and strutted around like a stud horse. I expected him to beat on his chest like Tarzan before the night was over. You'd think it was some kind of powerful thing that proves he's still a man or something," Jenny said. "He wouldn't feel so cocky if he had to throw up everything but his toenails every morning. And just once I'd like to see a man go through labor. Not all of it and not delivery. God, they'd all die. But just the last five minutes they could take on the pains and do the pushing for us. That sounds fair, doesn't it? I'm sorry. Here I am bitching and I didn't even ask about you and Bart."

"We worked it out. I talked and he listened and swore nothing had happened and would never happen. He apologized and promised. I believed him but if I catch wind of it again, it's going to be a different story," Fiona said.

Sharlene raised an eyebrow.

Fiona jutted her chin out and said, "Fool me once, shame on me. Fool me twice, I'll go to Mingus and become a bartender."

Holt held the door for the other five and heard the last comment Fiona made. Evidently Bart and Fiona straightened out their problem but Bart was skating on thin ice until he proved himself. And the Waverly women didn't mess around giving second chances. He followed them to the kitchen where the women were bustling around arranging food on the buffet table. Miles pulled two ice chests from the back porch, filled them with two bags of ice, and then went to the coffee pot. He poured two cups and put sugar and cream in one and carried it to Jenny before he and the other men headed to the backyard.

"Amazing how attentive pregnancy makes them, isn't it?" Jenny sipped the coffee.

"A hissy will do the same thing," Fiona said.

Molly smiled.

"What's so funny, Momma?" Sharlene asked.

"Our ladies of the round table talks. They always make everything all better, don't they?"

"Yes, ma'am," three voices said in unison.

"What are we yes ma'aming?" Lisa asked from the living room.

"The fact that everything is all better today. Miles just made coffee for Jenny and Bart helped carry in the food," Sharlene said.

"Well, hot damn! Maybe my problem will solve itself today too."

"Does Mr. Moody Grandson know who is invited to spend the day here?"

"No, I thought I'd surprise him," Lisa said.

Someone knocked on the door and Sharlene spun around to look at the rest of the family. No one ever knocked. They just yelled and came through the living room, dining room, and back to the kitchen.

"I'll get it. It has to be the Alvarez family," Lisa said.

Sharlene followed her to see what a thirteen-year-old little Mexican girl had that had set Creed's hormones into overdrive.

Same thing that set yours on a roller coaster, girl, she told herself. *It's pure old sex appeal. Don't matter if a person is thirteen or thirty or sixty-three. If the other party lights up the hormone drive, they are the best thing since ice cream on a stick.*

Lisa kept up a running chatter as she led the way to the kitchen. "Come right in. Take the food stuff to the kitchen and then you kids can all go outside. Maybe you can talk Creed into saddling a couple of horses for y'all to ride today, Christina. And the rest of you children will find someone your age out in the yard, I'm sure. Jeff is firing up a grill with the rest of the men. Just follow us through the kitchen and you can go out the back door."

Enrique made a hasty retreat away from the women when Lisa pointed to the back door. Kitchen and women were not his idea of a holiday. Men grilling meats and drinking ice tea was a much better choice. Three children, all younger than Christina, hurried out to where the other children played. Sharlene watched Creed's face from the window. When he saw Enrique and the Alvarez children, his gaze locked on the house.

Christina hung back to help her mother and the ladies until Lisa finally said, "Girl, get on out there with the rest of the young folks. We've got lots of help."

She looked at her mother, Martina.

"Go on. Shoo. You'll grow up too quick as it is and have to cook and run after children. Go and have a good time," Martina said.

Both mother and daughter were short, had long dark hair and big brown eyes. Their faces were round and their skin slightly toasted like coffee with only a dollop of pure cream. Martina had crow's-feet beginning around her eyes and a thicker middle. Christina's red tank top was tucked into jean shorts that nipped in at her tiny waist.

"Are you sure?" Christina asked.

"Yes, I am sure that I can uncover these tamales all by myself," Martina said.

Sharlene stayed glued to the window. Creed's whole face lit up when he saw Christina. He waved and motioned her over to the fence he leaned against. She joined him but kept a foot of space between them. Sharlene remembered back when she was about seven years old and Lisa first came to the farm with her parents for Sunday dinner. She and Jeff had to have been about that same age and they'd both had the same timid yet joyful expression on their faces. Was history about to repeat itself?

Lisa pretended to wash her hands. "What happened?"

Sharlene took a step to the side. "See for yourself."

"He reminds me so much of Jeff at that age," Lisa said.

"Well, she damn sure don't remind me of you. You were all legs and had long blond braids that you hated and braces. You looked like a young colt," Sharlene said. Her gaze went from Creed and Christina to Holt. He fit in so well with her brothers and their families that it was scary.

"I did not look like a horse. Good lord, you're the writer. Can't you think of something nicer than that?" Lisa asked.

"Hey, hey, we're here," Matthew called from the door.

Then people began to arrive en masse. In-laws, the neighbor Wayne who Molly made a great show of introducing to Sharlene before she sent him to the backyard, Dorie and her two kids, grandparents, and the ladies from the Circle. Everyone brought so much food that Clara had to drag out a folding table and set it up to hold all the dishes.

Sharlene knew them all except the Alvarez family and Wayne, but she wondered how Holt fared trying to put a name with everyone's face. It wouldn't be unlike the first day she arrived in Iraq and everyone introduced themselves. It took her weeks to get names and faces together and to stop calling everyone, "Hey you."

At exactly noon, Molly nodded at Claud when he poked his head in the back door, and he rang the dinner bell hanging on the back porch.

"Everyone gather round and we'll have grace before we turn the stampede loose on the food," he said. "Who's the youngest child we have here today?"

Everyone looked around. "I guess it's Betsy," Fiona said.

Claud motioned for her to join him below the dinner bell. "Then Betsy will give thanks for us."

She marched up to his side and bowed her head.

"Speak up so everyone can hear," Claud whispered.

"Now I lay me down to sleep," she said loudly. "And God bless Momma and Daddy and Gramps and Granny and the kittens in the barn. And oh, yeah, bless this dinner too. Amen."

"Amen," Claud said. "That was a good grace. Now you kids get in line first so your mothers can help you. And then the adults can fix their plates."

Holt took charge of Waylon right behind Matthew who had a hand on Matty's shoulder. Sharlene hugged Judd up to her side and got in line behind Jenny who would be helping Kayla.

When the children were all seated, the men navigated toward the buffet tables. Sharlene's maternal grandfather threw an arm around her shoulders and hugged her tightly. "What's this I hear about you owning a beer joint? In my younger days I mighta slipped off down there and danced around the floor with you, but Grandma would skin me alive if I did that these days."

Sharlene gasped. "You went to beer joints?"

"Back before I met your Grandma, I did a few times. I like the music and there's enough German in me to like a brew every so often. But Grandma was a preacher's daughter and I give it all up when I fell in love with her. Guess you took after me after all."

"News travels fast. I only told Momma last night," Sharlene said.

"Well, I already knew all about it. I was on the Internet and found that book you wrote. The thing written about it said you got the inspiration from your beer joint called the Honky Tonk. Don't worry. I didn't even tell Grandma. But Matthew came to help me with chores last night and he told me all about it. I didn't let on I already knew." He grinned big enough that the wrinkles around his eyes deepened. His hair was still as thick as it had been in his younger days but it was snow white. He wore bibbed overalls but they were starched and ironed. Grandma wouldn't ever let him out of the house without ironed clothes. They'd throw her out of the Ladies Circle if she committed such a sin.

"You have a computer?" Sharlene was amazed.

"Yeah, I got one last year. Didn't think an old dog like me could learn how to operate it, did you? I got Creed to show me how. He's a real whiz kid on one. It's my turn to get my plate. You take care of yourself down there. Don't let no drunks hurt you. I'd hate to have to come to Mingus and whup someone."

Sharlene smiled up at him. "Don't you worry about me. I've got a bouncer as big as a refrigerator who wouldn't let a fly light on me. And Grandpa, just between you and me, I can really take care of myself."

"I reckon you could or they wouldn't have sent you over there to that war place two times. You must've been good at takin' care of more than just yourself. I'm glad you got a good bouncer. I'd like to meet him sometime. I like the feller you brought with you too. Matthew says he's a real stand-up guy. He'll be a fine match for Dorie. Grandma already has them talking to each other," Grandpa said and then disappeared into the group of men folks loading up their plates.

Sharlene looked around quickly. Sure enough Dorie had plastered herself up to Holt's side while Grandpa was telling her about his shady past. Had Grandma instigated that by sending Grandpa to keep her busy?

Holt caught her gaze and nodded.

Dorie was all dolled up in her flowing multicolored tiered skirt and peasant blouse showing three inches of cleavage and Sharlene felt dowdy in her miniskirt and boots. She glanced out the window and noticed that Dorie's kids were sitting at the same table with Judd and Waylon. Ruth was talking to Judd a mile a minute and Waylon was listening to John tell some tall tale that involved lots of hand waving.

Dorie had never been a bit bashful or backward. Sharlene had always admired her nerve until she cut in line right in front of Holt.

"Y'all will have to excuse me for lining up with the fellers. I haven't had a bite of breakfast and I'm starving. I don't think this big old handsome cowboy will mind, will you, darlin'?" She blinked her long lashes up at him.

Sharlene would have gladly yanked every one of those bottle blond hairs from her head. It was the first time since she'd gotten home from Iraq that she seriously considered loading her army rifle. But when Dorie sat beside him at the dinner table, in the only seat left at that table, Sharlene decided that shooting her so-called friend was too easy. She needed to suffer. Maybe a quick roll in honey and sitting her on a bed of ants would be more in order.

"Come sit beside me." Jenny touched Sharlene's arm.

"Sure," Sharlene mumbled and wound up sitting right beside Wayne, the neighbor. He was a nice enough looking fellow and so sweet that Sharlene figured she'd smother in the course of one meal. No wonder women didn't flock to him like flies on a fresh cow patty. He was too damn nice. A woman liked a little bit of strength in a man. Not to the point of abuse but enough that she didn't feel like she was married to a wimp.

"So I understand you work for a newspaper in Dallas, Texas. How do you like living in the big city after being raised in the country?" His voice wasn't deep and resonant like Holt's and his eyes didn't glitter.

Bologna and steak, she thought. *Holt is steak and he is bologna. Both are protein and both will keep a woman from going hungry. But it's not easy to think about a lifetime of bologna when a woman has just kissed a T-bone.*

"Actually, I've moved to a town about half the size of Corn," she said.

Jenny grinned at her and glanced toward Holt.

Dorie had finished eating and had her hand over the back of his chair.

"Is there a newspaper there?" Wayne asked.

"Not in Mingus. The town doesn't have a newspaper. It's a border town that is known for its beer joints. I own and operate one of those beer joints. It's called the Honky Tonk."

His fork stopped midway between his plate and mouth. "You have a funny sense of humor, Sharlene. You said that so seriously I thought you meant it. There's really not a Mingus, Texas, is there? You're just making jokes."

"No, I'm just painfully honest. Want proof? Hey Judd, where do you go every day?" she asked Judd who sat at the next table.

"To your house. Uncle Holt is building a bigger beer joint for you so the people won't have to dance in the parking lot and they'll buy beer from you. Why do I have to keep tellin' that?" Judd asked.

"Because sometimes folks believe a little girl better than a big one," Sharlene said.

"For real?" Wayne's eyes looked twice as big through his thick lens glasses when he opened them wide. He laid his fork down and cocked his head to one side. "Are you really Molly and Claud's daughter or are these sisters of yours playing a trick on me because I'm the new guy in Corn?"

"That's what I do. From eight to two in the morning, six nights a week, I'm a bartender," she said.

Wayne's face went stone still and serious. "Does Molly and Claud know this?"

"They do now. Now tell me, Wayne, what is it that you did before you came to Corn and bought a farm?"

"I've always been a farmer. I had a bigger operation in Nebraska."

"Why'd you sell out and move here?"

"I wanted a new start," he said. "Truth is I was engaged to a woman for two years and she called it off. So how long are you staying in Corn?"

"We're leaving this afternoon. My other bartender is helping by opening up for me tonight but I've got to be home in time to close. This is old jukebox night. You listen to the old country music?" She kept an eye on Dorie's hand as it crept up to massage Holt's neck.

A man on the rebound. A long engagement and she called it off. Why? Was he too nice? And then there's Dorie, a woman on the rebound. Why couldn't she and Wayne bump into each other and see stars? Why does she have her hands on Holt? And while I'm asking questions, what in the devil was I thinking, bringing him here?

Wayne smiled brightly and said, "Oh, yes. Love it. Listen to it on my tractor radio. And used to square dance in Nebraska. I wish they'd get a club started here. I do a little calling when I'm not dancing."

"Any good at two-stepping or line dancing?" Jenny asked.

"No, just square dancing. You ever think about moving back home to Corn?"

"Hell no!" Sharlene said before she thought.

Sharlene stood up quickly and picked up empty bread baskets from her table. "Hey, Holt, these are begging to be refilled. Want to help me get some more hot rolls?"

"Will do. Ours is empty here too. Whoever made these homemade rolls deserves a gold crown," he said as he gathered up baskets.

She followed him into the kitchen and helped load a dozen baskets with hot rolls from the trays on the cabinet.

"So how are things going with Dorie?"

"She seems nice enough. We've been talking about our kids. Seems like she's got a lot of the same problems I do, except hers are reversed. Her son is the mouthy one and her daughter kind of introverted."

Sharlene turned to tell him to watch his back, that Dorie was on the prowl and found him so close that she could smell his aftershave.

"Did I tell you that you are beautiful today?" he whispered in a soft Texas drawl.

"No, but you can tell me now." She looked up.

He leaned in for a soft kiss and then started stacking baskets of bread up his forearm, holding them in place with his hand.

"Ready to go face the dragons again?" he asked.

"I'd rather go to the barn," she said.

"Me too." He grinned.

When they'd scattered baskets down the tables he took his seat beside Dorie and she went back to Wayne, but every few minutes they exchanged long glances across the yard.

"Why did I end up sitting beside Wayne?" Sharlene whispered to Clara when Wayne was in conversation with her grandfather sitting across the table from him.

"Momma arranged it that way so Dorie could sit beside Holt. She thinks that those two have a lot in common and you know what an old matchmaker she is," Clara said.

"I told Momma that there might be more between us than friendship. Why would she do that?"

"After she found out that Holt works for you and what you do, she's about to give up on you finding a husband. No decent man would marry a *cheap barmaid*, her words not mine. And she thinks Holt is a fine man and she knows you won't like Wayne so you're just here to keep him away from Dorie. Enough said?" Clara smiled at Wayne when he stopped talking to Grandpa.

Sharlene nodded. "More than enough. She'll accept what I do but she don't like it, right?"

"In a nutshell." Clara nodded toward the other table.

Dorie and Holt were gone. Sharlene's eyes darted all around the yard before finally spotting them. Dorie was leading Holt across the pasture toward the creek. Molly was right about two things. Holt was decent. Sharlene ran a beer joint. Did that make him too good for her? Pure old mad crept out of her soul and into her heart. Dorie had better enjoy her little walk with Holt Jackson because he was never setting foot in Corn again.

Holt listened to Dorie with one ear and wondered how he'd gotten himself in such a predicament. He'd awakened that morning wishing that Sharlene was beside him. He'd relived the night before several times before the kids had bounded in his room and landed on his bed, saying they were starving and asking what time the other children were coming back to play.

By the time they had breakfast Claud had enlisted his help to get the grills cleaned and set up for dinner. Then the backyard filled up with men and they were barbecuing hot dogs and hamburgers and the sound of children playing filled the yard. Just exactly when Dorie latched onto him was a mystery. He tuned in to what she was saying and tried to listen without thinking about Sharlene.

"We got married right out of high school and he died a year ago in a hunting accident. He was up in a tree stand and fell. The gun went off and shot him right through the heart. They said that he was gone before he hit the ground. That gives me a little comfort that he didn't suffer or call out for me," she said.

He wasn't interested in how or when her husband died and wished he'd been fast enough to think up a better excuse. When she'd asked if he would like for her to show him the creek, he'd said that he'd better watch the kids. Truth was, he'd been deep in thought about Sharlene and the night before and had stammered and stuttered like a junior high nerd.

"Nonsense! Go on with Dorie. She was here at the farm as much as she was home during high school. She and Sharlene were best friends. For a while we thought they might marry best friends but Sharlene got a wild hair and joined the army," Molly had said.

"But we have to leave in a couple of hours," Holt had protested further.

"Sharlene will help watch Judd and Waylon. They'll be fine," Claud said.

Now he was walking out across a pasture toward a creek over there by the willow trees and wishing he was back in the barn with Sharlene. She was probably ready to wring his neck and he couldn't blame her. Last night he'd come so close to making love with her that he ached from the desire after she'd fallen asleep in his arms; now he was arm in arm with Dorie. This was much worse than sending flowers to a woman and she'd threatened to help bury Bart because of much less. He made a mental note to hide the shovel when he got back to Mingus or else he might be planted beside the old tomcat by the end of the week.

"So tell me, do you like living in a small town? I understand you live in the same place that Sharlene has a beer joint. That girl was mouthy and sassy in school but I never figured she'd go out and buy a beer joint. I bet Molly and Claud are heartsick over that news," Dorie said.

Some friend you are! he thought.

"They seemed to take it pretty good. That and the book she's written too. You did know that she's sold a romance book and it will be on the market in November?"

Dorie toyed with his fingertips. "I heard she was into trashy romance."

"You ever read that kind of book?" Holt asked.

"I do not. It's only one step down from porn. I wouldn't have it in my house for the kids to see," Dorie said.

"So what do you do for fun?"

She stopped walking long enough to look up at Holt and smile brightly. "Fun? Well, I'm a mother so that leaves out most fun, doesn't it? The kids go to school. They're in the first and second grades. Then I go to work at the convenience store. When Jim died there was a big insurance policy and the farm was paid for instantly so I lease it all but twenty acres. Someday I'm going to remarry. Jim wouldn't have wanted me to be alone the rest of my life and maybe my new husband will want to farm. Farming is part of me and I'll get back into it someday, but I can't keep up the whole section of land without help."

"I see. Where is this creek?" Holt asked.

"Right through those trees." She started walking again. They passed through a copse of pecan and willow trees and sure enough, a small, bubbling creek ran through the land. She sat down and patted the ground. "It's pleasant and quiet here. All that noise back there is enough to drive a woman to Sharlene's place of business. But the kids are having a wonderful time and I'd do anything for them. I expect you feel the same way?"

"Not really. I'd do most anything for Judd and Waylon but I love all the noise and confusion of a big family. I even like going to the Honky Tonk when Chad and Gloria take the kids for an evening," Holt said.

"Well, that could change if you found the right woman," Dorie said softly.

"I doubt it. I'm too old and set in my ways to do much changing," he said.

"So tell me, if I gave you my phone number would you call me sometime?" she asked.

"Didn't Molly tell you? I'm involved with another woman right now."

"Who?"

"A lady I met in Mingus."

Dorie scooted in close enough to him that her body was glued to his side. "Does she have children?"

"No, she's never been married," Holt said.

The woman toyed with his fingertips and yet there was no friction. Not a single spark. No jolts that shot desire through his veins. Just a nice smelling body next to his that didn't put his nerves on edge.

Dorie pulled a pen from her shirt pocket and wrote her number on his palm. "Well, she's a lucky lady but just in case, you can always call me if things go south between you and her."

Judd and Waylon sprang through the trees like windup toys with Ruth and John right behind them. "Hey, guess what, Uncle Holt. Creed and Christina are putting saddles on two horses and they're going to let the little kids ride 'em. And guess what, they'll be leading them so we won't have a runaway and can we ride 'em. Please, please, please?" Judd said in a whoosh.

"We want to ride too, Momma. Creed said me and Judd can ride together. Did you ever know another girl named Judd? I like her name, don't you, Momma?" Ruth said.

Holt could have kissed every one of the four kids.

"Where's Sharlene? I thought she was going to watch you while I came to see the creek?"

"I'm right here," Sharlene said.

He looked up to see her leaning on a willow tree not ten feet away. Good grief! What all had she heard and how would she interpret it?

Sharlene covered the distance between them in a few easy strides. She'd heard enough to know that Dorie had changed drastically. Dorie would have never, ever said those things back when they were best friends.

"They ran on ahead. It's almighty important to get

your okay. I wouldn't give them permission without asking you, and I couldn't let them come running down here without me. Wasn't sure which part of the creek Dorie would take you to. So can they ride or not? If so, we'll get on back up to the barn. If not, you can deal with them." Her voice was even but cold.

"Of course they can ride," Holt said.

"You can too," Dorie told her children.

Four shouts went up and they tore back toward the house in a flurry of little legs chasing through the pasture grasses.

"That's good." Sharlene turned around and started after them.

"Wait," Holt yelled.

She stopped and slowly looked over her shoulder. He was standing up and offering his hand to Dorie, who looked as if she could put his hand against all her beautiful cleavage and enjoy every minute of what it might do there.

"I want to see their faces when they're on a horse for the first time," he said.

Dorie latched on to his hand and hung on when she was on her feet. "Me too. Of course, my kids have ridden all their lives but I'd like to see yours."

"What's that got to do with me?" Sharlene asked bluntly.

"Don't be testy," Dorie said.

Sharlene looked at Holt and almost giggled. He looked like a cottontail rabbit already caught between the jaws of a starving coyote. His expression pleaded for mercy and begged her to rescue him from Dorie's claws.

"They've got a head start on you, Holt. If you want to see them you'd best put on your running boots. You've got longer legs than either of us and you don't want to miss Judd's squeals, so get to running. We'll come along behind you," Sharlene said.

Holt dropped Dorie's hand and took off in a jog.

"That was just plain mean. He's just what I've been looking for and you're being hateful. You can't have him. You are a bartender. For God's sake, Sharlene, why did you buy a beer joint? Didn't you embarrass your family enough by joining the army?"

Sharlene set her jaw and said through clenched teeth, "Holt would never be happy in Corn and you aren't leaving that farm and your family and moving to Mingus, so why are you doing this? And I did not join the army or buy a beer joint to embarrass my family."

"How do you know what will make him happy or make him move either one? At least I've got a farm that looks pretty damn good compared to a beer joint," Dorie said.

"That's a low shot," Sharlene said.

Dorie gave her a go-to-hell-on-a-silver-poker look. "It's the truth. What happened to you? When we were in high school we were going to marry our sweethearts. You broke David's heart when you turned him down. It was only last year that he finally gave up waiting for you to come to your senses and married. Now you are a bartender. God Almighty, Sharlene!"

Sharlene shrugged her shoulders. "I wanted more."

"Why? What is out there that's better than the love of a good man?"

"Life," Sharlene answered.

Dorie took two steps, stopping only when her nose was inches from Sharlene's. "I love Molly and Claud. I should've been their daughter instead of you. And I know a good man when I see one. He won't have you anyway. No decent man hooks up with a cheap barmaid."

That said in a voice so cold it would have kept icicles frozen in Hades, she stormed past Sharlene, leaving her standing there beside a willow tree.

"You only met him two hours ago. How do you know he's such a good man?" Sharlene yelled.

Dorie spun around and pointed a finger at Sharlene. "I know what I want when I see it. I don't have to go to Iraq and back and still not know."

Sharlene slid down the backside of the tree and sat on the ground. Dorie *should* have been the Waverly daughter instead of Sharlene. She had the same ideals and played by the same rules. She was a farm wife from skin out and when the right man came along she'd make him happy. She had enough fire to keep him on his toes and to fight for their relationship if he ever sent flowers to a strange woman.

Anything worth having is worth the fight to keep it. Wasn't that essentially what she'd said to Fiona the night before? Stand up and fight for Bart. Don't let him walk on you and if you want your marriage to work, then be the woman he married.

Holt made every fiber of her being come alive when he kissed her, but could it ever develop beyond satisfying a physical need? She didn't know the answer to that question. There was only one way to make double sure that Dorie didn't mess it up before she could figure it out and that was to keep Holt in Mingus away from the woman. Dorie was a brazen widow in her stomping ground but she'd never chase Holt all the way to Texas. She might make some phone calls but she would not sit in the car or truck five hours with two kids to run after him.

Sharlene stood up, straightened her back, and started back to the barn. As soon as the kids had a turn on the horse, she and Holt were going to Mingus. She'd have room and time to figure it all out there without Dorie's smart-ass attitude and cleavage getting in the way.

Chapter 10

ONE MILE WAS EXACTLY LIKE THE NEXT. MILES AND miles of cotton and wheat; cattle and oil wells; scrub oak and small towns. Sharlene watched familiar landmarks speed past at seventy-five miles an hour and peeked through the pickup bucket seats every few minutes to see if the children were still sleeping.

The events of the past day and a half played through her mind like a movie in full living color. She hit the imaginary replay button several times when it came to the scene with Dorie. How could her mother and grandmother encourage a relationship between her and Holt? Sure, they each had two children but that's where the common ground ended.

Miranda Lambert was singing "Gunpowder and Lead" on the radio. The song was actually about an abused woman who was going home to load her shotgun, but Sharlene applied it to her friend.

What do I shoot her for? Pretending to be my friend all these years or blatantly trying to take Holt away from me? Damn it, Dorie, I could smack you for showing your true colors today. Now I've got to decide where this man fits into my life.

She shivered at the thought of really shooting anyone, even Dorie, who'd made her mad enough to chew up a full grown bull and spit out cellophane wrapped packages of hamburger meat.

Holt yawned, turned off the radio, and looked over at Sharlene. "Too much good food in the past twenty-four hours plus a very late night. You're going to have to entertain me or I'm going to fall asleep like those two kids in the backseat."

"What'd you have in mind?" she asked.

His grin was pure devilment and the lust in his eyes fried the sleepiness from her instantly. "I could think of some pretty interesting things."

"Well, that's not possible going down the highway at seventy-five miles an hour with two kids who could wake up at any minute," she said.

He raised an eyebrow. "Got your mind in the gutter, do you? Mine spent part of the day in the same place but I was thinking that maybe you'd tell me the story of the Honky Tonk angels. Or maybe the plot of your book. Not that I'm above anything kinky while driving down the road. But not with two kids in the backseat who might wake up and embarrass the hell out of us."

She slapped at his arm. "Honky Tonk angels?" she asked. "Why would you want to know about Dolly and those women?"

Holt shook his head. "Not the singers. The ones that owned the place before you did. Start with Daisy."

"Why not Ruby Lee? She had it the longest."

"Then start with her," Holt said. Anything to get her talking and keep her going until they got home. He'd never get enough of her voice. It was smooth southern bourbon mixed with just enough honey to make it sweet and easy on the ears. She'd said repeatedly that she talked too much but Holt didn't care. Her voice was one of the things he liked best about her.

"Okay, Ruby Lee built the Tonk back in the sixties. I've already told you this, haven't I?"

"Parts of it but if you start there and build the whole thing up to when you inherited the joint, it'll make better sense to me," he said.

She told him what she knew about Ruby Lee again and then paused.

"Now Daisy," he said.

"Okay, this is the way I heard it. Daisy O'Dell had a bad experience with a boyfriend and left Mena, Arkansas. She pulled into the Smokestack parking lot because her car overheated and Ruby was getting out of her Caddy about the same time. Ruby wound up buying her lunch and putting her to work at the Honky Tonk. Daisy was a vet-tech by trade so it wasn't long until everyone with a sick rooster, dog, cat, or goat was on her doorstep wanting advice or medical attention so she was essentially working two jobs. In those days, Emmett McElroy and his wife used to come in the Tonk real often. Then his wife died and Emmett got dementia among other things and finally his nephew, Jarod, came down from Cushing, Oklahoma, to help him run his ranch.

"Daisy had been going out to the ranch to help vaccinate cows and do whatever a veterinarian does to cattle and dogs. So anyway, Jarod comes in the Tonk one night because he and Emmett don't do anything but fight and argue and he's thinking about going back home to Oklahoma and leaving the old fellow alone. He and Daisy clashed in the middle of the floor. I mean literally, not figuratively. They ran smack into each other and the way I got the story is that she fell right on top of him. Then he brought Emmett to the Tonk one evening and Emmett made Daisy promise she'd come to dinner the next Sunday after she worked the cattle. With his problem he forgot all about the cattle part so she arrived in the corral ready to do a job and no one had gathered up the cows. By the time she got to the house, she was sweatin' and her temper was even hotter. She was loaded for bear and the only person in her sights was Jarod. They were already fighting a physical attraction so they locked up horns right there on the porch at the ranch."

"And?" Holt said immediately when she paused.

She went on. "And they clashed again, only this time it was over Emmett thinking they were married. He'd gotten it into his head that they'd snuck off to Oklahoma after a fishing trip that their friends had planned the previous Sunday. To make a long story short, Jarod talked her into pretending to be his wife. Then Emmett died holding both their hands and there was the house to clean out and the place to get ready for Jarod's nephew to take over. That would be Garrett McElroy, who fell in love with Merle's niece, Angel, and they met in the Honky Tonk too, by the way. It was a rocky relationship between Daisy and Jarod but they finally got over all the obstacles and Daisy admitted to herself that she loved Jarod more than the Honky Tonk."

"Angel and Garrett?"

"Relationship wasn't rocky. They fell in love over a pool table, didn't fight it, and are married now and living on the ranch. Angel is the head engineer for the oil company where Luther and Tessa work in the daytime."

"And the Chigger woman you all talk about sometimes?" he asked.

"She was Daisy's friend. She wound up married to Jim Bob Walker. He was one of the Walker triplets— Jim Bob, Joe Bob, and Billy Bob."

Holt was getting more and more into the story. "You've got to be kidding me?"

Sharlene shook her head. "No, I'm not. I've met all three of them. They are identical and that's really their names."

"So she married Jim Bob. What happened to the other two?"

"Back up a little here. After Jim Bob and Chigger got married they had a wedding dinner out at Chigger and Jim Bob's place. Chigger's momma said she would find the other two brothers a wife before the end of the year. Be damned if she didn't. She also told Cathy that she'd see her married too but Cathy didn't believe her."

"Okay, now Cathy is Daisy's cousin? Right? Was she at the dinner?"

Sharlene nodded. "Yes, she was. She had had a row with her boyfriend up in Mena too. He'd tried to beat her up but she worked him over instead. Kind of like Miranda Lambert's song we just heard about gunpowder and lead. She'd come to Mingus to get away from the situation and Daisy gave her a job in the Honky Tonk. By then she was trying to be Jarod's pretend wife and run the place all by herself too. Oh, and back then Hayes Radner was trying to buy the place."

"What in the hell would Hayes want with an old beer joint?"

Sharlene laughed. "Got to do a flashback in history here to get that straightened out. When Ruby Lee built the Honky Tonk she wanted to be close to Henry Wells.

They'd met and fallen in love in Dallas. So when her aunt died and left her a wad of money, she decided to build a beer joint. Erath County is dry and Palo Pinto is wet, and Henry lived in Palo Pinto and she wanted to be close to him. So she and Merle came to Mingus. Merle was her best friend and could do her work anywhere and Ruby Lee liked bartending. Henry threw a fit and told her he wouldn't marry a barmaid. I guess she told him he could squat and fall backwards," Sharlene said.

"Go on," Holt chuckled. "I'm finally beginning to understand this soap opera. You sure had plenty of material to work with for a book."

She giggled. "The truth is stranger than fiction."

"You got that right. So tell me more."

She took a deep breath. "Finally Henry gave up and married another woman. They weren't married long enough for the ink on the license to get dry but Victoria Radner had gotten pregnant during that time and Henry Hayes Radner Wells was the son they had from that misbegotten marriage. But Henry had told her about Ruby Lee and how much he'd been in love with the woman. Bless his heart, that was about a stupid ass thing to do and Victoria put all the ill feelings on Ruby Lee. She spent the thirty years trying to buy out the Honky Tonk so she could burn it down because she thought Henry was seeing Ruby after they were married and before the divorce."

"How was that possible?"

"Victoria had a business in Dallas and thought she'd change Henry into a citified dandy. Henry had a big ranch up north of Palo Pinto and thought she'd become a ranch woman. Neither one would budge. So he lived on the ranch and she lived in the fancy house in Dallas and they saw each other on weekends until they figured out they'd both made a huge mistake."

"What a tangled up mess," Holt said.

"Yep, so anyway, Hayes, aka Hank, paid Daisy and Cathy a visit one night trying to buy the place and they put him packing. Then Daisy and Jarod finally admitted they were in love and she gave Cathy the joint, the cars, and the motorcycle in the garage and she and Jarod went to Cushing to live."

Holt looked over at Sharlene. With the sunlight lighting up her hair and green eyes, she was even more enticing than she'd been in the barn. "What happened next?"

"Cathy took over and that's when Tinker was still the bouncer. He was almost as big as Luther and twice as mean. It was New Year's Eve and Gretchen Wilson was singing 'Redneck Woman' on the jukebox. The whole crowd was doing the countdown with Gretchen's words. Like 'ten, hell yeah; nine, hell yeah' when Travis arrived. He wanted to kiss someone at the stroke of midnight so he just walked right across the floor and laid one on Cathy. He didn't know she was the owner or that she'd be his neighbor."

"You got to be shittin' me," Holt said.

Sharlene crossed her heart and held up two fingers like a Girl Scout. "When Cathy told me the story I said the same thing. It's the pure gospel truth according to Larissa and Cathy both. I'm just giving you the bare bones but anyway, Amos hired her to work during the day for the oil company. The trailer was back behind the Tonk and she and Travis were constantly in each other's company. Then her old boyfriend had her kidnapped and

Travis rescued her. I guess she went up to Mena and knocked the pure old shit out of him before they came back to Texas."

"And then they got married and as Judd says, 'they lived happily never after'?" Holt grinned.

"Oh, no. He took a job in Alaska and she cried. But he found out somewhere along the trip that he didn't want wings to fly as much as he wanted Cathy so he came back, fell down on one knee, and proposed right there in the Honky Tonk in the same spot where he'd kissed her on New Year's Eve. Then they went to Shamrock, Texas, to run a company for Amos, which they've bought out since then."

"Now Larissa," he said.

"Well, she's rich as Midas and she'd been every-where for about six or seven years. And I mean every corner of the earth looking for happiness. So one day up in Perry, Oklahoma, she pulled down a map in her fancy house, turned around a few times, and stuck the pin in the map. It was smack dab in the middle of Mingus. So she moved to Mingus."

"Is this part of your book or the truth?" he asked.

"Pure unadulterated, one hundred proof, guaran-damn-teed truth." She raised her hand and even crossed herself.

"Go on then," Holt said. They'd just gone through Wichita Falls. He hit the brake and reset the cruise con-trol to a slower speed. He was fully awake and wanted to know the whole basic story even if it did take longer to get back to Mingus.

"So she came to Mingus and could not believe that fate had such a horrid sense of humor. She rented a hotel room down in Stephenville and was about ready to go home when she drove through town one more time and saw the house you are living in for sale. She bought it and believe me, it looked even worse in those days. Hadn't seen paint since the original was put on in the thirties. One night she got to craving a martini and went to the Honky Tonk because it was the only joint open on weeknights. At first Cathy thought she was there trying to buy the place for Hayes but they became friends and before long Larissa was bartending for her."

"I'm seeing a pattern here. Fate sends the women to the Tonk. They become bartenders and then fate sends them the love of their life," Holt said.

"That's the way it's worked in the past." Sharlene looked out the window. They'd all fought fate and they'd all lost. Was she next in line? She couldn't remember asking herself so many questions. Or having fewer answers.

"Keep talking, please," Holt begged.

"Okay. After Cathy and Travis got married, Larissa took over the place. Hank, who was also Hayes, came to the area for a month like he did every summer. When he was a little boy it was Henry's visitation rights. When he grew up he came to get away from the city. He kind of had two lives just like Larissa. They had a hell of a lot in common but neither of them were opening up and admitting who they really were.

"So he was coming into Mingus in one of his dad's old work trucks. I guess he was on his way to Stephenville for a tractor part. He was driving into Mingus and so was she. He was in the truck and she was in her fancy little vintage Mustang when a deer jumped out in front of him. He swerved but hit the thing anyway and it bounced back toward her. They both slid all over the road and ended up in the ditch. Her car wasn't hurt but Henry's truck was messed up because it came to a halt up against an old oak tree. Luther used the company tow truck and pulled them out of the ditches and took Hank home. You got to remember now that Hank slash Hayes had been trying to buy the Honky Tonk forever for his mother. By then they had investors and were going to turn Mingus into an amusement park if they could get everyone in town to sell their places. So he had been trying to figure an angle to meet Larissa and dig up some kind of weak spot to make her sell to him. And there they were crawling out of their vehicles, giving him a perfect chance to get to know her on the sly."

Holt grinned. "This damn thing really does sound like a soap opera on television."

"Doesn't it? Wonder if we could sell the premise to one of the major companies and start a new soap. We could call it *Honky Tonk Angels!*" she said.

"I get half the profit if you do."

"It's not your story," she argued.

"But I encouraged you to put it all in chronological order so I'm as good as the producer," he said.

"Twenty-five percent and I get seventy-five," she bartered.

"Thirty-five." His eyes sparkled.

"Okay, it's a deal. If we ever sell *Honky Tonk Angels* to the big soap opera world you can have thirty-five percent of the take," she agreed.

"Well, don't stop now. What happened?" he asked.

"Okay, there was enough heat between them to cause the people with the global warming stuff to start to worry. I mean every time they got together sparks flew and boom, they fell in love," she said.

"The end?" he asked.

"Not quite. He was in and out of the Honky Tonk as well as her house. She helped him haul hay and made him help paint the house. Imagine how he felt when she told him what colors she'd chosen." Sharlene smiled.

"I don't have a bit of problem imagining that scene. I bet his nose hairs curled as much as mine did and I didn't even have to deface a perfectly good house like he did, but tell me the rest of it. How'd she find out he was really Hayes?"

"She and her buddies put together a town meeting and invited the Radners to attend."

"Holy crap! And all this time she had no idea that Hank was really Hayes?"

"Not a clue until he walked into that meeting."

"What happened?" Holt was really into the story.

"They had a big fight out behind the garage and he left. When he tried to call her and explain she put the phone on the jukebox and played 'My Give a Damn's Busted.' She wouldn't talk to him at all, period. Then her mother came to Dallas to this big charity to-do and wanted Larissa to go with her. Stop right here and hear a little about Doreen, her mother. She's a short redhead like me and people thought I was her daughter instead of Larissa because Larissa's father is Indian and Mexican. Remember what she looked like that time you saw her at the ranch? She has dark hair and eyes. Doreen had Larissa while she was in college and her parents and a nanny raised the baby while she ran all over the world and had affairs with very young men."

Holt shook his head. "More and more like a soap. Write up the pilot and let's sell it."

"I don't do script. Only prose," she said. "So anyway, when they got to the charity thing Hank was one of the men being sold at the bachelor auction to raise money. Larissa paid something like fifteen thousand dollars for him and then left him sitting in a rundown fish café in Dallas. But it broke the ice and he finally moved back to the county and won her heart. It took some doing and there were times when I thought the charm had finally failed, but they finally settled the fight and lived 'happily never after.' The end."

"It's not the end. You are still in the picture," Holt said.

"But you know all about me. You just spent a whole day with my family and you are part of the extended story. You are building an addition on to the Tonk and living in the Bahamas Mama house. There's no hidden identity. No old boyfriend to kidnap me. Nothing exciting going on here."

"Then tell me more about Iraq."

They were driving through the hilly north side of Palo Pinto County where the road twisted and curved back on itself. Up in the area where Larissa and Hank lived. She wanted to ask him to stop, but it was already getting dark and it wasn't fair to leave Tessa alone at the beer joint too long. She didn't want to talk about Iraq or the nightmares or what she did there. She wanted to suppress it all and forget it.

"There's nothing more to tell about Iraq. I spent two years there and I can describe it in three words. Hot. Hotter. Hottest. Most of the time it was the last word.

Like I've said before, Iraq and the war over there is something you either did and saw or didn't. Words aren't worth a damn in that case. And besides, I talk too much and have already told you about Iraq."

"Sharlene, I love to listen to you talk. It's like listening to those tapes where someone is reading. Your voice is soothing and smooth and you have a way with words. No wonder you can write a book," he said.

"Thank you but you are covering your ass," she said.

He pulled the truck into the full Honky Tonk parking lot. People were crawling out of their trucks and cars and heading for the porch.

Holt turned to face Sharlene. "I'm telling the truth. I've loved listening to the Honky Tonk Angels story. We're home and I didn't even mind the drive. But now I have to take these kids who have slept for five hours home and try to get them to sleep tonight. Tomorrow is a school day."

"I forgot about that. Poor babies are up past their bedtime."

"They'll be home at three thirty every day ready for a snack and a nap after the weekend and a late night tonight." He unhooked his seat belt and hurried around the truck to open the door for her and retrieve her bags.

"Thanks for going with me, for driving, and for…" she giggled.

When she stepped out he wrapped his arms around her waist and drew her to his chest. "Thank you for a wonderful weekend."

He tipped her chin up and kissed her hard right there in front of everyone in the parking lot. "I loved every minute of it."

"Even those with Dorie?" she asked.

"Oh, yes, ma'am, even those with Dorie." He grinned. He wasn't about to tell her that that half hour he spent with Dorie had convinced him that Sharlene was special. Dorie's touch hadn't set off any bells and whistles and her voice wasn't honey in his ears like Sharlene's. Dorie did not pour molten desire in his veins like Sharlene did when she brushed up against him.

"Then why the hell are you kissing me?" she snapped.

"You go figure it out and I'll see you tomorrow," he said. Explaining would require a commitment. Holt wasn't ready to go that far.

The place was hopping. Every lusty redneck cowboy and cowgirl in five counties had evidently decided to start their week with dancing and drinking. Tessa and a stranger were behind the bar when Sharlene threw her duffle bag under Luther's chair and made her way across the dance floor to the bar.

Tessa waved from the mixed drinks section. "Hey, hey, you made it earlier than I figured you would. Grab a tray and get two pitchers of Coke and Jack ready. Meet my sister, Darla. She was sitting on my doorstep when I got home today. She's moving in with me and Luther for a while until she can get her own place. I told her she could work tonight for tips," Tessa said.

"Glad to meet you, Darla." Sharlene mixed Jack Daniels and Coke together in a pitcher being careful not to create a fizzy top on it. "Thanks for helping out while I was out of pocket."

"I need a job and I've done this kind of work. Need some full-time help?" Darla asked.

"Tess?" Sharlene looked at her.

She nodded.

"You're hired. We'll talk about wages and benefits later tonight," Sharlene said.

"Thank you," Darla said. She was as tall as Tessa, only slimmer built and no glasses. She had the same luminous green eyes and dark hair, smooth complexion, and smile.

"You are twenty-one, aren't you?" Sharlene asked.

"Twenty-three last month. Not married. No kids. Bad taste in men. I'm four years younger than Tess," Darla said.

Another soap opera segment begins, Sharlene thought with a grin. "Okay, ladies, they're starting a line dance. You know what that means."

"Set 'em up and get ready for the stampede," Darla said.

"You got it, girl," Sharlene said.

After the joint closed down Sharlene popped the tops off four bottles of beer and carried them to the nearest table. "So you still think you want to work here after tonight?" she asked Darla.

Darla tipped up the bottle and took a long gulp. "Yes, I do."

"Tell me now if you've got any bad habits like drugs or alcoholism," Sharlene said.

"Just horrid luck when it comes to men. There ain't many Luthers out there and if there was I couldn't find him with both hands and a flashlight. I don't have a damn bit of luck when it comes to men. Tess is the lucky sister," Darla said.

Tess laid a hand on Luther's arm. "I know it!"

Sharlene took a long drink of beer and set the bottle down on the table. "Well, if being unlucky with men was a sin, a hell of a lot of us would have hell's fire licking at our rear ends. I pay minimum wage to start with. Raise in three months if you're still around and one of the cowboys hasn't talked you into running off with him. One free beer a night if you want it after work and if you want to clean the place up before hours, that's extra money and up to you," Sharlene said. She remembered when Larissa gave her the same deal and she'd been glad to get it.

Darla didn't hesitate a minute. "Deal and yes, I will come in an hour early every night and do cleanup to get the extra money."

"Okay, now my turn," Tessa said. "I want off either Saturday or Monday night."

"You got it," Sharlene said.

"Just like that?" Tessa asked.

"Hey, you're good help. Six nights a week is a load. Plus you work from noon to five every day for the oil company. You're going to burn out if you don't take some time. You want a night off too, Luther?" Sharlene asked.

"Who'd you get to be a bouncer for you?" Luther asked.

"I expect Kent would do it in a heartbeat on Monday nights. Loralou doesn't come around that night because she has to work a three to eleven shift on Mondays. So you want a little time off with your woman?" Sharlene teased.

"Talk to Kent. If he'll take the job, I'll take a night off." Luther nodded.

"What about you? You want a night off too?" Tessa looked at Sharlene.

Sharlene held up both palms. "Hell, no! The Tonk is my life. Once in a while I might ask you to open for me but I'll be here. Except for that week when I've promised my friends I'll come for a visit and sign books in their home towns, I'll be right here."

———

She made it through the whole week and weekend without going back to the orange rocking chair on Holt's porch. But the next Friday night she was a mess. She locked the Honky Tonk doors and paced from one end of her apartment to the other. The only thing that was going to put her mind at ease was sitting on Holt's front porch so she picked up her keys and headed for the garage.

She parked on the road and sat down in the chair so easily that it didn't even startle the stray wild cat snooping around the end of the house. She sighed deeply when she looked up at the stars and the half-moon. The cat slinked past her and took off in a run toward the trees on down the road.

"Can't sleep?" Holt asked from the corner of the house.

"I was being quiet," she said.

"Come on in the house. I'll make us some hot chocolate and we'll watch a movie. Maybe that will help," he said.

She stood up. "I'll go on home. I can't keep disturbing you like this. I don't know what it is about Friday nights."

"Maybe it's knowing you won't see the kids until Monday," he said.

"Could be. I've gotten pretty attached to them," she answered.

"Well, I can't sleep either so you might as well come on in," he said.

"Are you sure, Holt?"

"Yep, fact is I was about half expecting you tonight," he told her.

"Really?" she asked.

He smiled. "Maybe I was just hoping."

She started in that direction.

He met her halfway and threw an arm around her shoulders. "How do you like John Wayne?"

"Love him."

"Well, let's go watch *The McClintock*."

"That's my grandpa's favorite movie. He says that the lady, what's her name? Anyway, she reminds him of his mother, the grandma that I was named after," Sharlene said.

"I can see that," Holt said.

He steered her inside, put the movie in the DVD player, and went to the kitchen to make hot chocolate while the first credits rolled. Some old lonesome cowboy sang about birds and bees in the country. Even though it was a historical Western movie, Sharlene could easily see country just like Corn in the background. Cows, horses, dust, and farming.

"Did I miss very much?" Holt asked when he put a cup of hot chocolate in her hands.

She kicked off her boots. "No."

"Does that make you homesick for cows and ranch life?"

She swallowed the first sip hurriedly and answered, "Hell, no!"

He laughed. "Maureen O'Hara does look somewhat like you. She's taller though."

She started fighting sleep about halfway into the movie and snuggled up against his side. "I'm sorry.

I don't know what it is about this couch that makes me sleepy."

"Stretch out with me. We'll just cuddle together and watch the rest of the movie. If you fall asleep that's fine."

He scooted as far back as he could and she stretched out with her back to his front, their heads sharing a pillow. He hugged her close, keeping an arm around her midsection and kissed her on the neck. "I love your red hair."

"Thank you, but many more of those kisses and we'll be doing more than watching a movie, and that might not be such a good idea with two kids who could come in here at any time."

"So you make a lot of noise?" he teased.

She slapped at his arm. "You'll make me blush and the glow will wake them."

Maureen was fighting with John about their daughter when she fell asleep. When she woke up two little kids were staring down at her with wide eyes and big smiles.

"Good morning," she said.

"Did you stay all night?" Judd asked.

"I fell asleep watching a movie. Holt?" She nudged him with her elbow.

He buried his face in her hair. "You're on your own. I went to sleep too."

"Can we keep her?" Waylon whispered.

Holt chuckled.

Sharlene elbowed him harder that time.

"Please, Uncle Holt. Please say we can keep her. We can 'dopt her and she can be a Jackson," Judd said.

"It's not that easy." Sharlene sat up and reached for her boots. "I've got to get back to the Honky Tonk."

"Stay around. I'll make breakfast. Do you like biscuits and gravy?"

Judd danced a jig right there in her pajamas. "Waylon, she's goin' to stay and eat with us. When she eats Uncle Holt's biscuits she'll let us 'dopt her, I just know it."

Holt couldn't keep the grin off his face. He was falling for the woman and didn't know what to do about it.

She couldn't tell them no so she dropped her boots. "What can I do to help?"

Chapter 11

THE DAY STARTED LIKE ANY OTHER ROUTINE DAY for a fine fall October day. A few trees were starting to show some yellow and burgundy color. The thermometer finally dipped down below the hotter-than-hell mark. It had been two weeks since she'd fallen asleep on Holt's sofa and the kids bugged the devil out of her every day wanting to know if she was coming home with them to spend the night.

Sharlene arose just before noon, spent two hours in front of her computer, drove to the school in her pink VW Bug, and picked up the children and brought them back to the apartment. She sliced apples, opened a container of caramel dip, and poured two glasses of milk for after school snacks. Normally the children changed clothes and raced out the door to play on the jungle gym and swings for a couple of hours while Holt and the guys finished their day. But that day it was pouring down rain and thundering so she suggested they take their Lincoln Logs and play with them in the Honky Tonk.

She'd known things were coming to an end for a few days but had no idea when the last piece of trim went up around the ceiling that evening that the job would be completely finished and right on time. When she and the kids opened the door into the empty beer joint, she found Holt and Kent sweeping the floor of the new room. Folding wooden doors that could be pulled shut had been installed.

All that remained was moving the pool tables, jukeboxes, and tables and the room would be in operation. The idea that Holt wouldn't be there every day hit her in the gut like a boxing glove on the fist of a professional boxer.

"Done and in record time," Kent said. "Now it's on to Merle's to put a new room on her house. She says she's too old to be climbing up and down basement steps so she's hired us to build a room that's basically all windows and faces the west so she can watch the sun go down every day."

"What?" Sharlene asked.

Kent repeated what he'd just said.

"She didn't tell me," Sharlene said.

Judd patted her leg and pointed into the new room. "Can we play in here today?"

"Of course you can. Set up your Lincoln Logs in the middle of the floor and build something while Holt and I get the finances settled," Sharlene said.

"Merle came by while you were getting the kids yesterday and talked to us. We don't have anything else on the calendar so we took the job," Holt explained.

"Can we keep our trailer spaces since we're staying in town?" Kent asked.

"Can I rent the house?" Holt asked.

"Yes to both. Now let's go sit down and take care of the final payment. When do you start Merle's job?"

The men followed her to the bar where she pulled a checkbook from a file cabinet under the cash register. She hadn't considered what would happen when the addition was finished. The thought of Holt leaving sent cold chills down her back. They'd become friends in the last few weeks, sharing the children and duties and talking a few minutes about his day and her writing each evening before he left.

"We start tomorrow," Holt said. "Should take us about a month. I'm hoping to be able to stay in the area until Christmas so the kids won't have to start school somewhere else until semester break. I think that would be easier on them."

That gives me three months. To do what? It's been a month since that night in the barn at Corn and he hasn't even kissed you since he brought you home that evening. What does three more months get you? Maybe Dorie has been calling him every night and he's decided that that hour he spent with her was the turning point in his life. Damn that woman anyway. I wish she'd get so fat that all that cleavage would be swallowed up in cellulite.

Holt figured the rest of his bill and laid it on the bar. She looked at it and whistled through her teeth. "That's considerably less than your original estimate."

"We finished quicker. Mainly because you helped with the kids so you reap the benefits," he said.

"Thank you for your honesty," she said.

"How much you going to charge me for rent now that we are done?" Holt asked.

She handed him the check when she finished writing it. "I'll make you a deal. You can have the house if I can continue to keep the kids after school."

"That's not a deal." Holt frowned. "I was going to ask you to watch them and I'd pay you."

"Shut up. Don't you see the golden goose when it's right in front of you?" Kent asked.

Holt had dreaded Friday all week, knowing that the job would be finished barring any major problems.

"So?" Sharlene held her breath.

"Sounds like a fantastic deal to me. But I'd still be glad to pay rent and baby-sitting fees," he said.

She waved the idea away. "We'll talk about it again later. Right now I don't have time to think about anything."

"Then how can you have time to keep two rambunctious twins who are forever arguing?" Hoit asked.

"They are my inspiration. They put order into my day. I've gotten more done this past month than my editor can believe. I get up and know that I've got to get so much done before I get the kids at school. I take a break with them, refresh my mind, laugh at their arguments, and after they leave I'm ready to write another couple of hours before the Tonk opens. I've got a routine and if I can keep it going, I'll have my book done by mid-December. Then my celebration will be even better. One will be on the market, the new Tonk can be christened, and the next one will be finished and on the way to the publisher."

"You talk too much." Holt grinned.

"That is not a secret and you knew it from the beginning," she said.

"Maybe that's where Judd gets it," Kent said.

"Probably. She already had the tendency but being around Sharlene all this time didn't curb it a bit. She'll be even worse by Christmas," Holt said.

"Is that a bad thing?" Sharlene asked. If only she could find a reason to fight with him or not like him, it would be so much easier to see him leave.

"It is," Holt nodded. "The hardest lesson some folks never learn is when to shut up and listen. Judd needs to learn that."

"Are you saying that I don't know when to shut up?"

"No, I love to listen to you talk. Your voice is sooth-ing but talking just to hear the sound of your own voice is what Judd does," Holt said.

Were they finally having a big battle? If they did would he get over the attraction he had for her and get on with his life?

"Hey, no fighting on celebration day!" Kent said. "Break out a bottle of champagne and let's celebrate, Sharlene."

"We'll celebrate on Christmas Eve when we christen the new room and have our party. You are all invited."

"Even the kids?" Holt asked.

"The party is going to be held in the afternoon. Larissa is bringing Ruby. Cathy and Travis will have their baby by then and Daisy and Jarod's child will be over a year old. So there will be children here. Also the old crowds, like Chigger and Jim Bob and their kids and Billy Bob and his wife and their combined family. Garret and Angel. Merle and Amos and everyone that has had a part in the stories of the Honky Tonk all these years. They're all going to come around sometime in the afternoon. I've already sent invitations so they could plan their holidays in advance," she said.

"So among all that talk, I take it that it's a yes?" he asked.

She shot him a look. "It's a definite yes. The kids are all invited."

"Sounds good to me. I'm picking up Loralou for sup-per and then we're going to a movie, so I'm leaving." Kent waved at the kids and headed out the door.

"Where's Chad and Bennie?" Sharlene asked.

"Chad went on up to Wichita about an hour ago. Bennie's outside putting the equipment in the trailer," Holt said.

He'd see her every day when he picked up the kids after work so why was it so hard to walk away? It seemed like a final good-bye and he wasn't ready.

"It's only a half an hour from when you usually call it a day. Let's celebrate by having an early supper at the Smokestack. The kids barely ate half an apple apiece so they'll be hungry and I got busy and forgot to eat lunch. And we really should have a celebration, don't you think?"

A slow easy smile toyed with the corners of his mouth. "You do talk too much."

"You've said that before. I've acknowledged it. Don't beat a dead horse until it's blue."

"Okay, point taken and I won't mention it again, ever. Got to admit I didn't eat much lunch either and I'm starving. So let's celebrate. Hey kids, put your toys away and we'll go out to eat." Holt's voice echoed in the emptiness of the new room.

"Where are we going? Can I have French fries and gravy? Is it McDonald's? I didn't know there was a McDonald's here in Mingus. You didn't tell me, Uncle Holt. Where is it anyway and how come you didn't tell me?" Judd asked.

Holt and Sharlene looked at each other and started laughing.

"What's so funny about McDonald's? Do they have a jungle gym and can we play on it if it's not outside and in the rain and move your ass, Waylon, we're going to McDonald's and you got to put your half of the toys in the bucket," Judd said.

"Judd!" Holt exclaimed.

Judd did a head wiggle and said, "Sorry about that. Sometimes he's slow and won't get busy. He thinks he's got to take it all down one piece at a time when he could pick up a whole handful and besides, it was a castle not a fort and he didn't even want it to be a castle so why does it matter how it comes apart?"

"Ah, stop your belly achin', Judd. You talk so much it hurts my ears," Waylon said.

"Arguing slows you down. And we're not going to McDonald's, Judd. So that answers your question about playing on the equipment. We're going to the Smokestack," Holt said.

"Well, damn," Judd said.

"Judd!" Holt said again.

"Well, Uncle Holt, sometimes them bad words just slip out and I don't even know it until they're already said and I can't put them back in my mouth. I would if I could but it don't work that way. I love this room. I'm going to grow up and own a honky tonk and have a room like this. Will you build it for me? And the people are going to come and dance just like they do here. Sharlene, will you show me how to be a honky tonk owner?"

Sharlene blushed. "When you grow up you're going to fly airplanes or be a lawyer or maybe even be the president of the United States, Judd."

"And the teacher said if she says another word like that then she has to stand on the wall next time. They might not let her be president if she don't stop saying bad words," Waylon said. "Today she said she was going to kick Jerrell's ass up between his shoulders and he said he'd whup her all over the playground if she tried."

Holt left the barstool and leaned on the doorjamb into the new room. "Why'd you say that?"

"Because he was picking on Waylon. He said Waylon wasn't a real cowboy and real cowboys was all that could belong to their club and Waylon wanted to play football with them and they wouldn't let him because he didn't wear cowboy boots," Judd said.

Holt's jaw worked in anger. "Next time you go tell the teacher."

"Next time I'll whip his sorry old ass only I'll just do it instead of using a bad word," Judd said seriously. "I might have to stand on the wall but it won't be for saying a dirty word and I bet Jerrell ain't so big in his fancy old cowboy boots after that."

"No more dirty words or you're going to stand on the wall in the restaurant," Holt threatened.

"Okay, okay. But it'd be worth it if Jerrell got his… hind end… whuped."

Holt went back to the bar. "What am I going to do with her?"

"My dad loved me like I was," she said.

"Claud Waverly is a bigger man than I am," Holt said.

Half an hour later they were seated in the first table on the west side of the Smokestack: Judd and Sharlene on one side with Holt and Waylon on the other. Sharlene and Holt ordered chicken fried steaks. Judd asked for French fries, a grilled cheese sandwich, and green beans. Waylon wanted a hamburger with mashed potatoes and gravy on the side.

When their food arrived, Judd laid both her hands on the table. "I'm the youngest so Gramps said the youngest got to say the prayer and everyone has to hold hands and bow your head and shut your eyes while I say it."

Waylon slipped his hand into Holt's and Judd's. She looked at Sharlene who obeyed with her left hand and reached toward Holt with her right. It was the first physical contact they'd had since he kissed her two weeks before but the heat hadn't cooled a bit.

Holt wondered what he was going to do about the attraction. Was it fatal? Would it kill his heart and soul when he moved away from Mingus and Sharlene? Or would the old adage about out of sight, out of mind work for him?

Sharlene didn't want to let go of Holt's callused hand or the emotions it caused. If she put her hand in his permanently there would be peace in her heart and soul and the nightmares would go away. But he'd never really ask a barmaid to raise his kids. It was all right for her to watch them a couple of hours after school but anything more than that would be like asking God to send an air conditioner to hell for Lucifer.

Waylon shut his eyes and hoped that if Jerrell yelled at him again that Judd did beat the crap out of him. He'd even stand on the wall for her if she'd knock Jerrell down and black his eye or make his nose bleed.

Judd looked around to be sure that everyone had their eyes shut and began, "Now I lay me down to sleep. Thank you God for these good green beans and for Waylon's mashed potatoes. Uncle Holt's have lumps in them and Waylon don't like lumps in his potatoes. And thank you God for Sharlene. Make Uncle Holt like her so she'll come and live with us all the time and make me pretty for school so that rotten Emily won't make fun of my hair. And help me to stop using bad words but if I get in a fight with Jerrell help me whip his mean old… hind end… all over the school yard so he'll leave Waylon alone. And…"

"Amen!" Waylon said and dropped both Judd's and Holt's hands.

Judd jerked her head up and glared at him. "You don't interrupt a prayer. You won't get to go to heaven with Momma if you don't let me talk to God before we eat."

"Yes I will and my potatoes are getting cold and I don't like them cold. And God says that you talk too much anyway." Waylon filled his mouth with potatoes and gravy.

"God did not say that. He don't talk to you. He only talks to the youngest and that's why they get to pray before we eat," Judd said.

"If you don't stop arguing, then your green beans are going to be cold," Sharlene said. "And Waylon is going to finish before you do and get his chocolate pie first."

Holt squeezed her hand before he let go and picked up his fork and knife.

"Thank you," he mouthed.

"Don't you even look at me like that, Waylon. I'm not eating too fast," Judd declared.

"If either of you eat too fast, your stomachs will hurt and you won't be able to eat your pie," Sharlene said.

"So you'd best eat slowly and do it without all the bickering," Holt said.

Judd nodded and chewed slower.

Waylon did the same.

"So tell me about this addition to Merle's place," Sharlene said.

"It's a twenty-by-twenty-four-foot room across the back of her house. Long glass windows on three sides.

The fourth wall will be up against the house so it'll be brick. She says her cutting tables and designing desk will go against that wall since they don't require electricity. It won't take as long as your job did because it's mainly just framing and setting windows," he said. "This is really good chicken fried steak. The kids and I haven't tried this place. I forget about it being this close. Tell me about your book. How's it coming along?"

"Wonderful. My editor is ecstatic."

"What's it about?"

"Promise you won't laugh?"

"I promise."

"It's about a hooker who goes to sleep in a brothel one night in the late eighteen hundreds and wakes up the next morning in the modern day world. She's in bed with a redneck husband, living in a double-wide trailer out on a few acres. She made the mistake of saying that she wished she lived a hundred years in the future, so the old witch traveling on the train with her granted her the wish without telling her about it."

He almost choked. "Don't tell me something like that when I've got food in my mouth. I almost choked to death. Is that really what your book is about?"

"It is. He thinks he's died and gone to heaven. She thinks she's died and gone to hell."

"What happens?" Holt asked.

"They learn to love each other in spite of the time differences."

"How does it end?"

"Happily never after." Sharlene grinned.

Chapter 12

LARISSA PUT HER BABY DAUGHTER IN SHARLENE'S LAP and sat down in the rocking chair next to her. There was a little nip in the air, the promise of fall after a long hot summer.

"Beautiful day, isn't it? You look pretty good holding that baby. You sure you want to be an old maid?"

Sharlene nodded but Larissa noticed the brief hesitation.

"So tell me about the addition. I can't wait to see it. How's it going with the crowd being so much bigger?"

"Very well. Tessa's sister, Darla, is working for me full time. Tessa and Luther take Monday night off now and Kent is stepping in as a bouncer. That's the only night we only have two bartenders. The rest of the week there's three of us. And on weekends we stay busier than a hooker at a Shriner's convention in Las Vegas."

"That's pretty busy. Holt ever come around to the Tonk?" Larissa asked.

"I know you too well for you to sneak up on my blind side like that," Sharlene said.

"Well, does he?" Larissa pushed back a strand of dark hair.

"Once when the kids were off with Gloria and Chad to the movies. Other than that, he's had kids every night. A single dad isn't any different than a single mom. He goes home after work to cook supper, do laundry, and all those things," Sharlene said. She didn't tell her that

she'd been to his house several times or that the only
time she could sleep without dreams was in his arms. Or
that they'd almost made wild passionate love and only a
big old ugly rat had kept them from it.

Judd ran up on the porch. If her tennis shoes had had
brakes on them she would have left a long black skid
line in her wake when she came to a stop. "Can I look at
Ruby again? I love her name. When I grow up and own
a tonk I'm going to have a baby like that and I'm going
to name her Pearl. Then she can be Ruby's friend like
Sharlene is my friend. Sharlene, can me and Waylon
have a drink? We're both thirsty, only he didn't want to
come and ask acause him and Hank are out there with
Holt lookin' at the cows."

Larissa pushed herself out of the chair. "I'll get them
a bottle of water. If I put them in a sack, you think you
could take four bottles so those big old men could have
a drink too?"

"I'm real strong like Sharlene," Judd said.

Sharlene looked out across the yard and the pasture
to the corral where Hank and Holt were talking about
cows. Holt hiked a leg up on the lower rail of the fence
in a position that stretched his jeans even snugger across
his rear end. Sharlene sighed and wished for what she
couldn't have. Not one kiss since the night he'd brought
her home from Corn. Not even a near miss. He'd kept
his distance and she hadn't stepped into it.

"Okay, what are you thinking about?" Larissa asked
when she sat back down.

"Why?"

"You looked wistful. Like a little kid in a candy store
where everything costs a dollar and she's only got a

dime in her pocket. You're in love with that carpenter, aren't you? The Honky Tonk charm did not end with me," Larissa said.

"It has to. Holt Jackson needs a mother for the children, not a bartender. He needs someone like Loralou or Gloria or probably even Coralynn even though I've never met her." Sharlene put Ruby on her shoulder and began to rock when the baby fussed.

"I see. Well, then tell me about Darla. What's her story? Sometimes I miss the Honky Tonk and all the drama. I wouldn't go back and I don't regret my decision but I miss the hustle and the noise every once in a while."

"Leave Ruby with Oma and Henry and come visit. She's three months old now as of today. Born July 16 in a heat wave and today is October 16 and it's still not cool enough to suit me. I bet you haven't left her alone once, have you?"

"No, I have not left her and I can't. Not yet. You sure about that charm slash curse idea? Holt looks at you like he could lay you out naked on satin sheets and have you for breakfast, dinner, and supper," Larissa whispered.

"That idea raises my blood pressure to the boiling point, but I'm very, very sure," Sharlene said.

"You slept with him yet?"

"Why would you ask that?"

"Because the way he looks at you says that he's unwrapped the candy bar and had a little taste. 'fess up, girl. I was honest about Hank," Larissa said.

"You were not. You beat around the bush so long and hard that it didn't have a single leaf on the damn thing. You didn't 'fess up to anything and I'm not either," Sharlene said. "Come to the Tonk on Saturday night. You can work behind the bar or dance with Hank. You'll get it out of your system in about an hour. I didn't realize that I'd ever miss the quietness of the farm until we went home to Corn and came out here today. But I do and all it takes is a little while and I'm ready to get back into my writing and hustling around behind the bar."

"Sounds to me like you've met your cowboy."

"Dream on," Sharlene laughed.

Holt smiled when Waylon propped one of his new cowboy boots up on the lower fence rail. "So tell me, son, which one of those calves do you think would be a good one to buy if we ever got our own ranch?"

Waylon studied them, cocking his head from one side to the other. "That one that's all black over there. He looks mean and tough and a boy cow has to be mean and tough acause that's what he's 'posed to be. If he wasn't he'd be a girl cow."

Judd handed Holt the sack of water bottles and climbed the fence, threw her legs over the top rail, and sat down. "That's not the best one. The best one is that feller in the back with his head down."

"Why's that?" Hank asked.

"He's the littlest one. He's got to be mean or the others will pick on him so he'll grow up to be the best one. That one that Waylon picked is good for this day but he's already a big old boy so he don't have to prove nothin'. It's that one in the back that'll be a good boy cow."

"Well, I appreciate your opinions, guys. I think I'll keep both of them and we'll see in a couple of years which one makes the best Angus bull. What are you going to name that calf back there, Judd?" Hank asked.

"Can I name the one I picked out?" Waylon asked.

Hank nodded. He had dark hair that needed a cut, light brown eyes, and was about the same height as Holt. He wore jeans and a faded orange Longhorn sweatshirt and cowboy boots.

"Well, my boy cow's name is Luther."

Hank chuckled. "Good name. He's about the size of a small refrigerator and looks like he might grow up to be as big as Luther."

"Ain't nobody as big as Luther. He's a giant," Waylon said.

"My boy's name is Beast and that's because he's got shoulders like the beast in *Beauty and the Beast* and I bet if we put clothes on him he'd look like that. And someday he might turn into a prince," Judd said.

"Bulls don't turn into princes," Waylon huffed.

"You don't know that. Sometimes magic happens," Judd said. "I been prayin' for magic to happen and make Sharlene like Uncle Holt. Every time we eat I ask for that and someday it's going to happen. Hey, you want to go see the goats? Look they're all comin' out of that barn." She pointed in that direction.

One glance and they were off like two bottle rockets toward the goat pen.

"Wouldn't want to pry but is there any chance her prayers might be going past the kitchen ceiling?" Hank leaned on the fence and wrote numbers and names in a little book he carried in his hip pocket. Calf number 12224 was Beast. Number 12225 was Luther.

"Afraid not."

"Larissa tells me that Sharlene loves these kids."

"That's right. But she'd have to love me for it to work and she's committed and grounded to that Honky Tonk," Holt said.

"Can't have it both ways, can you?" Hank asked.

Henry joined them at the fence. A tall, lanky man with silver hair and a long thin face that wrinkled even more when he smiled, he perched a leg up on the bottom rail and asked, "What's happening here today? You didn't tell me and Oma you were havin' company. She'll be upset with you because she didn't have time to make a big meal."

"That's the reason I didn't tell her. She works too hard and we decided we'd grill some hot dogs at supper and throw some chips on the table. It was impromptu, Dad. Larissa was pouting because she hadn't seen Sharlene in three weeks. So I called and talked her into coming out here and bringing the kids," Hank explained.

"Oma might let you get by with it this time but you'd better be careful of trying it again," Henry said. "So how are things with you, Holt?"

"Just fine. Is Oma your wife?"

"Oh, no! She's my housekeeper, cook, and secretary all rolled into one. At least she was until last year when Larissa came to the ranch. Now she does a lot of cooking but Larissa has taken over the office work. She keeps threatening to go live with her sister in Arizona but I don't think it'll ever happen. She's been on this ranch since I was a boy. It'd take a stick of dynamite to blow her off it, especially since Ruby was born," Henry said.

"I see," Holt said.

"I hear you are putting a room on Merle's house. How's that going?" Henry asked.

"Coming right along. We got it in the dry, thank goodness. I hear it's going to rain all next week," Holt answered.

He would have far rather been sitting beside Sharlene in one of those white rockers on the porch. She looked so cute with that baby in her arms. He wondered what their child would look like. Would it have her kinky red hair and green eyes or his looks? Would it be a girl who talked too much like Judd or a quiet little boy?

Hell, it'd probably be a red-haired boy with a temper from hell and that could put a politician to shame with his words. He'd most likely be on a soapbox about something from the hour after he was born and raise hell until the day he died.

"…need the rain but then ranchers never turn down a good shower, do we, son?" Henry was saying when Holt tuned back into the conversation.

"What is Holt's bane is our good fortune, I'm afraid," Hank said.

"Well, you two discuss the weather, politics, and women and I'm going to go hitch up the goat cart and let the kids have a ride. We don't get them out here nearly often enough. I can't wait until there's a dozen that live on this ranch all the time," Henry said.

"You better keep dreaming. Larissa says no more than four and maybe only two," Hank said.

"I'll take what I can get and be happy. Maybe we can talk Holt out of his two," Henry threw over his shoulder as he made his way back to the goat pen.

"Goat cart?" Holt asked.

"He's made a small box with wheels that'll hold two children. He harnesses up a couple of good sized goats to it and leads them around the ranch with the kids in the cart. They won't get hurt, I promise," Hank said.

"I'm not afraid of that. I'm just thinking about listening to them try to con me into a couple of goats all the way home," Holt laughed.

Hank changed the subject abruptly. "You and Sharlene likely to become anything more than friends? Sorry, but if I don't ask, then Larissa is going to throw a fit after y'all leave. Sharlene is her best friend and she's trying to play matchmaker."

"Probably not."

"Why's that?"

"She's a bartender. I want my kids to have a better role model than that."

"Wouldn't anyone love them any more than she does. Larissa says they love her and Judd is praying over her food that you like her," Hank said.

"Answer is still no," Holt said.

"Okay, fair enough. Let's go get out the four wheelers while Dad is giving the kids a goat cart ride and we'll ride down to the back of the ranch and do some target shooting. I got a tree stand down there and a bull's-eye set up on a big round bale of hay," Hank said.

"Sounds good to me," Holt told him.

Judd and Waylon bounced around as much as the seat belts would allow in the backseat of the truck.

"But Uncle Holt, we'll feed the goats and we'll make sure they have water," Waylon said.

"And I won't beg to bring them inside the house when it rains or snows. Henry says that they have fur and can stay outside and we can built them a little barn with our jungle gym wood when we tear it down out behind the Tonk and put some hay in it and they might even have babies someday," Judd begged.

"One final time, kids. No goats!" Holt declared. He'd listened to nothing but goats since Henry gave them a ride in the cart. They could hardly eat their hot dogs at supper for begging for two baby goats. According to them they wouldn't even ask for a Christmas present if they could have two goats.

Judd exhaled loudly and crossed her arms over her chest. Waylon set his jaw and stared out the side window.

"Okay, then, if I can't have a goat can I have anything else I want for Christmas?" Judd asked.

"You're not having a cow or a chicken or even a cat. We'll probably move after this school year and I'm not moving animals or listening to you whine when we have to take them to the shelter or out to Luther's farm," he said.

"But I can have what else I want?" Judd asked.

"Maybe you'd better tell me what you're trying to make me promise before I say no to everything for Christmas," Holt said.

Judd leaned over and whispered in Waylon's ear.

"Uh oh! They're going to do the gang-up-on-uncle trick and ask for the same thing then whine and beg until I can't take it anymore," Holt said.

Sharlene laughed. "Perfectly normal, I'd say."

"We made up our minds and we want the same thing," Waylon said.

"You can want the moon but that doesn't mean I'll lasso it and pull it down here for you," Holt said.

"Yuk! We don't want a smelly old moon," Judd told him.

"Why would the moon be smelly?" Sharlene asked.

"Sharlene! It's made out of that cheese that's got big old chunks of blue stuff in it. And that kind of cheese stinks. We don't want the moon, Uncle Holt. Guess what we want?"

He played along. "How many guesses do I get?"

"Three!" Waylon held up his fingers.

"Okay, Sharlene, help me. What is it that these two children want together when all they do is argue?"

"A swing set in their backyard?" Sharlene asked.

They both giggled and Waylon put down one finger.

"How about one of those game things that you hook up to the television and play against each other?" Holt asked.

Waylon leaned over and whispered and Judd shook her head. He put down another finger.

"But that might be the second thing on our list," Judd said.

"One last guess? You got any ideas, Sharlene?" Holt asked.

"Not a one."

"Okay, then you want…" Holt pretended to be deep in thought as he drew his eyebrows down and tapped on the steering wheel. "Let me see, not a swing set, not a Play Station game, could it be… no, that wouldn't be it."

The children giggled and put their heads together as they whispered.

"Give me a hint," Holt said.

"It's got something to do with dinnertime," Judd told him.

"You want a turkey?" Holt asked.

They both held their ribs and Waylon put down his other finger. "Guesses all gone."

"That's not fair," Sharlene said. "You teased that last one out of him so he gets one more guess."

"No, he don't. He said turkey and…" Judd started laughing again. "Why would we want a turkey?"

"If you let us have baby goats you won't have to guess anymore," Waylon said.

Sharlene came to the rescue. "Hey, I bet Henry would let you name two of his baby goats like Hank did the two calves. And if you name them then you have to go see them at least once a month so they don't forget you. You already have to visit Beast and Luther every few weeks and check up on them. So I don't suppose it would be any big problem for you to name a couple of baby goats and check on them, would it? You'd have to be careful and not let Beast and Luther get their feelings hurt and think you were paying too much attention to the goats, but I think you might manage that. What do you think?"

Judd uncrossed her arms and chewed on her lower lip. Waylon's attention went from watching Palo Pinto County going by at sixty miles an hour out the side window back to Sharlene.

"I'm naming my goat Billy," Waylon said quickly.

"Well, I'm naming mine Blake after that man that sings about the dog. I think he's pretty and I like his songs," Judd said.

They put their heads together and began to whisper. Sharlene heard snatches of the conversation and the gist seemed to be that they'd build a cart from the lumber pile. The argument was whether it would be painted like their house or plain old red like Henry's cart.

"Thank you," Holt said.

Sharlene smiled.

His heart melted. She really was good with the children. Even when she had children of her own he could never see her making a difference in them and Judd and Waylon. She'd never be a clinging, demanding wife because she was independent as hell and had proven she could take care of herself. Why did she have to run a damn bar anyway? Life was not fair.

He parked the truck behind the new addition. The kids bailed out and took off toward the jungle gym. He'd planned to take it down when he and the guys finished the job but Sharlene had asked him to leave it. After all, she'd have the children a couple of hours each afternoon and they could enjoy it a while longer.

"Texas has the most beautiful sunsets." Sharlene got out of the truck and walked around to the back side of the garage.

Holt followed her. "It is pretty tonight, isn't it?"

She sat down against the building and patted the space beside her. "They had a lot of fun today. And I got to get my baby fix for a few weeks. How'd you and Hank get on?"

"Just fine. Shot a few rounds from a tree stand. Hank is a stand-up sort of fellow. It'd be hard not to like him," Holt said.

"We'll be changing the clocks in two weeks and the sunsets will be a lot earlier," she changed the subject. She was itching to ask what he and Hank talked about all afternoon but then she'd have to be honest if he turned the tables on her. And there was no way she was telling him that Larissa tried to play matchmaker with every other word.

"It's bath time and believe me they need one tonight. They both smell like goats and sweat." Holt stood up and extended a hand to help her.

She took it and he pulled. But when she was standing he continued to draw her nearer until she was flat against his body with his arms around her tightly. She looked up to find his eyes searching her face. It seemed like slow motion when he bent forward and she tiptoed so their lips could clash in a hard kiss that sent them both spiraling out of control again.

She ended the kiss and stepped back. "Whew!"

"I know. What are we going to do about that?"

"About what?" she asked.

"You know what," Holt said softly.

"You tell me what we're going to do, Holt. There's nothing to talk about or to do, is there? You are a surrogate father and a damn fine one. I'm a bartender and a damn fine one. It'd be like trying to mix up a holy-roller preacher and a whorehouse madam. It wouldn't work."

"I'm not a preacher," he argued.

"I'm not a whorehouse madam."

"Then what are you talking about?" he asked.

"Go home and think about it, Holt. I'll see you when you get the kids tomorrow afternoon."

He yelled at Judd and Waylon and left her behind the garage still watching her sunset.

Chapter 13

HOLT READ THE CHILDREN A BEDTIME STORY, PUT A load of laundry in the washer, folded the towels right out of the dryer, and picked up the remote but couldn't find anything on television to hold his attention. Finally, he spread out draft paper on the kitchen table and did a rough drawing of the barn that he planned to begin for Elmer the next week.

Either there was work or else the people in town were trying to keep him there. If the latter was the case, then there was only one reason and that was match-making. That brought his thoughts back around to Sharlene. He imagined coming home from work every day to sit down at the supper table with her and the children. To be able to kiss her anytime he wanted; to hold her while they fell asleep or make love to her until they were both exhausted.

In reality life with her would be coming home from work to supper with her and the kids, kissing her good-bye at the door before eight o'clock, and being very quiet so as not to wake her in the morning. It would involve him still taking the kids to school and spending about two hours with Sharlene in the evenings, sleeping alone, and making love on Sunday night. Reality wasn't as pretty as the first picture he painted.

He put away his supplies and went to bed, only to lie awake for an hour trying to rid his mind of the woman he could not have. It was still dark when he awoke sitting up in bed with both eyes wide open and straining his ears to pick up whatever sound had awakened him. A quick check of the bedside clock said it was two thirty so it wasn't the children up and around before the alarm went off. He heard it again loud and clear and it was outside, not inside. Was Sharlene out there again?

The windows had been painted shut years before and with the arrival of the air-conditioning and heating unit there'd been no reason to open them again. He slipped on pajama bottoms and moved quietly through the house—from his bedroom to the kids' room to the kitchen to the living room, peeking outside each window as he went. When he reached the living room he discovered Sharlene was back. She hadn't been there since the night they'd fallen asleep and the kids had caught them the next morning. His breath caught in his chest at the sight of her. He grabbed a sweatshirt from the back of the sofa and jerked it down over his head, put on his cowboy boots, and eased out the back door.

"Hello," he said as he rounded the house.

Sharlene's flight mode went into effect and she jumped up so quick that she knocked the rocker backwards with a thump. "You scared the shit out of me, Holt."

"Sharlene, come inside and talk to me about what it is that keeps you awake at night and sends you to my front porch. Is it the moon or Iraq or what?"

"Technically it's my porch and it's my business. I'll go on back to the Tonk if it bothers you all that much," she said.

He raked his fingers through his thick dark hair. "Good God, Sharlene, it's not safe for a woman to be out in the middle of the night sitting on a porch staring off into the wild blue yonder. I'm glad I woke up. How many times have you been here when I didn't wake up?"

She shook a forefinger at him. "Don't yell; you'll wake the kids. And FYI, you have a sixth sense. You wake up every time I come around. And if this was my house and I was sitting on the porch at this time of night, no one would question it, so why are you? And besides, I wasn't staring off into the wild blue yonder. It's dark out here so I was looking at the stars."

He moved to the porch and set the chair back up on its rockers. "That's a moot point. It's not safe and you know it or you wouldn't be arguing with me."

She plopped down in the chair. "I can damn well take care of myself."

"You're not big enough to whip a good-sized Texas mosquito," he said.

She set the rocker to going with the heel of her cowboy boot. She wore gray sweat bottoms and a matching hooded sweatshirt zipped up to the neck. The night air was crisp for the first week in November. Tomorrow night they'd change the time and it would get dark even earlier. Before long, he'd be leaving and taking the children with him. Her heart hurt just thinking about that day.

He inhaled deeply and didn't smell smoke; so she'd showered after work. She looked cute and fragile at the same time in her gray sweats, with her hair pulled back in a frizzy ponytail.

"You don't have any idea what I'm capable of," she said.

"Oh ho, did the big bad army train you to be an assassin?" he asked.

She took a deep breath. It was time to sink the growing relationship or else let it grow. She'd never ever, not
one time, said the words aloud and didn't know if they'd
come out of her mouth when she tried.

"Did you ever see that movie *The Shooter*?"

"Back when it came out. Did you watch it tonight and
get scared or something?" he asked.

"Remember the very beginning of the movie when
he was sitting up on that high spot all covered up in
camo with his rifle trained on a convoy? He and his
spotter had a radio and were in contact with the home
base. They got left out in the dry with no support and his
spotter got killed. Well, trade that for desert sand. My
shooter was a married man from Kentucky. His name
was Jonah Black and he had three cute little boys and he
didn't go home either. They didn't leave me out there to
die. They rescued me and Jonah and the next day I stood
beside the plane with dozens of others as they flew his
body back home to his wife and kids. I couldn't even let
on that he'd been my partner or tell anyone about it. I'm
not supposed to be talking about it right now and I keep
reliving it in my dreams."

Holt swallowed hard. "Women don't do that kind
of job."

"No, they don't. I worked in hospital administration but from the first time I qualified with a rifle, they
knew what I could do. I was always good with guns.
Guess it comes from competing with my brothers. First
time I picked one up it was like an extension of me.
Daddy said I had a natural eye for shooting. The military recognized it. I could get into places a lot of times
where men had trouble going. So don't worry about

me sitting on a porch in the dark in Mingus, Texas, in the middle of the night. I mean it when I say I can take care of myself."

"You don't have a gun and there's drunks coming out of two bars on this side of town. What if…" He hesitated.

"You be the drunk man and try to mess with me if you want me to prove my point," she said.

He sat there long enough that she'd given up on him doing role-play. The tension left her body and she relaxed. She'd said the words out loud. It was as if an elephant had been lifted from her chest and she could breathe again. Sure, she'd been to therapists when she first came home but it wasn't the same. The two ton weight inside her was still there even after she talked to them. Now it was gone.

One second he was sitting in the chair with his hands on the arms, the next those same hands were around her throat. In three swift moves he was on the porch on his stomach and one arm was hurting really bad.

"Anything else you'd like, cowboy?" she asked.

He flipped over and suddenly she was pinned under him. He had both her arms above her head and his lips found hers in a crashing kiss. The stars paled in comparison to the sparks floating down around them.

He moved down to run his tongue across the soft, tender spot on her neck right below her ear. "Maybe a little of this."

She pulled her arms free and wrapped them around his neck, toying with his hair with her fingertips. When he pulled away she dragged his lips back down to hers and kissed him just as passionately as he'd kissed her.

He pushed off and sat up on the porch. He couldn't go any further. He refused to be nothing but friends with sex benefits and he wouldn't use Sharlene. She deserved more than that. She was a good friend, a good person, a good woman. She was kind, sweet, funny, and independent as hell—all the things that would have normally attracted him to a woman. But…

"What?" she asked.

"We can't do this anymore. I can't… you aren't… we…" he stammered.

She wiggled away from him. "I understand. I won't use your rockers again as long as you live in the house. Sorry I woke you up. See you tomorrow when you pick up the kids." She walked away without looking back. He didn't need to use words. His actions said it all.

In half a dozen long strides he was behind her. He scooped her up into his arms and carried her back to one of the chairs where he sat down and rocked her without saying a word.

She buried her face in his chest and let the tears bathe her face. Four years they'd been in the making and she didn't care if Holt thought she was a pansy as she mourned for her friend and spotter, Jonah Black.

"Thank you," she finally said between sobs. "I'm going home now."

"You can stay and talk about it," he said.

"No, I've got to go. I really have to go." Sharlene pushed out of his arms and hurried across the yard.

When she was in her apartment she threw her sweats on the sofa and went straight to the shower. Maybe if she washed away his kisses and touches it would remove the desire from her body.

I've fallen for Holt Jackson and I cannot have him. So the Tonk really did end the lucky charm after the third time. What I've got is the curse that follows.

She stepped out of the shower and wrapped a big towel around her body. She went to the kitchen and made a cup of hot chocolate. Surely chocolate would cure the doldrums brought on by rejection.

I've got to work on stopping the attraction, not feeding it with hot, wild kisses. So from this day forth I shall not think about Holt Jackson, dream about him, or get all gushy when I'm in his presence. I shall not kiss him, let him kiss me, or wish for even more than that. And I'll believe all that when there's a snow storm in Texas in the middle of July.

It was near daylight when she finished off the second cup of hot chocolate and fell asleep on the sofa with nothing but a quilt wrapped around her only to dream again of bombed out buildings, sand, and Jonah.

Chapter 14

Sharlene zeroed in on the target, inhaled and held it, blinked twice for good luck, and pulled the trigger. Then all hell broke loose. She kept yelling at her spotter to fall back forty feet and take cover but he couldn't hear her for the buzzing helicopters. They were all over them. Bullets flew through the air like sleet pellets in a fierce north wind.

When she awoke she was sitting straight up in bed, her eyes wide and dry from refusing to blink, her heart racing, and her whole body drenched in sweat. Would the nightmares never end? Did she need to go to those meetings for war vets who couldn't adjust?

She crawled out of bed and stood under a warm shower for half an hour. That always helped more than anything. Hot water and knowing that she was back home. There were no targets. No Jonah to spot for her. Holt knew and it had ended what might have been. Her future held a beer joint, romance novels, and nightmares.

Even if she went to those meetings no one would believe her. She could stand up in front of that little group of people who met in the basement of a church, who had cookies and coffee and no last names and tell her story.

My name is Sharlene and I was a sniper for the United States Army. I was defending my country's freedom and I'm very good at what I do but it doesn't stop the nightmares. Or the cold sweats or the sleeplessness. The only two times I haven't had them since I came home was when I slept with Holt Jackson.

No one in their right mind would believe a short red-haired woman, the emphasis on the last word, when I told them I was a sniper. That job is reserved for men with nerves of steel and a steady hand. Not a five-foot-three-inch woman who should be at home on the wheat farm raising kids and baking yeast bread twice a week.

They'd shuffle me over to the church basement two blocks down where they were having an anonymous meeting for liars. The cookies and the coffee would be about the same and no one would have last names there either. I could tell the same story and they'd all nod and recognize that I was a liar. Hell, I might even get the grand prize for the biggest lie told at that meeting. No wonder Holt had a change of heart about kissing me. I'm not sweet little wife material. I can shoot the eyes out of a rattlesnake from so far away he looks like an earthworm. Who wants to be married to a woman like that?

She turned off the water and stepped out of the shower to hear the phone ringing. It was in her purse so she hurried to the living room and grabbed it on the fourth ring.

"This is your wake-up call," Merle said.

"I'm awake. What's going on that you are calling me? What is today? My birthday is past and my books don't arrive until next week," Sharlene said.

"Today is Saturday, November thirteenth. It's my party day to show off my new room and you are coming to help me make cookies."

"I thought that was next week. I just got out of the shower. I'll be there in twenty minutes. Mind if I bring my clothes and change at your house?"

"Honey, you can move in my spare bedroom if you'll make the sugar cookies and punch you made for the wedding reception for Larissa and Hank," Merle said.

"See you in a few minutes then."

"Front door is open. Oven is preheated and I'm ready for you," Merle said.

Sharlene threw on a pair of sweat bottoms and a T-shirt, her boots, and chose a pair of jeans and a western cutoff white lace blouse with ruffles on the cuffs to wear that evening for the party.

Half an hour later she was in the middle of Merle's kitchen with flour smeared on her nose and her hands in a big crock bowl of cookie dough. The military anonymous club would believe that she was right where she ought to be. The liar's club would take away her award.

Merle's state-of-the-art kitchen had an island in the middle of the floor with a sink and stove top incorporated into it, an enormous refrigerator/freezer combo, double oven range, and every gadget that Sharlene could think of. Merle would have to offer drooling bibs at the door if her sisters-in-law ever came to visit.

Sharlene made perfect little round dough balls and lined them up on the cookie trays. "Did I ever tell you what I did in the army?"

Merle sipped her coffee. "Were you a cook? Betcha if you were them boys didn't have such a hankering for home-cooked food."

"Would you believe me if I told you I was a sniper?" Sharlene asked.

Merle set the coffee down with a thud. "Were you?"

"Yes, I was," Sharlene said.

"Well, I reckon I owe you a thanks for your contribution in keeping my country safe first, Texas safe second, and my sorry ass safe third. Did you actually have to use your training?"

"I did."

"How often?"

"I didn't keep count."

"Why are you telling me?" Merle asked.

"I have nightmares and wake up all sweaty and scared. Sometimes I forget to exhale in my sleep. I always inhaled and blinked twice for good luck. When I wake up I'm still trying to suck in air and forgetting to exhale. My chest hurts and my heart is beating so fast it feels like I've run a marathon."

Merle nodded seriously. "How many women do that job over there?"

"That field isn't open to women." Sharlene slid the cookies into the oven. "While they're cooking, I'll make punch. A can of pineapple juice, one can full of water, two cups of sugar, two packages of red Kool-Aid, and a two-ounce bottle of almond extract." She counted off the ingredients on her fingers as she added them to the gallon jug. When that was finished she made another one.

"Then you just put ice and ginger ale into that when it's in the punch bowl, right?" Merle asked.

"See you remembered. You could do all of this, Merle Avery."

She smiled and part of the wrinkles smoothed out. "Of course I could but I've got the jitters about having so many people in my house so I wanted the company. Now tell me more about this sniper business. How in the hell did you wind up in that?"

"Four older brothers and I had to keep up or get left out in the cold," she said.

Merle shook her head slowly. "I had older brothers and I can shoot the ass end of an elephant if he's not more than twenty feet from me. That's not the whole thing, is it?"

Sharlene poured herself a cup of coffee and topped off Merle's. "I'm very good at it. From the first time Daddy put a gun in my hands, I was at home with it. And I passed the psychological tests that said I could do that job without falling apart in the middle of a mission. They trained me in hospital administration work but the sniper business was classified top secret stuff. Only my spotter knew who I was and what I did and he was killed right beside me one evening. After that if they had something classified for me to do, I did it alone. I did two tours and did my job, Merle. It wasn't until I got home that I fell apart."

"So that's why you didn't stick with a job very long and was hopping from one thing to another when you lit at the Honky Tonk?" Merle asked.

"I guess so. I didn't realize it until this minute." Sharlene looked at the yellow daisies on the wallpaper and the lace valance on the spotlessly clean window above the stainless steel sink. So very different from the bombed out structures she'd hunkered down in so many times.

"Need to talk? It won't go any further than this kitchen," Merle said.

Sharlene sipped her coffee. The timer said she had five minutes before the first batch of cookies came out of the oven. "I don't know."

"Then you should talk. If you were totally all right with the job you had it wouldn't be giving you bad dreams. So talk while you cook and I'll listen. And don't think you'll shock me, girl. I watch all them news channels on the television while I'm designing shirts. I see what goes on over there," Merle said.

"I told Holt a week ago and he was completely turned off by it."

She told Merle about sitting on his porch because that was where she felt the most peaceful when the walls of the past were closing in on her and went on to tell the whole story leaving out only the part about the kissing.

"Holt Jackson is a good man. If he's turned off by what I did then will every man in my future act the same way?" Sharlene asked.

"Well, butter my butt and call me a biscuit," Merle said. "I've been living in fear that man was your cowboy like Jarod was Daisy's. I'm so damn sick of bartenders leaving the Tonk. I swear I was ready to buy you out if you'd fallen in love with Holt. Still will if you do."

Sharlene pulled the cookies from the oven and slipped them off onto a cooling rack. "You said you didn't want to own a bar."

"I don't. But I could buy it and get Luther and Tessa and now Darla to operate it for me. Hell, I might even force Luther and Tessa to get married before I let them manage it for me and that would cure this damn charm shit once and for all," Merle said.

Sharlene put more cookies on the tray, slid them into the oven, and went back to her perch beside Merle. "You didn't answer my question."

"I can't answer it. Men are all different. Don't seem like it but they are. Seems like they're like elephants or zebras. You seen one and you've seen them all. I'm not talking about the outside of them. Some are damn fine. Some are uglier than a mud fence with cow shit on it. Some are in between. But most of us women think they're all alike on the inside. They ain't. Some are assholes and some are fairly decent. If Holt don't like what you did and it drains his testosterone then you don't need him anyway. Next man comes along in your life might not be as pretty as Holt but he might not have any problem with what you did. He might even brag about it in church on Sunday morning," Merle said.

"Thank you."

Holt's deep voice called from the front door. "Hey, anyone home?"

"Speak of the devil and he shall appear wearing blue jeans and a big smile most of the time. We're in the kitchen," Merle shouted.

Holt stopped when he saw Sharlene. No woman at home in a kitchen and looking so damn cute with flour on her nose could look down the barrel of a sniper rifle and pull the trigger. She couldn't be that cold when her kisses were so fiery.

"Hello, Sharlene. Where's your ugly car?" he asked.

"In the backyard. I came in through the kitchen door."

"I see. Well, Merle, I brought the last set of blinds to hang and then the job is completely done. All right if I get it done before the kids get out of school?"

She nodded.

"So you're picking the kids up today?" Sharlene asked.

"You're busy with this stuff and I don't have anything to do until Monday. I'll pick them up today and tomorrow," he said.

"What's happening on Monday?" she asked.

"We're going to build Betty and Elmer Cantrell a new barn with a tack room and horse stalls. Should take until just before Christmas if the weather stays decent," he said.

"And after that?"

"Never know. I expect we'll have done about all we can in this area by then. I'll get those blinds and put them up now," Holt said.

"Can I watch?" Sharlene asked.

Merle shook her head. "Hell, no, you can't watch. You got cookies to make and you got to entertain me so I don't get all antsy. The room will be unveiled in a ceremony and you don't get to see ahead of time."

"Ah, come on." Sharlene grinned. At least Holt didn't snarl when he saw her even if the way he scanned her from head to toe didn't exactly give him droopy bedroom eyes.

"I'll go on out and bring them in. It'll only take a few minutes and then I'll be out of your way," Holt said.

"You serious about me not getting to get the first peek? I should, you know, since I'm the only one in here making cookies and punch. It could be my reward for helping," Sharlene teased.

"No way. Only reason Holt gets to see it is because he built it and he's putting in the last set of blinds. We had to order them special because the corner window panel was so narrow. Pay attention to your cookies. Just because the whole kitchen is het up from y'alls

hot little vibes don't mean you can forget your job,"
Merle scolded.

"It is not!" Sharlene countered.

"Oh, honey. You are either dumb or blind. Maybe
both. You can bury your sweet little red head in the sand
all the way up to your ass but it won't change things.
Whether you act on the feelings or not is what will make
a difference. Way that man looks at you is visual porn.
Y'all been to bed or something?" Merle asked.

Sharlene blushed scarlet. "No, we have not!"

"Methinks you are protesting too loudly, darlin',"
Merle laughed.

"Okay, okay. We've been to bed but we haven't had
sex. Once when I was passed out drunk in Weatherford.
Remember when I went to meet my friends? Well, he
showed up at the bar and took me to my hotel. We slept
together but nothing happened and then once when we
went to my folks house. I took a nap out in the barn.
Again nothing happened. Then there was a night when
we both fell asleep on his sofa but the kids were in the
next room. So we've slept together but we have not had
sex. And all those nights I didn't dream, Merle. What
does that mean?"

Merle groaned. "That means you will be selling me
the Tonk."

"It's not for sale. So forget it. And what makes you
think that?"

"I'm old, honey. I'm not stupid," Merle said.

"You are also full of shit," Sharlene said. "Why isn't
he back in here yet?"

Merle rolled her eyes. "Lord, you missin' him already?"

"No, I'm just wondering where he is?"

"He's in the new room. There's a door on the south side so I can go out into the garden. Next year I'm putting flower beds back there. Already got me one of them fancy park benches. I like to go out front and talk to Ruby when the flowers are in bloom. Next year I'm moving her memories to the garden. Don't look at me like I'm crazy. I still miss her and it makes me feel good to visit with her every day. So to hell with anyone who doesn't like it," Merle said.

"Hey, I'm not saying a word. Remember, I'm the one with nightmares and who can't sleep except when Holt holds me and now he can't even look at me because I was an army sniper," she said.

Why would I need a man to make me feel safe anyway? I could outshoot him any day of the week and most likely protect him. Maybe it's not the physical safe I crave but the one inside my heart that says Holt could make me whole again. He could make it all right that I was a sniper.

"Where is your mind?" Merle asked softly.

"Somewhere where it damn sure shouldn't go on a regular basis."

"Why?"

"Because it's scary as hell when I go there."

Merle frowned. "Why?"

"Can't explain. It just is. Let's talk about the guest list. Is Chigger coming?"

"She called last night. She'll be here but she's leaving her daughter with Billy Bob's wife. Larissa is coming and bringing Ruby and Henry. Hank has to be off in Abilene at a cattle sale. Daisy and Cathy neither one can come but said they'd drop by and have coffee with me when they come for the Honky Tonk Christmas," Merle said.

"I can't wait. We're going to have a grand opening for the new addition and I'm going to have books there to sign for anyone who wants to buy one, and we're going to play that song. The maintenance man already has an order for it to be installed that week," Sharlene said.

"You ever listen to the words real good? Alan Jackson says that he's going to have a Honky Tonk Christmas because his woman broke his heart. He says that he's going to be over her by New Year's Eve," Merle asked.

"Sounds like a damn fine plan to me. It's my new favorite song," Sharlene answered.

Chapter 15

"Whooeee," Chigger whistled under her breath when Holt walked into Merle's new room. "If that ain't sex on a stick then there ain't no heaven. Where'd he come from and where y'all been hidin' him?"

"He's the contractor and he's been right out in the open and girl, you are married," Merle said.

"Yeah, but I can still admire the candy in the window even if I am on a diet," Chigger laughed.

Holt scanned the room. JC, Frank, and Elmer were over beside the new pool table. Betty and Janice were staring out the window into what would be gardens come next spring. Finally, his eyes rested on Sharlene standing beside a tall blonde. She wore a lacy blouse and jeans. The sparkle of a double heart rhinestone belt buckle took his eye and he wished her entwined hearts was a symbol of their relationship. But after last night that door was shut forever. He'd lain awake for hours wishing he could redo the whole scene.

Merle motioned to him. "Holt, come in and meet Chigger."

The tall blonde extended her hand. "Hello, handsome."

"I'm pleased to meet you. I've heard a lot about you." Holt shook her hand.

Chigger laughed. "I expect you have and hopefully it wasn't all good. Darlin', if I wasn't married you'd be at the top of my list today."

She was as tall as Holt. Her hair was blonder than what God gave her, thanks to good hair dye. Dark brown eyes sparkled with mischief.

Merle stepped between them. "Don't you love my new room?"

"It's almost as pretty as the contractor," Chigger flirted.

Holt blushed.

Sharlene grinned.

"Down, girl," Merle laughed. "Jim Bob would hate to have to defend your honor."

Chigger laughed. "It don't hurt to look, Merle. The ring on my finger just says I'd better not touch. Where's Cathy and Daisy?"

"They are not coming until Sharlene's Christmas thing."

Chigger gave Holt a broad sexy wink. "Honey, wild horses or wild men couldn't keep me away that day if this is what's going to the Honky Tonk these days."

"You could have warned me," Holt whispered to Sharlene when Chigger moved across the room toward the refreshment table.

"I did. You didn't believe me. Aren't you glad you weren't adding on to the Honky Tonk back when she was there every Friday and Saturday night?" Sharlene's green eyes twinkled.

"Some friend you are. You'd let her back me up in a corner and do mean things to me," Holt said.

"I expect Jim Bob would keep that from happening."

"Sharlene!" Judd tugged on her hand. "Look at me. Do you like it? I fixed it up all by myself." She wore a denim skirt, a hot pink sweater, and her new pink cowboy boots.

"You are simply gorgeous, princess. And did Waylon get himself dressed too or did Holt help him?"

"Uncle Holt picked out his shirt and jeans. Boys ain't supposed to be all fancy. Just us girls. You look beautiful," Judd said.

"Can I have her?" Chigger asked as she rejoined the group.

"You got one," Sharlene told her.

"But she's not old enough to tell me I'm beautiful yet. Where's your momma, darlin'?" Chigger asked.

"She got dead in a wreck. Uncle Holt takes care of us now. I got to go find Waylon. He gets scared at big people things."

"You've got to fill me in on that story, Sharlene. I've missed the Honky Tonk and all the gossip. I'm probably so far behind I couldn't ever catch up now," Chigger said.

"It's a very long story."

"Then give me the sixty-second news clip version and save the rest until later," Chigger said.

"Okay. Their mother was killed in a drunk driver accident. Holt is her brother and only living relative so he took charge of the kids. I've been watching them some. They are a hoot. Someday I'm…" Sharlene stopped. She'd been about to say that she intended to have a dozen just like them. She couldn't have a dozen kids with no husband and besides, she wouldn't do that to a child. In today's world a kid had to have two parents to survive, or did they? Holt seemed to be doing a fine job of being a single parent.

"Someday you are going to what?" Chigger asked.

"I'm going to miss them when Holt's construction company finishes up their jobs around here and moves away from here. Look, there's Amos. How long's it been since you've seen him?"

Chigger smiled. "Too damn long. Amos, you old sinner, come over here and give me a hug."

"That's the pot calling the kettle black, ain't it, Chigger," Amos yelled.

Sharlene left them to visit and made sure the punch bowl was full. The room was absolutely beautiful. She loved the way the glass walls brought the sun into the room. The garden was just stone pathways and dirt now but next spring it would come alive with color and that would flow into the room with the bright light.

"So?" Holt asked from behind her.

Her heart skipped a beat. "So what?"

"Do you like it?"

"The room?" she asked.

"What else would I be talking about?"

"I'm pea green with envy. I wish I'd put my money into a room like this for myself rather than adding on to the Tonk," she answered.

He cocked his head to one side. "Seriously?"

"No, but someday I'm having a house with a room just like this. If you aren't around to build it for me, I'll bring the carpenter out here to see exactly what I want. You didn't file a patent on the room, did you?"

"Thank you and no, I'm not sure you can file a patent on a room design. And if you could, then that would be up to Merle. She's the one who designed it; I just followed her directions." His eyes locked with Sharlene's and neither of them could break the gaze.

The house was full of people standing in groups of two to five discussing everything from the new room, to how long Merle had lived in Mingus, to hay crops. Elmer Cantrell said a few words to Frank and JC and started toward the refreshment table. But Holt and Sharlene were alone. He wanted to lean forward and kiss her. She wanted to drag him out of the house and back to her apartment for more than hot steamy kisses.

Elmer was talking when they both blinked at the same time. "...got every woman in the county talking about how she'd like a room like this nailed up to the back of their house and what they'd do with it. Betty says she'd use it for a den. Sounds like a hell of an idea to me. I couldn't even see the television until after the sun set every evening for the glare."

Betty turned around and poked him in the arm. "Don't be thinking you can put that old fossil of a television in my new room. It's not going to have a television in it."

"But a den isn't a den without a television," Elmer argued.

"It's not going to be a den like that. It's going to be a place where friends gather up to talk and where when the kids all come home we can have extra tables set up so everyone can sit down at the same time to eat. But don't worry, Holt. I won't need the room for a few years. This year's oil royalties are going for a fancy new barn. Tell me something, honey, where are you going to put a television or an eating table in that new barn?" Betty asked.

"I suppose they could sit on hay bales to eat and if we put a couple of momma cats out there, the kids would have kittens to play with," Elmer said cheerfully.

"Momma cats? Where are momma cats? Do they have kittens? Can I see them? What color are they? If there's an orange one can I name it and play with it?" Judd talked fast and furious.

Elmer nodded toward Judd. "See, I was right. The kids will love a barn with a bunch of cats and eatin' on hay bales instead of tables with fancy cloths on them. Just ask Judd, here."

Merle elbowed Elmer. "So you don't like my room?"

"It's a very nice addition to your home, Merle," Elmer said.

"You see any fancy little tables other than the one with the cookies and punch?"

Judd crossed her arms across her chest. "I don't see any momma cats or kittens."

"I rest my case." Elmer hurried off to talk to JC and Frank about the new pool table in the corner.

Betty refilled her punch cup. "I've got to have this recipe, Sharlene. We've got a Christmas party at the church and I'm going to volunteer for punch. What's the secret?"

"A bottle of almond extract. It cuts the sweet," Sharlene said.

"You making this for the Honky Tonk Christmas?"

"Yes, I am."

"You closing down after the party that day or are you going to open up that night?" Betty asked.

"I'm going to close on Christmas Eve and Christmas both. There wouldn't be enough folks out to warrant opening the doors. Besides, Tessa, Darla, and Luther are going up to Ardmore soon as the party is over. I'd have to run it by myself," Sharlene answered.

"Where are you going for the holidays?" Betty asked.

Judd popped her hands on her hips and said, "Well, we aren't going anywhere for Christmas. I done told Santa Claus to leave our present in the orange rocking chair on the front porch. There ain't a chimney in our house so me and Waylon told him to leave our present in the rocking chair."

"And what's he going to leave in your orange rocking chair? A big teddy bear with a red bow around its neck?" Betty asked.

"Hell no!" Judd said.

Holt whipped around. "Judd Mendoza!"

Judd slapped a hand over her mouth. "Sorry, it just slipped out. It's hard not to say bad words when they're in your head, ain't it? Next week you ain't goin' to call me Judd Mendoza no more. You're goin' to call me Judd Jackson. I like that, don't you, Merle?"

"You are trying to get out of trouble. I'll let you off the hook if you'll tell me what is Santa supposed to put in that orange rocking chair?" Holt asked.

She shook her head. "We'll tell Santa when we see him at the Wal-Mart store. He always brings what we want," Judd said. "Now, can me and Waylon go out there and walk around on those steps?"

Merle squatted down in front of Judd. "Whisper in my ear and I promise I won't tell anyone. What is it that's supposed to be in the rocking chair on Christmas morning? What if you miss seeing Santa at the Wal-Mart store? I could tell him for you that way. "

Judd narrowed her eyes and set her jaw. "Okay, but the only person you can tell is Santa. You promise?"

"I promise I won't tell anyone but Santa," Merle agreed.

Judd whispered.

Merle's eyes widened out so big that half her wrinkles disappeared. "My lips are sealed."

Judd looked her right in the eye. "Only Santa?"

Holt sighed. Merle was a saint or an angel, maybe a mixture of both. He'd tried guessing for weeks what the twins wanted but they wouldn't budge.

Merle hugged Judd tightly. "You got it, kid, and you and Waylon can sure enough go out into the garden and walk around. You can even sit on the bench and talk about Christmas and what else you want. If you change your mind or decide you want to add something to that list, then let me know and I'll visit with Santa about that too."

"We ain't askin' for nothing else. If Santa brings that we'll be happy." Judd ran off to grab Waylon's hand and drag him out to the yard.

Betty and Sharlene were talking punch recipes but Sharlene didn't miss a single word of what had gone on beside her. Sharlene's heart dropped to the floor. There was a good chance they wouldn't even be living in the house at Christmas. Merle's job had taken five weeks. The next one could easily be done before Christmas even if there was rainy weather. How could Santa leave their present in the orange rocking chair if they had already moved to another location?

"Well?" Holt asked Merle when the kids were finally outside. He had plenty of time. It was only the first of November. He would have Saturdays to shop for Santa's present. He'd write a note to remind himself to leave it on the rocking chair.

Merle's eyes twinkled. "Only one thing and they're willing to share."

"I know. It's all I've heard since we went out to Larissa's place and played with the goats. They made a pact that they were only going to tell Santa and I've been worried that they'll be disappointed," Holt said.

"Hello, everyone. I heard what you said, Holt. I bet you those kids want a goat cart," Larissa said as she carried Ruby into the new room. Everyone navigated in that direction to get a peek at the cute dark-haired baby dressed in pink ruffles.

Babies always draw the attention, Sharlene thought. *Even a gorgeous new room and Santa Claus takes a backseat to a baby. Of course, Ruby is at that cute stage when she smiles at everyone. It doesn't matter if they're an angel or a homeless beggar.*

Holt slung an arm over Merle's shoulder. "They're going to see Larissa and the baby and come running here in a minute. Tell me, please."

"Do you promise to do your best to get it for them?" Merle asked.

"This is our first Christmas together. I want them to have what they want. Is it costly?"

"You're damn right. You can't imagine the price," Merle teased.

Holt shut his eyes. "Okay, enough. Tell me."

"Sharlene," Merle said.

"Yes ma'am." Sharlene turned away from Larissa and the baby to see what Merle needed.

Holt's eyes popped open. "Good God!"

"Did you need something?" Sharlene asked.

Merle shook her head. "Not me."

Sharlene let someone else have her place next to Larissa and headed toward Merle and Holt. Merle was grinning like she'd won the lottery. Holt looked like he'd been struck by a lightning bolt.

"What'd the kids want for Christmas?" she asked.

"I promised I wouldn't tell anyone but Santa. Now he knows and I kept my word," Merle said.

"So?" Sharlene looked at Holt.

"It's a secret," he mumbled.

"You can't even tell me? I could help you look for it," Sharlene offered.

"No, it's something I'll have to deal with," he said.

Luther didn't have to turn anyone away when the Tonk opened that night. With the new room the maximum capacity had doubled and now the problem wasn't getting inside, it was finding a parking spot. Cars lined the sides of the road up to the Tonk and some folks were even parking down in the Smokestack parking lot and riding with friends.

"Looks like everyone and their puppy dog is out tonight. Your cowboy coming around?" Darla asked.

"He's got kids and they've got school tomorrow and he's not my cowboy," Sharlene said.

"Well, since he's not your cowboy can I make a play for him? I saw him at Merle's this afternoon. That's exactly what I'm looking for. Responsible. Has a good job. I love kids and those two of his are so cute. I'd feel like I died and went to heaven on a big fluffy cloud if I could get that man," Darla said.

Jealousy shot through Sharlene's veins like a slug of cheap whiskey thrown back in one big gulp.

"You've rendered her speechless, Darla. I didn't know anyone could make Sharlene stop talking," Tessa laughed. "And stop teasing her."

Darla opened the dishwasher and removed dozens of pint Mason jars. "Who said I was teasing."

Kent claimed an empty barstool right in front of Sharlene. "Who's teasing?"

"No one," Sharlene said quickly. "What can I get you?"

"Nice party out at Merle's, wasn't it? I wonder if Elmer and Betty will have a barn open house?" he asked.

"Betty says they're having a Thanksgiving barn dance. Not on the holiday but the weekend after so she can decorate the barn in Christmas colors. She's looking for a live band and the whole nine yards. Says if Elmer gets a barn and she can't have a room like Merle's then she's going to have a party," Sharlene said.

"That ought to be fun. I'll have to make sure Loralou has the night off. There she is, coming in the door. Fix me up a couple of pints of Coors," Kent said.

"How's things going there?" Tessa asked.

"Looking serious. I'm thinking maybe an engagement ring for Christmas but don't you tell. I want to surprise her," Kent whispered.

"And the charm strikes again," Tessa whispered to Sharlene.

Sharlene set about making a pitcher of Coke and Jack. "It can hop around and make couples like rabbits make baby bunnies as long as it stays away from me."

Darla raised a hand. "And me. Keep that damn little naked angel and his arrows away from me. I wouldn't even look twice at your cowboy seriously."

"I keep telling you…" Sharlene started.

"We know," Tessa said. "He's not your cowboy."

"Who? Holt?" Kent asked.

Sharlene had forgotten he was still sitting on the barstool.

"Me and the boys got a bet going as to how long it'll take you two to wake up and admit you've got an attraction for each other," Kent said. "Want to give me some insider tips so I can either up my bet or lower it?"

"You'd better take all your money out of the pot if you don't want to lose it," Sharlene said.

Behind her, both Tessa and Darla were pointing at the ceiling.

Chapter 16

THE SMELL OF SWEAT, BEER, SMOKE, PERFUME, AND aftershave already filled the air and the Honky Tonk had only been open an hour. Line dances mixed with slow two-stepping songs kept the customers drinking and happy. The jukebox music was loud but could barely be heard among the buzz of laughter and talking. Merle was holding royal court at the pool tables in the new room with a line of admirers waiting for a chance to knock the eight ball queen off her throne.

Tessa was handling the mixed drinks, Darla the draft beer, and Sharlene was taking orders and taking care of buckets and bottles. They had no time for conversation past how many beers, was the dishwasher's last cycle finished, and did someone have time to gather up the trays from the tables.

"Pint of Coors," Holt said when Sharlene made it to his end of the bar.

"What are you doing here?" she asked.

"Buying a beer." He grinned.

Tessa called out from the mixed drink station. "Hey, Sharlene, we're out of trays again. Want to gather them up for us?"

"Gotta go," Sharlene said.

"I'll get them if you'll let me buy you a beer after work," he said.

"You take care of trays and I'll buy you a beer after work," she told him.

"You got a deal." He left his barstool and another person claimed it immediately.

By midnight he was behind the bar loading and unloading the dishwasher and drawing beer when the load got too heavy for the three women to handle.

"Hey, handsome." A woman pushed her way between two die-hard ranchers at the bar. "Come out from behind there and let me teach you to line dance. I'll pay you double whatever Sharlene is giving you."

"Mindy! Where in the hell have you been? I haven't seen you since June," Sharlene said as she stuck six bottles of Miller into a bucket and covered them with ice.

"Got married but it didn't work so here I am, on the prowl again. Where'd you find this handsome hunk? If you'll point me in the direction of the rock that you turned over to find him, I'll go see if there's any more hiding," Mindy said.

Sharlene grinned. "If I told you where I found him, you wouldn't believe me. What can I get you?"

Mindy pointed at Holt.

"He's not for sale. Beer. Mixed drink or both but you can't have my help. It's too hard to find these days," Sharlene said. "Did you marry someone you met in the Tonk?"

Mindy shook her head. "Then give me a pint of Coors. And hell, no, I didn't marry someone I met in the Tonk. Met him up at the Boar's Nest. If I'd met him here it would have lasted. I don't know of a marriage that started in the Tonk yet that ended up in divorce courts. He was from Abilene. Just passing through and three weeks later we wound up in Vegas for a weekend. Got married by Elvis while we were both looped.

Don't know if it was us getting hitched or two bottles of Jim Beam. Big mistake. Don't ever say 'I do' in front of Elvis."

"Sorry about that."

"Don't draw that beer just yet. Give me a whole pitcher of Jack and Coke and a pint jar and your pretty bartender," Mindy said. "I bet he could make me forget all about Elvis."

"You can have two out of the three. Why would you be on the prowl already if you just got out of a five month horrible relationship?" Sharlene picked up the square bottle of Jack Daniels.

"Relationship only lasted one month. Took me four months to get up the nerve to go honky tonkin' again but I'm back in full force. If you won't let me have him then I'll go find someone else. Talk to you later, darlin'." Mindy picked up the pitcher and jar that Tessa set in front of her. She handed Tessa a bill and told her to keep the change and disappeared into a crowd of slow dancers in search of a table.

"Hmmm," Sharlene mused. "I could make a lot of money pimping you out for a couple of hours at a time."

Holt threw up his palms. "What'd I ever do to deserve that kind of treatment? Don't answer that out loud."

Sharlene looked up to see that Tessa and Darla had stopped work and were listening.

"What did he do?" Darla grinned.

"Nothing," Sharlene said. "Here comes another wave of thirsty, lusty souls."

And thank God for them. I almost said things aloud that shouldn't even be thought about in a dark corner, Sharlene thought.

At closing time Luther unplugged the jukebox just as Waylon Jennings finished a slow song about making it through December and announced that the Honky Tonk was officially closed. "We'll reopen at eight tomorrow evening and be open until two o'clock Sunday morning. We are closed on Sunday night."

Smoke rushed out the door with every customer and by the time they were all gone the haze hanging close to the ceiling had practically disappeared. Luther carried his red and white cooler to the bar area, tossed six empty Coke cans in the trash, and picked a bottle of beer from the ice.

"I need this tonight. It's been a hell of a busy week," he said.

"Please don't tell me you're ready to throw in the towel. One night a week is all I can talk Kent into and besides, what would I ever do without you?" Sharlene said.

Luther shook his big round bald head emphatically. "Hell, no! I'm not ready to quit. I'd quit the oil business before the Tonk. I like it a lot better these days. You girls ready to go?"

"You drinkin' that here or takin' it with you?" Tessa asked.

"You drive. I'm drinkin' it on the way."

"I'll drive. I love these busy nights. I made a hundred dollars in tips," Darla said as the three of them traipsed across the dance floor toward the door.

"I owe you a beer." Sharlene looked at Holt who'd taken up residence on a bar stool. "Would you please take the tops off a couple of Coors while I lock up the cash register?"

"Yes ma'am." His Texas drawl was more pronounced when he was tired.

He had his feet propped on a chair when she joined him at a table in the new room. She kicked off her boots and propped her feet up on the table.

"My dogs are barking," she said.

"I didn't think it was polite to put your feet on the table," he said.

"I own the place and it'll get washed down good tomorrow before we open again. Try it. Feels wonderful."

He pulled off his boots and adjusted the chair so that his feet would touch hers. He'd touched Tessa and Darla's hands while they worked. He'd bumped against all three of them all evening. No one but Sharlene set a fire inside him, not even Mindy who'd flirted so blatantly that it was embarrassing.

"It does feel good." He wiggled his toes and enjoyed the fire they shared.

She tipped up her beer. "It's a tradition. Ruby started it. She taught Daisy to walk away from the mess after a hard night and do cleanup the next morning when she was rested. Daisy taught Cathy and Cathy taught Larissa. I still remember the first night she trusted me enough to join her after work."

"That mean you trust me?" Holt asked.

"I trust you, Holt. The issue between us has nothing to do with trust."

"It doesn't, does it? Want to talk about it now?"

"Do you?"

"I miss you, Sharlene. I miss our visits, even the ones in the middle of the night. I miss my friend. And I trust you."

Tears welled up in her eyes but she refused to let them escape. "I miss you too."

"Were you really a sniper or were you just saying that to get a rise out of me?" he asked.

She set the beer down with a thud. "I was really a sniper. I still have the nightmares to prove it."

"How many?" he whispered.

"Nightmares? Every night except when I slept with you," she said honestly.

"I didn't mean how many nightmares," he said.

"I made myself not count so I really can't answer that. Enough that the dreams haunt me."

"Why'd you do it?"

"I'm good at it. I did a job so that hopefully there won't be another nine eleven. That's what the captain told me when he gave me the pep talk for reenlistment."

He sipped at the cold beer. "You didn't want to make a career of it?"

"No, one stretch and two tours was enough for me. You sure you trust me?"

"With my life, yes I do."

But not with your heart, she thought. *That would take a hell of a lot more than your life, wouldn't it?*

She changed the subject. "Where are the kids tonight?"

"Gloria and Chad wanted to play parents tonight. They called this afternoon. They'd finagled four tickets to Disney on Ice in Dallas tonight. Then they had a hotel room rented with an indoor pool and were ordering out pizza. They'll play in the morning until they have to check out at eleven and then they've got appointments at a bridal shop to have the kids fitted for a tux and a fancy dress. Want to have a barbecue at the beach house up the road at supper time with all of us?"

"Why, Holt Jackson, are you asking me for a date?" she flirted.

"I guess I am," he said.

"I'd love to," she answered. "What can I bring?"

"Dessert?"

"As in food or something else? And are we talking about tomorrow or tonight?"

"Food. Tomorrow. Bartending is tough work. As beautiful as you are, I don't think I'm up for dessert tonight," he said.

"Me neither. Why are they fitting kids for a tux and a fancy dress at a bridal shop?"

"Gloria and Chad are getting married the last day of December in Wichita Falls. Big church foo-rah with all the trimmings. Waylon is ring bearer. Judd is the flower girl. Kent is best man. Bennie and I are groomsmen," he explained.

"When did all this happen?"

"He gave her the ring a couple of weeks ago. He thought they'd have a six-month engagement. Gloria says not."

Sharlene set her empty bottle on the table and put her feet on the floor. "Where are they going to live?"

"We're working on an idea. We'll have the jobs finished here and it'll be semester break for the kids so a move wouldn't be so difficult. Did I tell you that Kent is planning to propose to Loralou at Thanksgiving? Wouldn't be surprised if they aren't married by the end of the year too," he said.

"What idea? And where are you going with my kids?" she asked.

"I'm not discussing either one with you tonight while we are both worn out, my lady," he said.

She stood up. "I'm starving. Want something to eat? This is my normal breakfast time. How about western omelets and hot biscuits with sausage gravy?"

The way to a man's heart might be through his stomach and the way to get him to talk is along the same pathway. Before he left she'd know where he was moving and how often she could still see the children.

He set his beer bottle on the table and his feet on the floor. "Lead the way."

She locked up, turned off the lights, and went from the Tonk to her apartment with him right behind her carrying his boots. She pointed toward the sofa. "Remote is somewhere between the cushions. Make yourself comfortable. This won't take long."

He'd been in her apartment before when he was gathering up kids at the end of the day. It had a leather sofa on one wall, an entertainment unit with television and stereo on the opposite side of the room, a rocking chair in the corner, and tables filled with pictures of Sharlene's family. The tiny dining area and small galley kitchen was to Holt's right.

"I'll never get used to seeing this table and chairs!" he exclaimed.

She raised an eyebrow. "Remind you of anything?"

"You're not a bit afraid of color, are you?" The chairs were painted in the same colors as the ones in his house. One each of yellow, purple, hot pink, and turquoise.

She took eggs, sausage, frozen biscuits, and milk from the refrigerator. "I'm not afraid of anything except nightmares. What are you afraid of?"

"Bad choices. I'll help. I can grate the cheese," he said.

She handed him a bag of cheese. "I do a pound at a time so I don't have to wash the grater but one time. That is pepper jack. You got a weak stomach? Why are you afraid of bad choices?"

"Not me. My stomach is lined with steel. I can eat anything but habanero peppers. Those are grown in hell and not fit for human consumption. Because my sister made some bad choices and it might be genetic. My parents were older when they had us kids. Maybe that's because they made bad choices," he said.

"Habaneros are so hot even Lucifer couldn't eat them. Actually, they are grown in the backyard of a church house. They were invented by a preacher who was proving his point about how hot hell really was." She crumbled a fist full of sausage into a small iron skillet and handed him a wooden spoon. "You keep that stirred and I'll whip up the eggs and chop onions and peppers. Your sister's bad choices could have been because she was so young. And you have no idea about your parents' choices in their youth so they might have been as upright as a priest. So stop worrying or being afraid."

"That's easier said than done," he said.

"Sure is."

She bumped into him several times and felt the effects every single time her skin brushed against his arm or her rear end against his side. Without thinking she looked up at his mouth.

"What?" he asked. "I tasted the cheese when you weren't looking. Do I have some on my mouth?"

"I wouldn't care if you did," she said.

He bent forward and brushed a light kiss across her forehead and then one on her lips.

"I was just checking out the merchandise. I didn't ask for a free sample," she teased.

"Wouldn't do you a bit of good to ask or to demand. I'm too tired," he said.

"So a little bartending wore you completely out, did it?"

"You askin' me to take you to bed before or after we have breakfast?"

"Neither. I just want to eat, take a shower to get the smoke off me, and go to sleep. You want to stay? You can sleep with me, as in shut your eyes and snore."

"Can I have a shower first?" he asked.

"It's mandatory if you get between my sheets."

"I'll think about it," he said.

"Wow! You are so romantic tonight."

He chuckled. "Hand me the flour."

"You better not mess that up. I get real testy when my gravy is scorched."

He shook four tablespoons of flour into the sausage and kept stirring. "Right back atcha, darlin'. You get that omelet too dry and I'm an old bear."

The gravy and the omelet turned out perfect and the biscuits fluffed up just right. They helped their plates right off the stove and sat down together at the small kitchen table, him in the turquoise chair, her in the hot pink one.

"Tell me about Holt Jackson," she said.

He laid his fork down. "I was the high school football star at Mineral Wells. I could've gone to high school at Strawn or Gordon but my dad had retired by then and wanted me in the bigger school system. Later, he wished he'd have sent me to Gordon but it had nothing to do with me. If I'd been in Gordon then Callie would have gone there and that would have separated her and Ray and things wouldn't have happened the way they did. Ray's parents moved that summer and I was a senior so I could take Callie with me every day. It was the easy way but not necessarily the good way looking back on it."

"College?" she asked.

"Couple of years but not because I wanted to go. Dad and Mother wanted me to have a degree so I was appeasing them. I'd taken some carpentry classes in high school and loved the work so I concentrated on drafting in college. Got an associate's degree in two years but by then Chad and Kent and I were already working summers on small jobs. We met Bennie on one of those jobs and the four of us formed a loose knit company. Then Mother and Dad died and left me and Callie a little inheritance. Not much, but enough to buy some equipment and we went into business for ourselves."

"What did Callie do with hers?"

"Bought a brand new car. Blew the rest on God knows what and before the year ended it was all gone."

"I hear bitterness," she said.

"You've got that right. I'm raising her kids. Much as I love them, it's not what I had in mind for my life at this age."

She slathered a biscuit with butter and orange marmalade. "What did you have in mind?"

"At almost thirty? Maybe a serious relationship that could go somewhere. A house of my own with some property to raise a few head of cattle on the side. Time to date a beautiful woman when I want instead of just seeing her when I can fit in a few minutes every few weeks or when she shows up on my porch," he said.

She smiled. "Want to buy my house and get the kids the goats they asked Santa to bring them? It's a big lot with a garden spot already in place and room for a goat pen out behind the tool shed. I'll make you a great deal on it if you promise not to paint it some old dull color like white or gray."

He shook his head. "No thanks. I couldn't sign a contract unless it had a codicil that said you'd paint it within thirty days of payment. And you'd have to dig up Waylon and bury him somewhere else. I wouldn't buy something with a cemetery attached to it."

"You are a cold hearted SOB, Holt Jackson." She yawned.

"Let's get these dishes washed up. I get first shower," he said.

"Let's pile these in the sink until morning and I get first shower."

"Thank you for breakfast. You go wash the smoke off and I'll load the dishwasher. You'll be asleep by the time I get done and I'll lock up behind myself," he said.

She looked up at him. "Stay. Please."

They locked gazes across the table. His heart raced. His palms went all sweaty. "You sure?"

She nodded. "The invitation is for sleep only, though."

"I didn't bring my jammies." He smiled.

"Hank left a pair of flannel bottoms when he stayed over with Larissa. Meant to take them back to him but keep forgetting. I'll put them in the bathroom. You can borrow them tonight. And I won't be asleep when you get to bed."

"Okay, but don't wake up in the middle of the morning and attack me in my sleep," he teased.

"I won't if you don't," she sing-songed on her way to the bathroom.

He was on his way down the hall when she came out of the bathroom, a towel around her body and a separate one around her hair.

"Love the outfit," he said.

"I'm so glad. I picked it out of the towel stack just for you," she said.

He kissed her lips hard before she could say anything else. "Goodnight. Sweet dreams."

"Goodnight, Holt."

He took a long time in the shower, letting the hot water beat down on his tired muscles and wash the tiredness and smoke from his body. Sharlene might sleep but he wouldn't. No way could he even nap with her that close. He turned off the water, stepped out of the small shower, dried off, put on the soft flannel pajama bottoms, and padded quietly down the hall.

Sharlene was curled up on her side with her arm thrown up over her head. She was whimpering and muttering with urgency in her voice. He crawled between the sheets and gathered her up in his arms.

"Shhh, it's all right. I'm here. I'll keep the monsters at bay," he whispered.

She stretched out beside him, every part of her body pressed hard against him as if she were trying to melt her skin into his. He kissed her still damp red hair and rubbed her back until all the tension left her muscles. She mumbled something and wrapped her arms around his neck, bringing his mouth down to hers for a long, lingering kiss.

One minute the dream was there, the next it was gone and she was kissing Holt. He deepened the kiss, making love to her lips and mouth with his tongue. She moaned and melted tighter against him. He slipped a hand under her nightshirt and made wide lazy circles on her back with his fingertips. When he moved his hand around to the front to cup a breast, she shifted her position to accommodate him.

"Thought you were tired," she mumbled.

He kissed the soft erotic part of her neck. Shivers danced all the way from her toes to the top of her head.

"My body is tired. My heart and soul have a different opinion," he whispered.

Her arms were wrapped around his neck and her lips were on his but she opened one eye a narrow slit to make sure she wasn't dreaming. They were about to make wild passionate love and she wanted to be fully awake.

She reached down and tugged the drawstring on his pajama bottoms.

He slipped the nightshirt over her head in one fluid movement. "You are so beautiful, Sharlene. So soft that I want to touch all of you at once." He savored every inch of her body as his eyes tried to take her in by the light of the moon filtering through the window.

"Me too." She skimmed his pajamas down over his hips and covered his body with slow, hot kisses. When she stretched back out on top of him he moaned. She nibbled on his earlobe and he wrapped his arms around her slim body.

"Oh no, cowboy, keep your hands laced together up over your head. It's not your turn yet," she whispered as she left his mouth after another hard passionate kiss that created a hurricane of desire in both of them.

He shut his eyes and everything but the touch of her soft skin and kisses disappeared. Nothing existed but the deep desire to please one another. After several minutes, he flipped her over and hung a thumb under her bikini underpants, slowly slipping them down over her hips and legs. They landed on his pajama bottoms when he tossed them out of the way and kissed each toe individually before he started back up.

She writhed but didn't want it to end. She'd had sex before but no one had ever made long-drawn-out love to her body like Holt was doing. "God, that's wonderful."

"Darlin', God doesn't have anything to do with this," he said.

"Then hot damn! That feels so good!" she said when he reached that soft skin right under her breast. She'd known about erotic zones and how a touch or a kiss could set her on fire, but Holt had found places that she never knew could make such intense heat. The inside of her thigh, the soft place under her breast, her wrist right where her pulse pounded, all of those virgin places now belonged to Holt Jackson.

"Yes, ma'am, you sure do feel good," he drawled huskily as he found another spot on her neck that fanned the blazing fire, making it even hotter.

She gave her body, heart, and soul totally over to Holt and let him make all three hum. He strung kisses from her neck, across her cheeks, her eyes, the tip of her nose, and ended with eternally slow kisses on her lips until the only thing running through her mind was a continuous loop of his name and the word *please*.

"Now, Sharlene?" he asked.

"Two hours ago," she said.

He moved on top of her and began a long, easy rhythm that erased every word from her vocabulary. Sex was sex. This was love making taken to new heights.

Like a good country song, the crescendo built to a final drum roll of breathlessness so intense that neither of them could utter a word when the final thrust sent them over the top at the exact same moment. The sweet warm afterglow hung over them when Holt rolled to one side and continued to hold her tightly, his face buried in her hair.

"I wonder if they heard me moaning all the way up to Mingus?" she asked when she could speak again.

"No, but they probably see the embers of the fire still glowing out here and think the Tonk is on fire," he said softly. "I could hold you like this until morning and never let you go."

"Please do. It's only when you hold me that the nightmares disappear."

He wrapped his lean muscular body around hers and they both slept.

One minute she was on a hill looking down at a road where a suicide bomber waited beside an old jeep with a flat tire and the hood up. They'd gotten intel that the enemy would be setting up shop to stop a bus load of new troops coming into the city. She hadn't expected it to be a teenage boy.

They'd gotten the information late in the day and dispatched her and Jonah in a hurry. He took stock of the wind, the distance and made calculations on his notebook. She adjusted as he whispered. They were so far away that the kid couldn't hear them but protocol said they'd be as quiet as possible. He whispered frantically that he could see the bus and it was not more than two city blocks away. She had to take the shot now or they'd be so close that the effects could be disastrous.

She pulled the trigger and he let go of the pressure switch in his hand when he dropped. They barely heard the blast. The bus didn't even stop. No doubt their orders had been that the threat had been eradicated, and to proceed with caution.

But then someone touched her on the shoulder and she knew she'd been discovered. She and her spotter would be captured and tortured for information. She shut her eyes and practiced saying name, rank, and number over and over as she felt the cold metal of the gun barrel against her cheek.

She looked up at the movement above her to find Holt Jackson floating down from the sky with a finger over his lips. The gun barrel flew away from her cheek and the soldier holding it ran away into the brush and sand behind her.

Holt held her and said, "I'll keep the monsters at bay."

And she believed him.

Chapter 17

A SLOW COLD DRIZZLE CAME DOWN OUTSIDE HER window when Sharlene awoke. She looked at the clock and stretched. She couldn't remember the last time she'd slept until three thirty in the afternoon. Twelve hours of sleep without waking with the taste of sand in her mouth and the sound of gunfire in her ears. Without seeing haunting faces of suicide bombers, maimed children in the hospital, soldiers without arms and legs, or Jonah with the life gone from his eyes.

She rolled over to find one pillow propped at her back and a note pinned to the other one. She removed it and sat up, wiping the sleep from her eyes as she did.

She read aloud: "Kids will be home at five. Can't grill the chicken and burgers outside in the rain so I'm going to make lasagna in the oven. It's still a date even if we don't barbecue outside. Expecting you to bring dessert. We eat at six. Signed, Holt."

She laid it on the nightstand beside the clock. "My first love letter and it's so not romantic! But after last night it could be written on Charmin and it would still be wonderful. I slept all night without dreams. Can I have your body every night, Holt Jackson?"

She had two hours to make a dessert. That left out cinnamon rolls from scratch. Not even putting a rush on the dough by putting it into a warm oven to rise could get them ready in two hours. Pecan pie needed an hour to bake and an hour to cool. It wasn't completely out of the question. But then she remembered her mother's old recipe for gooey cake. She hopped out of bed and trotted off to the kitchen to check ingredients.

"One white cake mix. One stick of butter. Four eggs, cream cheese, powdered sugar." She talked as she set them on the cabinet. It only took thirty-five minutes to bake so that would give it plenty of time to cool to the proper temperature before she left.

She picked up an egg to crack against the mixing bowl and the phone rang. She jumped and dropped the egg on the floor. The phone continued to howl and she stepped in the slimy egg when she ran to fetch it from her purse.

"Hello, dammit!" she said.

"That's not a nice way to answer the phone," Molly scolded.

"I dropped an egg and stepped in it. I've got goo on my foot." She walked on her heel to the bathroom where she propped her leg on the vanity and washed the sticky egg from between her toes. She talked with the phone propped on her shoulder and had to pick it up twice when it fell.

"Are you just now making breakfast? Lord, Sharlene, a woman wasn't meant to work all night and sleep all day. I bet you didn't even do that in the army, did you?" Molly bombarded her with questions.

"Good afternoon, Momma. I'm making gooey cake for dessert tonight. I'm having supper at Holt's," she said.

"Well, the kids will love it. You kids always did. I called to check on you and to make sure you're coming home for Thanksgiving next week," Molly said.

"I'm fine and I'll be there Thursday in time for dinner and stay over until Monday. Tessa and Darla are going to run the Tonk for me on Friday and Saturday night so I can have a long weekend with y'all."

"You'll want pumpkin bread?" Molly asked.

Sharlene could hear the smile in Molly's voice. She always made one favorite thing for each of her children on Thanksgiving and Christmas. Molly had shipped pumpkin bread to Iraq both Thanksgiving days that she wasn't home with her family.

"Of course, and pumpkin pie and pumpkin roll and pumpkin pancakes for breakfast the day after," Sharlene laughed.

"Now tell me about this date? I thought he and Dorie were all hot and heavy into phone talking. She was sitting in church with Wayne last Sunday though so maybe she's decided to go for the man with stability. I would have sworn she and Holt would have made a better couple than you and him. No way would he ever marry a bartender and Dorie has that farm that would be wonderful to raise up four kids on," Molly went on and on.

Sharlene's mood got worse with each sentence. "Mother, I've got to make dessert so can I call you back tomorrow and hear more about Dorie?"

"Don't you take that tone with me, young lady. I don't agree with what you are doing one little bit. Just because I didn't pitch a big fit in front of the whole family doesn't mean I'm on your side. I had to keep my temper in check because if I got all fired up then your dad would too, and I'm not losing him with a heart attack because of your unwise decisions." Molly's voice was not smiling anymore.

Sharlene sighed. "Momma, you don't have to be on my side. I wasn't expecting you to like what I do or even support me in it. I was surprised as hell that you took it as well as you did. I don't need your blessing any more than I needed it to join the army. I do need you to be my mother and love me and stop trying to hook me up with every available man in Oklahoma."

"What makes you think I've limited my search to one state? I'm determined that you aren't going to die a lonely old maid. We'll talk more about this next week. I'll have all your pumpkin goodies ready. Just promise me you'll be here," Molly said.

"I wouldn't miss Thanksgiving with all the family for anything," Sharlene assured her.

"Not even that abominable beer joint?"

Sharlene laughed. "Not even the Honky Tonk could keep me away from your pumpkin bread. See you next week on Thursday in plenty of time for dinner."

"And you'll really stay until Monday, no matter what?"

"You've got my word on it," Sharlene said.

"Okay. I'll get your room ready and the bread made. I still don't like you driving all alone that far."

"Momma, it's five hours. I'm not crossing the desert on a motorcycle," she said.

"Promise me you'll be careful and you'll stay until Monday," Molly said.

"I told you I would. Now good-bye. I've got a gooey cake to make." Sharlene flipped the phone shut before Molly could make any more demands.

What did her mother have up her sleeve anyway to make her promise to stay that long? Was Wayne still on the top of the bachelor list down at the Ladies Circle?

Did the women plan some kind of magical voodoo to make the two of them fall in love so Sharlene would move back to Corn?

Well, it wasn't happening. The temperature in hell hadn't dropped that far yet.

———ɯ———

Judd threw open the back door of the multicolored house before Sharlene could knock. "I been watchin' for you forever. Come in and see my book about the ice thing last night. You should've seen it, Sharlene. It was so pretty. I'm going to grow up and skate on ice and Waylon is going to run one of them big old ice machines that sweep all the lines out of the ice. And Uncle Holt is in the kitchen with Chad and Gloria and they're making us some supper and is that a cake? What kind? It's not lemon, is it? I don't like lemon."

Chad poked his head through the archway into the living room. "Okay, magpie, give Sharlene time to bring the dessert in here and then you can show her the book."

Judd crossed her arms over her chest and stuck out her lower lip. "Well ddd... dang!"

"Good girl," Sharlene whispered.

"It ain't easy, not sayin' bad words," Judd said.

Chad took the cake from Sharlene and set it on the cabinet. "I want to introduce you to Gloria."

"Hello," Sharlene said. She was surprised when she finally saw the woman she'd heard so much about. Gloria had thick jet-black hair and a round face. Her Hispanic heritage showed up in slightly toasted skin and big dark brown eyes. She wore jeans that nipped in at a small waist between rounded hips and big breasts.

"This is Gloria Green," Chad said. "And this is Sharlene Waverly."

"I'm glad to finally meet you. I've heard so much about you from the children," Gloria said.

"Likewise," Sharlene said. "They talk so much about you and Chad that I was beginning to get jealous."

Gloria laughed. "Holt told us that he was afraid we were going to have a custody battle with you."

"What's a testofee battle?" Judd asked.

"Cus-to-dy," Sharlene drew the word out by syllables. "It means who gets to keep you and Waylon the most. But we were just joking. Your Uncle Holt has real custody of you and Waylon."

Judd ran to Holt and wrapped her arms around his leg. "I love all of you but Uncle Holt is my daddy. We done signed the 'doption papers yesterday at the courthouse and now he can't even call me Judd Mendoza no more. Now I'm Judd Jackson. But we're not going to tell it at school right now acause it would 'fuse the teacher so we're goin' to wait until we move and then I'll be really Judd Jackson. And guess what, we got a 'prise next week. Daddy is going to take us somewhere special for Thanksgiving."

"Okay, enough," Holt said hoarsely. "Cake looks good. What kind?"

"Gooey cake. My momma makes them. Lots of cream cheese and butter," Sharlene said. "She got the recipe from Dorie's mother years ago."

Holt turned back to the oven. He wanted to go to her and kiss her on the forehead, to show everyone that they'd moved from friendship to relationship but Sharlene looked severely pissed when she handed him the cake.

Sharlene pulled out a chair and sat down at the end of the table. "Why didn't you tell me you were doing the adoption yesterday? We would have had a celebration."

"It was supposed to be next week but they got the papers done early so we ran in and out and got it finished," he said. Was that what had her dander up? That she wasn't asked to go along? In his mind, the whole thing was a formality. Judd and Waylon had been his since the day he took custody of them.

"I see," Sharlene said and turned to Gloria. "So I hear there's a wedding in the works?"

"Last day of December," Gloria said. "You'll get your invitation after Thanksgiving. Judd said that you had to come and see her all dressed up like Cinderella. She wanted to know if she could ride a white horse up to the church."

Judd crawled up in Gloria's lap and another bout of jealousy turned Sharlene bullfrog green. Dorie had been making phone calls behind her back. Holt hadn't even mentioned that he'd talked to her on a regular basis. Now Gloria had stolen Judd.

Waylon meandered into the kitchen from his bedroom and laid a hand on Sharlene's shoulder.

"I'm going to grow up and drive an ice 'chine," he said.

His innocent touch and sweet little voice made Sharlene smile. She patted his hand. "I bet you'd be a good ice 'chine driver."

"I have to wear gloves. It's a cold job but Judd's skates will make lines in the ice and I'll have to fix it for her," he said seriously.

"You don't want to skate with her?" Sharlene asked.

He shook his head and shivered. "Too fast for me."

"You ever been ice skating?" Sharlene asked.

He shook his head again.

Judd jumped off Gloria's lap. "Have you been ice skating, Sharlene?"

"I don't reckon they had ice skating in Corn or Iraq, did they?" Holt asked.

"You were in Iraq?" Gloria asked.

She nodded. "I was there for two tours during my army career. And to answer your question, Holt, no they don't have ice skating at either place. But I happen to know where they do."

"Oh, I forgot about Frisco. Hey, Chad, can we take the kids skating next Sunday?" Gloria said quickly.

"Can't," Holt said.

"Why?"

"Next week is Thanksgiving. We've got plans from Wednesday through Sunday. If you want to take them the next week that's fine. Where is this Frisco place?" Holt pulled the pan of lasagna from the oven and set it on a hot pad to cool.

"At the Frisco mall. They've got a rink on the bottom floor. I went there a few years ago," Gloria said.

"You want to take a chance like that? What if you sprained an ankle or broke something that close to wedding time?" Sharlene asked.

Gloria shuddered. "You got a good point. You take them."

"Take us where?" Judd and Waylon both danced around the kitchen.

"Ice skating. But it'll have to wait until after Christmas, kids. We've got plans for this weekend. The next weekend your grandparents have asked for you on

Sunday afternoon and the one after that too, for their family holiday. They always do it in between the two big holidays so everyone can come home," he explained.

"Ahhh, shucks!" Judd said.

"That's a good girl," Sharlene said. "You didn't say a bad word."

Judd snorted. "But I wanted to."

Holt frowned.

Sharlene shot him a look.

"What'd Holt do?" Gloria asked.

"Long story," Sharlene said.

"Mr. Perfect has a fault. Tell me, please," she begged from behind her hand.

"He's not Mr. Perfect, darlin'," Sharlene said.

Holt tilted his head to one side. "Oh?"

Chad moved his chair over closer to Gloria. "What are you two talking about?"

"Recipes," Sharlene said.

"They were talking about me not being perfect," Holt said. Had he been too blunt in his note? Should he have signed it "love or like" rather than just his name?

"Well, it took a long time but the light finally dawned. Don't weep and have a gnashing of teeth because you found out Holt wasn't perfect. Save that for when you figure out I have a tiny flaw in my character," Chad laughed.

"Oh, really?" Gloria eyed him up and down. "Maybe we'd better put off the wedding date until I figure out where this flaw is. I might not want a man who's got stuff wrong with him."

"What's a flawed?" Judd asked.

"It's something that makes someone or something not perfect," Sharlene explained.

"Waylon, you got a flawed. I think you might have to go to the doctor and get a shot for it," Judd said.

"I do not have a flawed. I don't even have a sore throat and I ain't gettin' no shot," he yelled.

"Are too," Judd said.

"Stop arguing or take it to your room," Holt said.

They marched into their room and shut the door. The argument was muted and the word "flawed" was used repeatedly, but they could hear it. All four of them held a hand over their mouths to keep the laughter down.

"What have you been doing all day besides making a cake?" Holt finally asked when he could talk without chuckling.

She watched his expression closely. "I talked to Momma."

A nervous twitch made his eyebrow dance. "Are they getting geared up for the holiday out on the farm?"

She nodded. "They are. I'll be driving up on Thursday and staying until Monday."

"Turkey, ham, and all the fixings?" Gloria asked.

"Every year. I missed it when I was gone."

"I would too. This will be my first year outside my family circle." She reached across and took Chad's hand. "But we'll be together and that's all that matters."

"You're going to Chad's then?" Sharlene could smell a rat but she couldn't see or find the critter. That didn't mean it wasn't in the room with her.

"In a roundabout way," Gloria said. "Tell me. How in the world did someone as young and pretty as you wind up with a beer joint? Do you like it? And I hear you've got a big romance book that just hit the racks. That is so exciting. I love romance. Keep one in my purse all the time at work."

"I'll take that young and pretty thing as a compliment and yes, it is exciting and yes, I love all of it. The beer joint, the writing. I even love Mingus, Texas. Where do you work?" Sharlene asked.

"At a bank drive-by window. That's where I met Chad. He came by the window one day and I'd never seen a cowboy as handsome as he is." She smiled.

Chad put his hands on Gloria's shoulders and stood behind her. "And I thought I was looking at an angel. Took me three weeks to get up the courage to ask for her number."

"If he hadn't asked I'd made up my mind to march outside and get in the car with him," Gloria said.

"You going to continue to work after you get married?"

"Probably not at the bank. I'm thinking about putting in a day care. I love kids," she said.

"There should be plenty of customers up around Wichita Falls. That where y'all are going after Christmas?" Sharlene asked Gloria but she looked at Holt.

"We still got a few irons in the fire that we're letting heat up but probably not up that direction," Holt said.

"He won't tell us either and I got a best friend at school and she was going to ask her momma if I could come over and play after Christmas time and Uncle Holt, I mean Daddy, said we'd have to wait and see," Judd sighed.

"Secrets," Sharlene said.

"Not a secret. Just don't want to broadcast something that would get two little kids' hopes all up in the air and then have to ruin it all. But I'll tell you one thing, Judd, if it all pans out you will be a very happy little girl," Holt said.

He wished he could tell Sharlene the same thing but she was going to pitch the biggest fit this side of World War II when she found out where he was taking the children.

Chapter 18

SHARLENE LISTENED TO THE RADIO UNTIL SHE LOST her favorite country music station. She turned it off and dug around in an old worn case for a cassette to put into the tape deck. She found a Miranda Lambert tape and pushed it into the slot. Her next VW Bug was going to have a CD player instead of the old cassette system and it was going to be bright yellow.

When the music stopped she didn't put another one in but let her mind drift as she drove north. Where was Holt today? The children had been excited on Tuesday saying that Uncle Holt slash Daddy had a big surprise for them. They were going somewhere special the next day and they weren't coming home until Sunday. The passing idea of them being at Dorie's clinched her stomach up in knots.

She turned the radio back on to push the notion to the back of her mind. She looked at the car's clock. Her mother would be in the church kitchen with an apron on over her Thanksgiving skirt and top. She'd be basting the turkey or checking on the ham, peeling potatoes, and making sweet potato casserole. The sisters would be buzzing around her like bees serving their queen.

The Waverly family had long since outgrown the farmhouse kitchen and the weather was either too cold or too wet most years to eat outside in the backyard. For the past several years they'd been granted the use of the church fellowship hall for their family dinner. The kitchen had two stoves and two refrigerators and plenty of workspace. Sunday school rooms were located up and down the hallway so each of the sisters-in-law set up a play area in each of four rooms. The first one had toys for the young kids, the second puzzles and games for the next step up, the third had board games like Monopoly and Clue for the older kids, and the fourth had a television set and DVD player with a selection of movies for the teenage crew.

"Fellowship hall? That's where the Ladies Circle meets," Sharlene talked to herself. "Hopefully Momma hasn't invited Wayne in hopes that the very ambiance of the room will create vibes between us. If I see him I'm going to grab my pumpkin bread and tear out for Mingus, Texas. One never knows about those women and their magic."

When she was two miles out of town a fine mist began to coat her windshield. Enough that she only needed to use the wipers sporadically but if the temperature dropped it could easily freeze. It was ten minutes until noon so she'd made it in time for grace. Claud always called everyone around for grace at exactly noon. If someone wasn't on time they weren't there to fit into the circle. She liked that part of the celebration and didn't want to be late. She pulled into the parking lot at the church and rushed across the lot toward the doors with her head bent against the freezing rain.

Someone opened the door for her and she dashed inside.

"Thank you," she said.

"I'm glad you're here," Claud said. "I been standing here waiting for you. Your momma has fretted all morning about you driving in bad weather."

She hugged her father tightly. "It didn't get ugly until about five minutes ago. Mostly I drove on dry road. I'm glad I made it before grace. I like the circle."

He kept her close to him a minute longer. "I know, baby girl."

"I'm really not a baby or a girl anymore, Daddy," she giggled.

"You'll always be my baby girl, no matter what happens or how old you get. Don't you forget it, Sharlene," he said.

"Sharlene! You are here! We been waiting and waiting. Why didn't you ride up here with us anyway? We've been playing with a puzzle in one of the game rooms and Waylon is really good at finding the pieces and you've got to come and see it. It's a picture of Bambi." Judd rushed to her side and put both arms around her waist.

"Dad?" Sharlene asked.

"I'll let Holt tell you all about it," Claud said.

Loralou pushed open the door to the women's bathroom and stepped out into the foyer. "Hello, Sharlene. Six months ago if someone had told me I'd be having Thanksgiving dinner with my fiancé today in Corn, Oklahoma, I'd have thought they were drunk or crazy or both."

"Dad?" Sharlene's voice was shrill.

"Got to go help your momma. Holt can explain." Claud hurried into the fellowship hall.

Judd ran away back toward the game rooms and Loralou followed Claud. Sharlene couldn't make her feet move an inch. Surely she was in the middle of another nightmare. She shook her head and blinked a dozen times. Every time she opened them there was no change.

Holt waved as he came down the hallway in long easy strides. "Sharlene!"

"What in the devil is going on? This has always been a family occasion. Is Dorie hiding back in one of those rooms too? How about Merle and Amos?" she asked.

"I knew you'd be angry," he said.

"Damn straight. But I'm not angry. I'm mad as hell."

"Cussin' in the church?" he asked.

"You ain't seen nothing yet. I'm just getting wound up. Want to tell me what's going on here?" she asked.

A loud voice came over the intercom system. "If everyone will join us in the fellowship hall, we will say grace and have our Thanksgiving dinner."

She jumped and looked up.

"It isn't God about to light up your… hind end… for cussin'. It's Claud," Holt teased.

"We'd best go say grace and then you *will* explain exactly what is going on," she said.

"Those who demand get very little," he said.

She glared at him.

Claud's voice rattled the walls. "We're waiting on Holt and Sharlene to join us."

She marched down the hall with Holt on her heels.

The circle was broken with Judd on one side and Waylon on the other. Everyone else held hands and waited. Judd held out her hand to Sharlene who took it and bowed her head. Holt took Waylon's.

Claud cleared his throat and everyone bowed their heads. When he didn't begin the prayer, they looked up. He was staring at Holt and Sharlene. "We can't say grace without an unbroken circle," he said.

Holt reached across the distance and grabbed Sharlene's hand. She just thought she had something to be angry about. Wait until she heard the rest of the story. Then flames would shoot out of her ears and the church roof would rise up a foot off the rafters.

"Father, we are grateful for family and friends today. Thankful for answered prayers, health, and good times we all share. Bless this Thanksgiving meal and be with us in our decisions. Amen."

"Now let's eat," Molly said. "Kids first. Line up."

Sharlene pulled her hand free of Holt's and scanned the room. Dorie and her kids weren't there. That was one blessing. Kent and Loralou were to the left of Judd. Chad and Gloria to Waylon's left.

Judd tugged at her hand. "Sharlene, come and help me. I can't carry my plate once I get everything on it and can I please sit by Tasha? There ain't no baby kittens but we're making a puzzle of a cat and Waylon is helping us find the pieces and we all want to sit together."

Waylon did the same with Holt. "I want some of them baked beans, Uncle Holt. They was so good the last time we came up here and I want some turkey and some of that dressin'. And one of them hot rolls."

Sharlene and Holt were pulled in two directions. She shot a look his way. He was ready for it. He'd made his decision last night with Chad and Kent. It was an opportunity they couldn't pass up, not with Bennie wanting to form his own business.

Molly went to Sharlene and Judd and wrapped her arms around her daughter. "Hey, girl, you didn't even make it in time to give your momma a big hug."

"You want to tell me why Holt and his crew are here?" Sharlene whispered.

"He'll tell you after we all have a nice dinner together. I really like Gloria and Loralou. They helped me all afternoon yesterday and were up at the crack of dawn to help today," she said.

Sharlene filled Judd's plate and helped settle her on Tasha's left at the same time Holt was seating Waylon on Tasha's right. He raised an eyebrow at her and tilted his head toward the door.

"Not on your life, cowboy. I've been looking forward to this meal for a solid week and I'm going to eat before we talk about anything. I've got a feeling what you are about to tell me is going to sour my appetite," she said.

He nodded. "Have you seen Loralou's engagement ring?"

"No! Did Kent propose?"

Holt nodded."Yesterday on the way up here. Get Loralou to tell you about it. Not so romantic but an excellent story that you might want to use in one of your books," he said.

She went back to the table and heaped her plate up with traditional Thanksgiving food and carried it to a table where Kent and Loralou were sitting with Chad and Gloria. She'd barely sat down when Holt pulled out a chair next to her. His thigh touched hers when he settled in and her mind went to something a lot more exciting than turkey and dressing.

"So I hear there's a story about the engagement. Congratulations. Now do you believe in the Honky Tonk charm?" Sharlene asked Kent.

Kent shook his head. "No, but I do believe in fate bringing us together there. I was going to stop at a fancy steak house on the way up here yesterday but Loralou had to find a bathroom so pulled in at a McDonald's. I barely got the trailer parked…"

Sharlene butted in, "You brought your trailer? I didn't notice it missing this morning."

"Been gone since yesterday morning. You were probably asleep when I pulled out. Chad's is gone too. But there were a couple of big old semis pulled in the first two lots so you couldn't have seen past them anyway," Kent said.

"Okay, on with the story." Sharlene ignored Holt as much as possible but his aftershave wafted over to her nose every time anyone breezed behind him going toward the food table.

"So here we are at the McDonald's restaurant and she's hurried into the bathroom. I figured I'd best make use of the place too since I was nervous as hell and that always makes my bladder seize up," Kent said.

"You are so romantic," Sharlene said.

"Stop interrupting," Fiona said from down the table. "I haven't heard this story yet either."

Sharlene leaned forward and looked past several people at her sister-in-law. "But I bet you knew they were coming, didn't you?"

"That part is between you and Holt. I just want to hear the story."

"Okay, then I won't talk anymore. Tell the story." Sharlene filled her mouth with turkey. She would gladly trade the whole meal for one breathless kiss from Holt. What she'd give for another night of hot sex couldn't be measured in turkey and pumpkin pies.

Kent kissed Loralou on the cheek. "Go on, honey."

Loralou grinned. "I came out of the bathroom at the same time he did. He asked if I wanted something to drink and I said a cup of coffee would be nice. I had no idea he was going to propose or that he'd planned to take me to a steak house. So when we got to the front, I said I was hungry and we might as well grab a sandwich right there."

Kent took up the tale. "Foiled my plan. We ordered Big Mac Meal Deals and chocolate shakes. I couldn't very well tell her that I planned this big romantic thing with wine and white linen napkins and the whole nine yards."

Loralou patted his hand. "I love it even more than that. He reached in his pocket for money to pay for our meal and this red velvet box fell out on the floor. He just stood there and stared at it with this bewildered look on his face. The whole store kind of spun around because I just knew it was a ring and I was so nervous I forgot to breathe. I didn't know whether to reach for it or wait for him to shove it back in his pocket."

Kent slung an arm around the back of her chair. "Cat was out of the bag. Dinner was ordered and the cashier was waiting on payment. So I just dropped down on one knee, opened the box, and said, 'Loralou, I love you with my whole heart. Will you marry me?' and she said 'yes.' I put the ring on her finger and everyone in the place clapped like they were family and friends."

"Isn't that just the sweetest thing you've ever heard?" Loralou asked.

"It really is." Fiona smiled.

Sharlene said, "I'm wondering how to work it into a book."

"What kind of proposal do you want, Sharlene?" Gloria asked from across the table. "You want the violins and the fancy restaurant, or something more original like Loralou got?"

"Right now I'm too busy to think about that kind of thing. When are you two getting married?"

"We've decided to do a double with Gloria and Chad. Their invitations haven't been ordered and they came up with the idea. It'll work better that way and we'll always have each other to keep us reminded of our anniversary," Kent answered.

"In Wichita Falls?" Sharlene asked.

"Well, that's what we need to talk to you about. We'd like to have it at the Honky Tonk. It's midway between the girls' families and we could plan an afternoon wedding so it wouldn't interfere with the Honky Tonk New Year's Eve thing. I hear there's been other weddings there. We'll do the work and the cleanup and be out before eight," Kent said.

"That's fine with me," Sharlene said.

"We can have an open bar and that big old dance floor and two different jukeboxes," Loralou told Gloria. They put their heads together and began to plan colors, cakes, and caterers.

"Don't tell me you're going on the honeymoon together too. That's going above and beyond brotherly love," Sharlene said.

"Actually we kind of are. We'll have a week together and then work will begin but…" Gloria stopped.

Sharlene looked at Holt who was finishing his last bite of ham.

"You finished?" she asked.

He nodded.

"Let's go get it over with so these people can finish a sentence without looking at you," she said.

"Take it to the sanctuary," Fiona said. "I'll keep a watch on the children and make sure they get dessert. And remember, Sharlene, God is watching you. No cussin' or hanky panky."

Sharlene stuck out her tongue at Fiona and led the way to the hallway. When Holt caught up to her he grabbed her hand and walked beside her. She didn't say a word until she was sitting in the front pew in front of the pulpit with him beside her.

"Okay, spit it out. I've never known my folks to invite anyone but family to Thanksgiving dinner. Not that I don't want to share the day with you and the kids but you should have told me she'd asked you. It wasn't fair to walk into that kind of shock. There's something brewing and I'm not even sure I want to know why the whole crew would be up here. I can't even put my fears into words, Holt, and that's why I'm so angry. Not because you and the kids are here but because I'm scared of what you are about to say."

Holt threw his right arm around Sharlene, tilted her chin up with his left fist, and planted a hard kiss on her right there in God's presence in the front pew. "I've wanted to do that ever since I saw you in the foyer. You are beautiful today. I've never seen you in a flowing skirt like that. You look like something meant to sit on a shelf and look at all day long."

"Holt?" she mumbled into his chest.

He eased his hold. "Bennie wants to form his own company based out of Palo Pinto after we finish Elmer's barn. He's got a couple of brothers-in-law who want to go in the business with him. They're willing to buy enough equipment to get started. And Kent, Chad, and I will have our company. The equipment belongs to me so we'll take that with us. We're moving to Corn."

She shook her head. Now that the words were out, they were even more ominous than they'd been in her mind all during the meal.

"Are you going to say anything?" he asked.

"Did you really say you all were moving to Corn?" she whispered.

"I did," he murmured into her hair.

She pushed back and jumped to her feet. "Why in the hell would anyone move to Corn, Oklahoma? That's the stupidest thing I ever heard. It's a dried up farm community. What in the hell is going to support you up here?" Her voice got shriller with each word.

"We are buying four houses inside the city limits. They need lots of work and they are lined up like row houses, all four just alike. Little two-bedroom places like the Bahamas house me and the kids have been living in. We are going to live in them while we remodel and within a year or two we'll flip them and build something better. Claud has lined up two years of work right here in the community. Barns, decks, houses, garages. Most of it inside the family but word of mouth will travel fast," he said.

"Four houses?" She frowned.

"One for each of our families and the extra one for Gloria and Loralou to start their day care in. Jenny and Molly have checked around and there's enough women working in town that need child care to support it. Ten kids will give them a salary and pay the overhead."

The church walls closed in on Sharlene. Holt wouldn't be in Mingus or even near there to chase away the nightmares, to hold her, to let their relationship grow into something more. The children would be five hours away. Dorie wouldn't be half an hour from Holt. Things couldn't get any worse.

"I can see that you've thought this out pretty well," she whispered.

"I love it up here. The kids do too. They fit in well with your family and they need that. Everyone is happy about the move. Gloria and Loralou are ecstatic. Gloria mentioned a day care and Loralou asked if she could work for her almost before the words were out of her mouth. They both love kids. Kent and Chad say it's just the right distance from their mother. She's not too happy about them getting married so quickly. Especially Kent who hasn't even taken Loralou home to meet her yet."

"But Corn?" Sharlene frowned. It had to be a nightmare. No one moved to Corn, Oklahoma, because they wanted to. "Isn't there a small town in Texas where you'd be as happy?"

"If there is I haven't found it. I fell in love with this place when you brought me up here. I wouldn't make a decision until Kent and Chad saw it. Claud and I've been talking every few days on the phone since I went back. But yesterday when we looked at the town and the possibilities, we all came to the same conclusion. We had found home."

"Well, I'm damn glad you found home. I found mine in Mingus, Texas, at the Honky Tonk. Now what do we do?" she asked.

"I guess we go on with life," he said. "You can see the kids on holidays when you come home. I suppose I could bring them down to you for a week in the summer."

"We sound like two married people about to split the blanket," she said.

"They'll miss you. If we were moving anywhere else Judd couldn't take leaving you. It's only because she'll have your family that will make it less traumatic."

"Promise I can have them a whole week in the summer? I'll move into the house and get a sitter for when I have to be at the Honky Tonk," she said.

"You don't have to do that. They can stay in the apartment and you'll only be a few feet away," he said.

Tears began to roll down her cheeks and drop onto her lace blouse. "Nothing works out the way it's supposed to."

He put his arms around her. "Sharlene, move back here. I'll build you a damn beer joint and you can run it every night and write your books in the day just like you are doing in Mingus."

"I can't. I couldn't do that to Momma and Daddy. It's hard on them already but I'm not up in their face. I can't do it, Holt. I won't. Besides, it's not any old beer joint that I love. It's the Honky Tonk. The people that come and go. Merle. Amos. Tessa. Luther. Darla. All of them."

Chapter 19

CLAUD LOCKED THE DOORS TO THE CHURCH AND THE parking lot cleared out. Food had been divided to take to individual homes for leftover suppers. Sharlene had expected two vehicles to go to the farm that night. Her pink Bug and her father's ten-year-old pickup truck. But there were five headed that way and she had no idea how in the world she was going to get through the next three days. Now she understood why her mother had been so adamant about making her promise that she wouldn't go home a day early.

She'd bluffed her way through the afternoon but her heart hadn't been in it. Most of the time there was this big gaping hole where her heart had been up until the moment that Holt told her he was moving to Corn. The only place in the whole world where she'd vowed she'd never live again.

She parked her car behind her dad's truck and helped carry leftover food inside the house. The kids bounded out of Holt's truck and ran toward the porch in the drizzling rain with Holt right behind them. Two travel trailers were in the backyard with long extension cords snaking out across the yard to the house. Kent and Loralou parked their truck beside one and disappeared inside. Chad and Gloria did the same in the other one.

Sharlene wished she had a trailer to hide out in for the next three days. Maybe she should go to the barn and sleep in the tack room. There was an old electric heater out there for when her dad puttered around with the tack during the winter. And when they'd installed a new bathroom in the house, he'd recycled the old toilet and sink to install in a half bath in one corner. She could live quite well if the children would tote out a plate of leftovers a couple of times a day. In three days she could probably have every piece of leather on the ranch cleaned up and ready for spring.

"What are you thinking about?" Molly held the door for Sharlene.

"The tack room," she said honestly.

"Why on earth would you be thinking about that? Sometimes I don't know how your mind works," Molly said.

"I'm going to change into sweats. Where's Daddy and Holt?"

"They went right out the back door and to the barn to do the chores. I think Kent and Chad are going with them too. And the girls are coming in here soon as they change. Did you and Holt talk?"

"We did."

"And?"

"I get the kids a week in the summer and I can see them when I come home," she said.

"What about you two?"

"What about us?"

"I thought you were getting on past friendship into something more. The way he looked at you all day, I would've sworn y'all were meant for each other," Molly said.

"Don't look like it with him in Corn and me in Mingus."

Gloria and Loralou giggled through the back door before Molly could ask another question.

Gloria brushed water drops from her black hair. "The weather sure isn't cooperating for a wedding."

"Neither one of us runs very gracefully. I'm glad Kent and Chad were gone off to do chores and didn't see us," Loralou said.

"Wedding? I don't think it'll rain all the way to the last day of the year. That's four weeks away. And if it did freeze this early in the year, it would thaw long before that," Sharlene said.

Molly sighed. "I'm going to get into my caftan and then I'll explain about the wedding. Make a fresh pitcher of iced tea and one of lemonade. Go ahead and get a platter of cold cuts ready and put out some paper plates. I'll be right back."

"Where did the kids go?" Sharlene asked.

"They're holed up in their room with a puzzle. I let them bring home one from church. I'll take it back Sunday. Oh, by the way, you are teaching their class on Sunday. Miss Mable is off to visit her daughter in Kansas so you are filling in," Molly said.

Sharlene smiled. "Only in Corn can a bartender come home and teach Sunday school!"

"Better enjoy it. When it gets out about that book, Miss Mable won't ever leave town again for fear you'll put the wrong ideas into her precious little class," Molly said on her way down the hallway.

Sharlene laughed out loud at that remark. "You got that right, Momma."

"I'll do the cold cut tray if you'll make the lemonade. I always get too much sugar in it," Gloria said.

"So are you moving up here with us?" Loralou asked bluntly.

Sharlene almost dropped the glass pitcher. "No, I am not! Just thinking about coming back to Corn gives me hives and ulcers."

"If you change your mind, we could use a third partner for our day care," Loralou said.

"Thank you but if I ever did come back here, I would write books. I love kids but not on a twenty-four-seven basis."

"Not even Judd and Waylon?" Gloria asked.

"They are like my own. I could keep them forever. But it's a moot point. I'm not coming back."

Molly flowed into the room in a floor length caftan with big multicolored flowers printed on a bright pink silk background. "I hope you brought something decent to wear to a wedding. We're all attending one tomorrow at the church. If you didn't you can borrow something from Jenny or else wear what you've got on now. Family won't care if you wear it two days in a row and the rest of the congregation didn't see you."

Sharlene cut lemons in half and began to squeeze them into the pitcher. "Who's getting married?"

"Dorie," Molly said.

Sharlene's heart dropped through the floorboards, down a thousand miles of hard packed earth, and straight into hell. So that's the reason the rest of the crew was there. Holt had invited them to his wedding.

He was kissing me in the church and asking me to move up here. Why is he marrying Dorie?

She heard her mother say Dorie and looked in that direction but the whole room was spinning out of control.

She dropped the lemon on the floor and grabbed a chair. Nothing made a bit of sense. Holt wasn't the kind of man to make love to her, then go home and call Dorie.

"Are you okay?" Loralou asked.

A wet cloth appeared in Molly's hand as if it were magic. It felt cool on her forehead but the tears were steaming hot that ran down her face. If she'd had to speak or die she would have had to crawl up in a casket and cross her arms over her chest.

"Sharlene, what in the hell is the matter with you?" Molly was saying when she came to herself. "You didn't expect Dorie to stay single forever, did you? Or is it that you had a crush on Wayne?"

"Wayne?" Sharlene whispered around the baseball-sized lump in her throat.

"He is the groom," Molly said.

"She's marrying Wayne?" Sharlene asked.

"I told you that they were seeing each other. I know I did," Molly said.

Sharlene's tears dried up and the giggles began. "No you didn't!"

"Well, I meant to but every time we talk we get into a row about something. I swear that Irish blood in you is a blister," Molly said.

"When did all this come about?"

"Last week. They've been seeing each other since Labor Day weekend. After you and Holt left they kind of hit it off and one thing led to another. He proposed last week and she said there wasn't any need for a long engagement. Their land joins each other on her north side and his south side so they'll combine two sections of land and Wayne will farm it all. He gave her a diamond half the size of an ice rink and the kids love him and she said she could get a wedding ready in a week." Molly worked around in the kitchen getting things ready for supper.

Sharlene got the hiccups. "Then why did you tell me all that shit about Holt and her talking on the phone?"

Molly shook a wooden spoon at her. "Watch your language. I wanted to make you jealous. Did it work?"

Sharlene nodded. "I'm not moving to Corn."

"I'm not asking you to move back here. But I am telling you straight up that Holt is a fine looking man and Dorie isn't the only available woman in the area. It's your call, honey. Just don't be whining to me or fainting in my kitchen when I have to tell you that it's Holt getting married next. We intend to put him on the top of our list at the Circle. If he's not married by summer it won't be because us women folks haven't set our minds to find him a good decent wife."

Sharlene went back to work making lemonade. It was her call and she would not give up her life and return to central Oklahoma. Simple as that. She'd cross the bridge with Holt's name engraved on the sign at the edge of it when she had to. That day she just had to get past the idea of him not being in Mingus past Christmas.

"Honky Tonk Christmas just lost its shine," she mumbled.

"What'd you say?" Loralou asked.

"Nothing. I was thinking out loud," Sharlene answered.

―――∽∽∽―――

As luck would have it, Sharlene was seated so close to Holt that every square inch of her skin on her right side was shoved up against him. Waylon sat between Claud and Holt. Judd was on Sharlene's right, sitting in the outside corner of the pew.

Sharlene wore a long emerald green dress that she'd brought for church on Sunday. The children's class probably wouldn't mind that she'd worn it to the wedding on Friday evening. It was an ankle length sheath with gold buttons down the side. Her boots were the same color and she'd put some mousse in her hair to tame the curls.

"Did I tell you today that you are very beautiful?" Holt whispered.

"Three times." She shivered when his breath kissed her neck as passionately as if it had been his lips.

"Make it four. You look like a model out of one of those fancy women's magazines."

"Flattery will get you a trip to the hay barn for more than kisses." She smiled.

"Will flattery move you back here?"

"Angels walking a tight rope with harps and singing my favorite song couldn't get that done, darlin'," she said.

The music started and the groom took his place in the front of the church. Then the pianist struck a chord and everyone stood. Dorie's children, one on each side, led her down the aisle. She flowed toward Wayne with a smile on her face. Her gown was a cream colored creation with lace, beads, bows, and glittering sequins. She could have put Dolly Parton to shame with a good four inches of cleavage at the top of the sweetheart neckline.

"Dearly beloved, we are gathered today to create this family by joining Dorie and Wayne together in holy matrimony. Please bow with me while we go to the Lord and ask his blessing on this union," the preacher said.

Holt reached for Sharlene's hand and squeezed.

"What?" Sharlene mouthed as the preacher prayed for the family to be united in love and unity.

"Nothing." He grinned.

"The answer will always be no."

"I didn't ask and I won't again."

"Good."

"Amen!" the preacher said loudly. "You may be seated."

Sharlene fidgeted worse than Judd. It was the longest wedding she'd ever attended. If a gimmick had ever been used, Dorie had incorporated it in her ceremony. They sifted four small shot glasses of sand into one pile, showing that the four of them would be a complete family.

Sharlene stared at the shot glasses and wished she had one filled to the brim with Jack Daniels. Maybe all four of them, lined up in a neat row and she'd toss them back one at a time then fill them up again for another round. Hell, why dirty up the shot glasses. She'd just drink it straight from the bottle.

The two mothers went forward and lit two candles beside the unity candle. Wayne's momma had a trouble getting her candle to light from the long match with white satin streamers attached to it. Did that mean that she wasn't going to like Dorie and the two kids she got with a marriage license rather than a birth certificate? She was a sour looking old girl with a little gray bun knotted up on the top of her head and a navy blue dress that looked like it belonged at a funeral rather than a wedding.

After that Dorie and Wayne used those two candles to light their single candle. It was a carved creation with wedding bells and doves all around the edges and sat on a silver tray with pink roses and baby's breath circling it. Wayne picked up his mother's candle and Dorie got a hold on her mother's. They united the flame into one as their candle took on life and blazed.

The candle's flame made Sharlene think of how hot she and Holt could get just touching each other. Did Wayne and Dorie have that kind of chemistry or were they marrying to join two farms together? She wondered if Dorie's honeymoon would be as well planned and drawn out as the wedding ceremony. If so, it might take a whole week just to consummate the damn thing.

"And now the couple have written vows they want to say to each other in front of God and this cloud of witnesses," the preacher was saying when Sharlene shook the idea of the honeymoon out of her head.

Vows! That was another reason she didn't intend to get married. What would she say to a man in front of God and a cloud of witnesses?

Let's see. I knew you were the one when I curled up in your arms drunk as a skunk and didn't dream about being a sniper in Iraq. I realized I couldn't live without you when you made wild love to me in my apartment. I cried when you and the children moved and I can't live without you. Bull shit! I can live without anyone and I'll get over the nightmares someday.

"And now, Dorie, it's your turn to tell Wayne your heart's deepest thoughts," the preacher smiled.

Crap! I missed Wayne telling her that she was the light of his life.

"Wayne, darling, I knew last summer at the Waverly's Labor Day party that you were the man for me. I looked across the tables and when you looked at me, I knew that our hearts had united and it was just a matter of time before they would become one," Dorie said in a soft southern voice.

Oh, please! You were chasing Holt and in heat worse than a momma cat in the springtime. If he believes that crock of crap, he deserves a honeymoon where he don't get to dive into those big old boobs until he's toasted you a dozen times with pink champagne and told you how beautiful you were at the wedding for twenty-four straight hours. By the time he gets to take off your bra he'll be so tired he'll fall asleep before you get to the good stuff.

"And now the rings," the preacher said. "These two rings symbolize an unending love that Wayne and Dorie are pledging this day."

Judd snored. Sharlene wrapped her arm around her and cradled her to her side.

If the ceremony lasted much longer, Sharlene was going to flop over on Holt's shoulder and join Judd in a snoring duet. If she ever did get married, she intended to go to the courthouse like Chigger and Larissa had done. Walk in. Get the license. Say "I do" in front of a judge. Walk out and go make wild passionate love at the nearest motel until neither she nor her groom could stand up straight.

Holt covered a yawn with the back of his hand.

"Boring!" she whispered.

"Amen!" he whispered back.

"The bride and groom have exchanged vows and given their pledge to love all the way through eternity. Let us pray," the preacher said.

Why didn't he say until death parted them? Is it because her first husband is gone and that might be disrespectful or did she find that in a bridal book? If Wayne dies in a hunting accident or gets smothered to death in those boobs, angels on wild horses couldn't drag me to another of Dorie's weddings.

The preacher cleared his throat at the end of the prayer and then said, "Amen. By the authority vested in me by God and the state of Oklahoma, I now pronounce you man and wife. Wayne, you may kiss your bride."

"After all that he might need a refresher course in how to kiss," Sharlene whispered to Holt.

He grinned and squeezed her knee.

After a quick peck that barely qualified as a kiss the bride and groom pranced down the aisle with the children behind them and went into the preacher's office next to the sanctuary.

"The newlyweds would like me to extend an invitation on their behalf to everyone here to join them in the fellowship hall for a reception. You are free to go there now and the bride and groom will join you in a few minutes following a few pictures taken right here in the sanctuary. Thank you for attending. Friends and family will be the bond that holds this new family together. I ask that you not forget to remember them in your prayers."

"More like two sections of land will hold them together. Wonder if they had a pre-nup?" Sharlene mumbled.

"What are you muttering about?" Holt asked.

"Nothing that matters."

The fellowship hall looked like a high school prom. Crepe paper streamers twirled together in pink, silver, and white. A fountain took up the center of the floor with water spewing from two doves' mouths. The groom's table had a three-tiered chocolate cake covered with dipped strawberries. Two long tables were laden with every finger food imaginable. But the bride's table was truly something to behold. The cake sat on a mirror that was at least four feet across. Life-size sugar roses covered the six-layer cake and were scattered on the mirror. Two silver punch bowls flanked the sides.

Loralou and Gloria were standing with their backs to the wall, their eyes wide as they took in the whole scene. Sharlene left Judd in Jenny's care and joined them.

"Please tell me that you aren't going to do something like this," she said from the side of her mouth.

"Not us. We're having a two o'clock double wedding. We've already got it all figured out. No need for finger foods since everyone will have lunch before and go on home before supper. We are having one three-tiered cake for the bride's table. Since there's two couples we decided to use fresh daisies on the top instead of the bride and groom thing and a full chocolate sheet cake for the groom's table with chocolate covered strawberries on top," Loralou said.

"Add some mints, nuts, and Sharlene's punch Holt told us about and the jukebox to provide music for a little dancing and that's the extent of the reception," Gloria said.

"Decorations?" Sharlene asked.

"An arch with greenery, daisies, and ribbons woven through it for us to stand in front of for a few pictures. Hell, Sharlene, I want to be married, not put on a dramatic production that could win a spot on that redneck marriage television program," Gloria said.

"Good. I don't think I could sit through another three act play in such a short time." Sharlene smiled.

"Here they come," Gloria said.

Dorie had fastened her train up in the back. Wayne held her hand possessively as if daring anyone to try to take her from him. They went straight to the cake, cut it, and fed each other small bites for the pictures. They locked arms and drank punch from crystal glasses with their names engraved on the sides.

Well, those two gestures should glue the marriage together until... what was it? Oh, yeah, through eternity. I'm not sure it would last that long if their names hadn't been written on the glasses and if one of those pink sugar roses had a broken thorn. God, I'm getting cynical.

"What are you thinking about? You've got a wicked grin," Holt said.

"Pomp and circumstance," she said.

"I feel like I should have bought you a corsage and should ask you to dance," he said.

"Well, praise the lord. I thought I was the only one who saw a senior prom."

Molly joined them. "Aren't you going to get in line for cake? Dorie told me that cake cost her as much as she made on the lease last year for the farm. Something that expensive has to taste good."

Sharlene shuddered. "You are kidding me, aren't you? A person doesn't spend that much on a cake that will be destroyed in half an hour. And what in the world is she going to do with all the leftovers? There's enough cake and food here to feed half the troops in Iraq."

"Who knows. They are leaving the kids with her mother and going away for a cruise so I don't know where all the leftovers will go," Molly said.

"Which house are they going to live in?" Sharlene asked.

"His for now but he's building her one of those new fancy things. They'll leave the old house and offer it to the couple he intends to hire. The man will serve as foreman and his wife as cook, baby-sitter, and housekeeper for Dorie. No one knew just how rich Wayne is until now," Molly said.

"I bet Dorie did," Sharlene said.

"If I may have your attention, the bride and groom and their parents are now forming a receiving line. Please go through and give them your blessing and then help yourself to the food tables as well as cake and punch," the preacher announced.

When Sharlene's turn came to hug the bride, Dorie pulled her close to her side and whispered, "You should've paid more attention. I won. You lost. You can have your cowboy carpenter and his kids. I've got Wayne and he adores me."

"I hope you are always as happy as you are today." Sharlene headed to the punch table to get a drink of something to get the taste of a lie from her mouth.

Molly was right behind her. "Holt and your dad have gone on home with the kids. They've had about all of this they could stand and the kids were beginning to fidget. Holt is going to get them bathed and feed them more leftovers. That Waylon does love baked beans and turkey."

"They could have eaten here," Sharlene said.

"They'd rather have leftovers and play with puzzles in their pajamas," Molly told her.

"Me too. Can I go now?"

"In thirty minutes. That way she won't think she's got one over on you," Molly said softly.

"Momma!"

"What she said was rude and I was proud of you for not letting her get under your skin." Molly patted her on the shoulder.

"I'll be damned if I let her know it but I'm mad enough to spit tacks."

"That's my girl. I knew you got some of my genes."

Chapter 20

AT BIRTH, BABIES DO NOT GET A SIGNED DOCUMENT from the hospital saying that life is going to always be totally fair. If they did Sharlene wouldn't be staring out the window at two travel trailers parked in the backyard. Kent and Loralou could talk about their day and all those in the future. Chad and Gloria could do the same. It just plain wasn't fair that she was in one room and Holt in another.

While she was wallowing in the pity pool she realized how much she'd come to value their friendship. When they'd had sex it set the world off its axis several degrees and when they argued it was with passion. When she was in his arms the nightmares disappeared and all that was very good. But she would miss the friendship as much as the passion when he left Mingus.

She watched the clock as she waited for him every weekday to arrive at the beer joint to get the kids. While they gathered up their things she'd ask how his job was coming along and he'd tell her what they accomplished that day. He'd ask about her writing and she'd fill him in on the plot development. That fifteen minutes after his workday ended was the highlight of her day and she didn't realize it until right then.

"It was like the building of the addition. We started out with a foundation. Him taking care of me when I was piss drunk. Then the walls. Him sharing the kids with me. Then the roof. Coming to Corn with me for a weekend. Then the finish work. One day building on the next and now I'm in love with the man and there's nothing I can do about it," she said.

A gentle rap on her door brought her up out of the bed. She opened it to find Holt leaned up against the jamb. He wore flannel bottoms and a white T-shirt, his hair was all mussed, and he had enough scruff on his face to prove that he hadn't shaved since the morning before.

"Can we go to the kitchen and talk?" he asked.

She looked as good with her red curls all frizzled and no makeup as she had all dressed up for the wedding. From the time he carried her piss drunk into the motel until now, he couldn't think of a single time that she hadn't been beautiful to him.

She nodded and stepped around him and headed that way. "I could use a cup of hot chocolate. Want one?"

"I'd rather have a glass of tea," he whispered.

She turned on the light above the stove and heated milk in a pan for hot chocolate. He filled a glass with ice and poured sweet tea over it.

"What do you want to talk about?" She poured a package of hot chocolate mix into the milk and stirred.

He sat down at the small kitchen table in the semi-dark. "I missed talking to you. We haven't really hashed out this move and I didn't tell you that we are going to have the last of the barn done next week and Elmer and Betty really are having a barn dance. It's for kids and adults too so we want you to go with us. They're planning it for Sunday night before you leave on Wednesday to see all your friends and sign books. By the time you get back from that we'll be moved up here. That's going to be tough on the kids," he said.

She pulled out a chair on the opposite side and sat down. "And you?"

"Sharlene, my heart tells me it's the right thing. Everything is working to that end so smoothly," he said.

"Except?" she asked miserably.

"Us."

"I'm not sure there ever could be an us. We are fantastic in bed. You make the nightmares disappear when you hold me. But…"

"Does there always have to be a but?" he asked.

Her smile was bittersweet. "Most of the time. In this case the but is what I do and have been."

"Hell, I don't care what you have been, Sharlene. You deserve a medal for what you did for this country. That doesn't bother me a bit. I do not have a problem with that," he said.

"Go on to the next but then. My beer joint?"

"Used to, but not anymore. It's the location of the beer joint. I'm going to live in Corn. I'll build you one right next to the post office in Corn if you want one," he said.

She swallowed quickly to keep from spewing hot liquid all over the table. "Holt, look around Corn. It's Mennonite country. Religious as the angels in heaven. A beer joint would go bankrupt the first month."

"You can't tell me everyone in this county is a teetotaler," Holt said.

"No, but they don't frequent beer joints enough to keep them in business. If they do it's not in their own backyard. They might go partying over in Weatherford or in Oklahoma City, but not right here in Corn. And what happens if I move up here and we decide we can't stand each other?"

"Then at least we'd know," he said.

"Did my parents put you up to this? Did they make a bunch of calls and offer you the moon to move to Corn?" The light was beginning to dawn and it was so bright that it threatened to blind her.

"No, they did not. When we got home last September the kids kept talking about the farm and how much fun they had. Judd asked me if your parents could be her real grandmother and grandfather. I was the one who made the first call and asked Claud if he and your family was serious about needing a year's worth of work done up here."

The light dimmed. "And Dorie's calls?"

"She got my business number from the Internet and called me twice."

"Twice?"

"First time to flirt. Second to tell me she was going on a date with Wayne and basically to make sure there wasn't a chance for the two of us," he said. "I guess when she figured out the difference in our bank accounts the flirting changed horses in the middle of the stream."

"I see. So the job out at Elmer's is about done?" Sharlene heard the pain in her own voice.

"Next few days it will be. Putting up a barn doesn't take as long as adding a room onto Merle's house or an addition to the Honky Tonk. Oh, by the way, Betty said she'd pick up the kids at school on Monday so you don't have to hurry home. We'll be heading back that way right after lunch tomorrow so we can get the laundry caught up. I think Kent and Loralou are staying until lunch but Chad and Gloria are pulling out at dawn. She promised her family they'd be there for an engagement dinner tomorrow at noon."

"I'll be home in time to get the kids at school. I don't want to miss a single day with them," she said.

"If you change your mind, just call Betty. I've missed you these last couple of days. We've been living under the same roof and actually see each other more but we haven't had any time alone." He reached across the table and laid his hands over hers.

"Me too. Guess we'd better get used to it, hadn't we?" She didn't want him to ever take his hands away, to always be there to keep the monsters at bay, to hold her while she went to sleep. But she could not leave Mingus or the Honky Tonk.

He nodded and stood up. He led her down the hall and stopped in front of her bedroom door and brushed a soft kiss across her lips. "Good night, Sharlene."

"Good night." She gently closed the door and fell back on the bed. Even a peck on the lips was enough to create a topsy-turvy swirl that flashed bright colors and made her heart thump.

It would be better when she was home in the Honky Tonk in her old routine. Even though it would tear her heart out by the roots she would be better when they were gone and it was all finished. It would heal eventually and life would go on.

"No, it won't!" Her face crumpled and the dam broke. Tears flowed like a river down sides of her face and into her ears. She swiped at them with the back of her hand and buried her face in a pillow so no one could hear her sobs.

She slept poorly with even more vivid nightmares waking her more than once in drenching sweat and an aching chest. Finally at five o'clock she took a shower, dressed in fresh pajamas, and padded to the kitchen.

"Well, good morning, sunshine," Claud said from the stove. "Coffee just quit perking. You must've smelled it."

"You made real coffee." She smiled.

"Sunday morning coffee. Made on the stove until it's just the right color. Not any of that drip through the pot one time stuff," he said.

From way back when she was a little girl in one-piece pajamas that zipped up the front she could remember going to the kitchen on Sunday morning to find her dad making coffee in an old glass percolator on the kitchen stove. He'd pour her a cup full in a tiny little espresso cup that had belonged to her grandmother and they'd sit at the table together.

That morning he opened the cabinet to get their cups and spied the small gold cup and brought it down. She swallowed hard and pasted a smile on her face when he filled it and carefully passed it to her.

"I figured that would have gotten lost years ago," she said.

"Some things, like home and family and little gold cups, are precious enough for a father to preserve," he said.

"I wish I could be that little girl again," she whispered.

"You always will be to me. Now let's talk about Christmas before you cry. It's on Saturday. Can you get your help to take care of your business and stay a few days? By then the crew will be settled in and Judd and Waylon will be itching to show you their new house. Judd told me she wants to paint it blue and pink and yellow."

"And I bet Holt rushed right out and had the paint mixed," Sharlene said.

Claud chuckled. "He asked her which she wanted for Christmas most. A multicolored house or what she asked Santa for?"

Sharlene finished the coffee in the small cup and poured more. "Do you know what she and Waylon asked for?"

"No, I understand that it's between them and Santa and they don't have to tell anyone else. Remember when you asked Santa for a wagon that Christmas?"

Sharlene nodded. "I sat on his knee at the store over in Weatherford and whispered in his ear. How'd you find out what I asked for anyway?"

"You told Jeff on Christmas Eve morning. Your momma had twenty dollars in the cookie jar that she'd been saving to buy one of them fancy mixers. Jeff told her and she gave me that money and told me not to come home until I found a wagon. I went to Oklahoma City and visited six stores. The last one had one little red wagon left and it was under the tree for you on Christmas morning."

Sharlene swallowed but the lump wouldn't go down. "No one ever told me that story."

"Didn't need to tell you. Shall we have pumpkin pancakes for breakfast?"

"I'd like that, Daddy," she said. "If the kids tell anyone what they want, will you tell me?"

"I reckon I could do that if I get downwind of a conversation." He smiled.

—〜〜—

Sharlene dressed in jeans, a bright green sweater, and her cowboy boots. The week had passed like a whirlwind. She'd barely gotten home on Monday in time to get the kids at school and then every single night had been a record breaker at the Honky Tonk. Add that to polishing off the last two chapters of her book, proofing it, and sending the final draft to her editor on Saturday and the time had whizzed by.

She brushed on a little blush, applied mascara and a touch of green eye shadow, and slapped a layer of lipstick across her lips. She picked up her purse and slung a leather bomber jacket over her shoulder and headed out to the garage.

"Two more days to spend a little time with the kids and see Holt and then it'll be all over. I'll be busy with this trip and then I'll start a new book and it will take all my time. Maybe I'll go to the shelter and pick out a cat. I think I'd like a big black fluffy one this time since my next book has a black cat in it." She talked to herself as she crawled into the pink VW Bug and headed east toward Elmer and Betty's place for the new barn party and dance.

Judd met her at the door and grabbed her hand tightly. "We been waiting for you. Did you know that there's a real band up there with real guitars and everything and that they are playing for us to dance? And there's food over there and Betty says everyone can just eat when they want kind of like at Granny's house and this barn ain't got no cats yet but Betty says it will have when we come back to visit you and maybe even kittens and you have to bring us to see them." She inhaled deeply and took off on another tangent. "And did you know that we are moving up there to live in their town and me and Waylon get to go to their church and we get to see them on Sunday dinnertime? Ain't it going to be wonderful?"

"Are you going to miss me?" Sharlene asked.

"Yep, but you got to go on the book thing before you can come home for Christmas and after that I won't never miss me no more," Judd said.

"Why won't you miss me?" Sharlene asked.

"You'll be in Corn with me and Waylon!" Judd let go of Sharlene's hand and waved at Merle. "I got to go talk to Merle. She don't have a little girl like you got me and she needs someone to make her happy."

"You look stunning," Holt said right behind her.

"Thank you. You look pretty handsome yourself. Haven't you told Judd and Waylon that I'm not moving?"

"I did but they just giggle and put their heads together," he said.

"Maybe I need to talk to them," she said.

"Go ahead but they won't believe you either."

He wore starched, creased jeans, bunched up just right over his boot tops, a plaid western shirt, and he'd gotten a haircut since she'd seen him on Friday. She wanted to take him up to the hay mow and spend her whole evening with him. Time was speeding and every moment was precious.

"May I have this dance?" He held out his hand when the band started playing "To Make You Feel My Love."

She melted into his arms. "This is the song that

Larissa and Hank danced to at their wedding reception. It was one of those moments."

"So is this," Holt whispered into her hair. His heart was torn in half as he waltzed around the dance floor with Sharlene in his arms. He wanted to move to Oklahoma. It was the right thing to do but how could he ever live without Sharlene and when in the hell had he fallen in love with her?

Chapter 21

Sharlene looked out across the faces of the folks who met in the library that morning in Savannah, Georgia, her first stop. Her friends had made the plans and even paid for the tickets. She'd flown from Dallas to Savannah on the first leg.

Kayla was speaking to a book club group at the library, telling them how she'd met Sharlene and about serving with her through two tours of duty in Iraq.

Sharlene didn't know what she'd expected, but it certainly wasn't facing that many people. There must have been forty in attendance ranging from early twenties to one lady who had to be ninety-five.

"Trust me, her new book—which will be available for anyone who wants to purchase one—is not about Iraq. Not that we didn't talk about romance while we were there. But before I tell you everything and spoil it for you, I give you Sharlene Waverly." Kayla started the round of applause.

Sharlene had asked Kayla what she should wear and she'd said to be herself. So she walked up to the podium in a denim skirt, red boots, and a jean jacket over a red shell. She adjusted the microphone to a lower level.

"Hi, y'all. Thank you for being here today and for listening to me talk about my love for writing and running a beer joint," she said. She gave a ten-minute talk and a ten-minute excerpt reading. By the time she sat down her mouth was dry and a line had formed to buy books.

"I told you it would be a success," Kayla beamed when everyone had left and thirty books had sold. "I ordered thirty-five. I've only got enough to give away for Christmas. We did good, girlfriend."

"Thank you!" Sharlene said.

"I should be thanking you. When all those girls read this hot thing, they'll think I'm real special since I'm your friend." Kayla grinned. "Let's go eat and talk about old times."

"I'm not drinking," Sharlene laughed.

"No, you are not. Not after this summer. Did the bartender call a cab? We left money for him."

"No, Holt Jackson took me back to the hotel. Now that's a story," Sharlene said.

"You can tell me over dinner and don't leave out a thing. With a name like Holt, it has to be a cowboy, right?"

That night she slept in a strange room and wished she was back home in Mingus. Judd and Waylon had had their Christmas program that day at school. As much as she'd enjoyed Kayla and the book signing, she would have rather been at the program listening to Judd sing and Waylon say his part.

Holt took off time from packing and went to the kids' Christmas program. Judd was an angel draped in white with big fluffy wings and a halo. She'd bounced around enough that the halo was slightly off kilter but she did look adorable. Waylon was a snowman, dressed in a white sweat suit with big colorful pompoms pinned to the front of his shirt. He wore a stocking cap and his nose was painted orange like a carrot.

They sang "Jingle Bells," "Frosty the Snowman," and then the angels came forward to sing "Silent Night." Holt was amazed at the clarity in Judd's voice when she stepped up to the microphone to deliver her lines from the song. Their part of the program ended with the whole kindergarten, first grade, and second grade singing "All I Want for Christmas."

That brought about a vision of Sharlene sitting in an orange rocking chair on the front porch. As much as he wanted the same thing for his Christmas present, there was no way he could make a miracle happen. He looked at the empty seat beside him and wished she was sitting right there with her hand in his.

—⁂—

Sharlene's next stop was in Chambersburg, Pennsylvania. She rented a car at the Harrisburg airport and drove an hour from there to Chambersburg, arriving an hour before time for another book club meeting in a local bookstore.

Joyce knew the owner of the small store in downtown Chambersburg and introduced her to her friends. Sharlene basically told the same story that she'd told the night before and then signed twenty books before the hour was done.

Then she and Joyce went to Red Lobster and dined on seafood while she told Joyce all about Holt.

"I figured Kayla would have beat a path to the nearest phone and spilled the whole story to you before now. Please tell me I didn't sit here and bore you to tears with that story," Sharlene said.

"No, she just said not to let you leave without asking you about the cowboy. God, girl, what are you going to do?" Joyce asked.

"Live with it. Can't be in two places. I love the Honky Tonk and my life there."

"But you love Holt," she said.

Hearing the words said aloud brought tears to Sharlene's eyes. "Sometimes you don't get everything you want," she said.

"Looks to me like it's pretty clean cut. Him or the Tonk. You better think long and hard about it. Now let's go home. You've got to be up early to catch the flight to Florida and no, I'm not telling Lelah a thing about Holt. You're going to have to tell it all over again. And I'd love to come to your Honky Tonk Christmas thing but I couldn't possibly leave during that time of year."

"Some friend you are."

Joyce laughed. "That's what you get for getting drunk and passing out."

Half an hour later she'd kicked her boots off and peeled off her clothes, and taken a long hot shower before putting on a worn old nightshirt that reminded her of home. She dug her cell phone out of her purse and called the Tonk. The noise in the background brought tears to her eyes.

"Hey, famous lady," Darla said. "How'd it go today?"

"It went fine. I'm tired of talking," Sharlene said.

"I don't believe it. And you got the rest of the week to go?"

"Yes, I do. By the time I get home I may be mute for a month."

"I'll believe it when I see it. Miss us?"

"It seems like I've been gone a month," Sharlene said. "Hey, I've got a beep here. Tell Tessa and Luther hi for me. I'll call again tomorrow night." She hit the right buttons and said, "Hello?"

Holt's deep southern drawl sent shivers trailing down her backbone. "Sharlene, how did it go?"

"It was fine. Now tell me about the kids' program yesterday. Did Judd sing good? She's got the voice of an angel and how did Waylon do? Did he deliver his lines without stuttering? We've been working on them all week. I can't believe they had the program when I couldn't be there. It wasn't fair."

Holt laughed.

She shut her eyes. "Holt, I've got an idea. Your work is finished at the barn and the kids only have two more days of school before Christmas break. Why don't y'all fly to Florida tomorrow and see me. You can finish the book tour with me. The kids would love all the flying and seeing new places. Y'all could sightsee while I do my stuff and we could be together at night."

A long pause on the other end gave her hope that he was thinking about the proposition. "Sharlene, we agreed, no good-byes because you'll be in Corn for Christmas and no regrets. That would be fun but I've got to move and get things in motion. We start our first project on January fourth."

"I'm lonely," she said.

"It wouldn't change anything, would it?"

"No."

"Okay, then let me tell you all about the program and we'll forget that you came up with such an idea. Judd's halo was crooked but she put on quite a dramatic show when she was singing her song. She rolled her eyes toward the spotlights and tilted her chin up like she was a real angel just waiting to go to heaven. And Waylon stepped up to that mic and spit out his lines louder than any snowman I'd ever heard. You would have been so proud of them." He went on to regale her with every detail he could remember.

"Did you ever find out what they want for Christmas? I could look for it while I'm out and about between engagements," she said.

"Merle told me but I'm sworn to secrecy and I'm afraid it'll take a miracle," he said.

"Tell me. I might be able to do a miracle."

"You might but I can't tell you because it's a secret. Merle swore she'd put out a contract on me if I told."

"I miss home," Sharlene said softly.

"Home misses you," Holt whispered. She'd never know how much it hurt to tell her no. His heart was screaming at him to catch the next flight from Dallas to Florida and spend as much time as he could with her, but he couldn't. The split threatened to kill him; seeing her again would make it only more difficult. He couldn't even look at the orange chairs without his chest drawing up in knots and when the kids kept saying that they'd have Sharlene after Christmas, his mind went stone cold numb.

───

Sharlene fell in love with the white sand at Panama City Beach. Lelah's condo opened onto a deck with steps leading right down onto the beach. After talking to the library group, she and Lelah had dinner together then

Lelah got called to the hospital for an emergency shift. She felt horrible but at least she'd gotten to hear the Holt story. She told Sharlene to make herself at home and enjoy anything she could find.

Sharlene threw her clothes on the bed, donned a pair of cutoff jeans and a T-shirt, and went for a long walk in her bare feet up the beach at the water's edge. The surf licked her toes as it rolled in and out and the sun set at the edge of the world.

If they had joined her, Judd and Waylon would be squealing and dancing in and out of the water as the waves splashed up onto the sand. They'd have a competition going about who could build the biggest sand castle or who could make the most footprints in the sand. She picked up a handful of shells and tucked them into a pocket made by folding up the hem of her shirt. She'd give them to the kids at Christmas and tell them all about the beautiful shore.

The sun was a brilliant array of colors when she made it back to her deck. She filled a glass with water and watched the day end from an Adirondack chair and yearned for Holt to share the sight with her.

She called him that night and found that he had most of the packing done. Claud had talked to the right people and the utilities would be turned on in the house where he and the kids would be living. They planned to leave right after school the next day. Judd and Waylon were both floating around on clouds and couldn't wait to get there and have Christmas.

"One last favor, please," he asked. "Would you sell me one of the orange rocking chairs?"

"Hell no!"

"Please. They want their Christmas present delivered in the orange rocking chair. If I can work a miracle it won't be the whole package if I don't have a rocking chair to put it in on Christmas morning," he said.

It would be symbolic of the split. One would stay in Mingus; the other would go to Corn. If the kids wanted it she couldn't refuse them. "I won't sell it but I'll give it to you. They are just alike. Pick out the one you like best."

"I'll take the one you were sitting in the night you woke me up and told me that you'd been a sniper," he said.

"Why?"

"Because then I'll be taking a part of you with me," he answered.

"Then you go sit in the other one and leave part of you in Mingus," she said.

On Friday she flew to Nashville to talk in the back room of a bookstore that Maria frequented. There were twenty people present and twenty-five books sold, which made the owner of the little bookstore very happy. She and Maria had dinner with Abby and then went to the Grand Old Opry. It was after midnight when she called the Honky Tonk and Tessa picked up the phone.

"Was it wonderful?" she asked.

"Make Luther bring you here for your honeymoon when you finally say yes," Sharlene said. "The hotel is fabulous and the Opry was something every bartender with a jukebox as old as ours needs to experience."

"Who'd you see?"

"Alan Jackson stopped by and Blake Shelton and Miranda Lambert. Brad Paisley did a song," she said.

"I'm so jealous I could spit."

"Make Luther marry you and bring you here for New Year's. I bet that Friday night will be a hoot," Sharlene said.

"Maybe for Valentine's."

"Speaking of holidays, everything is still going smooth for our Honky Tonk Christmas, isn't it?"

"Smooth as a baby's butt," Tessa laughed. "See you in a week."

She hung up and wanted to call Holt but he'd be on the road or else trying to get the kids to bed. Claud and Molly had insisted that he stay with them the first two nights until he could get things unpacked.

She had finished her shower and was wrapping a towel around her body when the phone rang. Figuring it was Tessa with a Honky Tonk problem she grabbed it on the first ring, "Hello!"

"Well, you sound all spry." Holt sounded exhausted. She hadn't heard that kind of weariness in his voice even after a long day of work.

"Not really. This getting up early is about to kill me. I can't sleep at night and when I do the nightmares are horrible. The farther I get from home the worse they are," she said.

"We ran into a traffic snag in Wichita Falls and didn't get here until thirty minutes ago. Molly and Claud carried the kids in and put them to bed for me. I'm on the swings in the backyard. I just wanted to hear your voice."

She shut her eyes tightly and imagined him sitting on the same swing she'd sat on the night they wound up in the barn. She touched her lips and remembered how his kisses made her feel.

What am I going to do when I get home and he's not there? These nightly calls will fade away eventually. Nothing can withstand five hours of distance with no end in sight.

"Did you take a rocking chair with you?"

"Oh, yes! Judd insisted on it. She said Santa couldn't do his job without it," Holt said. "Tell me again when you'll be here. Oh yeah, Larissa stopped by and left me one of your books. I started reading it tonight. You are so good that it's like you are telling me the story. I can even imagine your Southern twang talking," he said.

"You are reading a romance book?" she asked.

"Yes, ma'am, I am. And it's a damn fine book. Now when are you going to be at the airport?"

"I'm staying here another day with Maria. We're doing the tourist thing in Nashville tomorrow. Then I'm flying home to Dallas. My ugly car is waiting for me and I'm missing it."

She got off the plane late Saturday night and fought the Dallas traffic until she was on the other side of Fort Worth, then it thinned out to what she considered normal. The further west she went the less town she saw and the more country and the better she liked it. It was only an hour to closing when she reached the Honky Tonk. She went straight for the bar and started helping Tessa and Darla, so glad to be home that she could have kissed the Honky Tonk parking lot. At closing time, Luther called it a night and the four of them talked until two thirty.

She walked them to the door and stood on the porch, sucking in lots of good cold country night air. She saw

the lights of the truck turn into the parking lot but figured someone was just using her space to make a U-turn.
When it pulled right up to the door she recognized the
truck and the driver. She could hardly believe her eyes
when Holt crawled out and shook the legs of his jeans
down over his boot tops.

She walked into his arms and everything in her world
was right.

"I missed you," she said.

He tilted up her chin with his fist and kissed her hard.
"I missed you too."

She wanted to propose to him right there on the spot.
She'd had a lot of hours to think about what was important in her life. Day one she fought the idea that popped
into her head about marrying Holt and moving to Corn.
That was in Savannah when she missed the kids' school
program. Corn didn't look so bad when she landed in
Florida. Day three she called Merle and tiptoed around
the idea. Merle said her offer still stood and she wasn't
surprised but to think about it for a few weeks before she
made a rash decision. The night before she'd called her
father and he told her the same thing Merle did. Now she
was in his embrace and she lost her nerve.

"Where are the kids?"

"Molly kept them. She said they'd be bored to tears
driving all the way down and back. So she invited
Tasha and Matty over and they're making Christmas
cookies. I had to see you, Sharlene. I couldn't wait until
Christmas. Tired?"

"Exhausted. Holt, I…"

"Sharlene, I…"

They both started and stopped at the same time.

He took her hand in his and started toward the door.

"Was it a big success?" he asked.

"My friends thought so. I must've sold a hundred books all total. That's not bad for a debut author. I'm so excited I could jump up and down about it all. What were you going to say a while ago?"

"This isn't a very romantic spot," he said.

Her breath caught in her chest. "It's more romantic than McDonald's."

He put his hands on her shoulders. "I love you."

"But…" she started and he shut her up with a hard, hot-blooded kiss that turned into two and then three.

"You were saying?" he said when he finally drew away.

"I love you back."

"What are we going to do about that?" he asked.

"I've got a plan," she said.

"Does it involve buying a small airplane and week-end trips?" he asked.

"What?"

"It's the only way I can stand being away from you. This week has been pure hell for me. I can't do it, Sharlene. We may have to invest in a small plane and learn to fly so we can at least be together on weekends." He kept one arm around her and kicked the door shut with his boot heel.

"I think you'll like my plan a little better," she said.

He kissed her again when they were inside the Honky Tonk. "When did you figure it out?"

"A long time ago. I'm just not good at giving in to my heart. How about you?"

"On the creek bank when we were at your folks for the weekend."

"But you said Dorie…"

He nodded. "She was. She made me realize that the chemistry between us went deeper than physical attraction. It wasn't there with her. It is with you." He landed one more kiss on her lips and went behind the bar to open two bottles of beer. "Okay, tell me your plan."

"First tell me you love me again. I need to hear it one more time."

"Darlin', I love you with my whole heart and mind. I will love you forever and won't stop at death. I will love you through eternity and beyond. Now tell me about this plan."

"I will but not until we finish our beers. I want to hear all about the kids, and Kent and Chad and the girls and how the wedding plans are coming along. Don't leave out a single detail," she said.

Holt began to tell stories about the houses they were moving into and the kids and Sharlene hung on every word. She sighed when he finished and carried the empty bottles back to the bar.

"Want another one?" she asked.

Mistletoe hung from the ceiling in several places, glittery garland decorated the jukeboxes, and two Christmas trees, one on either end of the beer joint, were lit up.

She couldn't leave this place. She just couldn't. Her plan went right down the drain. Tears ran down her cheeks and dripped onto her blouse.

"Darlin', why are you crying?" Holt crossed the floor and wrapped her up in his arms.

"I love this crazy old beer joint," she said.

"I know, baby, I know." He wiped away her tears and kissed her on the nose. "It's a matter of which do you love most. It or me?"

She looked around and then at him and settled it in her heart that very moment. The Honky Tonk was home but Holt held her heart. She'd miss the Tonk but she'd die without Holt Jackson.

He dropped down on one knee and looked up at her. "Sharlene Waverly, will you marry me?"

She nodded. "Yes, I will."

"And move to Corn with me?"

"Yes, I will."

He stood up and wrapped her in his arms. "I love you. It's not enough but it'll have to do because my heart is all I've got to offer you. I promise I'll love you forever, darlin'."

She pointed to the mistletoe right above his head.

"We don't need that but we'll take all the luck we can get," he whispered as he kissed her with so much heat that her legs trembled.

"Now, I'll tell you my plan," she said.

"I'm listening."

She smiled and laid her head on his chest.

The Honky Tonk had even more decorations than it did the night that Holt proposed. The whole place glittered with the warmth of lights and garland, and smelled like Christmas with the cedar branches strung down the bar. Finger foods were arranged on four eight-foot tables and by two o'clock the Tonk was filled with past and present patrons. Daisy, Jarod, Chigger and Jim Bob, Billy Bob and Joe Bob and their wives, Cathy and Travis, Luther and Tessa, Darla, Angel and Garrett, Merle and Amos. Larissa, Hank, and Henry and to Sharlene's absolute surprise, Victoria. There were so many people that she couldn't begin to count them all.

"Well, darlin', you did it. You've got a fantastic Honky Tonk Christmas. I remember when me and Jarod clashed right here where I'm standing," Daisy said.

"And when Travis kissed me," Cathy joined the conversation. "This is a wonderful idea, bringing us all together like this. Now where's the books? I want twenty and all of them signed."

"Twenty?" Sharlene was amazed.

"Yep, I'm giving them for presents all year."

Merle tapped a Mason jar with a spoon. "Hey, everyone. Sharlene is going to talk now so listen up."

Sharlene picked up a karaoke microphone beside the bar and blew into it. "Testing," she giggled. "I always wanted to do that. Now seriously, today is very important to me. I came to the Honky Tonk last year as most of you know and this place gave me the inspiration for a wonderful book. While I was off doing a little promotion and visiting some of my old friends, I figured out exactly what was important."

"Aha!" Larissa said.

"You win." Sharlene winked.

"Short version," Merle said loudly.

"Okay, short version it is then. I've sold the Tonk to Merle who insisted on paying exactly what the appraisal price is. She says it's the giving it away that has brought on the charm or curse or…"

"Charm!" Holt said from the end of the bar where he visited with Jarod, Travis, and Hank.

"Okay, then charm it is." Sharlene held out her hand and he joined her. "We got married this morning in

Palo Pinto. I'm told that tomorrow morning I have to be sitting in an old orange rocking chair on the front porch of this little ratty house in Corn, Oklahoma, because all Judd and Waylon want for Christmas is me. Now on to the next item. Tessa, Darla, and Luther will manage the Honky Tonk for Merle. Darla is moving into the Bahamas Mama house. I'm moving out of the apartment in the next couple of weeks when we can get down here to pack. My book *Honky Tonk Charm* is set up on the bar and I'll be glad to sign a copy for any and everyone."

"And the story ends right here," Tessa said. "Luther and I will be getting married in February so the charm is finished."

"What about Darla?" Chigger yelled.

"Oh, I expect there'll be some charm left, just not for the owner unless Merle is up for a wedding," Holt teased.

"Bite your tongue, cowboy," Merle said. "Luther?"

He went to the jukebox and plugged money into the slot. Garth's song, "To Make You Feel My Love," started and Hank led Sharlene to the middle of the floor.

"Thank you lord for the Honky Tonk," he whispered as he drew her near.

"Amen," she said.

"I love you, Mrs. Jackson."

"That does roll off the lips very well, doesn't it?"

"Yes, ma'am, it does."

They arrived at the house no bigger than the Bahamas Mama house in Mingus long after midnight. Christina and Creed were watching old movies on late night television when Holt carried Sharlene over the threshold.

"Why'd you do that?" Creed asked.

"Because I married this woman today," Holt answered.

Christina beamed. "I told you they wouldn't wait until summer."

Creed stood up and reached for his coat. "Where you going to live?"

"Right here until Holt can build us a house," Sharlene said as Holt set her down.

"Okay, take me home, Creed. My little brothers and sisters will be up at the crack of dawn to see what Santa left them," Christina said.

"It's cold and spitting snowflakes. You want me to drive you kids home?" Holt asked.

"Naw, I got my four wheeler out back and we'll stay off the roads. It's only half a mile up through the countryside. We'll be home in twenty minutes," Creed said.

When they were out of the house, Holt picked Sharlene up again and carried her to the bedroom where he laid her down gently on the bed and said, "Well, darlin', it's been a day. You had your Honky Tonk Christmas and it was beautiful. This isn't so romantic for our wedding night. I should have had roses on the bed and champagne chilling in a fancy bucket in a fancy hotel room," Holt said.

"What is that noise?" Sharlene asked.

"It's your Christmas present. We've got it in a carrier in the corner of the kids' room. It's going to be a surprise after they find you on the front porch in the rocking chair," he smiled.

"Is it…"

"Shhh, you're not supposed to know that it's a cat. It's six weeks old and black and furry. Judd picked it out. Have I told you that I love you in the last five seconds?" He stretched out beside her on the bed.

She snuggled next to his side, resting her face against his heart and listening to the beat. The nightmares might come back on occasion but Holt would always be there when she awoke and tell her that he'd chase the monsters away. "It was a beautiful day. I wouldn't have done one thing different. No big wedding to be nervous about. And my Honky Tonk Christmas was perfect. I thought it would be sad but it wasn't at all. I'm leaving one life behind but the one in front of me is so much better. And honey, those two kids in there are my roses and truth is I'd rather have a cold beer any day as champagne. And I already love my Christmas present."

"And I love you, Sharlene. We've only got four hours before you have to get up and sit on the porch. Got any ideas?" He kissed her earlobe.

"Yes, I do! We are going to live happily never after for the rest of our lives, starting right now with this hot kiss. Merry Christmas to me, Holt Jackson."

THE END

About the Author

Carolyn Brown is an award-winning author with more than forty books published, and credits her eclectic family for her humor and writing ideas. She is the author of *Lucky in Love*, *One Lucky Cowboy*, *Getting Lucky*, and in the Honky Tonk series, *I Love This Bar*, *Hell, Yeah*, and *My Give a Damn's Busted*. She was born in Texas but grew up in southern Oklahoma where she and her husband, Charles, a retired English teacher, make their home. They have three grown children and enough grandchildren to keep them young.

Either one," Kent answered.

Austin didn't. Wherever she is, Granny probably did

s laughing because I did what I wanted and showed

say goodbye."

What'd she look like?" Kent asked.

ou've seen her pictures," Rye said.

hat's not what I asked. A picture is just a likeness.

people have dimension," Kent said.

e poked him on the shoulder. "You're usin' a ten

word there."

nd you are avoidin' a simple question, which

s you liked what you saw and you ain't goin' to

it," Kent said.

t's go eat some fish. I'm starving," Rye said.

e sign outside the small building said "Doug's

Orchard" and that it had been in business since

The restaurant was packed full of people. He

ent walked past the U-shaped cashier's bar and

h a door into the dining room on the north side.

ise of conversations and the smell of frying fish

he place. They settled into chairs at the table be-

last booth on the west side.

waitress didn't look *quite* old enough to have

ere since the place opened, but didn't miss it by

u fellers look like you put in a morning. What

t you?" she asked. Her eyebrows were drawn on

arch that made her wrinkled face look surprised

eyes were bright and sparkling.

emoved his cowboy hat and hung it on the back

air. "It's been more than just a morning."

t's done got you all in a tizz?" Pearlita asked

booth.

Don't miss the first in a new "Spikes & Spurs"
series by Carolyn Brown

LOVE DRUNK
COWBOY

Coming from Sourcebooks Casablanca in May 2011

Rye O'Donnell pushed his black hair aw
and resettled his sweat-stained black Ste
He headed the pickup truck for town, p
that next week he'd make a trip to Gem
in Wichita Falls and get a hair cut, but
and his one hired hand, Kent, had been
tor most of the morning. The only thin
together since last summer were balin
parts, and cussin' that would fry the h
nostrils. There didn't seem to be any
available and the baling wire had a
thing left was cussin' and even that v

He was hot, sweaty, and hungry
the parking lot of the Peach Orchar
on the rear fender of the old ranch v
cigarette smoked down to the stub a
heel of his boot when Rye parked t

"So?" Kent asked.

"Went just like Granny Lanie
brought the ashes and Austin s
river," Rye said. He didn't say tha
from back in the shadows of a gro
taken his breath away and cause
deep in his gut.

"She see you?"

"Who? Granny or Austin?'

"Well, I'll be danged. I didn't recognize you without your hat and boots," Rye smiled at Pearlita. He'd seen them in the booth when he walked through the doors but Kent was right behind him and there was no going back.

Pearlita stuck out a foot. "Look more familiar now?"

"Yes, ma'am." Rye wondered how in the hell they'd gotten to the café before he did. "This is the morning for Granny Lanier's service, isn't it? And you'd be her granddaughter?" His eyes landed on a tall blond that sucked every bit of the air from his lungs for the second time that day, dried his mouth out like he'd just eaten a sawdust sandwich laced with alum, and made his palms go all clammy. Austin looked cool as a rainbow snow cone in her black suit and spike heels. He was damn sure glad he was sitting down or his knees would have failed him and he'd have fallen flat on his face right there in the café. He'd heard of being love drunk before, but he'd damn sure never believed such crap.

"I am," Austin said. Her stomach suddenly twisted up like a piece of sheet metal in a class five tornado.

Trouble was always lurking right around the corner when her gut knotted up like a pretzel. A dozen tiny pretzel-making elves had taken up abode in Austin Lanier's stomach that morning and she didn't need a deck of Tarot cards or a psychic to tell her something was fixing to turn her world upside down.

The Lanier gut was never wrong.

His mossy green eyes rimmed with the heaviest lashes she'd ever seen on a man were undressing her right there in the café in front of Pearlita, the customers, and even God Himself. And immediately after her grandmother's memorial. Did the man have no manners at all?

Pure animal sexuality exuded from him and she wondered who in the hell he was. He wore faded jeans stuffed down into the tops of scuffed-up cowboy boots with spurs that jingled when he moved. A green and yellow plaid shirt with the sleeves rolled up to his elbows covered a gray sweat-stained T-shirt. He drank long and deep of the iced tea the waitress set before him, then removed the shirt and hung it on the back of the chair beside his hat. A barbed wire tattoo circled his left bicep right below his shirt sleeve.

She blushed when she realized she was staring at the tat. She shut her eyes and suddenly, there he was in her imagination without a shirt, his belt buckle undone, showing a fine line of dark hair extending downward and a big smile on his sexy face. She opened her eyes with a snap to find him grinning at her. A slow heated blush crept into her cheeks.

He cleared his throat and looked past Austin at the menu on the far wall. If she had half a brain between those crystal clear blue eyes she could see the desire in his face. He'd never been thunderstruck before in his thirty-five years of life. He'd heard about it and thought it a bunch of pure unadulterated bullshit, but it had never happened to him until that moment. A grown man didn't look across a room at a woman and know in an instant that she was his soul mate. That wasn't just bullshit, it was insanity.

When he found his voice he said, "I'm Rye O'Donnell and this is my friend, Kent, who works with me. I'm sorry to lose Granny. She was a pillar in Terral and the best neighbor a man could ask for. This is probably a poor time to bring it up, but if you are going to sell Granny's land, I'd like to make a bid on it. Could we start negotiating at five hundred an acre?"

Don't miss the first in a new "Spikes & Spurs"
series by Carolyn Brown

LOVE DRUNK
COWBOY

Coming from Sourcebooks Casablanca in May 2011

Rye O'Donnell pushed his black hair away from his eyes and resettled his sweat-stained black Stetson on his head. He headed the pickup truck for town, promising himself that next week he'd make a trip to Gemma's beauty shop in Wichita Falls and get a hair cut, but not that day. He and his one hired hand, Kent, had been working on a tractor most of the morning. The only things that had held it together since last summer were baling wire, cheap used parts, and cussin' that would fry the hair of a frog's nostrils. There didn't seem to be any more cheap parts available and the baling wire had all rusted. The only thing left was cussin' and even that wasn't working.

He was hot, sweaty, and hungry when he pulled into the parking lot of the Peach Orchard. Kent was leaning on the rear fender of the old ranch work truck. He had a cigarette smoked down to the stub and put it out with the heel of his boot when Rye parked beside him.

"So?" Kent asked.

"Went just like Granny Lanier wanted it. Pearlita brought the ashes and Austin scattered them in the river," Rye said. He didn't say that just looking at Austin from back in the shadows of a grove of willow trees had taken his breath away and caused a boiling fire down deep in his gut.

"She see you?"

"Who? Granny or Austin?"

"Either one," Kent answered.

"Austin didn't. Wherever she is, Granny probably did and is laughing because I did what I wanted and showed up to say goodbye."

"What'd she look like?" Kent asked.

"You've seen her pictures," Rye said.

"That's not what I asked. A picture is just a likeness. Real people have dimension," Kent said.

Rye poked him on the shoulder. "You're usin' a ten dollar word there."

"And you are avoidin' a simple question, which means you liked what you saw and you ain't goin' to admit it," Kent said.

"Let's go eat some fish. I'm starving," Rye said.

The sign outside the small building said "Doug's Peach Orchard" and that it had been in business since 1948. The restaurant was packed full of people. He and Kent walked past the U-shaped cashier's bar and through a door into the dining room on the north side. The noise of conversations and the smell of frying fish filled the place. They settled into chairs at the table beside the last booth on the west side.

The waitress didn't look *quite* old enough to have been there since the place opened, but didn't miss it by far. "You fellers look like you put in a morning. What can I get you?" she asked. Her eyebrows were drawn on in a high arch that made her wrinkled face look surprised but her eyes were bright and sparkling.

Rye removed his cowboy hat and hung it on the back of his chair. "It's been more than just a morning."

"What's done got you all in a tizz?" Pearlita asked from the booth.